SHOUTING AT THE SHIP MEN

Tim Geary

VICTOR GOLLANCZ
LONDON

First published in Great Britain 1999
by Victor Gollancz
An imprint of Orion Books Ltd
Wellington House, 125 Strand, London WC2R 0BB

© 1999 Tim Geary

The right of Tim Geary to be identified as author of this work has been asserted by him in accordance with the Copyright, Designs and Patents Act 1988.

A catalogue record for this book is available from the British Library.

ISBN 0 575 06716 0

The publishers and author assert that every effort has been made to approach the copyright holders of material quoted in this book. Any queries should be addressed to the publishers in the first instance.

Typeset by SetSystems Ltd, Saffron Walden, Essex
Printed in Great Britain by
Clays Ltd, St Ives plc

All rights reserved. No part of this publication may be reproduced or transmitted in any form or by any means, electronic or mechanical including photocopying, recording or any information storage or retrieval system, without prior permission in writing from the publishers.

This book is sold subject to the condition that it shall not, by way of trade or otherwise, be lent, resold, hired out, or otherwise circulated without the publisher's prior consent in any form of binding or cover other than that in which it is published and without a similar condition including this condition being imposed on the subsequent purchaser.

For Sarah
Every letter; word; comma; space

ACKNOWLEDGEMENTS

For her invaluable advice and friendship, I am indebted to Tifanny Richards. Thanks, also, to Humphrey Price, my editor, my parents and to Sarah, on whom I relied through every page of this book.

ONE

―・―

Consider your problems one at a time. Sometimes lumping them together can make them seem overwhelming, but if you look at each of your problems individually it may be easier to see that each one is not as serious as you thought it was. Then you can begin to look for solutions.

AMA Family Medical Guide

―・―

We are restless, Iain and I, sitting at our desks while summer burns outside. It's a scorcher, a day for bare feet and icy drinks, the sky so radiant it makes me long to get out and up to Lake Simcoe where I learned to swim twenty-something years ago, Dad rocking our boat with such applause and pride I may as well have been taking on the Atlantic.

'Do it for me, my little Pea,' he whispered, as he slid my armbands off to wear them himself as canary-yellow bracelets on his library-white wrists. 'Do it for me.' As if I would have swum for anyone else.

My brain is the proverbial sieve, but when I am a hundred and five I will remember that day, me crying with happiness and fear, the sunshine a generous slick of gold laminating the mercury blue with an almost terrestrial veneer. This afternoon, the same sun seems malevolent, a reminder that reproduction, photosynthesis, life itself, these not insignificant things are happening elsewhere and to other beings while Iain and I inhale second-hand oxygen in our office in downtown Toronto.

'See that dust?' I lift a finger towards the shaft of sunlight that's clipping the corner of my desk, so missing the rubber plant that has been dying, slowly as a Chinese leader, since I bought it. 'Most of that's old skin. Most of those motes.'

Furrows corrugate Iain's forehead as he lifts his eyes, then fade as he returns his gaze to the newspaper. I look down at my ringless hands. We are twenty-seven, my fingers and I, as good as thirty. I don't know when my body began to decay but recently it has been making itself felt. My hands have grown wrinkles. Gravity smirks at me. Hangovers hurt me twice as long as they once did. My face has lost its flawless rubescence. Truth is, I am getting old rather than getting on. Each day I think something has to change while each day remains the same. Enough, now; enough.

'There's probably a finger's worth of skin in here. Or more.'

'Hm.'

'More, I'd say. If you added it all up.'

Not long after my father ruined my life by carelessly ending his, I swept the dust from his study into a tiny maple-wood box that I used to keep under my pillow. The dust held was not him, but some of it had been and I needed to cling to whatever was left. Back then, when I was thirteen, I knew the percentage of a teaspoon of household dust that had been living skin. Now I have to guess at such things. I ask Iain.

'Seventy per cent?' he suggests without lifting his eyes from the 'Fun With Pictures' page of today's *Toronto Herald*.

'It isn't seventy. It's more than that. Hey, what are you doing?'

'Connecting the dots. It's going to be a dog.'

I sneak a peek at the picture. It is the antithesis of my own life. I am failing to form a distinct image of the future I once drew, had fun with. My dots have become random. Iain's dog, however, is almost whole. It is a spotted puppy nudging a ball out of grass with its snout. I wish I had shaped it. I would have had it being obscene: humping another, taking a shit, something.

Least that might teach the kiddies never to expect the expected. That life won't remain puppy dogs in the grass.

I myself was clueless. With snout down and tail wagging, I was a puppy at play for thirteen blissful, swaying long-grass summers. Then my father ended our game, snap, and left me with this burst ball, this deflated life. Simply, that is how it was.

'Do you know when Sebastian's getting back?'

'When he's through with BIHFOS, I guess.'

Sebastian Crow, of TV's *Crow's Nest* fame, is our odious boss and the producer of the eponymous bi-monthly show on which Iain and I work. Today, Sebastian is interviewing an Algonquin performance artist who has taken, get this, to stripping naked and covering himself in horse manure before running headfirst into pyramids of Coca Cola cans positioned parallel to the US border. Iain has nicknamed the Algonquin, Big Heap Full of Shit: BIHFOS, for short. We can't wait for Sebastian to rinse his hands of him, for the show to be over.

'I'm going to go to England,' I say, stirring my coffee with one of the station's cheap Chinese pencils.

'Uhhuh?'

Puppy drawn, Iain is now concentrating on a pair of spot-the-difference drawings. He doesn't seem to appreciate the importance of my imminent emigration, how many differences he could score between my future life and the one I am living now.

'That's where I should be.'

'You should go then.'

'I'm going to. I mean, I'm much more English than Canadian.'

'Oh, without a doubt.'

I can tell from the way Iain has raised one eyebrow that he doesn't believe me. Sure, he knows my father was English, but he doesn't understand that these Canadian trappings are merely the iceberg's visible tenth. The meaningful bulk, my impervious English foundation, is subterranean. That is where I get my nourishment. My father's parents and their parents and their parents' parents are buried in England and I, Portia Mills, bear the name of the tree that's grown from their flesh.

'It's not as if I'll miss anything about Toronto,' I add.

I feel confined by this city. I don't want to live in a place so clean that film crews have to throw trash on the ground. I don't like it that I have already listened to every good band, visited every good bar, every decent restaurant, every hip and happening street and found myself bored. And I am up to here with Canadian pride. It's as if we have some kind of neurological disorder, an inverse Tourette's, a sickness that makes us babble in superlatives. Should I care that we have the world's longest road, the most land, the tallest building, the largest bookstore? When biggest is not best?

With my damp pencil I draw England's outline on a faxed memo in front of me. My father was born in Cornwall, near to the toe that is Land's End. That is where I would like to go.

Iain tosses the paper aside and leans back in his chair, his hands behind his head.

'So when are you leaving us?'

'Soon.'

'You said that last year. When we were going out.'

'Iain, we "went out" for one night.'

'That must have been the night you said it, then.'

'I've probably been saying it ever since I nearly went there with Derek.'

'Who he?'

I tell Iain of how I tripped into Derek and a love of sorts ten years ago when I was seventeen and had just escaped from my mother's house. He was a sordid, English skinhead who had hitched his way up from New York. Somehow, my apology for knocking over his tin of coins evolved into a longer conversation and by three, on the afternoon we met, he and I were raucously fucking on the floor of my tiny rented bedroom, my ankles against his neck and the sweat dripping from the dome of his shaven skull. He moved in that night.

At the time, having most of my space and all of my orifices filled by this man and his tough little skinhead prick felt like freedom. Although I had been healthily rebellious at school I had never met anyone as anarchic as he. At least, I assumed there to be a hint of philosophy behind the bricks thrown through Mercedes' windows, the shoplifting, the broken noses; something more than mere thugishness. I was searching for an ideology to mate with my own. Having fled both my mother and my academic future, I was in the mood to find Derek appealing. I loved the flashy tattoo on his fleshy right arm that read 'Fuck the Fucking System', the words curved in a horseshoe around a Doc Marten boot. Each night I pressed my lips to the blood-red pattern and slithered my tongue over the skin. Within a week I, too, had shaved my head.

Of course, there was more to it than sex and chaos. There was Mother. Four years on from Dad's death I despised her, blamed her entirely for what he had done. I knew how she would hate Derek, not just his refusal to toe the line she followed, but his thin-lipped ugliness. She's vain, it's the French in her, so when I arrived unannounced at her door one evening, newly shaven and with Derek in my tow, I could see the disappointment glaze her eyes. Not just Derek with his black fingernails and fetid breath and anger, but me, her gorgeous butterfly turned worm.

Although Derek and I had plenty of postcoital discussions about my following him to England, I did not follow him when he was deported. I assumed I would leave soon enough. England was my true home. That was ten years ago.

'I'm going to have to tell Sebastian,' I say.

'Tell me what?'

Typical. I am always doing this. Sebastian is back now, standing behind my chair wearing a blue blazer and a swirly silk cravat that must have looked ludicrous beside the Algonquin's rufous birthday suit.

'Nothing important.' I clunk the front two legs of my chair back onto the floor and turn the map of England face down on the desk. 'How was the besmirched Indian?'

'You're very droll, Portia.' Sebastian taps an oval cigarette on its pack. With it bouncing baton-like in his lips, he says, 'Now would you come with me?'

Reluctantly, I follow Sebastian to his office and then travel with him beyond Mississauga to meet with an artist working in neon. By the time I get back, Iain has fled, most probably to some bar to further dampen his grisly, Scottish sense of inferiority. I wish he hadn't gone. I want to spend an evening with someone. Of late, I have been feeling left out.

I think my friends are scared that my own sense of fracture might be contagious. Of course, since I have only my word for it, I may be unduly neurotic, and yet I feel as if I am entering another of those periods of segregation that punctuate our lives. This time it's the looming bank of cloud that's our thirties with which my contemporaries have become obsessed and I, scared. They are running to houses with barely manageable mortgages and a room or two for the kids when they pop, which they will, so segregating us further; to the right, we childless nomads, to the left, the new sleep-and-diaper crazed parents convinced they have discovered the meaning of life. I don't like it. Time was we didn't waste time trying to make each day more than a passable imitation of our past. Now my life in Toronto has become nothing but memory, the memory nothing but loss. I long to begin again.

From the office I take Queen Street home. It is comfortable out, the kind of warmth that invites you to slip out of your clothes and lie naked with a lover, drinking alcohol while playing with cubes of ice. Iced vodka I have, it's a someone I am missing.

Needing to be cheered up, I stop at a pharmacy. I love browsing among the drugs that other people need. It makes me feel the same as I do when watching the nightly news: fortunate, healthy, better than the bombed and drowned, the murdered and sick. I choose an aisle. Look at this stuff! Excema creams; vaginal suppositories; pills for grass allergies; liquids for sleeplessness; powders for diarrhoea. I read some of the labels. There are hair dyes; enemas; denture creams; corn plasters. Drugs containing quazepam; benzocain; ampicillin; trypsin; guanabenz; naproxen; psyllium; naphazoline. What would happen to the world if these pharmacies were closed? Would we drop dead suddenly, instead of gradually? I raise my nose at a shelf full of acne cream and haemorrhoid soothing pads. Pah! Instead, I take honey-filled cough sweets, because I like the taste, and Dead Sea Bath Salts because they make me feel soft, and religious.

There's a girl in front of me at the check-out. She looks young, maybe fifteen. She has casually lustrous hair, styled in a seemingly naive fifties cut and curling my way at the nape of her neck. On her back is a fluffy brown and cream bear knapsack, the straps looking like legs ending in cute, pink, padded feet that hug her floppily. I guess: cover-up stick, silk conditioner, chewing gum, an antibacterial face wash, but then I see it is condoms she's buying, twenty-four of them packaged in two scarlet packs of twelve. Those, and nothing else. God, she must think she's found all she will ever need in the magical, satiating bliss of her own honey-liquid centre. Exactly as I did, once.

She tosses a twenty onto the counter then, forgetting her change at first, turns, glances at my salts and smiles a broad, childish grin that makes me feel irredeemably pessimistic and old. When I dump my salts by the register I am unable to look the cashier in the eye. 'Relax with minerals enjoyed since biblical times,' proclaims the blurb. It should read, 'Look how alone.'

Through the side window I catch a glimpse of the girl skipping (yes, even that) back home. I want to stop her, slap her, swap places with her, something. She'll be using her bed, I'm sure of it, because making love in the only place she has kept sacred and private her entire life will seem infinitely more illicit than screwing on the table or porch or floor. Disconsolate, I pay up and leave.

Back on Queen everyone is walking in the opposite direction from me. I know they have places to see, people to go to, condoms to use. I wonder if the girl is home and sliding her lips over the prick of some vigorous boy who thinks his life has just begun. Or is he naked in bed waiting for her with a Pepsi cold against his washboard stomach where a tantalizing strip of hair has recently sprouted and the sheets are pushed provocatively low? It turns me on to think of him. I haven't been kissed in six months. I realize this empty groan at the base of my washcloth stomach is nostalgia. The condom kid's euphoria is in my past.

I turn off Queen. Ahead of me a tidy young man is scrutinizing the menu of a new Italian restaurant I usually hate to pass. My face becomes brittle with the effort of appearing content to those diners gazing through the immaculately polished windows. Tonight, though, I am distracted by the man. He has glanced at me a couple of times. He's cute in a boyish, law-abiding kind of way. I wonder if he is waiting for a date but then figure, no, else he would be inside. I meet his eye for a moment as I pass, then am surprised to hear him speak.

'Um, hello. Excuse me.'

I turn. He has slipped his hands into the back pockets of his dark blue suit trousers. It makes him look harmless and uneasy, his shoulders pushed into an awkward shrug. 'I'm terribly sorry.'

He isn't sorry, obviously, or he wouldn't have spoken, but the chaste British tone makes him sound apologetic and that's enough for now. I raise my eyebrows.

'I was wondering if you know whether this restaurant is good or – or not. I'm just visiting.'

'From Mars?' I say for a reason that I can't fathom. But that's what came out.

'Well, from England actually.'

'Oh, right. That's closer, isn't it?'

'Yes. Anyway, I was wondering whether you'd eaten here. By any chance. Whether you'd recommend it.'

'No, I wouldn't. I mean, I haven't. Eaten here.'

I don't know why I am not being more friendly because I kind of like the look of the man, not so much the clothes since his striped shirt and polished leather shoes augur a Preppie staidness within, but his winsome aspect, the penitent stutter in his eyes. He seems about my age – hanging, I'd guess, by the tips of his fingers to his twenties. Yet there is something boyish about him, as if the stubble is sponged on; the ropy, chestnut hair smoothed back; the round metal glasses worn to add academic credibility;

the soft creases on his forehead painted with a calligrapher's precision; the sideburns long, à la mode, a tepid nod to the seventies in this age without a clue. Only in his manner does he reveal his prescribed maturity, the smooth, if guarded, confidence of someone who was evidently born clutching a silver spoon. Not that he seems arrogant. Rather, there's a tang of anxiety to his manner, as if he remembers his birth and hasn't recovered from the sloopy wetness against his cheeks.

'You haven't been? Oh, OK.' He tips back on to his heels. 'I'm sorry to have bothered you.'

'No problem.' I smile and half-turn towards home but instead of leaving I hesitate, as does he. I raise my eyes to his, unsure of what I am feeling. I am excited, though the excitement is not explicitly sexual, not the groan of a couple of minutes ago. Nor am I conscious of having collided with someone cut from the same cloth as I, someone who will instinctively understand my jokes and references and concerns. Yet I can't leave, not with the gnawing fear that I'll never again be as happy as the bear-hugged girl.

Besides, haven't I tried to make spontaneity the cornerstone of my adult credo? Never expect the expected. Fuck the fucking system. Screw the script, the treadmill, the knee-jerk nine-to-five, eight-to-six, seven-to-seven death that most of us call a life, the days wasted waiting for life to begin. None of us has the slightest clue when it's all going to slip away. We can't trust the future, only the past, only the present that becomes it.

Perhaps even if this man and I are not made for each other, our destinies are. A collision between the stars has lit our immediate future. I ask, 'Are you eating alone?'

'Actually, I am.'

'So, what would you say to me joining you?'

'Oh.' He looks a little alarmed, but then suddenly perks up. 'I'd say great. I'd have probably ended up in McDonald's.'

'I'm glad you didn't.' I give him my favourite smile.

'My name's Luke, by the way. Luke Bingham.'

I shake his soft hand. 'Hi, Luke. Portia.'

'Portia,' he repeats, and then, after a few pensive seconds, haltingly adds, '"She is fair, and fairer than the word/Of wondrous virtues."' Then he laughs. 'How's that for a bit of memory?'

I am speechless. A bit of memory? How much more memory could be wrapped around eleven words?

'Is something wrong?' Luke asks.

'No, I'm sorry, I'm fine,' I say, though I don't know whether to laugh or cry. 'Do you know how that speech goes on?'

Luke shakes his head. 'No, not a chance. I'm amazed I remembered that much. I think I wrote it on a Valentine's card once.'

'"Sometimes...",' I say to him — recalling everything about the note my father left me, from the creamy waffle of the paper to the smudge of ink above the final i that spoke both of the terrible speed of his leaving and of his wonderful, reinless spirit — '"sometimes from her eyes, I did receive fair speechless messages."'

'This is like being at school,' Luke says with a self-deprecating little laugh, and I forgive him for having no clue why the quote matters. Of course I forgive him. It can't be chance that I have encountered an English man on a Toronto street who can quote Shakespeare to me, and not just any lines but the very lines that Dad wrote to me who knows how many hours or minutes before he hanged himself. It is meant, it must be.

Beyond the door our Italian waiter charms us as if we are old friends of one another, of his, of the entire kitchen staff, only not strangers, and we are ushered to a table by the window. The room is warmed by the noise and smells of cooking coming from a kitchen which can be seen through several sheets of thick, greenish glass. It's a modernist touch, having the guts of the place exposed.

'You know something funny? Often when I'm on my way back from work I try to guess what the person sitting in this precise chair might look like but, ah, tonight I couldn't picture anyone. D'you think that's because it was going to be me?'

'Well, I'm sure you're much more attractive than the people who usually sit there,' says Luke, with such casual sincerity that I find myself enjoying the compliment. Most of the time I consider such smoothness unctuous and unforgivable. It is the insinuation that we can't see the puppeteer's arms that disturbs me. And yet charm seems an integral part of this man.

Water is poured and bread arrives, modern cubes flavoured for demanding palettes, with a shallow bowl of garlicky oil.

'I was going to take a bath,' I say as I reach for my glass, though which came first, the aqueous thought or the thirst, I can't say. 'I was going to soak in these biblical salts, sort of as a substitute to having any religious convictions.'

'Oh, I'm sorry,' Luke says, leaving a long enough pause for me to wonder whether it's my agnosticism that has him worried. 'I should have let you go home first. I'd have been more than happy to have waited.'

'More than happy?' I repeat with a laugh. 'Now there's a state.'

'Honestly, I—'

'No, please, I was just saying that. Besides, this is a much more divine experience.'

'Is it? Good.' He smiles then offers me a cigarette which I take and he lights, deftly with a Zippo lighter that seems too cowboyish for a dapper Brit in a suit. We order wine. White, we agree, to begin with: Côtes de Montravel. Seems this Luke knows his way around the vineyards.

'So,' he says, exhaling a cloud of smoke, 'here we are.'

'You're not usually here, are you?' I ask, snapping a tile of sesame toast between my fingers. A couple of seeds land in my water. I watch them as they spin in tension before joining to float together. I think it rather sweet and symbolic. 'Or am I wrong?'

'Not at all. I'm on business. My uncle's wife . . .'

I raise my hand, just a little. 'You know, in Canada we call them aunts.'

'Ants?' he asks, mimicking my accent. 'Creepy crawly ants?'

I smile right back at him. 'That's right, aunts as in asshole.'

He blinks. Damn, I've only just met this guy and he's English and they can be uptight as hell and hasn't my best friend Moira warned me a million times that I seem aggressive when I think I am being funny? Why do I assume that people sense when I like them? I am never able to tell. I tend to think I am hated or, at best, tolerated unless I do or say something to make others change their minds.

A smile breaks on Luke's face. 'Point taken,' he says. 'Except in England we say the r in arsehole and, unless I am mistaken, it was our language first.'

I smile back at him. Thank God it was a dry, English brand of humour I inherited from my dad. My dear, darling, intolerably dumb Canadian mother was the butt, not the source, of all the jokes in our family. I am unlike her.

'I'm sorry, Luke, you were saying . . .'

'Well, um, just that I'm staying with my uncle and ant until Friday, but they were busy tonight.'

'In formication, probably.'

'What?'

'It's the feeling of having ants crawling all over you. Your uncle might like it.' I laugh. 'Ants in his pants.'

'I thought you said fornication.'

'No.' I take a sip of the wine. 'I was only thinking about that.'

'Oh, right.' There's a moment's silence. 'Are you a writer, or something?'

'Sort of. I used to be a journalist but I'm about to get started on a novel.'

'Congratulations. That's excellent.'

I feel myself blush but thank Luke all the same.

He says, 'You're obviously very adept with words.'

'Am I? I guess I used to be.'

I tap the ash from the end of my Camel Light then tap it again. Daddy is back. His grip is never released for long. Yes, I used to be good at words. I knew more words than any seven-year-old in the land, he used to say. He himself was a wordsmith by profession, a lecturer on English language and medieval literature at the University of Toronto, and so loved the sight and sound of obscure and magnificent words. I think he saw them as characters lifted off the page.

I loved to learn things no one else knew; neither my friends in their playgrounds, nor his friends in theirs. At first, my mother played along. She, who had me instead of a college education, thought it flattering that her six-year-old daughter could flummox grown-ups with a knotty, esoteric vocabulary. She claimed some genetic credit while I tap-danced with my words: formication, athamantic, flibbertigibbet, mordacious, cacodorous, slubberdegullion. It was my party trick. I was able, too, to remember manias and ologies and phobias at the snap of Dad's fingers. Only as the years passed did it begin to matter to Mother that only my father and I understood, that the words were Greek to her. What scares me is that I myself have forgotten most of what Dad taught. My language has become less rich with each year since he died. I can only dig up random words. Monophobia; beblubbered; funipendulous. This last means hanging from a rope.

A waiter has arrived.

'Do you know what you want?' Luke asks.

'I want to go to England,' I reply, though it was a stupid thing to say, especially with the waiter hovering.

'I meant from the menu.'

'I know you did. I'm sorry. Ah, why don't I have—' The list is appetizing, but long. I feel indecisive. 'Whatever you're having.'

'I don't know what I'm having.'

'So, I'll enjoy the suspense.'

This is unlike me. Usually, I am neither loose with my trust nor comfortable with having my hand held, but the girl in the pharmacy has jolted my sense of balance. And yet, as I watch Luke order from the waiter I am struck by how warming and addictive the traditional wife routine could become. Although I have probably had these moments before when a soft ray of sunlight has greeted my wakening in a strange man's bed or when I have seen something of Dad in a lover, I don't think I have ever contemplated finding pleasure in being supplicant, feminine, easy to please. Now I wonder if it might take some of the strain out of being alive.

'My father was English.'

'Was he? What's your surname?'

It's an odd question. 'Mills.'

Luke nods.

'Do I pass?'

'What? Oh, yes. Yes, no, I was just asking. It's funny how often one meets people who are friends of friends,' he says, twiddling his left and right forefingers in tight little circles. 'That's all.'

I think of telling him that I am friends of friends, only not of his friends. Instead, I say, 'So what about you? Do you live in a big castle with a moat around it?'

This amuses Luke. 'No, not quite. A couple of people I know do but, no, my family comes from near Oxford.'

'My dad went to Cambridge. I always wanted him to go back there to teach.'

'Perhaps he enjoyed Canada too much.'

'Not a chance. He adored England. He used to talk about it all the time.' With my knife I sear a few lines across the butter's surface. 'He used to make up these amazing bedtime stories about me being an English princess in a castle. They were all connected, like medieval soaps I guess, but so detailed, and so loving about the gardens and the architecture and the fabric of my robes that he sort of put these ideas into my head that England was this utopia while Canada was, I don't know, some damp tower I had to be rescued from. He always said we'd go back one day but he ... we didn't.' With the addition of horizontal lines in the butter, the indentations look like a portcullis. 'What got me started on this? Oh, I know, the moat. What about you?' My ending seems to have caught Luke by surprise.

'Me? Oh, I can't imagine wanting to live anywhere other than where I grew up. It wouldn't be home.'

'That's because you're English.'

'Maybe, but didn't you grow up here? Aren't you Canadian?'

'Well, my mother's from here but . . . it's complicated.'

'I've always thought you Canadians were the most patriotic people in the world. You can't move for all the flags flying.'

'Yeah, but isn't it always miserable people who have to tell you how happy they are? Waving a flag and saying it's great to be Canadian doesn't in itself make us great.'

'I suppose I had better defer to your native judgment.'

'You had? Wow, I think I could get used to being deferred to.' A new basket of bread has been brought to us, bricks of focaccia and sourdough. I break some, though I'm not getting ideas above my station.

'But tell me about you,' I say, sponging up some peppery oil. 'Even if you don't have a castle I bet you're one of those English boys who spent your childhood cooped up in dormitories with lots of other sweaty boys.'

'Sort of,' Luke says, with what seems like embarrassment. He lifts his hands off the table and pauses while we are served our carpaccio. Oh, can't say I care for raw beef. There was a spinach and pinenut risotto I had my eye on, but I guess this has become my choice, my cake, and I had better eat it.

'I did go to a boarding school when I was seven.'

'That young? Wow. Did you cry?'

'My mum probably cried more than I did.'

'No kidding. You probably had to be reintroduced to her at the end of it all. "Do you remember your kid, Mrs Bingham? He may have grown a couple of inches in the last ten years."'

'We did have holidays, you know,' Luke declares with a buttoned-up expression I've noticed tensing his face once or twice. 'And, in fact, it was a lot of fun. People who aren't English don't really understand.'

This bugs me a little. I hold up my fork as I try to swallow a mouthful of carpaccio. 'Well, I'm half English and I understand that I would have hated being sent away from my father when I was only seven.'

Luke mumbles something about how it made him a man, but I can see he doesn't want to argue with me. That's sweet of him. I ask him instead whether he went to Oxford or Cambridge. He assures me that the university he attended in Edinburgh is 'only a notch below Oxford' and that, having spent those four years getting drunk or stoned or both, he strolled into his current job at a Canadian bank at which his uncle is a director. It is clear I don't need to ask awkward questions about qualifications or skills.

Our carpaccio is followed by gnocchi which is heading straight to my thighs. Not that I am bothered tonight. I am revelling in the sidewalk-skipping thrill of being here at all. Luke is smarter than I first took him to be. He is well-travelled and a good storyteller in a 'here's another funny story I've told before' way. And he has made me relax and laugh and forget about my self-pity. I am grateful for that.

'Pudding?' he asks, after I lay my fork down beside the cluster of gnocchi I've hidden under a large leaf of lettuce. 'It's all on the bank.'

'I'd love some coffee. If it's OK to plunder some of granny's savings account.'

'Of course.'

I order a double espresso and glance through the window. There is a woman, not much older than myself, scurrying by, her arms weighed down by grocery bags. She looks miserable. I can't lie, she has made me feel smug.

'Thank you, for this,' I say. 'I didn't feel like spending the evening alone.'

'I should be thanking you.'

'Can I look you up when I get to England?'

'Of course. Have you already got something lined up? A job?'

'Why? You got some spare uncles floating around?'

'There's my aunt.'

'I thought she was Canadian.'

'She is, but she's a journalist. I'm positive she'll have connections in England if you want to write for a newspaper again.'

I dunk a cube of sugar in my espresso and watch it darken. 'I'm not really the ambulance-chasing type. Though I wouldn't mind doing features, or something.'

'Well that's exactly what my aunt does. She's the features editor of the *Herald*. I'll ask her, shall I?'

Is this why I was led to Luke? So he can be my bridge to England?

'That'd be fantastic. You could say I've got some, you know, cuttings from when I worked on the *Herald* and you can say I wouldn't need much money just enough to pay my way and – and whatever.'

Listen to me. I am gibbering with my excitement, being inarticulate in a way unbecoming of an employable writer. Luke, however, either doesn't notice or chooses not to.

'I'm sure she'll help somehow.'

After our two bottles of wine, I think Luke looks almost impossibly handsome when he says those words. Suddenly in my soft-edged state I am yearning to kiss him, to take him home. I imagine he will be as considerate under the sheets as above them and, if no Picasso in the position department, then clean and tasty and comforting to wake beside.

'Do you have a girlfriend, Luke?'

'Excuse me?'

I freeze. Too often, I speak my mind when it serves me least well. 'Doesn't matter.'

'If you really want to know,' he says, pausing to light another cigarette, 'I ended something with somebody about two months ago.' He twists the signet ring on his left hand. 'So I'm free as a bird.'

'Is that good?'

'I rather like having someone around. Don't you?'

'Depends on the someone,' I say, flirting with my eyes.

'Of course.'

He is flirting back, I am sure he is. It makes me feel weightless. I say, 'Let's get the check,' then glance at my watch. 'Oh God, it's ten thirty-four.'

'Do you have to be somewhere?'

'No, it's, it's just that ten thirty-four is the time that most people in Toronto are, you know, at it. Doing it.'

'Most people?'

'Well, perhaps not most people but among the people who regularly do it, the most common time is ten thirty-four. Apparently.'

The waiter is quick with our check. Luke studies it carefully before tossing a card on to the plate. He leans back. 'Thanks for telling me that.'

'Actually, I shouldn't have. If you're anything like me you'll keep being drawn to clocks at ten thirty-four. Whatever I'm doing some evil voice inside me whispers, "Look at your watch, look at your watch."'

'Perhaps you shouldn't wear a watch.'

'Then I'd see yours, or something.'

'Well, I hope I haven't kept you from somewhere you needed to be.'

'Me? No. Here was good.' After the coffee, the last drip of wine tastes fruity on my tongue. 'Here was perfect.'

Does he get it? I think he gets it.

I go on, 'Anyway, me – soon as I see it's ten thirty-four I stop the action. It's creepy doing it knowing that others are at it too.'

'I can't imagine your other halves being best pleased.'

'Oh no, I only stop when I'm on my own.'

Luke looks embarrassed. Hasn't he drunk as much as me, or something? I say, 'Shall we get out of here?'

It is only two blocks home. Luke offers to walk me, as I thought he would. I think he likes me. How suddenly it has happened. Lives do change when we least expect them to. I think he will come in. I would like him to, though I am nervous about the state of the apartment. My bed is unmade, there are dishes in the sink, panties on the floor. I left late as usual this morning and there'll be an air of abandonment that might attach itself to me. And I am wearing horrible, grey knickers and only yesterday I noticed a couple of hairs on my left nipple which could use attention. Still, I want him to come in.

We reach my building. I jangle my keys, but not sluttishly. 'More coffee?' I suggest, to save Luke the embarrassment. 'It's already past ten thirty-four, so . . .'

He seems to have found something on the tip of his foot to interest him. He is embarrassed. Aren't the English adorable?

'Or come in and don't have coffee. I am licensed.'

Eyebrows raised, he asks, 'Licensed as what?'

'General good-time girl.' I twirl in a silly way. 'Or is it not good to be a good-time girl?'

'I think it's good,' he answers with the most kissable smile I've seen in years. 'But I'm afraid I had better get back. I wouldn't be very polite to my aunt if I didn't.'

I try hard to keep the surprise hidden.

'Here.' He takes out two business cards, one of which he hands to me, the other he flips over and writes my number on. I think his hand may be shaking a little. Then, sweetly, with a kiss on each cheek, he thanks me for having made his evening so very enjoyable, watches over me as I walk a little baffled and a little embarrassed into my building, and leaves with a kooky nod of his head and a promise to call.

Inside, my apartment feels different, somehow more welcoming than usual. Nor is it as untidy as I had remembered. Just a little less than perfect, the way I like it. Perfect scares me. Anything too good, too neat, scares me. Except, I guess, the natty neatness of this meeting, this Luke.

I finger the raised ink on his business card with a sensitive fingertip and say the name aloud. Luke Bingham, who'd have thought? Then I slide the card like a body between sheets into a smooth leather slit in my purse and wonder why he ran scared. Men always want to come in. It is the only reason to say no.

I glance at my answering machine. A keen red three is blinking. Three! I choose to ignore you, Machine. I am not interested in you tonight. Instead, I run myself a Dead Sea Salty bath in which, minutes later, I gently finger myself, with neither purpose nor passion, but just because life feels extraordinarily good and I don't want the bear-hugged teenager to have all the fun.

Later, I am woken by my dream. It is late, early, that hollow time between the two. The tick of my alarm clock is the only sound I can hear beyond the muffled thud of my heart. I sit up. It is almost four, too late for a sleeping pill, too early to get up or to read my way until dawn. My oversized T-shirt is sticking to my back, damp from sweat. I lift it off and, with a fistful of cotton, wipe my cheeks where the tears have been running. Then I plump the pillow, turn it dry side up, and lie down again. It is cold and makes me feel the same. I curl onto my side and stretch an arm over the vacant sheet.

I frighten them off, my men. By being me? How else can I be? In this darkness nothing seems remotely possible. I am frightened even of tomorrow which seems insurmountable, a maze of tunnels, the bricks of which are rough enough to cut into my hands. Blood, sweat and tears; life's one reliable triumvirate. I will try lying on my back. It is my father I cannot escape.

I don't know what to think of him any more. I think I hate him for killing himself when I wasn't old enough to be without him, and then I think I cannot because I adored him every day he was alive. He loved me as much, more. He used to sing that I was his sand, his sky, his munchable, kissable, sweet apple pie. I can hear the tune in this darkness and feel his breath on my neck and a pressure at the back of my thighs as if I am sideways on his knee. Sometimes I wake with the shock of falling off, though every time he caught me when he was alive.

Hate? No, I cannot hate air he doesn't walk through or shoes he doesn't wear or pages that lie unturned by his hands. I cannot hate cloud and memory. I loved him. Surely his death could not have undone that? But why, thirteen years on, am I being haunted? Why, when I don't believe in voices from the grave?

He comes in a dream and the dream comes every night. He is

lying on the floor of a large room. The walls are primrose-coloured, the floors bleached planks. It is a formal room, as if in a European palace. Although there are no windows, it is bright, almost spring-like, and there is a breeze. He has spectators. Sometimes I recognize Mother or my grandparents and, occasionally, myself. We sit on Regency gilt dining chairs arranged in a jumbled order. Some chairs are not facing the spectacle of this man on the floor. Each night the chairs are in different positions, but there is always space around Dad in which I move. I think I am naked. It is not a nightmare of details. The pastel colours and the slowness of movement suggest serenity, but the content terrifies.

I enter the room through two magnificent doors, carrying a thin tray. My father is calm. He, too, may be naked. I try to give him something from my tray but he doesn't move. He is dying quietly, not violently as he did. The others take what I am offering; some murmur. With my tray empty, I take a seat. Time passes. It seems I dream for hours.

I am then outside the room; no logic to it. When I return, Daddy is still. The people have drawn closer to him. It seems he has given birth; I suppose I am the child. I understand that he is dying but I am powerless to help. There is commotion in the room but no one dares step closer to him. I want to take the baby but it has been dumped on the floor. I begin to cry from the pit of me, a sensation my conscious body is able to recall absolutely. In the dream I want to give my life to save this man's, but he curls into a foetal ball. I can do nothing. It is theatre and I am audience.

When I wake I am always in tears, feeling bland, insipid, a shell of myself. And this is how I feel now; exhausted but unable to sleep.

I suck in a deep breath and try to think of beautiful things; of anything but the dream. I picture a blue sky, a lake, a million pink flamingoes. And, as I start to float back to sleep, I think of Luke Bingham.

He is a stranger again. The ease we shared has dissipated. I am scared of him now. How could I have suggested he talk with his aunt? I am not a journalist. Luck was all it was when I began: a scoop, a downtown skinhead brawl and Lady Luck had it that Derek's useless friends were there and I was the only journalist they'd talk to. When a gap opened in the market, I was there to fill it. Young life in Toronto. Offbeat stories, nothing newsy. Lies half the time. I was twenty and most of my peers were at college instead. Luke's aunt won't miss the fraud. I am ashamed of his asking her. And tomorrow there's the new show to book for *Crow's Nest*. Women writers from the festival, I know their agents won't agree. Oh, I can't believe I told Luke I was writing a novel. Nine years the same twelve pages. It's a fucking joke. I turn back on to my side. There is a hole in my stomach into which my heart falls. Hearts do sink. It only became a cliché because there are billions of hearts and only so many words. I would shore mine up if only I knew how.

Could it have been different? When I was in sixth grade my friend Amy was hit by a car. She fell into a coma out of which she emerged with almost no memory of her mental or physical past. Everything had to be relearned: how to walk and eat, how to recognize her family and friends. Then, none of us envied her. Now, I wonder if I do.

Would I be happy if I wasn't weighed down by the memory of my father? Probably. And yet, I couldn't lose my memory and hang on to myself. Doesn't my understanding of everything depend on the miraculous fusion of what I perceive and feel with my memories of those signals? And since I learned my responses from Daddy, since my tastes are his tastes, my desires his desires, he exists in every millisecond of my life. He lives. Would I choose to lose that in return for a life unburdened by this loss? I don't know. I don't know. I do not know.

I need pills. The light in the bathroom hurts my red-streaked eyes. Look at me. I have that vacant expression sometimes even I don't recognize and, though I am lucky in having deceptively healthy olive skin, I look pale now, as if I am the ghost, not he. Dad's legacy is internal, it is Mother's Quebecois mother I resemble – our dark hair and chocolate-brown eyes astonishingly similar. The curve of my jaw is Mother's. Only the mole on my forehead, this sweet genetic kiss, comes from him. I like to think of it as a microchip passing to me the make-up of his soul.

Back to earth, I tip a sleeping pill into my hand, my wrinkling hand, swallow it with a palmful of scooped water, and return to bed. I find a classical music station on the radio and turn it low. Chopin – it's pretty. Dad liked piano. I think of him playing his scratchy records in his study at the top of the stairs. I knock, enter. He is working at his desk. He grins. 'It's you, my precious Pea.' He holds out his arms. I climb into his lap and rest my head against his shoulder to sleep, yes, to sleep.

'The wanderer returns.' Iain is swinging himself from side to side in his chair. He looks smug and well-rested, while I am puffy-faced and tired. I need this cappuccino I've brought up from Dominic's Diner downstairs.

'Crow's been looking for you. I told him you had to go to the women's bits' doctor.'

I make a disapproving face. 'Thanks. I guess.'

'No problem. He says he's sorry about your VD.'

I slump in my chair. 'Iain, I am not in the mood.'

'For what?'

'You. Jokes. You making jokes, especially.'

'Not enough sleep, eh? I shouldn't have woken you.'

'No, thanks for doing that. I slept right through the alarm.'

'Out all night, were you?'

I sweep some hair, still wet from my rushed shower, behind my left ear as I look through the morning's mail. Last night is already a different country. I feel a little battered, although this morning the phobia's dissipated like mist. We survive our nights. 'I wasn't out late. You know I don't sleep.'

'Oh, like I'm there to know these things.'

'No one's there.' I rip open an envelope. 'Why do they keep sending me these appeals? Don't crack-babies know how broke I am?'

'You didn't go out with some English guy, then?'

I lift my eyes. Iain is smirking. I say nothing. I don't know what he knows or how. I don't like this feeling.

'Only, you see, this charming chappy called Luke Bingham called this morning; said he'd had dinner with you.' Now he throws a paper aeroplane at me which lands, annoyingly, in my coffee. He claps in delight. 'You'd better take a look before the ink runs.'

I open out the sheet. HRH Luke Bingham, Iain has written, called to enquire as to the health of his charming companion of yestereve. He prays you will do him the honour of returning his call at your earliest convenience. After this, Iain has written a number, and a heart with an arrow through it. Funny.

'He's somebody with a possible job for me. In England.'

'He sounded choppy.'

'Whatever, Iain. Did he say when I should call?'

'Aye, forthwith. Most expeditiously.'

With an unashamedly childish roll of my eyes I take my coffee to Melissa's phone, out of earshot from Iain, and dial the number. It is true, Luke's consonants make him sound brusque on the phone, choppy, I guess, yet he is all geniality and charm. He tells me he spoke to his aunt last night, that the news is excellent, the timing uncannily perfect, that I should give her a call. He's a sweetheart, as it turns out. I don't know why I frightened myself so last night.

After I hang up I stare at the number Luke has given me, but before I have time to get nervous I have dialled it and spoken to the ant's secretary. We arrange a meeting for this very lunchtime.

Snap, quick as that.

I worry, of course, that I am dressed inappropriately (black jeans, white top), though there is a certain newsprint motif to my colour scheme. And yet when I am shown in to meet the editing ant, I am able to present the version of myself I prefer: Portia Mills the writer, the daughter of an English professor at U of T, the classy mix of refinement, English name, aristocratic nose, poise – and can-do feminist chutzpah.

The job on offer, a weekly column from London, genuinely suits my writing style. And I like the ant. She has that brisk efficiency good journalists learn early and seems genuinely pleased to meet me. I am so convinced she is on my side that I leave more confident than I have from any interview in my life.

As it turns out, my instincts are good. Within hours, the ant calls to say the job is mine. I can leave for London when I like and we agree on a month.

My luck is still slowly sinking in when Luke telephones the following night, from the airport, as a lover would. He is full of apologies that he hadn't called before, but he had to rush to Ottawa. Now he is on his way home. I am disappointed. I had been wanting to celebrate with him.

'Do you know where you'll be living in London?' he asks.

'I haven't even thought. I have an aunt somewhere near London but I don't know. I'll find somewhere.'

I am not worried. The job, a thousand words a week for the paper's Sunday edition, is paying well and I hope to earn yet more writing freelance.

Without hesitation, Luke offers, 'You're more than welcome to stay at my flat if you want. I've got a spare room that no one's using.'

I make the usual unconvincing noises of protest, but I don't take long to accept. Nor do I admit that I'd have been happy to sleep among the rose bushes under the stars, just so long as I was in England.

Luke sounds delighted that I've accepted. He promises to call me soon and then we laugh at how quickly this has all happened, like in the movies we agree, though neither of us mentions how the next celluloid step would be our falling in love. Is it on Luke's mind? For my part, I am leaving it to the gods since they seem, for a while, to have defected to my side.

'See you in Blighty, then,' he says.

'I guess so,' I reply, smiling a smile that recedes long after I have pressed the receiver back into its snug cradle.

TWO

Do not complain about your problems. Instead, talk things over with your family and friends; seek positive feedback and listen to their opinions.

AMA Family Medical Guide

A month later I am at Mother's thinking of all that has passed between these walls, of the plates and glasses and insults thrown, even of the blood that has occasionally been shed. This kitchen is Lady Macbeth's bedroom, it's hosted so much madness. In a drawer by the fridge is a fork which, eight years ago, I threw at Mother. I had made some joke about the sheets of lasagne being tough as old linoleum and we slipped, as often we would, from a swipe about my ingratitude to a screaming match over blame, which ended with my lobbing the fork in her direction, harder than I had meant. If you look closely at her crestfallen cheeks you'll see the tiny maggot of a scar beneath her right eye. For some time I considered it something of a victory that she had no choice but to lay that same fork at the table and draw the prongs between her lips. Now I am ashamed of what I did. I would tell her if I knew how.

She collects my plate, and I thank her; the good daughter. She has developed a nurse's graceless bustle in the twelve years since joining the staff at the Ashbridge Bay Nursing Home and grabs at my plate as if the task is keeping her from more pressing duties: bedpans, enemas, drugs that need to be forced through blanched lips. Truth is, she has nothing to do this afternoon but say goodbye. I leave tomorrow.

My mother took to nursing as a penance, saw an opportunity to extend lives having helped abbreviate one. She has paid with her appearance. Although she is a good size for a forty-eight-year-old, her hair is mostly grey and her skin wan, as if she has contracted senility from the elderly people at the home. She has sought a younger image by cropping her hair, but the new pixie style has added to the briskness that now defines her. Her spry enthusiasm, evident on Dad's old 8mm films, has been replaced by a weary, scuttling efficiency.

'Coffee?'

'Please.'

She fills the espresso maker and lights the ring beneath it. Drips of water fizzle and pop near the flame. The gas whispers. If it were to speak it would shame me with a trinity of sins. One: my turning the oven's heat up full, to four-fifty or more, three years after the suicide when Mother had found courage to ask guests. The Christmas turkey was cooked and being kept warm while the grown-ups got sozzled. I ruined the bird, burnt it crisp, was forgiven. Those were the last days of Mother's tolerance, before I was dispatched to the mind-doctors, before our descent into absolute war. Two: later that same holiday I loosely rewrapped Mother's best gift to me, a stylish black blouse she could barely afford, around a wooden spoon which I held above the gas's eager flame until the black burned a brilliant yellow. Her shock was so absolute that I can picture it perfectly now. It leaves me with a bilious shame.

The third, cruellest sin I committed two years previously when I staged my own suicide. I remember my heart-thumping eagerness as I watched for Mother's car from the window upstairs then the dash on bare feet to the kitchen, the twisted angle in which I lay on the lino, the greasy cold of the oven rack against my cheek, the brief terror as the gas hissed in my ear while

Mother slowly climbed the stairs to the bathroom before coming down to find me. Perhaps I coughed myself into obvious consciousness a little too loudly and a little too soon, but it almost scared the life out of her, she who had already lost so much. I was capable, back then, of such things.

Now I offer to help at the sink but am told, firmly and in a voice that has become more peremptory, more matronly over the years, to stay put. We are treading carefully, relieved, but still uncomfortable, with our new détente.

At least in the days when we fought we knew where the battle lines were drawn. Often, I would visit Mother with my latest boyfriend, either one of the men she considered too old (a shoddy accusation since Dad was twenty-two years her senior) or a spiked-hair loser I had picked up somewhere around the city. She never refused to have me, despite the inevitable arguments. I think she decided years ago that she was going to perform the soup-and-turkey-and-ironed-clothes gig however much I hated her. That didn't work. She could not and cannot make herself less culpable through maternal diligence and good cooking. Nothing fundamental has changed. Dad would be alive if Mother had left us. I was thirteen. He and I would have managed.

'What is this friend like?' she asks me, vigorously drying the plates instead of leaving them to drip, as I would.

'Luke? You'd approve.'

She takes this well and her features soften. 'Are you two . . .?'

'No, we're not. I'm just going to stay with him a while. Until I find my feet.'

'Glory, that long?'

It is measure of the distance we have come since my grandfather's death that I tolerate the joke.

Mumpsimus, as Dad had nicknamed him, died eighteen months ago when he was only seventy-four. We buried him on a freezing, unkind day beside my grandmother in a plot in local Mount Pleasant. After the ceremony there was a small gathering here at the house. I stayed until the end, hating it but helping with glasses, drink, small talk. The party seemed unnecessary, forced. Mumpsimus was never a gregarious man.

After the final goodbyes I collected my things and called for Mother. I found her alone, hunched within herself in the garden, crying in a scary, undramatic way. She seemed oblivious to the snow dampening her clothes. I fetched her a coat from the house, but she seemed so desolate that I could not leave. Have you seen that expression on a person? When a son is murdered for twenty-five cents; when a family is buried alive in an earthquake. It terrifies, turns what we think we understand upside down. That evening it spoke to something better in me than the rage I was most used to venting. We were daughters who had lost. Now she knew. I said I would stay the night.

We watched television, cooked scrambled egg, chatted loosely about unimportant things. To anyone ignorant of our past it would have seemed an unexceptional evening. To us it was anything but, the first night in nine years that Mother and I had slept under the same roof. It should mean nothing that we behaved like adults since adults are clearly less forgiving than children, and yet the evening marked the end of a relationship that had begun when I was still a child. Whatever was to follow was the start of something new: this truce, this acceptance of one another. I am glad for it.

Chocolates have appeared with the coffee. Mother is never without a box. They are given to her by the grateful, guilty children of residents at Ashbridge Bay. It comes as no surprise that this strawberry cream is stale, but I say nothing. We tread with care.

'I saw your amusing Indian running around.'

'That Algonquin? Iain and I thought he was a jerk.' I put my feet against the table and push myself back on the chair, but then, without being asked, I sit straight again. With each visit it becomes easier being adult rather than rebellious child. 'It's weird, Iain's about the only person I'm going to miss. Oh, and Moira.'

'What about . . .?'

I avert my eyes. 'Friends, I meant.'

'What about Jennifer, or Tom?'

'I don't even have their numbers.'

Jennifer and Tom were friends of mine from North Toronto. She was my closest girlfriend, but when she found God, she lost me. And Tom? Well, he and I found each other under the sheets one night and, unglued, we stayed unstuck. I think he joined the Mounties, of all bizarre things, but I haven't seen him in years. Mother habitually brings up names I have let sail away.

I swill my coffee in its cup and knock it back. It is good. She inherited the taste and the skill from her own mother, a Francophone from Quebec, and was never won over by Dad's passion for milky tea. Nor, strangely, was I.

I ask, 'Have you seen Leonard recently?'

'No, not for a while.'

Leonard is Mother's latest, a widower ten years her senior who made a fortune selling sonic cat deterrents. Although I have stopped trying to sabotage her romantic life, I think Leonard weaselly and have taunted him with a contrived devotion to the furry pets.

'He's moving to Ottawa,' she says, then, unconvincingly, 'for the best, I think.'

'More cat-haters there?'

'Portia. He's a nice man. He was nice to me.'

I wish Mother would find a man. It feels odd worrying about her, makes me less sure of myself.

I stand. 'I want to take some photographs to England. Can I?'

'What photographs?'

'You know, ones to remind me. From the chest.'

My mother raises her eyebrows. I suspect she would burn every image of Daddy if I let her. 'Take them all.'

Our photographs are jumbled in three shoe boxes kept in a pine chest at the top of the stairs. It has a rich, complex odour like nothing else I know. Musty clothes, cardboard boxes of children's games, Operation, Cluedo, my Mork and Mindy dolls,

Kerplonk, the Game of Life – and dusty cloves from a wizened Christmas decoration mingle with the sweet scent of the polished pine. It reminds me of where the chest used to be, in my bedroom at our old house. Its lid was a second home to the furry animals I exiled from my bed. I still do that, tire quickly of the creatures sharing my mattress. I am always the one to question the love, to compare it with what I once knew. No one survives that.

It was on this chest, too, that Dad left his last note to me, the quote from Shakespeare and six kisses beside a simple D. I am convinced he wrote it in his final moments because the pen bled ink where the nib bobbled over the rough grain and then ran up against a knot in the wood. If he'd had any doubts, this brief obstacle might have been enough – a heartbeat's pause in which to think of me and change his mind. If.

I grab a handful of photographs and sit with my back to the chest. My memory is so poor that sometimes I have to look at these to prove I existed as a child. Although the prospect of England is a constant reminder that life is suddenly good, it is heartwrenching to be presented with these images of happier times. Nostalgia must be the price we pay for a place in history. Here I am on Dad's shoulders, aged three or four. At forty-six and with his balding head and thick-rimmed glasses, he looks an unlikely father but there is no doubt how I adored him. I am leaning forward with my hands under his chin, wearing a wide grin that is pushing my eyes half-closed. Mother is walking listlessly behind, looking pensive.

She didn't want me. Aged only twenty-one, I think she saw death in my beginning, a symbolic end to her usefulness and purpose, an actual end to her youth. Certainly, the weight she picked up during pregnancy did not fall off easily and the effect of cutting her long hair to the shoulders seemed to turn her, within a year, from a child of the sixties to a woman and mother of the seventies. And it is I who carry the blame.

Her transformation is evident when I hold two photos side by side. They are rectangular Polaroids with white borders, one is in colour, the other black and white. In the colour, I am standing next to Mother wearing a red-checked dress that looks like a tablecloth. I must be less than two. I don't look steady on my legs, the way my feet are splayed apart and my diaper is centre of gravity. Mother is wearing an injudicious, lime-green sleeveless dress that looks patterned with house plants. Her putty-like arms are thick at the shoulder, her face is chubby. She looks tired and uninterested, as if I have been handed to her and she can't find a place to put me down.

In the other image, dated April 1969, my parents are together on a lawn somewhere. Dad is sitting up behind Mother and she is leaning back against him, her body between his legs, one hand on each thigh. He has his arms wrapped around her waist. She is laughing. It makes her look vibrant and very young; a person I never knew.

I come to these photographs to weld together my strained, fragmentary recollections; to reassure myself with the proof of them. But in the jigsaw of my youth, the love my parents shared is the piece that never fits. Occasionally, if I crept downstairs when they thought I was asleep and they were relaxed, one lying on the other on the couch or else playing cards or joking with the Breyers or Ted Cardoza and Sally Green or the Mitchelsons in the magical haze of cigarette smoke and liquor and loud, incomprehensible, grown-up jargon, I saw them happy, but mostly they were not. Yet look at them before I was born! There is nothing forced about the smiles and locked arms, about the coupling itself. Single since, Mother must miss that. Then again, don't we all miss the past every day? We were all happier then.

Oh, I mustn't do this. Already my eyes are brimming with tears. Quickly, I gather the few prints I want. I reach for a folder in which to store them. This one's old, it has 35 millimetre proudly written on the front and the words 'Try flash this year'. The colouring is muted, dated. I pick at the tape sealing it shut. Inside, there is a printed stamp reading: Boots, Nottingham. Must have belonged to Dad. There is a picture of him inside. He is dressed in winter clothes, duffel coat and woolly hat, standing in snow with his arm around Mother's shoulder and . . . wait, that isn't her, it is a woman, a girl, almost. Someone I don't recognize.

Downstairs, I ask, 'Who's that with Dad?'
'Where did you find this?'
'Upstairs.'
'I don't know who it is.'
'I'll ask Aunt Barbara when I'm in England.'
'Don't,' Mother snaps, then, more gently, 'I doubt she'll know.'
'No harm asking.' I rap the photo lightly against my fingertips.
Mother looks annoyed. She is always trying to bury Dad deeper while I want the reverse. 'Where did you say this was?'
'In a folder in the chest.'
She nods then, sitting on the arm of her ugly beige sofa, looks up at me and says, 'She was called Diane. She was a friend of your father's.'
'You mean a girlfriend?'
'In a sense.'
'In a sense what? Stop being all oblique, will you?'
'She was his first wife.'
I think it is some kind of joke at first. 'What do you mean?'
'Before me.'
Mother is looking defensive, scared that we may fight. I am too uncomfortable to sit.
'What? She . . .? But she looks about fifteen.'
'She was old enough, it was legal.'
'Of course, but I mean, why didn't I know about it? What happened with them? I can't believe I didn't know. How long were they married?'
'No time, less than a couple of years.'
'Two years? And I didn't know?'
'Portia, even I didn't know until after your father died. So I am sorry. With all that was happening then, telling you didn't seem a priority.'
'Why not?'
This annoys her. She's unpredictable like that. 'You tell me

why it matters so much what Clive did before you were even thought of. God knows he got up to enough you have no clue about.'

'Can we not get into that?'

She is always reminding me of how I was too young to understand Dad, though she refuses to help me know him more. Breathless and hoarse from insults, I have demanded countless times that she explain to me what went wrong in his life apart from them, their loveless marriage. Dad was not a depressive, not a criminal, not a freak. He was a romantic who taught and lived and breathed medieval poetry about chivalrous love; the love of one man for one woman. Yet, every day he returned home to this woman who had chosen to fall out of love with him. Is there anything else to say?

'Listen, I'm just going to go. OK? Before—'

'Portia, I'm sorry we didn't tell you. She was in Clive's past.'

'Which obviously impacts my present.'

'Oh, Pea, grow up.'

'Don't call me that. And, don't tell me to grow up. You know it makes a difference that Dad was married before.'

'And how is that?'

'Every way. Every way. I know you'd prefer it if I knew nothing about him at all.'

'Don't be cruel.'

'Well, stop trying to undo us, then. Please.'

Mother has crossed her hands on her lap, a gesture which suggests to me both repentant schoolgirl and impatient teacher. We say nothing. In the kitchen I take a few deep breaths and sit to drink a glass of water. Being angry with Mother doesn't relieve the pain as it once did. It turns itself back on me.

Returning next door, I ask, 'Was she pregnant? Is that why they married?'

'No.'

'So he must have loved her.'

'Yes, I think he did. In his way.'

'His way? Why do you say things like that?' I pick up my bag, slip the photo inside. 'Do you know why it ended?'

'They weren't happy. Diane left him.'

'Then he came here?'

'Yes.'

'Poor him.'

She pauses, blinks once, 'He wasn't blameless.'

Though I smile, I don't mean to be generous. 'I knew you'd say that.'

'It's true. He wasn't a saint with Diane.'

'And she was with him?'

'No, none of us is.'

'Not even you?'

Quietly, 'That's not something I have ever claimed to be.'

There is a strained silence before I announce that I am leaving.

'You have to leave now?'

'Yes.' Oh, I didn't want our farewell to end this way.

'Can I drive you to the airport tomorrow?'

'Iain,' I lie, 'is taking me.'

She nods, then strokes a hair off my forehead. I feel myself flinch, wish I hadn't.

'When do you think you'll come back?'

'Mother, I'm not even out of the door and—'

'I meant Christmas, Portia, not for ever. You never tell me your plans.'

'Because I haven't made any. I don't know. But not soon.'

In silence, she shadows me to the door where she gives me a tight hug, kisses my neck and then jerks her head back fast. Go now and quickly her body language suggests, yet she has taken my free hand in hers. 'You won't expect too much, will you? Over there.'

The remark surprises although – it is true – I am expecting my world to find its axis again. 'No.'

'Promise me?' Quickly, she cups a hand over the heart of her face as if to catch the tears she is now pressing against the bridge

43

of her nose. She sniffs, smiles bravely. 'Call me, won't you? Say you've arrived safely.'

'Yup.'

A couple more tears break and course down her cheeks. They bring a lump to my throat.

'Makes me feel orphaned, your going,' she says with a breathy, silly-old-me laugh. She wipes at the tears with the back of her hand.

'Don't say that. Don't make me feel bad.'

'Oh, Portia. Always you,' she begins.

'I'll see you soon.' I kiss her again, taste the salt on my lips as I used to after he died, when we cried together night after night.

When I turn to wave goodbye I am shocked to see how Mother perilously resembles her own mother, Grandmamma Bec, reproachful and drawn before cancer took her away at the age of fifty-four. I can't look again. If I were to, she might see tears in my eyes as well.

I walk on. These were the streets of my childhood. It is unnerving how little they have changed. Ahead of me on a blood-red bicycle a young girl is weaving in and out of the trees' dappled shade. I step aside as she passes. Nothing about me means anything to her, not the way I keep my hair long or wear black most of the time or have, so I am told, bedroom eyes; nor that my father hanged himself less than five minutes from here. I am an adult, foreign. I don't know how it happened. Inside, I am obviously child. It is a mystery how Mother, twenty-one when I was born, coped with having me. I couldn't be a parent. I have neither the meekness for such an abandonment of self nor the moral confidence to print my pattern on another. Will I ever?

I envy the girl. The world feels orderly and light on your shoulders before you are ten. You don't begin to imagine how clueless adults are. The possession of answers is what makes grown-ups adults at all. These detached dark brick houses are set back from the road and have the appearance of homes drawn by kids; square with sloping, tiled roofs, white windows and sturdy front doors enclosed by porches from which three stone steps decline to the street. Each house has a single chimney, a drainpipe, a square of lawn and a maple tree. It's very Canadian, the democracy of this arboreal distribution. No wonder it bugged me when I was a teenage girl.

  Today, its appeal is obvious. It is too generous an afternoon for being inside so the air is crowded with the chug of lawn mowers, with birdsong and kids' playful yells. I recall days such as this, starfished on the lawn listening to the phutphutting of sprinklers and watching jets stream across the blue, else riding my bike with Dad or swimming with Jenny van Darlen at her home. It is all so long ago, all yesterday. My throat is torn from swallowing memories bent out of shape by his leaving.

  I was staying the night with Jenny when Dad killed himself. She lived in a huge house a couple of blocks from me, her father having made his fortune in communication technology before such men were two a penny. Her friendship was priceless to me, her house a den. Since Jenny's older sister had died from leukaemia, her mother was (I knew) a pushover and (this I didn't know) an alcoholic too. She furnished us with junk food, late-night TV, dinners out at the Chinese. Whenever we could, Jenny and I would play in the Jacuzzi, drinking sodas out of crystal champagne flutes sneaked from the cupboard downstairs while floating under hot bubbles as if we were the stars of *Dallas*. It was there, too, that we prodded and poked at our burgeoning, febrile bodies; rather Jenny than an icky boy with playground dirt under his nails. Still, our naughtiness never felt sinful and though sometimes a lesbian fantasy sneaks into my mind, I doubt such thoughts were sown by those Cola-breathed pecks of years ago.

  I turn down Tranmer. Oh, listen: fourteen years and has nothing changed? Through an open window at Cynthia Maynard's I can hear the sound of a child learning the piano. Mrs Maynard was already grey when she taught me, but obviously she is still at it. And here's the sign, PERENNIALS FOR SALE, ALL PROCEEDS TO CHARITY, that she has had since time began, only now it is an urban youth drug programme she wants to support, not Ethiopia. I was a good student, and patient. Dad loved listening to me play. He would sit on the piano stool beside me, else I'd climb on his lap and giggle furiously when he failed to press the pedals when asked. After his death, I quit. Mother kept trying to coax me back, but I refused and, in time, she sold the pretty upright Grandmamma Bec had given me. We never spoke of it again. Now the sound brings regret stinging in my throat.

I have reached Eastbourne Avenue. If I keep walking this way I'll soon arrive at the house where we lived and he died. Should I go?

I stop by a gleaming yellow hydrant on the sidewalk to light a cigarette. My hands are shaking so much it takes three matches before the tobacco is lit. Would a visit do more harm than good? As I am wondering, a car passes slowly, a Toyota family saloon. A boy in the back seat is staring at me with big eyes. He twists his neck as he passes, opens his mouth to speak. Oh God, he recognizes me, he's pointing out the poor Mills girl to his mom. She's the one whose father hanged himself.

But what am I thinking? It has been thirteen years. It is only me who remembers the day as if it was yesterday. Isn't it time to begin to forget?

Timidly, I walk the two blocks north to the junction of Anderson and Eastbourne, and raise my eyes. There, under the maple tree by our house, Dad stood waving at me. I was turning this corner on my bicycle, and though I turned my head back, I pretended not to see him. I should have waved goodbye. It was the last time I saw him alive.

The day had been strange and tense. The night before there had been a run-in with the university, yet another visit from the Dean and some stranger which had left the air acrid. Dad and Mother couldn't even look one another in the eye over dinner. I was stuck in the middle. And then the next day, when Mother was out, Dad came into my bedroom when I wasn't expecting him, didn't even knock and there I was exploring myself in the mirror, feeling the tiny bumps on my chest, the one on my left twice the size of the other and worrying me. Nothing was more private to me than that, even with Jenny I had been coy. I was too embarrassed to tell Mother, even though I was scared that something was remiss, that real, soft breasts would never emerge from hard lumps such as those. Why then, of all times, did Dad have to come in? I yelled and swore at him. He was the worst person to discover my secret because hiding it from him felt like a betrayal of our love. With my shame I hated him, suddenly, urgently.

He should have left at once, but instead he came over to hug me. I know he didn't like to fight, he was soft in that way, so he hugged me to him before I'd got my top back on, not in a bad way, not in the way those shrinks later suggested, but just because he loved me. In return I thumped my fists against his back, hard as I could. What's the point of me having a door if my room's going to be a fucking corridor? I screamed as I ran from the room. I hate you. I hate you. Those were the last words I spoke to the only man I've loved with all my heart.

I wrote a note for Mother saying I was going to sleep over at Jenny's. Dad followed me out. 'Don't be angry, my Pea. I'm sorry.' I couldn't bear to look at him as I bicycled away, only once, here, did I turn to see him waving. That's when I didn't wave back; I didn't wave back.

It is quiet now. A ghost town. I do not believe in ghosts and yet I can still spook myself. An English accent, a particular tone of voice, will make me turn sharply. A similar profile might make me start. And when I am feeling stoned or fanciful I have been known to ask Dad to contact me through the wind or the play of a shadow tossed against a wall. My bluff has sometimes been called. A sudden gust, the rattle of a can on the sidewalk, the brush of something against my skin and I will scare myself. It is foolish. If there is an afterlife, it is inside us. I cannot be scared of that.

This is the poorer end of the avenue. The houses here are more crude and some of the gardens unkempt. Dad kept ours immaculate. He liked gardening, mowing in perfect strips and planting the beds with rose bushes and flowers that reminded him of England. Now I lean against a lamp opposite our old house and see with sadness mossy fringes of green where Dad kept the edges sharp.

We left the house in good shape. For an academic, my father was dexterous. In his forties he had something of the nineteen forties about him, a can-do, one tea bag for four, I'll be buggered paying someone else good money to do that British spirit. He built me a wendy house, made all the bookshelves, repaired the windows, fixed whatever needed fixing; he even taught me knots and their names. I know the rope he used when he hanged himself had been kept in the shed for years.

For some minutes I stare at the house, shards of memory coursing through my veins and making my fingertips tingle. I would wait at that top window for him, my breath steaming the glass, then race down to reach the door first where I would wrap my little hand around one of his fingers and pull him to see what I had been drawing or making or learning to do. He never failed to follow. He was exceptional like that.

I cross the street. We had a swing on this front lawn and here, yes, just here, I learned to ride my bike. I stare at the empty sidewalk. It was a crisp day, though soggy red leaves starred and hugged the grass. Dad was holding my shoulders. He must have been holding me because I was moving, riding fast. And then I felt my shoulders were free and it was like flying. He was shouting with joy. 'Go, Pea, go.' I turned to look at him and, as I did so, the bars twisted in my hand and the wheel turned in on itself and I fell with a cry but it didn't matter because he was there, hugging me, lifting me, kissing my neck. 'You did it, my beautiful girl. You did it for me.' As if I would have learned for anyone else.

'Damn you, Daddy,' I whisper aloud. 'Damn you.'

The house looks deserted this afternoon. Quickly, I follow the path towards the back garden, trailing one of my hands against the rough brick wall, pushing my fingertips hard against the grain so they hurt. When I kick the bottom of the warped wooden gate it yields, scraping with a familiar sound, leading me back in the garden once again.

The green paint is peeling around the window from which he let himself fall. How I wish it could talk to me. Countless times I have tried to piece together those final hours and minutes of my father's life. Not knowing has fuelled my nightmares. I cannot help but imagine the worst kind of torment, the most excruciating pain.

It was my mother who found him. Crusty-eyed from sleep, she shuffled into the kitchen and screamed for Dad when she saw legs against the kitchen door's glass pane. At first, she thought a man was going up, not coming down, that she had caught an intruder attempting to clamber through my window upstairs. But then no sound came from within the house and she realized that these legs weren't moving, that they were clothed in pants she recognized; that it was he. She ran to open the door, but the weight of him against it made it too heavy so she bolted upstairs and into my room where at once she saw that my bed had been moved to the window and that from one of its legs was a rope that was taut from the weight of him.

What she did after the discovery she has never said and I have never asked. He was already dead. She called the police. He was taken away. He left without saying goodbye. Does anything else matter but that? I lift my eyes once more to the window and suddenly feel my fists clenching in anger at the nights lost and tears spilled and years wasted. The feeling scares me. It is not love or longing. I want to scream at Dad for being so careless with my life, with Mother's life. Was it so terrible being alive? Why did he have to pass the pain to us? We did not ask for it, deserve it. More than anyone, he should have cared for us.

Suddenly, I pick up a stone from the flower bed and hurl it towards the window. The smash of the glass is so loud it shocks me. With the pane still falling to the ground, I run as fast as I can through the open gate, past the kitchen, past the driveway where he was standing and waving at me. At the sidewalk, I turn right and then right again on to Eglinton. I don't look back. Running, running, I go past the entrance to the park where I was screwed by Josh Medwood, past Verdura, the restaurant from which I was fired, past the bus stop onto which I myself scrawled obscene graffiti – Portia Mills eats dick and swallows cum – because I knew it would tear at Mother's heart, and on towards the subway station, away from this neighbourhood, this half-life, this present past; away, away from him.

THREE

> Concentrate on the present. Do not brood about the past. Think about the future in terms of changes you can make. Do not worry about a future you cannot control.
>
> AMA Family Medical Guide

I notice Luke the moment I pass through customs at Heathrow. He is looking fit and tanned and handsome.

'Hello there, you made it.'

'I made it.'

He rests a hand on my left shoulder and leans in to kiss both cheeks. His skin is newly shaven and smells, I think, of sandalwood.

'You look as if you've just got out of bed.'

'Uh-oh, do I?' I am doubtless a disappointment to him. He must have been eager, remembering how I looked across the flickering candlelight.

'I meant you look as if you had a better night's sleep than I did.'

'Oh, wow. Probably I'm still drunk. Can't resist those free drinks.'

'Well, I think it's wonderful you're all smiles. Come on, let me take that trolley.'

When I described Luke to Moira I said he was charm's

essence itself, that if the virtue was bottled, no better name could be found for it than his. Now he has confidence, too. His ums and ers have so far been swallowed.

'I've parked this way.'

As we are leaving the terminal I glance up at a monochrome security screen and immediately love what I see. We look like an attractive couple. Perhaps I was right in imagining this reunion would be as magical and alluring as the fantasies in the romance novels Mother likes to read. My man is a prince in black and white. There'll be plenty of time to add colour after this.

We are soon out of the airport. Luke is driving fast in his cool black convertible. He has one hand on the wheel, the other cupping a cigarette against the wind. He looks handsome with his Ray Ban shades and new haircut. Outside, too, it is majestic: sunny and better than I had dared to hope. The world gleams with its fresh coat of paint. I know this M road is ugly as sin, but it doesn't seem to matter. This beholder finds it beautiful.

When a song I know screams in on the radio, I turn it up loud and start to sing. 'Get up and get down and get up out of your seat/Get up and get down get up and move your feet.' It is perfect: the hippest, happiest, blackest kind of soul. Luke is swaying a little but he is not doing what the Dramatics want of him. 'Clap your hands. Stamp your feet/In time with music, get on down with the beat!' Since he has put his cigarette in his mouth and is running a hand through his hair he surely wants to be part of the vibe, but he is behind the beat. When he tries to catch the words he misses. He is like one of those kids you see wearing thick glasses in the park, their hands grasping air while the ball falls to the earth. I find it so endearing I have to hold myself back from putting a hand to his cheek when he screws up.

As we near the city, Luke says, 'I'm going to be late for work if this traffic doesn't start moving.'

'I'll call your boss and tell him how much I loved being picked up. Oh, Luke, look.' To our right there is a warehouse flying two flags: one English, the other Canadian.

'You're not going to drag me to *Riverdance*, are you?' he says, referring to the show advertised by a theatre beyond.

'No, the flags.'

'That's a carpet warehouse.'

'It's welcoming me.'

It's kooky that the Canadian flag should give me any pleasure. Most often, I find it disturbing. But I like the flags side by side. Me and me? Luke and me? Or both together on a carpet? Ha, there's a thought. Closer still and I begin to recognize the places. Earl's Court. Kensington. Shepherd's Bush. It is exciting that it is not all a blank, yet I can't wait to learn more. I want to know the city inside out.

Luke pulls off the busy road and with one right and one left we're in a gorgeous square. He brings the car to a halt and squeezes it into a space with an unaccountable fanfare.

'You live here?'

He looks proud to have caused my wide-eyed grin. 'So do you, now.'

'It's beautiful.'

'It is quite nice,' Luke says, giving a quick tug to the back of his shirt where sweat has darkened the cotton. He lifts out my cases. 'Come on.' The door of his building clunks emphatically behind us. 'It's the third floor, I'm afraid.'

'I can live with that.'

I feel suddenly smaller, more timid, now we are inside. It is a rich man's hallway: soft carpet, thick walls, money in the powder-blue paint, in the coy octagonal chandeliers, even in the bulbs. Their light is the amber of good hotels. It is a rich man's quiet, too. These people can't know how crazy it makes you when someone else's noise moves into your home. The deathly wheezings, the guitars and fights and cries, the fucking you don't care to know about and the laughter that makes you feel more lonely than before. Silence such as this is a luxury.

Luke is carrying my bags ahead of me, his back stiff as a bellhop's. It is reassuring, a tiny break in the struggle. My hand trails the polished bannister as we curve around each corner.

There is a smell of coffee sneaking from under the door of Number Two that reminds me of breakfast on the flight, of the cooking smells thick in the air, of how far I have come.

'Here we go.'

Sunlight gushes into the corridor as Luke opens the door. He steps aside to let me in.

'Oh, my God. Look at this place.' I turn to place a hand on his arm, 'Wow.'

It is huge. The sitting-room is lofty and inviting, with a heavily corniced, high ceiling. Opposite the door is a carved wooden fireplace and either side of that are rounded niches in which brightly coloured prints have been hung. Hunting scenes, I notice them to be, framed in heavy, bevelled wood and hung level, with military precision.

At right angles to the fireplace, facing one another, are two large sofas, one mossy green, the other a rust red. The floor is covered with rattan matting that looks – what else? – golden, gloriously golden, in the warming columns of sunlight slanting in through the windows. Under my feet is a gorgeous patterned woven rug that is clearly an antique.

'It's lovely, Luke.'

He handles the compliment messily. 'The loo's this way, if you need it.'

'No, thanks.'

To the left of the door, in front of the rectangular windows, is a long, wooden table on top of which are piles of letters, papers and magazines. They are stacked perfectly. I will have to be careful when nosing through them. Luke seems to be a man who will notice disorder.

I wander to where the three tall double-hung windows are presenting between their glazing bars twenty-four miniature framed images; here the gorgeous royal blue of the sky, there the fluted pinnacle of a church across the square, or the branches of the trees, restless with chirruping sparrows, to the right the crisp, eurhythmic lines of the square itself with its weather-ravaged cornices sharp against the cloudless sky. I feel as thrilled as Oliver Twist in the movie when he flings open the shutters of his Mayfair bedroom. I want to buy this beautiful morning and put it in a box.

'Your room's this way.'

I hardly need to see it. I know this view, this fictional London come to glorious life, will inspire me to write a hundred articles a week, a novel or two before year's end, a brilliant new chapter for my life. I follow Luke to my bedroom which, as it turns out, seems poky on such a beautiful morning. There is no window to let in the light. Absurdly, I feel cheated, as if I am some kind of parlour maid. I put my bag in the sag at the heart of the single mattress.

'It's, um, it's horsehair,' Luke tells me. 'I'm afraid it's done the rounds,' which means, I guess, that it has been slept on and pissed in and fucked upon by generations of Binghams since the fifteenth century, or whenever it and they were first stuffed. At the end of my bed is the wardrobe, a shoddily constructed plywood closet painted white on the outside. On the walls are six glass clipboards filled with glossy snaps of Luke, his family and friends. They are mostly wearing sunglasses and skiing or lounging in the sun or looking drunk at weddings and parties. Or they are standing in fields, for no obvious reason, wearing hats.

I glance at the group above the bedside table. 'Lucky me. I get to sleep with you and your girlfriends, do I?'

'Oh, those are all old.'

I circle my focus around the framed menagerie. 'All old girlfriends?'

'That one was,' he says, pointing, I think with pride, at the prettiest of them all. She looks about twenty in the picture and the pose, topless on a yacht somewhere hot and sunny, is undeniably sexy. I feel a pang of hatred for her, not because of the luxurious tan and tidy, taut breasts, but for the air of arrogance with which she is carrying herself, with the way her creams and books and friends are scattered on the polished deck, for the lazy manner with which she implies that such privilege is deserved, as if the boat is hers.

'That was Jemima's boat,' says Luke, 'her father gave it to her,' and though I smile at my guesswork, the truth makes me feel as if I haven't a hope with this man. It isn't that I am convinced we should become lovers, rather that my own unexceptional family holidays – a week in a bed and breakfast with my aunt and cousin Paul in St Ives, another in the Lake District after they'd bought the caravan, trips staying in HoJo's and Motel Sixes as we toured Maine and Vermont in Dad's Mazda, a coach tour of Europe (this, the biggest disaster of all) taking in nine cities in fourteen days with the bus smelling of chemicals and shit and brake fluid and all of us throwing up after bad shrimps in Marseilles – will condemn me as being somehow unsuitable. The Bedouin with not enough sheep. The tribal girl short on neck rings. I am lacking in everything, in layers of tanned skin, wealth, culture, diamonds. It makes me nervous. What if it's money, not blood, that links people? Yacht owners of the world unite. I can't fake this money thing. It shades everything green.

'Where's she now?' I ask, hoping Luke will be flattered by my jealousy.

'Oh, she got married a couple of times. So far, anyway.'

'She obviously gets bored of her toys. Luke?'

'Yes?' he eagerly replies.

'Do you have any orange juice or . . .?'

'Of course. Sorry. Sorry. I even went to M and S.'

M and where? Never mind. I follow him back next door. The juice tastes good when he gives it to me. There are two heart-shaped cubes of ice in the glass. I am going to check the freezer when he's gone, see if he had a pick of moulds. For now, I just ask, 'Are you some kind of wedding mascot, or something?'

'What's that?'

'All these,' I raise my hand towards the stack of stiff cardboard wedding invitations on his cluttered mantelpiece. I can hardly count how many people are expecting the pleasure of Mr Luke Bingham's company this year.

'It's that time,' he explains.

'You don't say.'

'Not many of us left now,' he adds, with what sounds like regret. 'Um, I'd better change for work.'

While Luke is in his bedroom I run my eyes over the clutter on his mantelpiece. It is the only untidy part of the flat but, like a priest's dog collar, the tiny space gives a lot away. There is a small double-handed silver cup won for playing a game called rackets, a praying Buddha from Thailand, splitting in the middle, a bronze cast of a Yorkshire terrier, a framed photograph of a woman I take to be his sister (it's in the nose) standing in front of a lovely old church in her wedding dress, an empty bottle of Veuve Cliquot encrusted in layers of red wax, a gold carriage clock that is six minutes fast – an oversight? – and layers of invitations, each one sporting a tick or a cross in the top right-hand corner of the stiff white card. I am reading one (get this: the groom is a Viscount) when Luke returns in stripes, a ballsy blue on his white shirt, chalk lightening the suit's grey.

'Hey,' I say, because it works, the suit. It suits him. There is a particular breed of man, to which Luke belongs, that appears slightly off-kilter in casual clothes. It has something to do with the uncanny kemptness to their faces, the neat consistency of the whole: cheek-bones, eyebrows, ears, skin. Now here I am with one of them, Mister Pin Stripe himself. It is odd, a little.

'Portia, you've been invited to a dinner party tonight,' he says, tying a flowery tie around his neck. 'If you'd like.'

'Wow. Who by?'

Young marrieds, he tells me, nothing formal. Camilla, the hostess, is great in the kitchen (I don't ask how) and just back from a course in Tuscany with some celebrity chef. Since I am 'more than welcome,' I say I would love to go.

'Great. Now, do you want to walk to the tube with me or would you rather have a doze?'

I join Luke. The atmosphere has been warmed by the sun, though there are still pockets of cool air mixed in from dawn. I haven't been thinking of London as a city of fresh air. Now this sweetness confirms that I am entering the greenest of pastures.

'We'll have to find you some ladies who lunch.'

'Luke, I'm a working girl.'

'So are they. Camilla does interiors, I think, or fashion, or something. Or she used to. But she definitely lunches.'

Maybe my first article should be about lunching. I am carrying a spiral notebook that I bought yesterday in Toronto and on the cover of which I wrote, 'England: Ideas and Observations,' when I was cruising somewhere high between my two nations, between my future and past. I write down, 'Lunch'.

My brief from the scribbling ant is absurdly simple: I am required to write a thousand words a week about life in London for the *Herald's* Sunday edition. Already I want to try to capture something about the Englishness of this area. There is even a seal and the words 'Royal Borough of Kensington and Chelsea' on the parking meters. The symbol has weight and meaning here. In Canada, it looks unconvincing.

'There's the tube I take.' Luke points towards a small cluster of shops covering South Kensington Station. 'This area's absolutely chocka with cafés. And then there's Conran and Joseph down at Brompton Cross, then you can either go to Knightsbridge or Sloane Square. Take this.' From his briefcase he hands me an A-Z map of London's streets. 'I wrote the address down in the front, in case you get lost.'

When I have watched my man head off to win bread for those who surely don't know what hunger is, I find my new address at the heart of one of the large-scale pages. I have never lived anywhere worthy enough to be magnified, always I've been closer to Z than A. It feels better than I had dared dream.

All morning I wander the neighbourhood. It is a tree-lined, white-painted, flowery window-boxed, blue-skied, decorous oasis completely unlike anywhere I have called home before. Perhaps I have been wielding a chainsaw for so many years because I never expected to reach the top of such trees. Now I want to cling on. The view is lucid and peaceful. I don't know how far I walk or where to by the time I cheat and take a cab back to the apartment. But it has gone three, and the flat is hot and humid from the afternoon sun.

'Hey there, home,' I say, pinching myself with the words. I toss the keys onto the sofa and step across to the mirror. 'Portia Mills,' I say in my English accent. 'Lovely to meet you.'

I wink at my reflection. Yes, I am *happy*. I wish Mother could see. She has always accused me of fostering my melancholic state. 'You're only happy when you're unhappy,' is what she says, as if that means something. How can that be? It isn't as if I chose the weave of my past.

Now, I skip into Luke's bedroom. It is as tidy as the rest of the flat, curiously for a single man, though these are boy's colours: the quilt cover patterned in wide maroon and blue stripes, the curtains a hunter green, the furniture a serious brown. There are more framed photos on his walls, these of sports teams Luke must have played in at school. Fresh-faced boys wearing colourfully fringed V-neck sweaters. Nine hundred years of class rule without a revolution.

Luke's bed is neatly made. I wonder if I will be too, laid neatly. I think I may have bartered away my right to sleep alone by accepting the ant's job, the room, the ride from Terminal Three. Not that it is an unappealing prospect. I haven't had sex in months. I have been chased but chaste, like a cute nun.

I sit on the bed and wonder how, when, whether. Will I have to lead? If so, I should discover what Luke likes. In his chest of drawers I find that, predictably, he is a boxers man. The shorts are all similar, made of oily cotton striped in various colours. They're roomy, making me wonder if room is needed. Clearly, he hasn't been swept up in Calvin Klein's revolution, doesn't appreciate how salacious and promising, how deliciously weighty, a man's package can be when swaddled in suitably warmed fabric. I like to undress my men, to taunt and tease and kiss. With Luke's little hiptents I'll be reduced to guessing at my target, like a blindfolded kid trying to grab a floating apple between her teeth. If I miss I could end up dull as the prelapsarian Eve; all virtue and no mud.

A surprise is what I am after, some proof that beyond the banker's seemly façade there exists a vein of independence. Instead I find socks that are grey and black, some of which still sport little green school tags; six identical crew-neck lambswool sweaters in solid colours; trousers folded neatly on hangers, rust red and royal blue moleskins; a pair of tartans that he probably wears to be wacky; polished leather shoes held in shape by shoe trees made from fine cedar. I have to wonder why is he bothering with shoe trees. It isn't as if the vamps of my own treeless shoes collapse in on themselves while I sleep. And then his suits. My God, all nine are arranged by colour, the darkest to the left. I doubt my Canadian ex-boyfriends could raise nine suits between them. Could I possibly love a man who arranges his clothes like this? Do I want to?

I lie back on his bed and close my eyes. It is comfortable, spongy, not too soft. I am tired. My eyes feel like pinballs rolling back into my head and for a delicious few moments, as I listen to the sound of a branch gently scratching the window's pane, I know I am rapidly falling to sleep.

Except now I hear a sound, a man's voice. I open my eyes. It is darker than before. I look at my watch. No. Three hours? Is that Luke home? The embarrassment of being caught on his bed rattles me. I shuffle next door and am relieved to find that the voice is coming from a telephone answering machine. It's a friend arranging football. 'And Charlie's playing too. Oh yeah, he says he'll take over stuffing your Canadian goose when she gets bored of you. Later, mate.' Then he is gone.

I grin. Ha! Stuff the Canadian goose? Have the previews been good? I love it that the slates are clean and enticing. I will try to invent a person I can love. It feels like it should: a chance to get things right. For now, I tense the creases from the sheets and check the room for evidence of me. Then I run myself a bath in which I am relaxing with a delicious cigarette held high and dry when I hear Luke open the front door and call out my name.

He says, 'I bought you a present. You might want it.'

'I'm still in the bath.'

'Even better.' He knocks, swears not to look, and pushes into the bathroom a small cardboard box of bath salts. Pine and lavender, this I see once I've splashed across to get them. 'They're because you skipped your bath to have dinner with me in Toronto.'

'That's so sweet of you.' I picture him smiling beyond the door as I splash the water into a romantic, milky green that makes me think of Cleopatra, then I slide back into the softness with the box in my hand. I love hearing that I have been thought of during someone else's day. I wonder, did they picture all of me or just a detail: my mouth, eyelids, smile, feet, breasts, elsewhere? These salts suggest licentiousness. Dissolved, they have access to every inch of me. Is Luke hoping for the same? Doesn't he want me to smell my sweetest when he kisses my neck and breasts, when he pulls me onto his face? I sink lower in the bath, the cool water creeping up my torso like fingertips. I close my eyes, rub the sponge over my expectant skin, and float in the sugary anticipation of his touch.

'Lord, sorry,' Luke says when I almost collide with him outside the bathroom. He has a cigarette in one hand and a drink in the other and with his ruddy cheeks and slicked back hair looks rich and comfortable and from another age, one of Gatsby's guests. I am standing with the towel wrapped around me and my wet feet darkening marks in the coir floor. I can smell the lavender on my skin. It crosses my mind to drop the towel, leave him little choice.

'How was your day?' he asks.

'Wonderful. It's so gorgeous out. Like being in Florida.'

'The tube's like Africa. How did the, um, the writing go?'

'Good. I should be able to take most of the week off.'

'Lucky you.'

Can he read my mind? The air is at body temperature. I am good as naked and can see the end of Luke's bed beyond him, a glimpse of beach from a coastal road when the car's stuffy and you'd kill for a swim. He is looking awkward, the way bad dancers do; too much elbow. I want to give him a massage, sit naked on him, press my sensitive flesh to the knobby base of his spine. It is something I'm good at, massage. You get a sense of someone from the way they take to your hands, the manner in which their tautness yields. And it excites men, of course, so quickly, the promise and teasing in it.

Luke takes a step back, and breaks the brief silence. 'Can I get you a drink?'

'Lovely,' I say, chirpy as anything because I don't want him to know that it irks, my being resistible. 'And, Luke? Tonight, is it smart?'

'No, not at all. You could go as you are.'

I put on a floral dress, short, no bra, and drink vodka shoeless on the green sofa. On TV there is a recording of last month's Wimbledon. Don't ask why. Some English player is hanging in there with one of the top seeds so the crowd is beside itself. I watch, wishing I could get patriotic, but I like the Dutchman's disdain, his cool.

When Luke comes in, he flops onto the sofa opposite me.

I say, 'Your guy's winning.'

'Him? He's a Canadian like you. He wangled himself a British passport.'

'But look at the flags. They love him.'

'We take what we can get. Another vod?'

Why not, I say, and we drink more and flirt some and talk of sights that Luke will show me: lakes, fens, downs, cliffs, and by the time I feel the cab's leather seat warm as a hand against my thighs I am glad he denied me the sexual satisfaction I was craving. My skin has been left stripped a layer, the pores flooded with tender sentience. A swirl of excitement has opened me out and revealed, like the lime green underbelly of an oak leaf before a storm, an aspect usually hidden and protected.

It is a pirouette of a night, the sky clear save for the tumbling swallows and a few wisps of cloud drunk and ruddy from the sun. The light encourages me to imagine the city as it used to be before this century's swathe of ugliness. With the sun recently set, a smoky orange light has charmed and softened the buildings. The roads and sidewalks are thinly peopled. I feel a peace as harmonious as the stucco façades of Belgravia and Knightsbridge that we are passing.

I smile at Luke. The idea of us escaping early, drunk on wine and the summer sky, to make love through the night, brings a palpable flash of red to my cheeks. Oh, I feel enchanted as the condom-kid herself. I am lucky.

With a loud squeak of brakes, the cab's classy rumble dies to a ticking purr. We have stopped in a pretty, residential street somewhere close to the Thames. As Luke rings the bell I put my hand against the smooth front wall of the building and say, 'It looks like wedding cake, the icing on this.'

'The stone, you mean.'

Although the terraced house is beautiful, it's a tad too House and Gardeney for my taste. A front door painted a shiny loden green. Immutable iron railings. A polished lion's head knocker. It seems wrong for people our age to be living in such a place.

After a lock's click, James Huntley appears, smiley and tall in a pink shirt with cufflinks as gold as the chains on his shoes. He is a large man with heavy eyes, a flop of dirty blond hair and a genuine smile that spreads to his eyes when he shakes my hand and welcomes me into the house. 'Everyone's outside in the garden,' he says, leading us along a corridor that is fragrant with the spicy scent from a decorated glass bowl of pot pourri. It sits on an antique side table. I dip my hand into the bowl as we pass, taking with me a crackly leaf that I am holding to my nose when James turns his head to say, 'How does champagne sound?'

'Cool,' I reply, the word and my accent sounding ugly in this setting.

'We'll go outside, yeah?' says Luke, suddenly chummy and relaxed. 'Portia, the garden's this way.'

Hearing the voices – how many? I sense fifty – I cling to Luke's shadow as we step outside. The garden is more a square of gravel, so clean it seems the stones have been washed for us. Sweet-smelling honeysuckle, clematis and pale yellow roses have been trained up the brazen red brick of the walls. In the narrow strip of earth fronting the U-shaped wall, I see tidy plants, no weeds. I imagine the couple hire a man to tame nature, prune the naughty roses, contain the lavender, straighten the sunflowers from following the arc of the sun.

The guests themselves are seated around a white wooden garden table, their circle making physical my sense of exclusion. These are the people from Luke's photographs. I want to lose my accent, to announce that I have English blood in my veins. My roots go deep in English soil. Florists, fisherman, teachers too. A couple of our fellow guests have turned to inspect me. I am not dressed right, am I? This flowery dress advertises too much. My thin, tanned legs, these breasts. But you can't win, meeting people if you're at all attractive. Hide your beauty and such modesty is considered false. Flaunt it and you're despised. It is the women's eyes I feel on me. I do what I can to look coy.

I hated my good looks after Dad died. It was my mind he loved, the mind he had fashioned and made, rather than the face of the pretty girl with the chocolate brown eyes that Mother's friends oohed and aahed over as if they wanted to swallow the beauty for themselves and their own. To accompany my curving body they tried to curve my mind, to make me celebrate the fact of my subtly inferior unmanliness. Dad was different. He had me help him banging nails, reading books, digging weeds, writing stories, throwing balls, learning words; myself is all he wanted me to be so long as I had courage and independence and an inquisitive mind. I tried, of course, to emulate him, wanted nothing but his approval of me as something more than the cute, miniature woman Mother longed for me to be.

It was after Dad died that I felt myself being valued at school only for the looks I had and most thirteen-year-old girls wanted. I don't know what happened to everyone, even my friends thought my sex appeal (the desire suddenly, unwelcomely, out in the open) was somehow compensation for Dad's death. I didn't want that to be. It is why I cut my hair and tore my dresses to keep hold of myself. Dad would have been proud that I resisted my role; that I kept away, early on I did, from the boy's hands and glances. And I think he would be proud of me now for having made it this far.

I wish Luke would put his arm around my waist or at least take hold of my hand. He is standing a half-step in front, his hands clasping the shoulders of a man who has his back to us. I notice again his fresh haircut. The thought that he exposed that frightened strip of pink skin for me causes my heart to swell with such an immense fondness that I step to him and brush the back of my hand against his.

'Everybody, this is Portia.'

I blush, smile, let the pot pourri leaf fall to the clean stones. And then the names come too fast for my addled mind. Fee, Camilla, Charlie, Emma (was it?), Damian. I nod at each and try to look relaxed as if there is nothing separating us. Then, as if to confirm this, the circle breaks and widens to include me. Our hostess, Camilla, chattering about how brave I am to have come to dinner on my very first night (just ask Jim, she had felt like lead when she flew overnight from the Maldives, didn't know what she would have done without melatonin, if I hadn't taken some really I should) empties herself from the chair beside Charlie and, with what seems like a disparaging glance at my cleavage, leaves to 'attend to the veggies,' by which I assume she means the dinner vegetables and not some clan of vegetarians locked in the basement. I take her chair, surprised that it doesn't feel warmed. Beside me, Charlie has stood and then sat again, out of good manners I suppose. I think it looks silly, but thank him.

He is very cute, this Charlie Garton, quite small, with dimples and a glint of mischief in his eyes, as if he has read our medical records and knows things he shouldn't. He is smoking a cigarette with great purpose, drawing deeply each time and looking at me through the smoke. His scrutiny is more severe than Camilla's but seems to lack the malice.

He offers me a cigarette, which I am thankful for and take.

'Young Luke's been talking about you.'

'Oh? Like how?'

'Like you were worth the wait.'

'Charlie,' says Luke, sternly. 'Don't embarrass Portia.'

Charlie leans towards me. 'I'm terribly sorry. Am I . . .?'

'It's fine.' I tilt my cigarette into the flame of his gold cigarette lighter. 'I think I can handle it.'

'Have you handled it?'

'What?'

Luke again: 'Charlie.'

'Luke, you're terribly on edge. All I want,' he continues, leaning back in his chair and crossing his legs, 'is to establish something.'

Charlie's charm does not completely mask his capacity for cruelty. He has a sharp, bullying air.

I pinch an imagined speck of tobacco off my tongue, like I'm a young Lauren Bacall, and ask, 'What would you like to know?'

'Thank you, Portia. A willing witness for once.'

'Uh-oh. Is this a trial?'

'Watch him very carefully,' says Luke, his lips tightening with unease. 'Charlie's a lawyer.'

Charlie doesn't move his eyes from mine when he rapidly stipulates, 'Bingham, as the defendant you have no right to speak unless called upon to do so.'

'He sounds just like you, darling,' brays Camilla who is back and stretching out a spidery arm to stroke Jim's head as he passes her with my champagne.

'Now, Portia, we have been led to believe that you ran across a Toronto street to invite yourself to dinner and that the defendant took pity on you and accepted.'

'That's right,' I say, 'I couldn't resist. I was like a moth to the flame.'

'Ah, certain death, then.'

'No, I never got that close. I managed to fly away; like a Canadian goose.'

That surprises him, but his stride isn't broken for long.

'Ah, now that's interesting. You see, geese mate for life.'

The thought is sudden: I could marry Luke. Snap. Just like that I could be a part of his world, these people, this England. Mrs Portia Bingham of Chelsea, London. I kiss Luke with my gaze, and he is smiling at me as if we are alone when we are startled by the sound of Camilla clapping. 'Jimbos, there's that beastly cat again. Shoo!'

'I'll get the girls,' says Jim.

He returns with a revolting little dog in his arms. Another is snuffling at his feet.

'Go on,' Camilla urges. 'Go find the pussy.'

'Sounds like my sort of game,' Charlie remarks.

'Chasing pussy away, you're good at,' Luke retorts with a laugh.

Of course, Camilla's repulsive creatures have run straight to me and are sniffing and slobbering on my feet and ankles. I despise pugs, with their grotesque, wheezing flat faces and boasting black arseholes. Gently, I try to nudge one of them away but in no time they are waddling and heavy-breathing themselves back to me.

'I've always thought pugs look like handmuffs,' I say as a joke, though as soon as the comment has left my lips, I regret it. The faces around me resemble those of a jury with a guilty verdict in its hands.

Charlie raises his eyebrows and, in a deceptively benign tone, asks, 'Fur trappers in your family, were there?'

'No, I'm English, mainly. Not Canadian.'

Charlie holds up his hands as if in surrender. 'I'm sorry. I should have guessed from your accent.'

'Portia's father was English,' says Luke. Lovely Luke. Helping me out like this. I want to kiss him.

I say, 'He went to Cambridge.'

'Which college?' asks Damian.

'To the university.'

'Right, but which college in the university?'

'The main one, I think.'

Did someone snigger? I want to ask: why be particular? Dad was smarter than us, than you, than your fathers. He knew Greek, Latin, French, German, Early English, Middle English, Elizabethan English, every type of English. That is enough, isn't it?

'My father was at Peterhouse. Maybe they knew each other. How old is your dad?'

'He's not. He died.'

There is a brief silence during which everyone at the table looks into their laps.

It is Fee who breaks the silence, asking, 'Portia, have you spent much time in England?'

Just as I am suspicious of Camilla, so I am comfortable with Fee. She is, I suppose, a woman's woman, alluring in her flashlessness. Mousy hair, a kind, round face. She is wearing no make-up and no jewellery, aside from an unremarkable gold cross on a thin chain, and wants nothing of me with her question.

'I used to come with my parents and spend time in nice hotels when my dad wasn't teaching.' These little white lies can't do any harm. I have to sell myself big with this crowd, I think, their expectations are not the same as most people's. They know royalty. They buy emperors' dogs. They live in houses that smell of spices, of pot pourri shipped from a place they think of as the Raj. 'I've always wanted to live here. That's why it was lucky meeting Luke because I got a job through his aunt.'

'Shortlist of one, was it?' asks Charlie.

I am not quick enough with a reply, so I raise my eyebrows and take a sip of champagne, hoping I'll be found mysterious instead of slow-witted.

'Portia's going to be writing about the English, from what I hear,' says Jim, 'so we'd all better be on our best behaviour.'

'Please don't be. The badder the better.'

'Badder? Is that a Canadian word?' This from Charlie. 'Or just journalese?'

'Oh, button up for a second, Chas,' says the one I'll call Emma. She's a glamorous little thing in a leather mini-skirt. 'We all know you think you're cleverer than us.'

'Not cleverer, Ems, just badder.'

I glance at Luke. His smile makes me feel very safe. If a plane fell from the sky, somehow I think he would be there to catch it. My own Superman.

'But tell me, Portia, what are you going to write about?'

'I don't know yet. What I see.'

'If I were you,' says Charlie. 'I'd write about how the British are clinging on to an outdated self-image to protect ourselves from the despair we feel at the end of our least impressive century since the eleventh. That'd be interesting.'

'I was thinking I'd begin with the exact opposite. Something about how London looks as good as it does on the postcards. You know, the buses are as red and the cabs as black and the buildings as handsome and—'

'Only if you're a foreigner.'

Emma again. 'Charlie, no one thinks it's clever when you try to be subversive.'

'Ah, the teacher speaks. I am only pointing out that England Plc has done a bloody good job of marketing herself in the last couple of hundred years. The world should know that we're a nation of shopkeepers and pirates and thugs. You know how we behave abroad.'

'Luke was great in Toronto.'

'Men are capable of the greatest illusions when they're blessed with a hard-on.'

'Charlie Garton! Watch your Ps and Qs,' Camilla snorts before leaving. Seems she's a killjoy, our hostess. Wants it all her way.

'Oh my God,' Emma shrieks. 'Did you hear that Jamie Anderson's getting married before both his brothers?'

The assembled agree it is despicable (this from people labelling themselves as thugs), but since I haven't heard of the perpetrators I let the conversation bubble and burst around me. High on booze, I keep having this strange sensation that I am observing the scene from above but with myself sitting in the middle, a little more upright than usual and staring with a deliberate look of interest at this knot of people babbling in the seductive, fading light.

Jim returns from the kitchen with orders from the 'Missus' that the food's ready and that we're not going to wait for Kaz, the final guest. It's agreed she is never on time.

We are shunted in from the pleasing cool to a hot and cosy dining room with low ceilings and – get this – a portrait of Camilla on the wall opposite me. It was a wedding present, Charlie tells me, from Camilla's parents and had been cloaked in secrecy until the big day. Am I the only one to wish it still was? The artist was too skilled. In the corners of Camilla's mouth and eyes he has perfectly caught her haughty, arrogant sneer.

'Portia, you're over there between Damian, who's very nice, and Charlie, who isn't.'

'It's a Jesus, Devil thing,' Charlie whispers in my ear.

'What?'

'Patience, now.'

The dining table is gorgeous, a textured pool reflecting the ornate bloom of the silver candlesticks above, although, like England herself, it requires its history, the hours it has been dusted and polished by hands that have become dust themselves, to make it notable. I stroke my fingertips over its surface thinking how wonderful it would be to own such a solid piece of the past. The few items I possess which are older than myself I inherited from Dad, so they are soaked in a history that gives me no pleasure.

In front of each of us are place-mats depicting engravings of nineteenth-century London. Also: three silver forks, two knives, a spoon, two wineglasses and one for water. It seems Camilla has measured the distance between each piece of cutlery. I turn my spoon upside down and then, before anyone has noticed, right it again.

'Please, please start,' Camilla urges, popping her large head around the door. 'I'm just tied up in the kitchen for two minutes.'

I think, want me to check the knots? although I have to admit that Camilla has produced some appetizing food. We are beginning with smoked salmon and caviar blinis. She has taken care with the presentation. What would she think of my internal disorder, I wonder? She, whose entire manner glows with the equilibrious surety of the silver-spooned, whose life is, and has always been, so unlike the life I was living until yesterday.

The formality of the cutlery is setting us on our best behaviour. My lazily slack back has stiffened. I thought this was what people became when they were middle-aged. Have Luke and his friends ever been irresponsible and young? I had a peek into the living room and thought even the television looked out of place amid the pristine sofas and gold-framed watercolours and oils. I hope the leap I need to take won't prove to be too far.

Damian, to my left, lacks Charlie's bite, if not his charm. He is a tall man with a slight lisp, but handsome in the scrubbed style adopted by all the men at the table. He is the sort of man mothers urge their daughters to bring home. Then again, isn't Luke?

'Are you happy being a journalist?' he inquires once we have dispensed with chit-chat about a holiday he once took in Vancouver.

'Happy? Yeah, I think so. As happy as you can be, given . . . well . . .' I smile and scoop the last grains of caviar onto my fork. Somehow, it doesn't seem the time for complaint. 'Given that it isn't possible to appreciate happiness without a more persistent sense of misery.'

'I could sense that, a little. It's in your manner, if you don't mind me saying so.'

I do, as it happens, and it's on the tip of my tongue to tell him where to stick his sense. It annoys me, being so easily read.

'Fee and I couldn't possibly be more happy.'
'Oh, are you two together?'
'Actually, there are three of us.'
'You've got a kid?'
'No. Jesus is with us.'
'Aah.' The way Damian's eyes have locked onto mine is sapping my confidence. It feels Satanic. I reach for my wine. 'Does he have his own room?'
Damian shakes his head disparagingly, which makes me feel about two inches tall. Not that it should. I don't mean to sound like an antsy agnostic bitch, but it bugs me how Christians manage to act as if God chose them rather than the other way around. It just doesn't add up that God would have chosen these half-lifers to spread the message. His PR started so eloquently, so simply: one man and his cross. What went wrong? If He's up there, why doesn't He get some big hitters on His side? People who, like Jesus, only need one name: Cindy, Madonna, Prince? The fact remains that only Christians like Christians. The rest of us prefer to commune with lions.
'I wish you knew how much you were missing,' Damian says in a smug, disabling tone that denies me the opportunity to raise my voice in reply. 'It takes most of the weight off your shoulders to have someone showing the way.'
'But it's the weight that makes us human. It demeans us as rational beings if you claim that we're only alive to serve some absolute being. There has to be a more convincing reason.'
'Such as what?' wonders Charlie.
'I haven't a clue. But that's my point. I don't want some easy answer. It may be tougher facing life knowing that there's no God or heaven at the end but at least it makes you realize this is it – this is the whole journey.'
'An hour here and our Canadian goose is flapping about the existence of God. That's not bad going.'
'I'd believe in Him, Charlie, if there was one, tiny crumb of the world that couldn't be explained scientifically.'

'What if God is science?' challenges Damian. 'Biology and evolution and chemistry and—'

'Love,' suggests Fee, softly.

Stupidly, I have taken a mouthful of salad. I wave my fork, and then swallow. 'That's science too. Obviously. The sexual imperative.'

'I love my mother but I don't want to sleep with her,' protests Emma. She is looking indignant, as if I have been condoning incest. For a teacher, she's no Erasmus.

'But that's because maternal love exists to keep mothers and kids together until the children are mature enough to reproduce themselves. God's not involved in these equations. And if He is, well, you guys better hurry and ask Him what He's playing at. If you look at the data, we're all going to be frozen solid or burned alive in the not-too-distant future. That's not nice. And I don't think God's going to air-lift out people with the shiniest tambourines either. So, as far as I can see, it's a waste of time saying prayers for murderers or lying to virgins about how they should lay off sex until they're married. From what I've heard that's when it stops being any good.'

'Now there is something I'll drink to,' says Charlie.

Damian begins, 'If you honestly think that religious conviction can be reduced to the issue of sex before marriage, then—'

Camilla taps her knife three times against her glass. She looks peeved, probably at having her marital sex life so casually dismissed. 'Mummy always says that religion and politics are no-no's at the dinner table, and I agree with her. Damian, you naughty you.'

Mummy says? You naughty you? Thirty-year-olds speak like this here? Of course, Camilla is admonishing me, only some small print in the etiquette book prevents her from looking me in the eye.

I am afraid I have taken against Camilla with her fierce red hair and narrow, upturned nose. She has been making me feel uneasy, foreign. And there is something consciously vindictive about the way she flaunts her conjugal status. She wears the word, marriage, like a scarlet M. I am sure she sees it as the mother-hen of all states, incubating the very malodorous eggs – settled, anchored, numb, snug – I have vowed to avoid.

Dad used to say that some women are born with grooves in their backs where the pinny strings could run, that I didn't have any, he could feel how smooth my skin was. 'You'll run the world, my little Pea,' he used to whisper, 'won't you?' He often did that; promised me the world before he took it away.

Like rapids easing, the conversation calms. My head starts to feel heavy, the jet lag thickening during the marinated chicken and polenta main course. I am drinking too much wine and it is making me slow. Charlie Garton is being self-deprecating and funny in a way that none but my gay friends in Canada are. I am angry with myself for not being able to keep up. I feel knotted inside, the way I get in countries where I don't speak the language. Emma, who'd like to be clever but isn't, is now telling a story about the son of a famous Hollywood actor who trapped his finger in a test-tube at school.

'And?' I ask, thinking I should sound interested.

Luke says, 'That's the story.'

Is he angry? I can't tell. His tone sounds sharp.

'Oh, sorry. I must be jet-lagged. Let me clear the plates.' A little unsteadily, I get to my feet. 'Damian, are you through with this?'

Next door, to the sound of Camilla calling me 'super' and 'a darling,' I clank the dishes into the sink, then ask, 'Where's your bathroom?'

'There's a boy's loo down here if you want to take your chances, or else turn right at the top of the stairs and the bathroom's straight ahead.'

'I'll take my chances.'

The toilet is tiny and sombre and hot, encased with striped purple and maroon wallpaper, a velvet-lined coffin turned on its end. The boys have indeed left their mark, an octuple of boastful quotation marks dripped on the carpet. On the wall is an old engraving of a line of cross-legged dogs waiting to pee against a lamppost. Each is standing on two legs. I study it for a while, searching for irony, for any kind of humour. Here, also, is a frame filled with two printed pages from Ed and Camilla's wedding service sheet, one displaying their names and the date and location of the church, facing that the poem 'Desiderata', chosen, I'd bet, by Camilla because it reads like a priggish credo for goody-goodies. 'Speak your truth quietly and clearly; and listen to others, even the dull and ignorant.' In other words, make no difference in the world. Let it wash over you. Be bothered and inspired by nothing. Enjoy the Camilla Huntleys.

I pee placidly, flush and in front of the mirror lick my finger and smooth my right eyebrow. 'Hey, how's it going?' Hm, I am drunk. Obviously so because I'm able to stand back and observe this other me. How am I doing? Camilla senses that I don't like her. She keeps giving me that look. Well, right back at ya, Ginger. Maybe I should have kept quiet about God. But, no, that's mainstream now, church-bashing. Theocracy isn't confused enough for us these days. If only Damian had been mixing and matching his beliefs, I'd have given him some slack. 'Don't mind Buddhism, aspects of . . .' I say aloud. A verbal shrug of the shoulders.

Would it have been Luke had I met them all tonight? I don't know. Charlie is funny but he's mean. Luke's a puppydog beside him. I like it the way he looks at me, too.

I laugh, suddenly. See where I am! These people are so fucking rich, aren't they? Caviar? A toilet that looks like it belongs in a five star hotel? Cham-fucking-pagne. And little old me slipping in like I belong. Sham nothing. I'm the real thing all of a sudden. 'Yes,' I touch the mirror with my fingertips, 'this is my boat.'

I am greeted in the dining room by the punchline of a joke, 'Let me push that stool in for you,' and guess from the disgust what it was about. Everyone is eating Camilla's lemon and lime sorbet served from scooped out lemons and limes. She really hasn't anything better to do, has she? The sharp cold on my tongue makes me feel a little more sober, which I like.

Coffee comes in a cafetière with a plunger, and Charlie makes a rude joke. There are mints. For half a second, I worry about the bill that will be coming our way but, of course, it's a life being handed me on a plate. I finish my glass of red wine which was probably a dumb thing to do. I have drunk more than enough.

'That's probably Kaz,' says Charlie when we hear the doorbell ring. We listen as Jim answers the door. I am disappointed to hear an unfamiliar voice. It is late and I have the measure of these strangers. It will take energy to impress someone new.

'Jimbo, it's unforgivable, I know.' The door slams shut. 'I tried to get away but I couldn't, I just couldn't.'

'Well, we're all still here. Just.'

Kaz makes her entrance and the room shrinks. It is not merely that she is physically impressive – almost six foot tall and floppily thin with it – but that she exudes an immediate energy that would be infectious even if we weren't the alcohol-soaked lumps of matter to which our digesting bodies have reduced us. She grins widely, displaying a set of teeth that are North American in their glinty whiteness.

'Sweets, hello,' she says, hugging Charlie from behind and kissing the dome of his head with her pretty, plump lips. Huh, he had made no mention of a lover. 'Are you going to divorce me?'

'I'd have to marry you, first,' he replies, tipping his head back to look up at her.

Luke, good child that he is, stood when Kaz came in. 'Kaz, you haven't met—'

'Ludo, I love the haircut. Makes you look yummy, like a prep-school boy.'

'So it does,' Camilla agrees. From her, it sounds vindictive.

'Kaz, you haven't—'

'I think I'm going to call you Wills. Can I? Can I call you Wills?'

'You haven't met Portia.'

'Oh, of course, today's the day. How exciting.' Generously,

she kisses me on both cheeks. 'We all thought Luke was making you up at first.'

'Oh, no, I'm all flesh and blood.'

'I can see that now. Will you be my best friend? I've decided I know everybody else far too well.'

'No, sweetheart,' Charlie says, 'you just think you do.'

'Lord knows I know your smelly body better than's good for me. All those vile nooks and crannies.' She scrapes back the vacant chair next to Jim, who has poured her a glass of wine. 'Milla, I can't believe I missed dinner. Did you cook something Tuscan and divine?'

'Chicken with polenta.'

'Darling, why didn't you save yourself the air fare and go to the River Café instead? Hammersmith's so much nearer.'

'Yes, but Francesco isn't,' Jim says. Camilla has been teased all night about her Tuscan cooking teacher. She flushed tomato red when Charlie suggested Francesco had scrambled her eggs.

'Dustin Hoffman was at River Café.'

'When?'

'He's tiny, but he's got this head on him like some alien.' Kaz hears other people, I think. She just seems to have too much to say to bother listening to them. I can't help liking her. She is fresh air in our stale group. 'Oh, I brought treats.'

She delves into her deep leather bag to retrieve a tiny envelope of what I suppose is cocaine, then reaches for the silver-framed photo of Jim and Camilla on their wedding day. The drug seems misplaced here, and perhaps it is a novelty since the others are now acting around it as if it were a celebrity. They are not looking directly at it, and making work out of small talk.

I was fifteen when I first tried coke. At that age you can't understand the difference between using drugs because it seems hip and rebellious and adult, and doing so because something within you has fractured, so stripping more amusements of their benign and childish fun.

Two years after Dad killed himself, Mother and I had begun to find each other's presence intolerable. I was living with her, but the house was joyless. With hindsight, I can see how she tried to satisfy me, how she never failed to try from the moment I began to form in her reluctant womb, but in succeeding to nurture my outer health she allowed space for my inner consciousness to develop in tune, pitch perfectly, not with her own soul but with my father's. Dad's suicide seemed to negate much of that. The event was so horrendous that it turned Mother and me into people we ourselves hardly recognized – so much so that, when the horror had been explicitly absorbed, we did not merely lose the curious compassion that such common ground had, for eighteen months, engendered, but recoiled with embarrassment at our intimacy. At least, I did. Only he had united us; now he was dead. I stayed at home because I had nowhere else to go.

I retreated into myself and into my room where I would listen through headphones not to Wham and Boy George and Madonna like most of my friends, but to the Dead Kickers and Psycho Rot and Attitude-BS! recorded on tapes from live gigs. I liked it that the bands were out-of-date. The narrowness of such taste strengthened my friendship with those who shared it. Of course, the less Mother approved of my new friends, the closer I became to them. I think I needed to rediscover a sense of individuality after the months of being a new, then not-so-new, member of that fraternity of the bereaved which is barely acknowledged by those whose focus is the living.

Drugs helped. With startling speed I progressed from bribing immigrant cab drivers to buy me smokes and beers to sharing with Zak and Kerri and Alisa and Moon and Johnny all the hash and grass and glue and E and acid and 'shrooms and coke that we, at fifteen, could lay our hands on. I lost my virginity to a man (a boy) willing to steal bourbon from his parent's shop. I learned how to deep-throat for acid, was happily free with myself on E. I suppose that my agile mind, edgy from inaction, from no longer being exercised by the man who had trained it, was seeking a dramatic response to an undramatic, draining sense of bereavement. I know I sought such hazardous pursuits (though I balked at heroin, partly through fear of needles, mostly through fear of how deeply I would sink) because familiar pursuits had lost their allure. I am just thankful that my character is too self-conscious to be addictive. I escaped – partly through meeting Derek who, perversely, disliked most drugs besides alcohol – in time. Others did not. Zak and Alisa, I know, are dead.

I am offered the coke first – six lines, not eight, the Happy Clappies claiming fulfilment enough. I coil a ten pound note, Dickens towards the Queen, and am amused by the shocked figure remaining on the outside of the papery tube. The illustration is of something very English: a cricket match inspired by *The Pickwick Papers*, Dingley Dell against All Muggleton. Come to think of it, Dickens himself looks a little disapproving.

The lines are long and I take a half up each nostril, which arouses comment. Charlie thinks I'm a pro. The drug is lumpy and weak yet Camilla and the boys seem excited by the ritual. There is a dip in the conversation while everyone wonders whether this is glamorous, taking coke that doesn't make much difference to how you feel. Kaz casually takes two lines, then wipes up the residue with a fingertip to rub onto her front teeth.

'Can you imagine how wild a sniffer dog would go in this room?' says Luke. 'He'd be at every frame and mirror in the house.'

Camilla tuts. 'Portia's going to think we're addicts.'

'I don't.'

'Lord, no, we're not nearly that interesting,' Kaz says. 'Even if Tara's back in Farm Place for the third time.'

Camilla brightens at the news. 'She is?'

'I promised I wouldn't tell a soul so you didn't hear it from me.'

'She's only after the attention,' says Charlie. 'Just watch, she'll try killing herself next time.'

'Don't,' says Kaz. She looks genuinely angry. 'I hate you saying things like that.'

'We should go,' says Damian, sounding disheartened by this further proof of human suffering.

He and Fee have been quiet for so long, no one thinks to protest. Both of them say they were glad to meet me, that they'll surely see me again, but in truth Damian's been as cold as a fish since our discussion. I think of recommending he look up forgiveness in his Bible Clift notes, but I hold my tongue. For once, I do.

Jim turns on an overhead light. It makes us all look alike – tired, jaded. I can feel my face sagging. The coke turned out to be like a bad smell arriving. I think Luke can tell that I am fading, and we agree to leave too.

'Portia, what'll you be doing with your days?' asks Kaz.

'I'm writing a column.'

'Oh, like Zoë Heller.'

'I despise Zoë Heller.'

'Charlie, don't be predictable. Portia, I've got to drop a necklace off in The Boltons tomorrow,' Kaz continues, 'shall I buzz Luke's buzzer, see if you're at home?'

'That'd be nice. Thanks.'

At the door, Camilla asks me how long I intend to stay. 'Oh, for ever,' I say. 'Or thereabouts.'

There is a subtext to Camilla's look. Though she says, 'How nice,' the meaning, Keep you hands off my friend, you Canadian whore, is as explicit as a crooked toupee. I touch her arm.

'Thanks for dinner,' I say, adding, 'if only your Italian cooking teacher could have been here,' before walking away, leaving the subtext of that lingering like a musty fart.

'Did you have a nice time?' Luke asks in the cab.

'Camilla didn't like me.'

'Did you like her?'

'That isn't the point.'

How quickly it has begun to matter that I make more enemies than friends. I'm sure the four of them are dissecting my character back inside. Only Kaz seemed to like me. 'Maybe I came on too strong.'

Luke says nothing. Oh, I want to start again. I lean forward to pull down the window, but Luke twists across me to do it himself. Whoever taught this guy should be given a medal. There was a photo of Luke's parents in the apartment. His mother seems frightening, but his father looks cute. I'm always a sucker for older men.

Yurgh, but I need this air. The cab is speeding, lurching around the corners, and I'm starting to feel sick. I cling to the handle up above the door and wonder whether to risk a burp. Wasn't feeling drunk like this at the table. Just kept pouring the red wine down my throat. My head feels too heavy for my neck. It's lolling.

Luke has a hand on my back as we walk from the cab to his front door. Nothing too sexy or pushy, maybe it is there to protect me; against what, I wonder.

Out of breath and upstairs, the apartment seems bigger than before. It looks like there's too much space and we haven't got anything with which to fill it.

'Fancy a nightcap? I don't know if you drink scotch.'

'I do, but I don't, I mean I won't. Thanks.'

'Sure?'

I nod. Under the table lamp by the sofa is the glass I drank my vodka from. The lime's vibrant green mocks my flat-footed heaviness. I wish I could go back, pour away the wine. I'd been bubbly as tonic before, keen for just this moment. Now I feel like throwing up.

'Excuse me.'

I jog to the bathroom and, inside, push shut the door with my back. Christ. How did I let this happen? Bent over the sink, I scoop a few handfuls of lukewarm water into my mouth. It tastes like blood. My eyeballs feel detached, swimming in fluid as they scrape and bump against my closed eyelids. Yuuuaaaaaaaaaaaaaagh. Please, God, let me breathe in one long breath and clear my head and stomach. I didn't mean what I said to Damian. We need you. I need you.

The toilet seat clanks noisily down as it slips out of my fingers. Oops. I sit on it, my head in my hands. What an idiot. Suddenly, a burp. Polenta, smoky salmon. Nasty, but better. I brush my teeth, enjoying the mint. Luke I find hovering outside. I say, 'I think I drank too much.'

'Yes, well he keeps it coming, Jim does.' Oh, what a darling Luke is, blaming Jim like that. 'I'll get you some Nurofen. You'll be right as rain in the morning.'

'That long?'

He brings it to me in my room. Water and a pill and a heart-shaped cube of ice. It means something, to be tended too. I feel like a patient lying here on this lumpy mattress here in this strange room. Homesick, too, a little. If I am going to throw up, I want it to be into my own toilet with my own smells and stains.

'I hope you sleep all right. I'll try my best not to wake you in the morning.'

I push myself up on my elbows. 'Thank you, Luke. I'm sorry if . . .'

'I'm glad you had a good time.' He stops at the door. 'It'll be fun, won't it?'

'What?'

'London. Um, you being here. I'll call tomorrow from work.'

And then he is gone and I am left with the light on and a ceiling that is moving. Oh, I wish I, really, how I wish I'd never . . . I'm never going to drink again, ever again, for sure.

Ow! Ow! Should have drunk more water before sleeping. Shouldn't have said so much. Why did I have to blaze into town with all guns firing? Why couldn't I have been mature and diplomatic? I had an empty sheet to write on. I could have been nice. Capital N, nice. I am sure they all hate me. Maybe not Charlie and Kaz, but the others. Luke too?

Yet Luke has left a charming note outside the bedroom with his number at work and an offer of dinner, on him, somewhere cheerful and cheap. I click on the plastic kettle. Its inside is as yellow and furred as a smoker's lung. My lung. I light a cigarette. The sun turns milky in the room. I watch it. My God, I have time for this. One of my monthly resolutions in Toronto was to get up ten minutes earlier each day, give myself time for a smoke and a coffee, yet each morning I left with my hair barely dry and the niggling suspicion that I'd left something behind. And I had, my peace of mind. Now, with a lackadaisical shrug of my shoulders, I let the water heat; to a rolling boil, no less. If I am going to produce an article on how London lives up to its postcards, the thousand words will write themselves. I'll be able to go back to bed, a much greater luxury than staying under the covers for hours. The retreat feels forbidden.

The Gold Blend coffee granules fizz then smudge the cup's edge. In the fridge I look for milk but instead find two bottles of Veuve Cliquot, a slab of hard butter grainy with toast crumbs, a ready-made Sainsbury's lasagne a month past its sell-by stamp, a bottle of white wine, a sweating bag of sliced granary bread, a jar of pickled herrings from Norway via Harrods and four bottles of tonic, all opened. These things, but no milk.

I thud shut the fridge door to which a poster of Goldie Hawn in a wet T-shirt is stuck by four angled strips of Sellotape, as crispy and yellow as cornflakes at their edges. With money inherited from a grandfather, Luke bought this apartment nine years ago and I guess and hope the poster dates from then, as does the only cookery book in the kitchen, *One is Fun!* by a Delia Smith. I blow some dried food matter off the closed pages and open it. On the inside page the words DO TRY, DAR-LING!!!! are sandwiched between Luke and Lots of love, Mummy, XX. I can't stand cookery books with their prissy, frightening commands. What's this – ¼ tspn bruised rosemary – if not the title of a battered woman's memoir? Bruise and batter a quarter of Rosemary then watch her live life cooking for one. Is Delia using suspect mushrooms in her omelettes? The book should be sold beside the Dead Sea Bath Salts, part of the *Look How Alone* range. I could send one to Mother, to bruised and battered Angela herself.

I drink my coffee black and stare out into the square. Oh, I am happy. I am the luckiest woman alive. I could write just that for the *Herald* but I don't want to turn readers against me with my opening shot. No, I can find better subjects. I can do anything I want.

Twenty minutes later, I stagger back to the bedroom with a glass of water, turn my clock face down and climb back into bed. The deep horsehair grooves welcome me back, their edges curling around me as I feel myself sinking into a cosy sleep.

It seems only moments later that the doorbell startles me awake, though I see I have been sleeping for more than two hours. It's Kaz. I forgot she was dropping by.

'Lord, were you snoozing?' she asks, striding into the flat. Contained within her red cheeks is the new day I have yet to face. Though I am only three inches less tall, I feel tiny in my shoeless state as she bends to kiss me. Truth is, I am a little intimidated by Kaz and her sudden interest in me. I'm the baby sister now, equalling her in nothing. Not that I resent her for it. She is too much the happy English woman I would love to be.

'I should be up, anyway.'

'I suppose it's some ungodly hour in Canada.'

'Always,' I say with a laugh. 'That's why I left.'

'Canadians drive with their lights on all day, don't they? I thought that was quite bee-zarre.'

'We're very safe in Canada.' I wanted to say 'they', but Kaz, unconsciously, makes me feel less English.

She looks good this morning. She has succeeded in making her Indian-patterned, ankle-length dress look as elegant as, say, the sail of a yacht against a Californian blue sky. She has the height for which designers design and although I would not be surprised if she considers herself too tall, she is willowy and lissome, not gangly. And she's lucky, she has well-proportioned tits for her height. She has a sexy voice, too. As with Luke, there is something sensual in the cadence and rhythm of her speech, the stretched vowels like sunbathing bodies, the unexpected stresses lacquering commonplace words. And the way in which she seems unconscious of her beguiling beauty, her fair skin and slightly scraggly blonde hair, her friendly eyes and bright lips strikes me as particularly European. She is understated in the best ways. I can imagine her carrying a baby against her shoulder with utter ease. Unlike me, she would know just how to silence its cries. I am sure she has one of those kitchens that feature in magazines, and movies set in Paris – one with chipped enamel jugs holding wooden spoons beside randomly picked bunches of flowers in funky earthenware vases on the windowsill. A kitchen with a spice rack that is actually used and an old butcher block chopping board sliced a thousand times against the grain and a stove-top espresso maker and a lovely wooden table in the centre of a room to which everyone in the house is, of course, always drawn. I bet that, with one fluid dip of her finger into her salad dressing, just so, Kaz knows exactly which ingredients are missing. Even the walls I picture, painted by Kaz herself in a rich blue or green that is chipping and fading in just the right way and just the right places. Her life will not be so perfect, lives never are, but it is something that she gives such an impression of, that I feel I will never catch her up.

I run my fingers through my hair, feel how squiffy it must be. 'Can I make you some coffee, or something?'

The casual manner with which Kaz tosses her bag onto the sofa then heads to look at herself in the huge mirror suggests to me not only that she is familiar with the flat, but that my own dishevelment must have sparked in her mind some concern about her own appearance. It's like seeing spinach between someone's front teeth; always, it makes you check your own.

'Does Luke have herbal tea?'

'I doubt it.'

'Never mind then.' She lifts an unframed photo off the mantelpiece. 'Have you met the gorgeous Mr Bing?'

'Not yet.'

'He's a prince, you'll love him. It's a crime he's with the battle-axe herself. Avoid her like the plague. She's one of those meals-on-wheels, WI, church flower, Tory, point-to-pointing types.'

'Doesn't mean much to me.'

'You'll get war-child food at the Old Rectory. Dry pork chops and soggy veg. It's worse than BA, let me tell you. I take my own. She thinks I'm a vegan.'

'I can't cook, either,' I admit in the kitchen as I make some more coffee.

'Well, they say men marry their mothers.'

I laugh the suggestion away. 'I don't think Luke's planning on marrying me. We haven't even—'

She touches my arm. 'Go on. Haven't you? What about last night?'

'Last night I drank too much. That's why I'm the way I am this morning.' It's an excuse for being less than her; for now, it is.

'So? I was drunk as a skunk when Charlie finally inveigled a way into my Sister Mary.'

'I don't think Luke was all that keen.'

'Of course he was. The thing is, he's frightfully shy. Poor lamb only wears his heart on his sleeve when it's been broken, then blink and you miss it. But he's been longing for you to come. Absolutely longing.'

'Has he?' I grin. It makes me like him more already. 'I couldn't tell.'

'You're all he could talk about when he came back from Toronto. He's smitten as a smitten-thing.'

'He could have pounced last night, if he'd wanted to. Especially before we went out.'

'Darling, if Luke was a lion he'd be anorexic. It's a miracle he spoke to you at all. Your meeting sounded so romantic. I want to hear all the details. Exactly when did your eyes first meet?'

Beyond my collision with Luke (which does sound fatalistic and romantic when told, our not fucking adding a suitably chivalric nobility to the union) Kaz insists on hearing about my less than thrilling life in Toronto. She insists that it doesn't sound dull at all, yet in comparison with the poolside-lounging, party-going, Caribbean-cruising, private-school educated, Alp-skiing, pheasant-shooting, restaurant-loving, home-owning, monied lives that so clearly she and her friends live in London I can't agree. In gossiping about Luke and their mutual friends, Kaz constantly reconfirms the popular notion that England is an aristocratic, superior country largely peopled by the privileged. It requires no leaps of imagination to draw lines between their dots. The holidays during which Kaz or her friends have become engaged, or drowned, or fallen in love or off cliffs have been in places as exotic as Zanzibar or Namibia, Mustique or Mauritius or else on yachts cruising around the islands of Greece. I think of the photos in my new bedroom, put the content faces to the blessed lives and, for now, despite myself, I feel lucky to have landed among such folk. Whether or not I deserve inclusion, here I am. Here I am.

Kaz is a jewellery designer, I discover, her speciality chunky, colourful bead necklaces that suit her. She is wearing one now that clacks with the same liberated joy she seems to live by. When she leaves, she insists again that we will be great friends. It makes me feel glad, safer, as if it is through her, not Luke nor even Dad that I have positioned my foot inside this door from which I never intend to turn.

FOUR

Occupy yourself and your mind as much as possible. Social activities such as sports, volunteer work, discussion groups, or outings with friends are often better than being alone.

AMA Family Medical Guide

It is now my third evening here. After Kaz left yesterday, I had a perfect day discovering London. It is the little things that keep exciting me – hearing the city's name on the radio weather forecast (which, like my own disposition, is unswervingly sunny) or the British accent of a black bus conductor or reading my bus ticket itself, London Transport: Adult! It is not simply the newness of it all that excites, but the city's refinement, its solid sense of itself. I am where I want to be.

Of course, hearing from Kaz that Luke has a crush on me brightened an already brilliant summer's day. As soon as he got home and suggested a vodka, I thought we were going to start where we left off before Camilla and Jim's dinner. And yet, although we again loosened ourselves with alcohol and, in talking of ex-lovers and future dreams, we were being undeniably flirtatious with each other, there remained a sense of something not quite right between us. It was a sensation of being almost in lust, almost impassioned enough to kiss and be kissed. Today, I've been thinking this might be how the English feel all the time.

Their reputation for stuffiness must have some foundation. Perhaps Luke does want to throw himself at me, but can't. Of course, it's the classiness of imperturbable British restraint that the world loves, but repression loses much of its appeal when it's from oneself that something is being restrained.

I decided, then, to take matter's into my own hands. If Luke and I are meant to be, then tonight would be a final test of fate's promise. I offered to cook risotto, wanted to see what might catch fire. Now, as I sit biting my nails on the steps of his building, I am frightened it may be the kitchen.

I started early, could have been hosting my own cooking show I was feeling so chipper, so *One is Fun*, when, with a glass of mouldy-labelled wine down my throat I realized I'd forgotten the cream and the shop down the road was shutting in four minutes and what could I do but pour some stock in the rice and run like the wind to the store with its quaint, tidy stacks of chocolate biscuits, its tinned soups, its unappealing fruit and Indians?

Along with the cream I bought an instant National Lottery scratchcard, attracted to the idea that, since I remain in fate's sights, I was doubtless tempted out of the kitchen for something significant. It was with such hope that I used the keys from my pocket to scratch the useless numbers to life on the ticket. And it was then, while strolling back to my tasks, that I realized what I had done. The keys in my hand weren't the flat keys at all. They were perfectly cut to start Luke's new car, to get me to Scotland or Wales or even to Sweden if the Saab felt homesick, but no cigar if I wanted to get back up to the risotto with its boneless chicken breasts, button mushrooms and wine.

The truth is, I thought Luke would be home or I would find a neighbour with keys. A pleasant resolution would make me feel blessed. Instead, almost an hour on, I feel helpless. I keep wondering what would happen if this meal was truly important, if, say, I had children to feed. Mother never failed to get decent food on the table, however mean Dad and I were. We used to laugh so hard we couldn't swallow, not just at those schoolyard adverbs – gloppy, barfy, sludgy, gunky – that were delicious as wet mud, but others dredged up from our dictionaries. Words like 'crissum'. Dad, is this crissum? Because it tastes like it, like a bird's bottom. Other favourites? Nidorous, the smell of burning animals; athamantic, a horrid taste; borborygmic, a rumbling in our bowels. We were relentless; and yet she stayed loyal, she didn't leave. It doesn't add up.

'Hello there.' Luke, finally. He is looking ruddy-faced, more farmer than banker.

'Are you waiting for someone?'

'No. Yes. You. Um, I haven't got my keys.'

'Poor you. How come?'

I'm thinking a straight answer will suit best. I lift up the paper bag. Members of the Jury, may I present. 'I went to get cream and picked up your car keys instead of the apartment keys.'

'Oh dear, how long ago?'

'About an hour.'

'Bloody Hell, I wish I had known. I was round the corner at Dominic's bar. I thought you were probably cooking.'

'I was. That's the thing.'

'Never mind, eh?'

Now we're inside – how simply the lock turned – I am sure I can smell something nasty, something nidorous, coming from Luke's flat.

'Don't worry if supper's going to be late. I've been munching on Bombay Mix.'

'So you're not hungry?'

'No, but . . . hang on, where's that alarm coming from?'

Hesitatingly, I say, 'Up, I think. Thing is, I was cooking when—'

'Fuck and bugger.'

Luke has ditched his briefcase and is taking the steps two at a time. I am slow behind him. I hear first the radio and then the alarm's vicious whine stop dead. When I reach the open door, he is nowhere to be seen. It stinks in here, but there's nothing on fire. Above a vacant chair, the face of the smoke alarm is hanging open like a broken jaw, the partially disconnected battery a tongue hanging out. I hear a snigger and discover Luke in the kitchen standing over the risotto pan with a fork in his hand. He is licking his lips. 'Mmmm.'

I peer into the pan where the rice has shrunk into a hard and blackened cake.

'Yikes.'

'Great. Jim gets Camilla who's done a cooking course in Tuscany, and I get Miss Chernobyl 1986.'

'Don't, Luke. It was going great.'

He lifts the pan, says, 'Now it's going, going, gone,' and drops it into the sink.

'Only one thing for it, I suppose.'

'I take you out to dinner?'

'No. Drink. Lots of it. We may as well finish that fifty quid Chablis, don't you think? Now it's open. Or do you want shampoo?'

'I'll take the wine.'

He fills my glass to the brim and pours one for himself. We take them next door where the windows have been opened and the smell of burning is receding. When Luke puts the Cranberries on the stereo it sounds too loud. I have come off the boil.

'I think there's a lasagne in the fridge, if you're hungry,' he says, standing on the chair to reconnect the alarm. He has apple-sized circles of sweat under his arms. For some reason, I hadn't imagined him sweating.

'I was going to ditch that. It's old.'

'Why don't you cook it, then we'll ditch it?'

'Thanks.'

'Cheer up. Let's get some Chinese.' He jumps off the chair and almost falls into my arms. 'OK? Now where's that glass of wine?'

I do cheer up when we order food. It doesn't take long to finish the Chablis then Luke says we should open champagne to celebrate the fact that I wrote my first article today. I say that sounds like a 'damn fine idea, Jeeves' and we laugh like Cary

Grant and Sophia Loren in a fifties' movie when the cork surprises us and shoots out of the bottle's neck, knocking a tall candle out of its stick as if we had choreographed the farce; as if all this is scripted, meant.

Tipsy, we kick off our shoes and sit on the floor with our backs to the sofas. I enjoy the tan and musculature of his arms.

'Can I read your article?'

'I'd rather you didn't. Not just yet.'

'What was it about?'

'Piccadilly. How London lives up to its hype.'

'London's supposed to be the hippest place in the world these days, isn't it? Sort of New York and Paris combined.'

'I guess.'

I hope I haven't screwed up. The editorial ant can't have expected me to have found the city's pulse after three days, so I wrote instead about its heart, Piccadilly, the place that seems a microcosm of a romantic England the outside world thinks it knows. Just the names – St James's, the Ritz, Bond Street, Burlington Arcade – arouse images that are almost mythic and, in fact, as good as fiction. The whole felt privileged and untouchable. I came back overflowing with the joys of life. The article took forty minutes. It's my week's work.

Luke refills my glass and we're good drunk, bubbly drunk, by the time the food arrives. Our delivered dishes are hot silver ingots. Luke and I rip open the bags, jostling like hyenas. He insists we eat off warm plates and is running them under water.

I stick a large prawn cracker in my mouth, feeling its tiny kisses on my tongue.

'Yaaaaa.'

'Ugh. Don't go kissing me with that.'

I flip it in and crunch. 'Why'd you say that? Wasn't thinking about it.'

'Here you go.' He waves a long spring roll at me that leaves his fingertips shiny with grease. 'That'll keep you happy.'

'Are you being gross, Luke Bingham?'

'Not at all.' He wipes his hands on the chequered blue tea

towel. 'Whatever you choose to think is up to you. Let's open more shampoo.'

I pull the last bottle from the fridge. 'What shall I aim at?'

'Aim at getting some in my glass while I do all the work.'

He is fanning the crispy duck pancakes across a plate, making neat piles of the cucumber and onion strips.

'Why is it that boys always make a big deal about doing the most simple things while women get on and do them?'

'Is that bottle open yet?'

I wave the bottle in front of his face. 'Be nice or I'll fire it in your eye.'

'Don't,' he retorts, suddenly serious. 'It's bloody silly. You might slip.'

'Sorry,' then whispering, 'Sir.'

He takes the bottle from my hands. We are carelessly tactile, and aware of it. Luke wants to open it anyway. I knew he did. This time, it's unshowy the way he eases the cork off. There's a tiny pffft. A buttock raised off the cushion when you think no one will notice – that kind of pffft.

We carry the food to the table next door and attack the appetizers and worry aloud that we haven't ordered enough, but of course there's plenty once the rice starts to fill us up. We drink, too, the whole bottle of champagne. It is good with Chinese. Will I ever be happy returning to cheap beer and greasy chow mein?

When we have eaten, Luke says, 'Let's sit soft.'

'Gotta pee first.'

'You do that.'

He is bunched up at one end of a sofa when I come back so there is nothing untidy about my choosing to sit next to him. It is the most obvious, comfortable place to be.

'You've got a hole in your sock,' I tell him, tickling his big toe. 'That's not like you.'

'You think I'm unholy?'

'That's not funny.'

'So stop smiling.'

'Don't want to.'

'Why?'

''Cos. 'Cos I'm happy.'

I could kiss Luke when he smiles back at me. I would like to. I am not breathless with longing but I would like to kiss him and to fuck him, I guess. But all night beside him is what I want the most. Whether or not I am wrong to leap fast as I normally do, I am uncomfortable with the supposition that one should know a man before having sex when there is no faster way into their psyches. Selfish men are selfish lovers, the cruel display their cruelty, the tender their tenderness. Besides, tonight it would feel like loss to sleep alone.

'Shall I go and get a video?'

'No. Let's talk.'

'What about?'

'I dunno. You.'

'God, no. Boring.' His right hand reaches for the ring on his left almost at once, and twists it.

'Go on. Tell me what you think you'll be doing in ten years.'

'Oh, I don't know. The usual. Married, I suppose. Probably a couple of kids and a house in the country.'

'That's not knowing. Sheesh. You got names for the kids, too?'

'No. Well, I'd probably call one Charles if he's a boy.'

'So you have got names.'

He sounds defensive now. 'I'm just saying I'm not going to become a missionary in Africa, or anything, so that's what's most likely.'

'And you don't think that's depressing?'

'Of course not. Why should it be?'

I could say that it sounds like a march towards death but I have no right to underestimate Luke's ability to forge a life that is exhilarating to himself. Perhaps the freedom I crave is not as liberating as it seems.

'What about you?'

'I don't even know what's going to happen in ten minutes.'

He looks me in the eyes and for a thump of my heartbeat I

think his answer is going to be a kiss. Instead he says, somewhat earnestly, 'I think I've got Häagen-Dazs.'

I grab his arm. 'Poor you. How did you catch it?'

Luke starts to laugh and either because we're drunk or because we're drunk enough to use alcohol as an excuse for any behaviour, we laugh until the laughter has become genuinely infectious. Luke lets himself fall off the sofa then takes my naked ankle in his hand and announces, 'Miss Portia, yew ave ze verry nassty cayse of Häaaaagen-Dazs. A zurra examination is required.'

'Not doctors and nurses,' I wail, lifting my feet onto the sofa. 'I shan't play.'

Hard to get, I'm thinking, must be good. Now it's good. Before, it was the other way around. Once I grew up and after Dad died. One minute I was Daddy's honeyed apple, his Hebe, his precious Pea, the next I was trapped with a woman who felt released by his death. That's the word Mother used, 'release', with its evil sibilance, its serpentine hiss. My own release was elsewhere, on car seats, behind gyms, in Verdura on Eglinton, at home on Mother's bed. I had no shame. Remember, boys, how you couldn't believe your luck? How I fished you in, shoals of you in front of Mother's eyes as I stretched and painted myself into a woman over whom you could slobber and gasp and come? Remember how easy. A wink from these lush, almond eyes, a pout from my truculent lips, an unabashed glance that lingered until you dreamt I was yours alone. Josh Medwood, sixteen and a half, you who stole bourbon to buy your brother's bed, his silence, my childhood; you, the first to tear into me until I cried. Sam Kelps; Johnny Prewitt; Preston Small; Tom Montino; Mark London; Nathan Kurtz; Ronnie Carp; Wilson Mondale; Kevin Knight; Ryan Jones; Bobby Decello; remember? How you thought it must be love and never was – your prize not pollen but petals that died. I was not being used. Sometimes I picture the look in your eyes when I turned you away. Snap. You could never understand, could you, how I could do that? But leaving you was easy, easy as Mother taking him from me.

Distracted, I have stopped laughing. Luke, sensing that our

moment has been lost, releases my ankle and sits up on his haunches. The skin under his ear is the colour of cranberries. He looks worried. I wonder if he is thinking of kissing me. I would, Luke, let you. Is it obscene to think sex inevitable? Sixties' sexual liberation led us to such unthrilling expectation. Not fucking – that's what's odd now. I offer my sole against his knee and then, suddenly, push him so he falls on his back, all arms and legs like an upset beetle while I run laughing into the kitchen. He'll run after.

I have the tub of Häagen-Dazs Cookies and Cream in my hands by the time Luke reaches me. I flick off the lid and take a spoon from the drawer. 'Goody. Just enough for one.'

Luke is trying not to smile as he takes a menacing step towards me, but he wants to play this game and can't help showing it. Slowly, I close my lips around a mouthful of ice cream.

'Boy, this is good,' I say, speaking as though through a yawn. The lump in my mouth is large and cold against my teeth. 'You should have had some.'

Luke holds up a finger. 'One. You've got one warning.'

'Before what?'

'Before I spank you.'

'Promises, promises.'

As I lick at another spoonful, Luke lunges at the tub. I used to play this game with Dad, he and I running all over the house, the forty-three years between us no obstacle to fun, though he always caught me and trapped me in his big arms. And I'm still fast, twisting under Luke's arm to run through the living room into his bedroom.

Now, in here, the game has turned serious. The bed seems to have grown in size just as thoughts of what we might do have swollen in my mind. I want to dent the taut cover with our bodies. I am bored with our mating dance, the studied avoidance. I want Luke to touch me now, physically my body wants him. We have been brushing skin against skin all evening, letting our fingers meet as we passed each other plates and glasses. My running in here is a sign of supplication.

'Portia, now give me that ice cream.'

'No.'

'Right. That's it.'

He corners me. I turn my back to protect my plunder but he clasps a hand around each wrist and starts to pull my arms back.

'Ow-ow-ow-ow. I give up.'

As soon as Luke releases his grip I make a leap across the bed but I'm not fast enough, or don't want to be, and with one tug on my shirt he has me flattened to the mattress. I turn on my back. Luke climbs on top and pins my arms down. We are breathless. I am simmering with happiness. A giggle escapes.

He says, 'You cheated.'

'Did I?' I do that thing with my tongue on my upper lip. Porno star. 'Which game were we playing?' I let the ice-cream tub fall from my fingers. Luke begins to move for it. 'Let's leave it,' I whisper.

He looks scared, hovering above me as he is; not the hunter at all. Looking him in the eye, I lift my head and then graze my lips against his. My stomach tightens sweetly. I close my eyes and as Luke presses his mouth against mine I let my head sink back on the quilted spread. We are glued together, gently, as if scared that with too much movement we will break for ever. And then we open our lips and touch with the tips of our tongues. I feel myself opening to him.

When he strokes my cheek, his hand is like sunshine. My skin tightens and eases at once. Sex is fighting to hold on to yourself and being thrilled when you can't. Now I want Luke to lie on me, I need to feel the weight of him. I lift my hands from the bed to his shoulders and pull him down. He hesitates but then stretches himself flat. It's exciting to feel him hard against me. I push my tongue against his and he responds, his own surging into my mouth.

Luke rolls me onto my side as we kiss, and then his hands are under my shirt and on the bare skin of my back. I gasp in a lungful of air. I want these clothes gone. I start to pull at Luke's shirt and struggle with the buckle of his trousers, but he stops me and sits up on his haunches and undoes the button of my jeans instead, unzips them, and then stands at the side of the bed to pull them down. I lift my hips to help him. Then, coming behind me, he asks me to sit up and take off my top. He reaches for the straps of my bra, lifts it off and throws it to the side. For a second it catches the light that is falling carelessly across the end of the bed. I am almost naked.

'You look beautiful,' he says, as if this has just occurred to him. It makes my heart swell, as it did when I noticed he'd cut his hair for me, as it did when he met me off the plane. It makes me want to make him happy. He is good and kind and acts as if he loves me.

'Come on,' I repeat, holding my arms out to him.

He has his back to me as he undresses. When he turns, his penis is neither hard nor soft, just a little nervous perhaps, but it isn't, thank God, small or crooked or weird. I don't get much of a look because quickly he is on top of me. We kiss again. Deftly, he has his hand under the elastic of my pants, and then he pushes them down and brings his hand back to touch me. I relax for him, lift myself towards his fingers. We kiss until I can bear it no longer. It has been so long. I am suddenly impatient. Urgently, I whisper, 'I want you inside me. Can we?'

'Um, are you on the—'

'No.'

'I don't have condoms.'

'So be careful. We'll be careful.'

'I don't know if I can—' He gasps when I take his erection in my hand and says, 'It's been ages since I last did it, Portia, I don't—'

'Sshhshh. Doesn't matter. Kiss me.'

The second time will be better, I think. I can wait for that. Luke pushes his mouth against mine and then, oh . . .

I am wet and it is almost a surprise how quickly, how

completely, he fills me. And it is good, his erection feels large and deep in me. He is big. It matters. It is better. Oh yes, it is better. I lie back and it is better, for a while I can't respond, he is moving so sweetly in me. You wouldn't have thought you could forget something this good but you do until it happens again. If Luke keeps moving like this like this like this I think I might even come without him touching or licking me just the delicious sense of how much he wants me is beautiful. Here I am, the last person to have thoughts so poetic, I know it's plain fucking most of the time, I've felt like a slut saying so to friends but it just satisfies, answers the void, feels like enough, just bodies being together. Only tonight it feels better than don't know when. For ever maybe. For ever I think. It's been so long.

'Like that,' I whisper. 'I love it like that.'

It can't be only England only London, only Luke being English like Daddy, it can't. And it can't be not having a man for so many months, it is Luke, it must be Luke, the way he is holding me as if nothing could make him let go and his hands wrapped under my back lifting me to him holding me so our hearts are pressed together tight, tight like my cunt and his prick in it. 'Fuck me,' I say. His fabulous foreskinned prick is so deep I think I'm going to come and he's kissing me like our mouths are only ever for sex they're wet with each other and like this like this is so fucking marvellous. I slide my hands down his back to the curves of his ass and with a finger, just so, push between the cheeks feeling for the clammy muscle so that—

'Oh, Porsh, oh, no.'

'Wait, Luke.' I try to cling to him. 'Please.' I want to cling to him but he pushes up and is out of me in a second and I feel empty so fast, I wasn't ready for that. I would have gone to a doctor's tomorrow, taken hormone-bending pills, whatever, if he had come inside. I would have loved to have felt the throb of him. It wouldn't have been the end of the world anyway, not with my period a couple of days away.

My heart is beating five hundred times a second I was so close to coming myself and now I have only the weight of me, my back sweating against the sheets, the feel, the shape of Luke so recently inside. I wish he would touch me. I feel flayed, inside out, wounded.

Luke is breathless on his back with ribbons of spunk like vanilla Häagen-Dazs on his stomach and here is a little oyster of sperm on his chest into which I dip my finger. I bring it to my lips like balm. Luke acts as if he doesn't approve, wiping at the spot with the back of his hand. I lean to kiss him but there is nothing left, his tongue feels weary. He is letting me kiss him because he can't say no.

'Sorry,' he says, covering himself with his hand. 'I'm sorry.'
'Don't be.'
'I haven't done it for ages. I—'
'Don't worry. It was wonderful. I loved it.'
'Did you?'

I kiss him again but this time he makes an excuse and moves away. 'Back in a mo,' he tells me, pressing a hand to the gunk on his stomach as he walks to the bathroom. Naked, he is more slender than his clothed self suggested, his hips more narrow, although he has the beginnings of a pot belly, like a woman three months' pregnant, what will come is inevitable. I couldn't mind less. I dislike perfection in men, it seems unnatural.

But this man, this Luke, has made me happy, happy, happy. I lie watching my stomach rise and fall with my breath, my heart thumping like a fist in frustration. So close you were to getting it right the very first time, Luke, my sweet, if only you'd known how close. I could touch myself now. My fingers drip to my wet fur, but I draw them away and close instead my eyes and urge this feeling to ebb. But, oh, never stop. Should never stop fucking. It buries the demons so much deeper than anything else can.

The sweat is cooling my skin so I draw the sheet up to my chest before Luke returns. I see he already has on a clean pair of boxers.

'Would you like to sleep here tonight?'

Did I hear that right? Does he think I am going to retreat to the horsehair mattress now he is done with me? 'Aren't you going to pay me first?'

'What's that?'

'Forget it. Dumb joke. Yes, I would like to sleep in your bed. But are we sleeping now?'

'I don't know. Do you want to watch TV?'

'No. No, I . . . It's only ten fifteen. Can't we sit together next door? Smoke some spliff, something?'

Luke shrugs his shoulders. Really, damn men. Soon as they come the sweetness goes. I can't help but want to be held by him. We were together too recently to be apart. I want him back in bed.

'Got to get some serious kip tonight,' he says. 'I'm playing footie tomorrow.'

I sit up with my hands flat on the bed behind me. His eyes fall to my breasts and back. 'Give me that ice cream, would you?' I ask, gesturing towards the tub on the floor.

'Oh, buggerations. Look at the mess on the carpet.'

'It'll wash. Can I have it?'

'The spoon's dirty,' he says, bending down to right the tub.

'We don't need a spoon. You can be my living lollipop.'

Luke smiles. 'That sounds naughty.'

'You don't know the half it. Come here Ice Cream Man.' I tease him with a flick of my tongue.

'I'd better get a cloth first. I don't want the carpet to stain.'

'You do that!' I say, flopping my head back onto the pillow and wondering, wondering, wondering, what will become of this something we have begun, my out-of-the-blue dinner companion and I.

FIVE

Sexual intercourse at bedtime may have a relaxing effect. However, other strenuous exercise or arguments just before going to bed are likely to interfere with sleep.

AMA Family Medical Guide

My life is full of laughing. The nightmares have dissipated and been replaced by this living dream. London is the most gorgeously beautiful, complete city in the world. I am overwhelmed and entranced by its history and mystery and soul. I sing aloud on its streets. I adore its green-parked decency and poise, its people. And Luke, my very own man; fuckable, suckable, velvety-pricked Luke who has filled me with himself and a sense of life being worth living, such as I haven't felt for over half a lifetime. I love him for it. Oh, he's such a pernickety little rat half the time, has to keep the toothpaste lid tight and likes the washing-up done before we go to bed and turns his nose up at my drinking pints of beer at the pub and gets all edgy when I tell him stories of my past as if he doesn't want to admit that, had I been raised here and not there, I would be beneath him, have a common accent not this Canadian voice that saves him from shame. I don't care. I love him. I love him fucking me most of all. Christ, yes, that. I want him inside me all of the time.

Don't expect too much, Mother said. But I expected less than this. Last week, Luke took me to a beautiful opera in the Sussex countryside. Glinnbourne, Glyndburne, Glen-whatever. Kaz and Charlie came, too, which made it even better. It is not often that life feels like the movies but that day it did. The grass was greener under my feet than anywhere on the planet. During the interval, I kicked off my shoes and skipped on the sprinkled-green lawn and felt as if I didn't have a care in the world. We drank champagne (again champagne, oh me, oh my) and pigged ourselves on picnic food from Marks and Spencer in High Street Ken (only see how easily the local slang drips off my tongue) and from Luigi's on the Fulham Road (these my neighbourhood stores now, I reside in London Town, don't you know . . .) and even though I have lived my life spitting in disgust at name-droppers, at people who assume that knowing the famous reflects well on themselves, I adored being surrounded by celebrity politicians and TV stars and actors since they helped me believe I was where it was at, truly believe that because I chose to turn some stranger on the street in Toronto into my lover that I had taken on the blues and won. My present is sneering at the past. With such happiness that night, I naturally started feeling horny, what with the champagne and all, and got to thinking that nothing could cap the evening better than a sweet alfresco fuckarooni, somewhere dangerously close to the babble of voices. So it was that under a candyfloss pink sky I tempted Luke until he hardened (a task easier with him than with most men, his appetite for sex is a joyful surprise) and, just before the second act kicked in, hit my very own internal top C as my lover, his willy brisk as a baton through his black-tie pants, gracefully parted my flesh on the soft camel seat of a vintage Bentley which some unsuspecting rich folk had left open, presuming, I suppose, that they were among people who loved art, not sin. As if the two aren't regular bedfellows. Not that there was anything sinful about our brief coupling, just something irrepressibly gleeful. It is how the entire month has been.

This train travelling towards my aunt in Essex is singing the progressive rhythm of my new English life. *Vivacissimo.* I feel in tune with London. It doesn't matter whether I am flirting with cheeky market traders on Berwick Street or Portobello, or getting lost in the romance of Cumberland Terrace or excited by the finger-tingling thrill of visiting the Tower or the Globe or St Paul's, or any one of the sights that were fodder for my childhood imagination. Being here is enough. I have been living life with a sense of Dionysian abandonment. The sex has caused me to adopt towards both people and time a slack, forgiving air, and although there is a certain cosseted arrogance to Luke's friends that niggles, when I am with them I am hindered by none of the toe-curling bitterness I usually feel towards such privilege.

Luke is still trying to charm me. He doesn't seem to realize how genuinely and deeply I like him already. It is not love, not yet, but I don't mind. Perhaps I will never know love as I knew it before. Instead, under England's careless skies, our relationship has had the feel of a beach and cocktail flirtation. Only my constant presence in his apartment has shored it up, given it a one-way-ticket permanence. I have not been contemplating the real world of drizzle and pale grey skies and pain. Winter is far away. Things feel easy. Work, play, the future.

I arrive at Colchester and try to keep my shock hidden when I wave at my Aunt Barbara beyond the ticket barrier. She has aged more than I had expected. She is sixty-seven now. The change in the fourteen years since I saw her is marked. I had prepared myself for the shock of seeing Dad living in someone else but in truth I can't see him. He has not grown so old in my mind. I used to think Barbara and Dad were alike, both firm-jawed with large eyes, the lower lids of which dipped as if attached to tiny weights. Dad looked the better, his own eyes furnished with thick, rectangular glasses. Strangely, now my aunt has become jowly, the pouches are more in keeping with the rest of her face. She has broadened in the beam, too. Her hips stretch the fabric of her pleated skirt. No question, it's a snug fit.

My aunt wafts an odour of sexless cleanliness as she leans to kiss me. It's a flowery smell, not unlike one of those toilet freshener sprays. It's fitting. I remember her having a smutless, dainty nature.

'It's lovely to see you, Portia. How are you?'

'I'm great. How about you, Auntie?'

'Oh, I can't grumble.' We walk to her car. 'Isn't it hot again today?' she says. The continuing heatwave (84 degrees today) has the whole country talking. It has helped me understand how tiny Great Britain is; how it could fit, just so, into Canada's pocket.

Barbara settles herself in the driver's seat beside me and pulls her satiny blouse straight beneath the seatbelt's unkind sash. 'You found your train all right, then.'

'I found it great.'

I know that's not what she meant but I so enjoyed the journey I am still feeling high from it. It was magical to pass the rich golden cornfields, the tiny medieval villages and farms, to see how the past has tamed every foot of land in England. It didn't take much for my imagination to conjure up images of long-dead ploughmen and shearers and tillers. In Canada, we lack such a sense of the past in the air. It lessens us.

'Your mother telephoned last week and asked had I seen you yet. She'll be pleased you're looking so well.'

'Am I?'

Barbara is careful in the car, she is a mirror-signal-mirror kind of driver and risks taking her eyes off the road only for a second when she looks at me. 'Lovely, I'll tell her.' Then, self-reproach in her tone, she adds, 'It's been too long.'

Barbara last came to Canada to see her brother buried. I don't know how Mother and I would have survived without her. In those two weeks, she spoke of him, of their childhood in Cornwall, of his academic promise and vivacity when we needed that, and in so doing helped lessen the horror of his death when the weight became too heavy. With her accent, her presence brought a little piece of him into the house. With her generosity, she made us grateful for what we had had rather than allowing us to linger on what we had lost. She filled the silences that would have screamed at us in the house. She even kept the balance as it had been; two adults, one child.

Only after Barbara was asleep did Mother have to tend to me. She and I slept together in her bed. I would wake night after night to find her in tears, and only if I cried too would she stop. It seemed to make her brave, mothering me. She would pull me against her, sometimes so hard it hurt my ribs, and we would lie together, our words submerged in grief. The thirty-two-year-old widow and her pubescent child. 'Look what he's done to us,' Mother would whisper as we rocked back and forth. 'Look what he did.' It felt as if Daddy had tied the rope not to my bed but to something inside of me that was ripped out when he jumped, something without which I would never be whole.

Barbara was witness to it all so that, even now, fourteen years on, I feel as if I know her. She was present when I became the adult I am. I recognize my aunt's address, Devonshire Close, as we turn off a tiny roundabout into what must be a new development of houses. It still has the look of an architect's model about it: the clean, graffiti-free glass of the bus shelter, the trees of varying colour still tied to their posts, the neat houses set in a celliform pattern of cul de sacs branching off the roundabouts. Net curtains hanging within almost every window add to the sense of desertion.

Once we are inside my aunt's proudly detached house, I accept her offer of lemonade. She suggests we sit outside on the patio. The house has a just tidied smell, part furniture spray, part hot electrics. I notice the beige carpet is hummocky in places from a vacuum's brush. It makes my shoes look tatty. Barbara should have known I am not the type to expect such tidiness.

Her garden is, as I might have guessed, immaculate beyond the patio. Half of it is paved in differing coloured stones, pinks and browns mainly, and there is a circular fountain elevated in three steps of coloured brick. At its centre is a stone bullfrog spitting a pathetic spurt of water from its mouth.

Barbara brings lemon barley water that tastes as good as it used to when Mother brought me tall, bright plastic glasses of the drink back home, always swimming in ice, as this one isn't. Or else ice pops she made in the freezer. She was good in that way. There was never any neglect.

Barbara and I sit on hot plastic chairs and squint at the neat scene around us. There is an umbrella staked in the table's centre but it is too small and the dark crescent of shadow at midday is curved across my aunt's cream skirt, missing me completely. I close my eyes and lift my face to the sun.

We chat about my older, married cousins, but I am much more interested in Diane, the woman to whom Dad was once married. I ask, 'Was she nice?'

'Oh yes, lovely. Keith and I were at their wedding, up in Robin Hood country. I remember you used to love those stories. Clive was ever so good at telling them.'

'Mother said Dad and Diane didn't get on after a while. Is that what happened?'

There is something suspicious about the way Barbara doesn't meet my eye when she replies, 'It's a long time ago now. Must be thirty years, isn't it?'

'Have you seen her since?'

'We exchange cards at Christmas sometimes, that sort of thing. She was a nurse like your mother.'

'She was? How weird. I'd like to meet her.'

'I wouldn't bother.' Barbara makes a face. 'People can be funny about things like that. Now, what time would you like your lunch?'

'Whenever.'

'We'll wait for Keith, shall we? I want to hear about all your goings on.'

When I tell Barbara about my two weeks of goings on in London she oohs and aahs and says it's quite a world I've got myself into. She has heard of some of Luke's friends, the only thing is, that set's not the most stable, so she's read. Flighty is the word she uses. Obviously, she has not met Luke. He is oak.

When Keith arrives it strikes me that he has aged less than his wife. He is a wiry man who greases his hair. Since I have received twenty-seven cards reading 'Happy Birthday love Barbara and Uncle Keith' he is part of who I am, an extra in my play; but we are not close.

When we are seated in the dining room with the chicken salad, Barbara says, 'Portia was asking me about those old films, Keith. The ones from Cornwall.'

'Yes?'

He makes me smile, that upright way he has of sitting at the head of the table, drawing his plate towards him as if it is the minutes from one of his meetings.

'She wonders if she might be able to take a look at them.'

'Nineteen seventy-six or nineteen eighty-one?'

'Um, nineteen seventy-six, I guess.' I am conscious of the um. Have I picked it up from Luke? 'When we were all in St Ives.'

'I do have it, but . . .' Keith pauses as he slips his fork between his lips. I am impatient as I wait for him to chew and swallow. 'Unfortunately the projector is broken.'

'You'll have to come down again, Portia,' says Barbara. 'That was a lovely holiday, wasn't it?' She looks wistful. Is she thinking of Dad, as I am? That holiday, he and I buried and hid countless bottles filled with messages for one another. The assumption that we would return one day to collect them was never spoken. It didn't need to be.

'Do you remember when Angela thought you were going to fall off the cliff at Maslyn?' Even now, she clasps a hand to her mouth. 'She was so scared, wasn't she?'

I do remember, and well. Dad was chasing me while Mother lagged behind with the picnic. As I turned to see him getting close, I tripped and tumbled to the edge of a steep fissure in the granite. Mother screamed so loudly and with such an infectious terror that I burst into tears, terrified more by the tone of her cry than the narrow escape itself. We had to turn back to the tea shop, she was so unsettled. I was rewarded with an ice-cream cone but, for some time afterwards, whenever I woke gripping the sheets at night it was down that Maslyn cliff I was falling with Mother's screams in my ears. And since, on darker days, I have imagined myself falling quite willingly, following Dad to death in the place where he was born.

I ask, 'Why do you think Dad never came home?'

'Would you like some more, Portia?' Keith offers me the bowl. I thank him and say no. He serves himself a measured spoonful and passes the dish to his wife.

'Sometimes, I think that's the biggest mystery of all.'

Bigger than the why of his suicide, I mean, and they know it. I have dismissed most reasons – love of Mother, or the university, or Canada – and am left with the unbearable notion that had he left he would have lost me. He couldn't have lived with that. Did he choose not to live with that? 'Didn't you ever wonder?' I ask.

'I never could read Clive's mind,' says Barbara, giving me the impression that she doesn't want to carry the topic further.

I have to wait until lunch has finished and Keith is out tending to his lawn before raising the topic again. 'Granny must have tried to persuade Dad to come home, didn't she? I mean, she can't have liked it that she hardly ever saw him.'

'He could have brought you both here, if he'd wanted to.'

'Mother wouldn't have let him.'

'I thought you had stopped blaming Angela for everything, dear.'

'No, I said I had started pitying her. You can't hate someone you pity.'

'You should treat your mum better. She's not had the easiest of times, has she? I'm sure you know that.'

Widowed when she was thirty-four with a teenage daughter who soon after wished her dead. Vilified by a community that considered her responsible, at least in part, for what her husband had done. Single since. No, I never considered hers an easy life. Rather, I used not to care and now I can't do anything to unhate the hate except let Mother know that it no longer burns in me, that I now carry some of the weight.

'Oh, Portia, I have something I want to show you,' Barbara says.

I follow her into the lounge and to a glass-fronted cabinet. She pulls out a rectangular lacquered box. 'There's a picture in here that Keith found and I thought...' The ringing phone interrupts her and, with some effort, she creaks to her knees and returns to the hallway to answer it.

The plastic lid makes a light, hollow sound as I take it off. Inside, beneath two or three full envelopes, are some old photos of Dad and Barbara as children which make me smile, along with unexceptional colour snaps of my cousins and their children. In one, Paul and Tony are together with a third man younger than they. All three men are holding bottles of beer in a salute to the photographer. The man in the middle has a smile just like Dad's, he looks uncannily like him. My heart skips a beat. I turn it over. Meeting Richard, 21 February 1996. I keep doing this: seeing and hearing Dad in English people. Am I too simple to understand that Britain is a small island? That its people do share features? Canada's a hodge-podge, we'll blend in anywhere, apologize as we slink into a corner.

I am like a thief, the way I put down the box when I hear Barbara hang up.

'Now where were we?' She flicks through the pile and finds the photograph she wanted. 'There. That's my mother's father, your great-grandfather, in the middle.'

It is a formal sepia photograph of maybe forty people, men save for one woman, standing in hats and suits beneath a wooden sign bearing the name of my great-grandfather's eponymous flower business, Dickerson's. They look proud and optimistic. It was taken, I see from the oval stamp on the back, in 1911. John Dickerson, a small man with a large moustache and happy, round eyes, is flanked by his two teenage sons.

'Those were his children,' Barbara says, 'my mother's brothers. They died in the war, both of them. That one, Alan, only a week before Armistice Day. It destroyed my poor grandmother. She died soon after. That's when your great-grandfather brought my mother to Cornwall.'

'And that's where Granny met your dad.'

'That's right.'

Barbara's father, my grandfather, was from the village of Maslyn, near Penzance. An accident in his youth kept him off the fishing boats on which all of his brothers sailed, and led to him getting a job in the Dickerson's flower nurseries where daffodils bloomed early in England's warmest soil. He fell in love with the owner's daughter, Dad's mother. It was a courtship as romantic as those of the knights and ladies of medieval myth. I like to think that's why Dad chose the subjects that he did.

'Mr Dickerson didn't really approve of my father,' Barbara reminds me. 'Not that he stood in his way. Anyway, you can have that photograph, if you'd like. The boys don't seem very interested.'

'I'd love it.'

'Good. Now, dear, do you fancy that walk?'

'Sure.'

Barbara asks, 'Do you know about Constable?'

'The painter?'

'That's right. He painted that,' she says, pointing to a framed reproduction of a horse and cart in a stream somewhere. I recognize it. 'That's not far from here at all. In Constable country. It's very popular with tourists, if you'd like to take a look.'

'I'd love to.'

'Oh, good. Then I'll go and ask Keith,' says my aunt as she waddles away to call to her husband outside.

We are in the Saab driving into Oxfordshire.

'Fuck you, Luke. She's my aunt.'

'Cool your boots.'

'But it bugs me how you get disparaging like that.' I flick the Alanis Morissette CD on by one song.

'What do you want me to say? It just happens, OK, it just happens that my grandfather has a Constable. That's all.'

I loosen the seat belt and shift in the seat. 'But the way you said "a real one, not a table mat stuck to the wall" you know that was disparaging.'

'I'm sorry.'

'You're not. You're not.'

'Then I'm not sorry.'

'Say you are like you mean it.'

He knows there is forgiveness in my asking. 'I'm sorry.'

'Thank you.'

'No prarblem,' he answers in a terrible Canadian accent.

I look at him. He is smirking. I know something more is coming. 'What?' The annoying thing is, I have to know.

'Oh, nothing,' he says. 'Only I heard they're having an exhibition of coasters at the Tate. They'll be selling the real lads in six-packs at the shop.' He checks his mirror and then accelerates into the fast lane. He is so happy driving his car. Every successful manoeuvre is cause for celebration, an imaginary step towards some auto nirvana. He returns the car to the left lane and looks again at me. 'Thought I might pick up a Turner.'

'You're a pig.'

'Oink.'

'How far is it from here?'

'Twenty minutes. We'll beat Chris.'

Christian is Luke's younger brother and twenty minutes away is their home, a house that used to be a vicar's rectory somewhere near Oxford. His parents, thank God, are away for most of the weekend but his sister, Serena, is at home. It's why we are coming: Christian and his cute girlfriend, Jim with Camilla, Luke and myself.

The Bingham parents don't like Serena to be left on her own. I am curious about her, even more so now Kaz has described her as 'rowing with only one oar in the water'. Even if she wasn't the sister of the most together man I have ever fucked, her psychological confusion would intrigue. She is almost exactly my age and grew up enjoying the life I wished for. It makes me wonder what went wrong.

'See, twenty minutes exactly,' Luke beams as we turn into his parents' driveway. 'Told you.'

My lover is ceaselessly congratulating himself on these unexciting feats: recalling the batsmen who scored the highest innings in a cricket series in Australia, parking in tight spaces near the flat, starting more quickly than the car parallel to us at traffic lights and now guessing the time it has taken from point A to point B in a car that he himself has been driving. Am I supposed to care? It is odd that he derives power from information to which I have no access.

The gravel swooshes like a breaking wave. We are not alone. There is another car parked by the house.

'What a wanker. How did Chris get here?'

Christian has a Ford Capri that Luke says he only bought because it is cool these days to be common. I haven't been able to get my head around the whole people/class business except that I can see that, however hard they try, Christian and his friends are too privileged to be anything but the rich kids they are. When the pubs close there is always cocaine and twelve-year-old single malt waiting back home.

I step from the car. Look at this house: it's a great box of a building constructed of a gloriously textured yellowy stone, clinging to which are thin patches of moss. Today is another heaven-sent, fluffy-cloud-blue day, and in places where the lichen is dense the façade seems to have inhaled the late summer sun, making the bricks yet more radiant.

The design is classical, neat. There are two floors with eight sash windows on each. The bedroom windows, which extend to only one stone's distance from the roof, are perhaps three-quarters the height of those downstairs and are shaded at the top by a wide overhanging eave. There, that's what I mean – with the sun where it is the line of its shadow is as straight as a ruler, precisely darkening only the top pane of each window. It is more nature than nurture that we live by our own internal rhythms, that some notes and patterns or colours seem particularly sublime and find an exact path to our hearts. I have no internal need for symmetry as this. I doodle in circles not squares, I liked punk and listen to anarchic jazz, I try to cross roads when the Don't Walk sign flashes, am riled by rules, unmoved by sushi, leave wet towels on my bedroom floor. And I never expect the expected. How, then, can I be moved by a house that is fascistic in the evenness of its design? But I am. Its simplicity kisses my heart.

I crunch across the gravel to hug Luke. Our relationship is so new that it takes only a little sugar to restore the sweetness when things have been sour. I am learning with my new man how restorative emotional generosity can be, how gentle its dew. Ours is a curious, old-fashioned dance; a waltz in which satisfaction comes from being in step. My past entanglements were all frenzied, fuelled by polarity, kept alive by passion only to be destroyed by the endless fear that if I sank too deeply in love I would be deserted again. Now, I am less scared of letting my affection show. Is it because I am wading in shallow, current-less waters? Perhaps.

'It's gorgeous, Luke.'

'Yes. Well, I love it.'

It is no surprise that my pin-striped lover should feel at home but as I curl my arm around his now familiar back it dawns on me that I am happy because this might be what I, too, was needing. Luke, by including me in his euphonic British life, has unknowingly helped me untangle the knots. He has given my life such structural harmony.

From the night we met, I have been attracted to the balanced wholeness of Luke's life. It was so clearly in contrast to my own confusion, both external – most obviously my dissatisfaction with my life and career in Toronto compared with his own complete and happy existence in London – and internal. He knows precisely where he came from (even this house has been in the family for two hundred years) and to where he is heading. His steps forward are secured by those taken in the past. His self-deprecation, his aristocratic profile, his mannered kindness, his dry sense of humour, his rigorous sense of decency, his conviction in his own values are in him the embodiment of much that I think wonderful about England. The country's past, back beyond D.H. Lawrence and E.M. Forster and Dickens and Eliot and Jane Austen, further still than Swift and Dryden and Johnson and Milton and Shakespeare to Langland and Chaucer and the troubadours themselves, lives in the English, in men like Luke. Their past is themselves.

Ironically, it was with a rope that Dad untied my own mooring, and in my resentment I became everything he would have wished me not to be. A very un-British drug-taking and tattooed teenager in Toronto. This is my chance to find England in myself again. To be connected, to belong. Perhaps, even, my chance to find my dad in me. And it is Luke I owe for that. I give him a plump kiss on the lips.

'Oi!' comes a shout. 'We'll be having none of that.'

I wave. 'Hey, Christian. I like your place.'

Luke's brother is standing between the stone columns of the porch, hands in the pockets of his baggy shorts. There is no denying his shoolboyish huggability, yet he is too pretty for my taste. His hair is fair and straight and usually in as deliberate a mess as a teenager's bedroom. He has thin, red lips that look sculpted and feminine and about which I would guess as many men as women have dreamed. An awareness of that must lubricate Christian's fluid manner. He is affable and loose-limbed where Luke appears implacable, contained within himself.

'Can't that pile of Swedish crap get you here any faster, then, Ludo?'

'Where were you calling from?'

Moments before Luke and I left his apartment, Christian telephoned to ask us to bring an extra tennis racket. For some reason, Luke challenged him to a race.

'McDonald's. Had a big night last night. There was need for a couple of McMuffins down me.' Christian gives me a kiss as he takes my overnight bag. 'Got a fag on you, Portia?'

'So that's what the kiss was for.'

'No, I fancy you. You're too good for him.'

'Shut it, Chris.' Luke slams shut the trunk of the car. 'Is Serena around?'

'Nah, the van just came for her.'

'You're no bloody use to anyone.'

'My apologies, sir, Luke, sir!' barks Christian, then he salutes his brother as Luke passes us to go inside.

Christian makes me feel younger in the same way that Luke makes me feel my age. He seems totally unaffected by doubt. I envy that. I give him a cigarette.

'Angel.' He lights one for me too, and says, 'He's very protective of Rena. Don't let it get to you.'

'I won't.'

It seems somehow anachronistic to be smoking this cigarette inside the cool stone-floored hallway, like seeing the tip of a microphone boom in the frame of a Jane Austen film. I look across in awe at the huge, spiral staircase elegantly curving into the room then hear some dogs running my way, their claws rasping on the floor. One of them, a warty beagle with a puffy eye and an unconvincing waddle, is barking ferociously.

'Shut it, Fat Girl,' Christian shouts.

The dog retreats with a sneer. I don't like dogs. As if sensing it, the warty beagle has taken a shine to me and has darkened a patch in the crotch of my jeans with its slobbery muzzle.

'Leave off, Ben, you dirty fuck.'

'Don't worry, all males greet me like that.'

The third dog is a Jack Russell, which seems to have a nervous disposition. It is backing away from me with tiny steps, eyeing me as it goes.

'That's Badger, the lab's Ben and the old bitch is Betty,' Christian informs me. 'Betty's about to kop it so don't say anything to Ma. She loves her more than the rest of us put together.'

My heart takes a nosedive. Is Mrs Bingham here? She sounds fierce on the phone, even last week she made the suggestion that I 'should go out and have some fun' sound like an order.

'I didn't know your mother was here.'

'She's not. But you'll have to meet her sometime before the wedding.'

'Whose wedding?'

Christian flashes his wicked, chipped-tooth smile at me. 'Oh, didn't I tell you I saw Luke wandering around Hatton Gardens?'

'Where's that?'

Chris taps his finger. 'Diamonds. Come on, Jo's in the kitchen.'

Marry Luke and live here and be the English lady Dad claimed I should be? Huh. Is that what this journey's about?

We advance down a gloomy corridor lined with prints of hunts and of ships into a large kitchen which reeks of dogs and cigarette smoke.

When Christian kicks a mangled teddy through the open door the dogs scamper out to the apple-green lawn. Bordered by the shadowy frame of the door, the garden looks as colourful as the flags of a hundred nations.

'Portia, you remember Jo.'

By anybody's standards, Joanna is beautiful. She is a willowy, tropical beach of a woman: sandy hair, ocean blue eyes, not much to occupy the mind beyond the notion of people lying on top of her. I am undecided about her, unable as I am to separate the woman from her title. She is the daughter of some earl whose family can be traced back to England's first coupling amoebas, and I suppose it is because I would love such a provenance that I hold this distinctly unmalicious envy for her. I forgive things – her shameless vapidity, for one – that in others I couldn't stand.

'Hey,' is as much of a greeting as she can manage. She is lying flat out like lunch on the large pine table, a smoking cigarette in one hand, a Bloody Mary in the other. On a high-backed bench against the wall beside her, a portable stereo machine is blaring out some House dance tunes. Jo is moving only to bring the cigarette to her lips, and then to tap the ash in the direction of a saucer by her side.

'Want a drink, Portia?' asks Christian. 'I made some wicked Bloody Mary.'

'Why not?'

'Good call. Never ask why when it comes to booze.'

The kitchen is divided into two parts by a pale Formica work counter. At my end is the kitchen table, surrounded by a mismatched collection of antique wooden chairs with the bench down one side. Behind the door are the dog baskets and against the free wall is a tall pine cabinet that is overladen with trinkets and invitations and brass candlesticks and one or two of those ugly painted figures. Staffordshires, I think they are called. Christian is pouring my drink at the other end, closer to the garden. I join him by a massive, blue, four-doored oven that is baking hot on this warm day. I point this out to him.

'It's an Aga, doughbrain,' then, 'there's ice up there if you want it.'

The fridge is tattooed with photographs of the Binghams and their pets. Dog with baby rabbit in its mouth. Dog sleeping with other dog on its back. Dog three as puppy. Then horses. Horse in field. Horse continuing to stand despite having Mrs Bingham on its back. Horse carrying three young Bingham children wearing riding hats and smiles. Amid these, edited highlights from the family's past. Luke at graduation looking about six years old. Christian photographed with a spade over his shoulder, a send-up of Working Man, this is a cut-out from a magazine that was probably celebrating his career as gentleman gardener. Three weeks ago, before I knew better, I would have told Christian that my own grandfather was a gardener, but to do so would target me for derision of some kind. I am learning.

'Has Christian been looking after you?' asks Luke, coming into the kitchen.

'Like royalty,' I say, my fingertips sticking to a cube of ice as I twist it out of its shell.

He welcomes Jo, adding, 'Glad to hear you've brought your music with you. She's like someone in a musical, isn't she? The band has to strike up whenever she appears.'

'She's my fair lady,' says Christian, but sheepishly. He knows it's not funny.

'No, that's me.' I run my smoked cigarette under a tap then hold it conspicuously in front of me. I need a trash basket. Christian kicks open a door under the sink. 'Luke's trying to turn me into a lady.'

'Daahdadada!' sings Christian. 'Daahdadada!' It's that marriage tune, whatever it's called. Obviously it's going to be Christian's joke for the weekend.

Luke lets fly a playful kick. 'Shut your face, Shrimp.'

'Reminds me,' Christian says, 'you find Mad Fish?'

'She's sleeping. And do you have to call her that?'

Christian plucks off a grape from the bunch in the fruit bowl, tosses it in the air and catches it in his mouth. 'Yup.'

'Luke, can I see outside?'

'You can see whatever your heart desires.'

'I've got something to show her,' chips in Christian.

'That belongs to me,' says Jo, breaking her silence.

The garden is a delight, a huge sloping sweep of lawn shaped into a horseshoe at the end where a border of shrubs and flowers backs up to a five-foot-high stone wall. Against it, low fruit trees, heavy with ripe apples and pears, have spread their knuckly branches. The air is soft and filled with birdsong. There are swallows and swifts screeching in the air and diving towards the lawn. I reach for Luke's hand and squeeze it as we walk on the stony path that is lined with tiles, through a pretty stone archway where a rusting iron gate is held open by a huge log of wood ringed at its heart with proof of centuries of growth.

'Voilà, we have the vegetables.'

'Oh, Luke, look. Raspberries. Let's pick some.'

'I suppose Mum won't mind.'

He gets a bucket from the greenhouse. The plump fruit stains our fingers. We eat as much as we save. Then Luke shows me the carrots with their bushy green stalks looking as they never do in the shops, the bright orange a surprise and a miracle out here. There is no doubt it's a juicy colour, it makes jewels of vegetables and fruits. I wipe the earth off one of the roots and crunch the succulent end before feeding a chunk to my caveman. For lunch we pick lettuces from soil that has turned grey from lack of rain, then bursting, ripe tomatoes grown in pots in the old greenhouse. Can I ever go back to a city again?

'Come here,' I say. Turning my back on Luke, I throw a handful of the raspberries in my mouth and then draw him in for a kiss, surprising him with the squelched berries on my tongue. 'Needs cream,' I whisper, reaching my hand down to touch him.

'Don't. Don't.'

'Why not?'

'I'll never hear the end of it if Christian catches us.'

Despite what he says, we kiss again more passionately than before. With a hand around the back of his neck I walk him backwards through erect onions that have seeded into flower.

'It's all this nature,' I tell him. 'Made me horny. Like a queen bee.'

The house must be thirty feet away but I can hear the tuneless scratching of Jo's music. Luke is nervous, looking over his shoulder. Truth is, I like the idea of fucking him amid such grandeur. I have led him, as if I'm a seasoned tart (could I find a place beside Bruised Rosemary in that cookery book for fun-seeking singles?) to a shady spot behind the greenhouse. With each pace Luke's erection has been making itself more visible within his linen trousers. The forbidden enthralls him like nothing else, and exciting him so excites me too.

With my back to the glass of the greenhouse, I push my jeans and underwear down to my knees. My skin looks ugly and shockingly white in the bleaching sunlight and I don't like the bulbous curve of my stomach from this angle, so I close my eyes then draw in a gulp of air as Luke parts the lips of my vagina, easing an earthy finger within. Eat your heart out, Lady Chatterley.

Luke's lips press against mine, then he bends his knees and I can feel his sun-licked erection nudging me, feeling for a way in. But he's got it all wrong, he is high and right. It makes me laugh.

He whispers, 'Open your legs further.'

'I can't,' I say, laughing more. 'I can't. Not with my jeans like this.'

Luke is all serious now, the sweet thing, his eyes are sharp with excitement, and his willy, looking red and truncated jutting out through his flies, is bobbing with the agitated pulse of his heart. I kiss him again, and tease him with my fingers.

'I'll lie down,' I whisper, although if anyone was near enough to hear us talking they would see us too.

'Why don't you turn around?'

I turn as he asks and then yelp as I see on the other side of the greenhouse all three dogs lolloping through the arch. The way they are coming, in that dumb, purposeless way dogs have, suggests they are proceeding somebody.

'Luke. Get dressed.'

'Jesus Christ,' he says, flipping up his willy. It makes me giggle, imagining it flattened under the waistband of his trousers. The whole thing's funny to me, but Luke looks terrified. He sweeps his hair neat and then, crouching low like a marine in combat, scampers to kneel by the lettuces, as if he is picking one.

'Hello?' comes a voice. It's Jim. We didn't hear his car.

'Hi,' I say, presentable now.

'Goose!'

Goose is what Luke's friends have begun to call me. It's everyone's joke, now, that I listened to the answer-machine message. I don't mind. The nickname makes me part of the gaggle.

'You're looking lovely today. Very tussled.'

'Is that a compliment?'

'Tussled? You bet. I mean, you'll never find a tussled nun, will you?' he says, laughing heartily. He is always in a gregarious mood, Jim, rather like one of P.G. Wodehouse's affable fools. I think he must be rather simple. Kaz said he couldn't get a place at a university so he followed his father into some army regiment, his plumpness was muscle in the days when he was a serving captain. Now he sells water filters.

'Have you two been cavorting in the rose bushes?'

'No, we've been blessing the vegetables, like Vertumnus and Pomona.'

'Who?'

'Actually, we've been gathering vegetables for your growing stomach.' I pat his paunch.

'Hello, mate,' says Jim. 'Your wife's being cheeky.'

'I'm not his wife.'

'Been playing cricket in those, have you?' asks Jim, nodding at Luke's trousers. Oh, shit, there is a streak of red, the raspberry juice from my hand probably, across the front of Luke's trousers where I was touching him. 'Giving the old ball a shine?'

'Raspberries, mate,' Luke explains. 'Come on. I'll fix you a drink.'

Since I've been pronounced cheeky, I offer Luke a cheeky smirk when Jim's not looking. He won't take it. Never seen her before in my life, your Honour. It's all lies. Being caught with his pants down is the sort of thing Luke hates.

Inside, I ask for the bathroom then make a mistake and open the wrong door, this one leading into a living room that is out of a museum it looks so unaccustomed to occupation. I step lightly on to a salmon-coloured carpet, the give of which makes it feels expensive. The lovingly polished furniture – of course, those are the smells in here: beeswax polish and soot from the fireplace – is exquisite. Across the room is a mahogany bureau and here to my right, shiny as water, stands a beautifully textured walnut cabinet that is filled, behind the glass doors of its upper half, with sets of leatherbound books. Jane Austen, Elland's *Wild Flowers*, Hardy, Balzac, Milton, Hume, Eliot. Does Luke just take all this for granted? Why didn't he bring me in here as soon as we arrived?

This room has a roped-off feel to it – the books in the bookshelves perfectly arranged by size, a wigwam of evenly sawn logs over crumpled-up yellowing newspaper, silver-framed photographs of a family too refined to swear and smoke and expose themselves by greenhouses under the midday sun. On the piano are black and white images of Luke's mother looking attractive in a 1950s rich debutante way. Here on her wedding day she looks radiant. His father was gorgeous too.

The upholstered sofas are positioned opposite one another, just as they are at Luke's. They are delicate, both with six curved and carved wooden feet on castors. The back of each has a crescented, inlaid crest rail, like a wave rolling to shore. I sit on one, put my feet up, then, when I think I hear someone, briskly lower them again. My God, these are uncomfortable. Why would anyone do this to themselves? It's no wonder the room seems unused.

I turn my attention to the paintings. They have gold tubular lights above their gilt frames. It is a museum. The paintings are landscapes, some with boats, some with passionate waterfalls, some, like the one above the fireplace, crowded with animals, as the fridge door is. In one I like, butterscotch-coloured cows are drinking from a lake under pale skies flecked with cotton-wool clouds. No thoughts of McDonald's or mad cow disease. It is the kind of idyll which seems thrillingly possible. Aren't I living it? Ha! I wish Dad could have seen me here. And Mother. It would make her happy, too.

Back in the hall and behind the next panelled door is the bathroom I was after. The toilet seat is a great, thick, square piece of wood, like the head hole from medieval stocks. When I touch it, my fingers spread tiny clouds of condensation. I sit. The tinkle echoes in this grandeur. There is an aerial shot of the house in here which is a little ostentatious. See how much we've got! How many fields and horses and slates. There are also framed photographs of school teams in here, as in Luke's apartment, except these are black and white, a generation older. I guess these will be replaced by Luke's own, and then by his son's. Framed, too, are some cartoon portraits entitled 'Men of Their Day' – two of a barrister called Bingham – and three bawdy prints. I wash my hands in the great basin of a sink, and dry them against my jeans. There is no towel. In the kitchen, I say, 'I've been trespassing.'

Luke is by the sink, shaking individual lettuce leaves dry. 'Do you want to see where you're sleeping? I've put you and Jo in one of the spare rooms.'

'What are you saying? You want me to sleep in another room from you?'

He grins. 'We can always corridor creep.'

'Dirty buggers,' Christian says. 'And not even married. We won't do that, will we, Jo?'

'I might. Only not to your room. I might search out Jim.'

'I've never had a threesome,' Jim chuckles.

'And you're not about to start,' Killjoy whinnies. It is my name for Camilla these days.

I light myself a cigarette. Wasn't this a full packet? There are only two left. It's a miracle there is anyone over fifty left in England. There is probably a Silk Cut mushroom cloud hanging over the country.

'I'm sorry,' I say. 'I don't understand. It's OK, is it, to try to fuck me up against the greenhouse in broad daylight, but if we do it at night in your bed then we're breaking some taboo the rest of you know about? Is that how it works?'

I must have said something right or wrong because Jo has sat up and is swinging her legs off the table.

'Porsh, it's Dad and Mummy's house and I just think we should respect their rules while we're here.'

'Even if they're not?'

'Can we discuss this later?'

'Whatever, Luke. Only maybe you could give me a list of terms and conditions in advance next time? It gets kind of hard keeping up with your small print.'

Although Luke and I are happy, I can't deny there is something a little uncomfortable about our binding, as if we are pieces of Lego crushed together by a toddler who doesn't understand the shapes but has managed to make them stick. I'm scared our structure is weak.

'Portia, did you say that was inside or outside the greenhouse?' asks Christian.

Pointing with a bread knife, Luke warns, 'Don't push it.'

'I need to know whether the tomatoes are safe to eat or not.'

'Luke and I didn't actually—'

'Can we be spared the details?' Killjoy implores.

'There weren't any. Were there, Luke? I made it up.'

My comment is supposed to be placatory, and seems to work. I offer to help with the lunch, but he declines. Instead, I ask where 'this room of mine is' since I want to change. It is Christian who takes me, leading the way two steps at a time up the curving, narrow back stairs.

It is, of course, another jewel of a room. Brown carpet, pink-painted walls, lots of flowery fabric on the long curtains and valances and headboards showing pink and beige roses in bloom. The two beds look enticingly comfortable. Between them is a pretty cluster of small round and oval gold frames containing silhouettes. It is quite sparsely furnished but there is a delicate walnut table between the beds on which someone has left us a bottle of Evian, which must be warm, and two glasses. I dump my bag on the bed nearest the window, then take it off and put it on the floor. Don't want to damage anything.

The window is shaded by the overhanging branches of a cedar tree. I look out. Beyond the wall where Luke and I had our heated moment I can see a tennis court and a swimming pool that is still covered. It must be worth a fortune, this place, no wonder Luke doesn't want to change the status quo when this is his status. Luke's father is a lawyer of some sort, but I think there has always been money in the family.

I change to some thinner, cooler clothes, find the bag of grass I was after, and am walking head down towards the stairs when I am shocked almost out of my skin. At first, I think it's a pale ghost I've seen but then recognize Serena. She is standing completely still and naked, a glass of water in her hand.

'I'm sorry, I didn't see you.'

She says nothing, nor does she move. She is thin, too thin, it is disturbing to see the shape of her hips.

'I'm Portia.' I hold out my hand. 'Luke's friend.' Look at me.

Always introducing myself to these Binghams in strange situations. Serena takes my hand. She is quite cold.

'We're making lunch if you—' Stupidly, I point my thumb in the direction of the kitchen. It's her house, she knows where it is. 'Jim and Camilla are here too. And Christian.'

'Chris is here?'

'Yeah, shall I go tell him you're awake?'

It's as good an excuse as any to get away. I am uneasy standing here.

Serena takes a sip of water. 'No.'

'Oh. Um, it's kind of hot out,' I add, I guess to make light of her nakedness.

Serena takes me seriously and, frowning, says, 'I'll get dressed.'

In the kitchen, Luke immediately makes for the stairs when I announce that I've seen Serena. When he has gone, Christian shakes a bottle of white wine in front of me and says, 'Want some?'

'Thanks.'

We carry plates and knives to the round, teak table on the flagstones outside. The garden is spread out in front of us like a landscape painting. I smile inside.

'Did Luke say anything about Rena? You know, tell you anything?'

'Not really.'

'Oh, OK.' Chris flips his sunglasses on to the top of his head and squints at me. 'Well, earlier this year she was pregnant and then something happened and she's been sort of odd since. So it's probably best, you know, not to talk about babies around her.'

In blinking, Christian reminds me of Luke. How must it be to have a brother, seeing fragments of oneself in another? It wouldn't have been the same with Dad if I had had siblings, I am sure of that.

'I'm not really a babies kind of girl.'

'So what were you and Luke trying to grow out by the greenhouse?'

'Ssh. You'll get me into trouble.'

'Come on, Goose. We all know you can manage that by yourself.'

Clothed now, Serena joins us outside. We eat salad and cheese and a revolting game pie left for us. Luke teases me about leaving the pie jelly on my plate, but when I throw it to the dogs I am back in favour.

'How are your letters from London coming along?' Jim asks.

'Great, I think. They seem to like them, anyway. I just did one about those ads for prostitutes you see in the telephone boxes. And then I wrote something about how I'm always on the bus that gets caught at every single red light.'

'That's my bus,' Jim says.

'Right. That's sort of the point, oh, and the other one I wrote is about how convincing British politicians are because everyone speaks so properly. And I want to write something funny about a sign I saw saying, "Come to the Lancôme counter and create your own ideas." I was wondering what kind of ideas people were going to create. "Being is nothingness without hazel eye-shadow."'

'I bought some Lancôme lipstick for you last week, didn't I, Milla?'

'Yes. Tart red.'

'That's how we like 'em,' claims Christian.

'Haven't you written anything nasty?' asks Killjoy, who has probably been to a Lancôme counter herself to think long and hard how to make herself more attractive.

I am unsure of what she is implying but will give her the benefit of the doubt. She wants to know whether I like England as much as I claim.

'No, I haven't found anything nasty.'

'Want help?' asks Serena, speaking for almost the first time.

'Maybe I will, one day.'

When we have finished yet another bottle of rosé, Serena, under Luke's concerned eye, slinks back upstairs while the rest of us saunter towards the pool. The weather is so glorious and the house so divine the rest of the day is a peal of laughter on which we all surf. We throw each other into the crystal blue waters of the pool, our wet hands slithering on each others' limbs. We lie topless on deckchairs (Killjoy timing her turns when she's tanning) by sweet-smelling pink roses, we drink white wine, read trash novels and Saturday newspapers, smoke our lungs black and our brains happy and high. The Lady Joanna comes to life when there are games and tricks to be played, she has an aristocrat's disdain for the mundane, and together we tip Christian off his sunbed into the pool and deflate Jim's floating inflatable chair while he is sleeping and hang the garden sprinkler on a branch of a pear tree, waiting in ambush by the tap for the boys to finish their tennis, so soaking them as they pass underneath. We pay for it, of course, Jim and Christian chasing us across grass that is scratchy and brown from lack of rain, catching us and carrying our kicking bodies to be dunked in the pool. When we burst through the surface together, gasping for breath and treading water side by side, I feel like encircling my arms around Jo's silky body and kissing her shiny red lips. There is definitely something orgiastic about the afternoon, a rosy unshackledness to it.

And just as the sun is setting and the black swifts are tracing wide curlicues against the magnificent pink of the mackerel sky I tempt Luke inside to finish what we began outside. I feel like a naughty schoolgirl as the warm air licks at the cold, spongy skin from which I peel my damp bikini. Then, lying on his bed, the forbidden bed, I have him spoil me with his tongue, his breath gloriously hot after the cool water. Swimming is foreplay's perfect foreplay and the thrill of his skin against mine is everything sex should always be and hardly ever is. It cannot be this good very often, it would cease to seem so, but I will remember this afternoon, this time we made love.

'I was worried about your sister, this afternoon,' I say, as we lie naked on his bed, me playing with his funny, shrunken penis.

'You never know with Serena. One minute she's absolutely fine and the next she's bursting into tears.'

'Was it just . . . do you think it was losing the baby?'

'I don't know.' He strokes my back with his soft hands. His palms have never seen a good day's work but then, why should they have? No one thinks labour noble any more. 'Everything was so right for her. Happy marriage, nice house, really great husband, no money hassles as far as I know and then, boof, she suddenly changed. I think it was bloody lucky she didn't have the baby in the end.'

'Makes you think we're all a whisker away from being like that, doesn't it?' Luke has eyelashes some women would kill for. I pinch a speck of something white from them. Cotton, maybe. My lover has lashes of pure cotton. 'From not being able to cope.'

'I don't think it does. I've never thought life could be unmanageable, whatever happens. You have to deal with it.'

'Well, maybe nothing bad has ever happened to you,' I say, twisting away from him.

'You're not the only one in the world who's had something bad happen, you know, Porsh,' he says. 'I mean, look at Kaz.'

Lovely Kaz, saves me whenever I feel down. We've been getting drunk in the afternoon recently, then phoning in bets on horses we know nothing about. We are up by seventeen pounds thirty-three pence, proof if it was needed that it is a mug's game.

'What about her?'

'With her mother.'

'She's never said anything.'

'That's my point. I mean, she killed herself too, so—'

'Kaz's mother?'

'About five years ago. In a car. I mean, it was called an accident but Kaz said they found a note. Killed her sister, too.'

'Kaz's mother killed herself?'

Luke stands, checks his paunch in the mirror. 'I know. And she was just like Kaz, you wouldn't have thought . . . anyway, let's not talk about it.'

'But she never—'

'I know. That's Kaz.'

Luke says he should go check on the others – who knows where the grass and alcohol goes with him, it's as if he has a back-up generator within him – and, though I was loving lying with him in this room, I let him go. Why hasn't Kaz said? In all the times I have talked about Dad, why hasn't she said?

The wind is picking up outside making the sash windows, which are loose in their frames, rattle. It is cold, suddenly. I roll into a ball under the covers of the forbidden bed wondering whether, if I was so blind to Kaz, there are answers to Dad's death that I have just been too stupid to find.

This Sunday morning, grey clouds have swept in like a hangover. It seems both we and the weather outperformed ourselves yesterday, leaving us burned up, leeched, abused.

Last night the seven of us drank fifteen bottles of wine and sniffed up twice as many lines of coke and, although we are nonchalantly proud of our stab at decadence, our energy has been so sapped that, after a morning spent sullenly wading through the dirge in the papers, we are wondering what, if anything, we can do to salvage the day. Only Serena is busy, out with the horses. Luke says they cheer her up as people can't. I recognize something in Serena's unsaddlement. After Dad's death, I preferred the company of our two cats – named Morocco and Arragon, Dad's joke being that neither was worthy of my love – to that of any of my school friends.

Jenny van Darlen used to herd our school friends to my bedroom like spectators to a freak. I hated it. Jenny and Kate and Sasha and Kim and Caro tried to get me 'out of myself' with gossip of who'd been with whom to the ravines, or with talk of our changing bodies, of this corner turned towards liberation, as if I should have been somehow grateful for the ultimate unburdening of a father around whom most of them, to be honest, seemed wary. I didn't have the words to explain that within myself was the only place I wanted to be.

'I need sleep,' the lady Joanna announces with sudden seriousness. 'You must understand, I need sleep.' Jo has the shifty, fragile air of someone who has suffered a bereavement; ever since she got up, her wounded presence has muted us. I knew she wouldn't want to do anything energetic. 'I'm going to retire to my boudoir.'

'Want me?' Christian asks.

'To sleep, bubba, to sleep. Not to talk or kiss or fuck.'

'Are you two married?' asks Jim.

'Say sorry,' Killjoy demands.

Jo kisses Christian's cheek who then declares, 'I'll whip someone's ass at tennis, then,' without raising his eyes from the *News of the World*. It's a horrible paper he is reading, a mean-spirited, cynical, sex-obsessed rag of half-truths. It bothers me. It's so un-British. I already got into an argument about it with Charlie Garton. He argues the opposite, says that it's because the English are mean-spirited, cynical and sex-obsessed themselves that they enjoy such papers. Had the fucking nerve to call me right wing, to suggest I would censor fun. But I care – more, weirdly, than most of Luke's friends – about the denigration of pretty much anyone who has made anything of themselves in England. Anyone who hasn't, too, come to think of it. The editors seem free with their moral censure. I find it nasty and mean. And it isn't just people who suffer, it's the institutions they represent. I told Charlie how it upsets me that a thousand years of British history might all have come to this facile entertainment, that there is nothing private, nothing sacred, nothing above reproach, just an endless nitpicking attack on all things that the English should be proud of. Despite their shoulder-chippy, grass is greener, look who's bigger bullshit, at least the Canadians are proud of Canada, at least they believe in her.

'I've got my new DKNY shorts I bought in New York,' Killjoy chirps. 'I'll put those on if we're playing tennis.'

Killjoy loves tight white Lycra. I've seen her show up to a pub in it for no good reason at all. Me, I get a kick out of being her spectral opposite. Today, I am wearing black: greying black jeans, devil-red Puma sneakers and a shrunken black Tee from Dominic's, the coffee shop beneath NTTV in Toronto. For sure,

Dominic's slogan 'Put some froth on it!' could use work, but on a gloomy afternoon I feel that I am the one sensibly dressed.

'I'll umpire,' I say. 'Can't manage anything more than that.'

We have eaten bacon sandwiches and picked at the chicken from last night and a couple of us have started on the Bloody Mary's in an attempt to kickstart our bodies, but doing anything is difficult to imagine.

'Why don't we play croquet,' suggests Jim.

After a little cajoling, it is agreed. From a room filled with Wellington boots and dog brushes and washing machines and leathery thingummies for the horses, Jim and I lug a heavy coffin-shaped box filled with hoops and balls and sticks out onto the lawn. It is damp outside and the colours seem richer after the night's rain. Yesterday feels like a vacation that has passed. Even the birdsong has diminished.

I light another cigarette and watch as the boys hammer six iron hoops into the lawn. It's the kind of task Luke relishes and he completes it with care and precision. Straight lines, neat angles. I think the game was French at first but it's perfect for the British.

With my cigarette between my lips the smoke keeps getting in my eyes as I practise hitting the chipped wooden ball I have chosen. These hoops are not as wide as they seem, I keep clanking the ball against the side. But it will come. The game is probably in my genes.

'Got to follow it through, Goose,' says Christian, surprising me from behind. He takes the cigarette from my lips and now I feel his hand pushing gently on my head. It makes me feel soft, as if a thousand hours of tension disappears, as if the hawsers mooring my thoughts are unleashed for a few precious seconds. 'Keep you head down and follow it through.'

'Get off my bird,' Luke shouts out.

'You can have mine,' Christian replies. 'She's already in bed.'

'No deal, sprout.'

Doesn't like me being touched or talked to, my Luke, even by his brother. When we have been to parties he's had his eyes glued to me. I don't like that in him, his possessiveness. His being richer makes me weaker as it is. He enjoys the sense of owning me.

'Let's go. Porsh, you start.'

A length is measured from the starting hoop and then shortened for me. I hit, miss, hit again, miss again, am given another shot, this being how it is these days: instead of what I have being taken away I am offered second chances. As if I am no longer required to play the cards I am dealt. On my third shot, I sneak through and then I am bumping and rolling up the lawn towards the second hoop. It means I am winning. The birds chatter in celebration. I lean on my mallet, smile. The others eye me.

But then something happens that I hadn't expected. My rivals power their balls through the first hoop then begin to roquet one another. It is not the game I thought it was at all, it is angry, vicious, driven by belligerent malice. It is bringing out a nasty side in everyone. My ball keeps being used so that the others can get ahead. I am sent once, twice, then again and again to the other side of the lawn, or into the flower bed, and it seems that it is never my turn and by the time I make it back to the second hoop, the rest of them are way ahead and it is lonely and boring when I miss again and am stuck where the game isn't.

They are having a wild time down at hoop four. No wonder croquet was all the rage last century when the English were defining themselves as indomitable colonizers. I'm the fucked colonial now.

'Guys?' I call out. 'Guys?' No one is listening. 'I'm heading in.'

That gets Jim's attention. 'You can't.'

'I'm bored.'

Now they all join in telling me I can't, but of course I can and I do. Might go for a swim. The water's heated, and there is a faint drizzle in the air. Everyone knows it is great to be in a pool when the rain comes down. Makes the whole world seem wet when you are bored with it being dry.

I saunter into the kitchen. What a dump, I should clear up. My God, what is Luke turning me into? I don't mind mess. And yet here I am filling the dishwasher and wiping the surfaces and emptying the ashtrays. I am gathering the newspapers off the table when I am surprised by a man's voice.

'And who do we have here?'

I spin around. 'Hi. Hi. I'm Portia, I'm—'

'Of course you are. How nice to meet you at last. I'm Luke's father.' He smiles at me, and holds out his hand. 'Charles.'

'I think I guessed,' I say with a nervous laugh. 'You look like Chris. Tian.'

'Give or take thirty years, perhaps.'

'No,' I find myself saying, and then I wish I hadn't because I am blushing, and I know he can see and it makes me feel like a child when I want to be regarded as an adult, on his level.

'No? Give or take more than thirty years, do you think?' When he takes off his jacket he slings it onto the table. Luke wouldn't do that. Luke would hang the jacket neatly on the back of a chair like, well, like a man twice his age.

'Less than thirty.'

I want to add that he is younger and better looking in life than he is in photos. He has a glow, an aura, the same that famous men often have, only with them it is explicable whereas this . . . I don't know what it is that makes him magnetic and sexy. Sexy? No, Portia. He is fifty-four. But, yes. Sexy. His composure is sexy. His confidence is sexy.

It helps, of course, that he is explicitly elegant. He does not look so obviously English as his son. There is a sharpness to Charles's features that suggests wealth and good breeding more, I think, than nationality. Of course, it might be that I am just being fooled by his richly suggestive suntan Charles has acquired over the summer, by the fact that he is clearly fit and in shape. He is lucky, too, in having kept a boyish head of hair which he brushes loosely to one side, and for the endearing laugh lines that fan from the edge of his soil-brown eyes.

'Have you been deserted by my sons?'

'Ah, no, we were playing croquet and I couldn't keep up.'

'Ah.' He steps closer, lowers the tone his voice. 'Then you probably weren't cheating.'

'Should I have been?' I ask with a laugh.

He has turned his back on me to fill the kettle. Its base rattles and spits when it meets the stove's hot plate. 'Next time, Portia, you must cheat.'

'Luke wouldn't like that.'

'No,' he says with a chuckle, 'he is rather a stickler for rules, isn't he? Takes after his mother.'

It is wrong, this; all wrong. Charles Bingham the lawyer should be ruled by rules. Instead, there is something wicked about him, a faintly lupine leer, the suggestion of a fault line that might shake loose the decorum above. I like him, as Kaz predicted I would.

I ask, 'How was your trip?'

'We went to Cumbria to see Victoria's father. The old boy's quite a character. He floats in and out of the real world, rather.'

'Sounds like me.'

'Does it?' He laughs, politely. 'Now, can I make you some tea?'

'Not for me. I was thinking of going for a swim.'

'Were you? Were you really?'

'Yup, if that's . . . if that's OK.'

'Of course it is. I think I might join you, if I may. We've been stuck in the blasted car all day.'

'Then I'll see you down there, shall I?'

I change. Outside, Luke has won the croquet game but, luckily, it was a close contest and they all want to play again. Charles arrives at the pool soon after I do. He is wearing a sky-blue bathrobe and scarlet espadrilles which he sheds before advancing to the edge of the pool. I wasn't wrong, he is well-shaped for his age though he has more of a belly than I had expected and his seeming hairlessness is a touch peculiar. He smiles at me as I tread water in the middle of the pool. I am not sure whether I should be staring at him or not. Yesterday, the sun brightened the veins on the water's undulating skin and bleached out the imperfections on our own and gave us, through its heat, an excuse to strip down and dive in. Today, it feels more as if I am about to share a bath, the water is warmer because the air is cool.

Crisply, Charles dives in and swims underwater for most of the length of the pool before breaking the surface quite close to me. He wipes the water out of his eyes.

'It's lovely if you make the effort, isn't it?'

'Mm.'

We girls sunbathed topless yesterday and yet I feel more naked and exposed now. My orange and red bikini looks bright and boastful and almost obscene. Perhaps I did buy it a size too small.

I take a deep breath and dive underwater myself, swimming away from Charles towards the deep end of the pool. My heart beats loudly in my ears. At the end I grip on to the turquoise-tiled wall of the overflow channel and pull myself to the surface. Summer's suddenly on her way out. Everything looks different today. The rain has flattened and darkened the leaves. Some have been blown to the edge of the pool and a few into it. I scoop a couple into my palm and shake them out on to the surrounding concrete.

'Aren't you swimming?' Charles's fingertips press the wall. He turns. 'Come on.'

I join him. We swim breaststroke, like a retired couple.

'I try to swim fifty lengths a day when I'm here,' he tells me.

'Fifty? Yikes, count me out.'

'You have no need,' he says, turning his head to smile at me and sending a little wave of water against my face.

'Oh, I need.'

'Why do I doubt that?'

We swim on, silently for a while. For one brief moment, his fingers brush my hand and I wonder if he did that on purpose. I move slightly away.

A loud whoop comes from the croquet lawn. I hope it doesn't

mean the game is over and the others will come here screaming and dive-bombing and shattering this peace. I like being this side of the brick wall which, set back fifteen feet or so from the pool, hides us and gives the swim a seductive, forbidden feel.

We swim for maybe ten minutes in silence before I get tired and stand where the water is fairly shallow. My nipples stand erect against the fabric of my swimsuit. Should I get out? Charles surprises me by stopping too. His rising sends a rose leaf on a wave to the smooth deltoid where the water's surface meets my breasts. His eyes follow it, I can see that they do, and then rise to my own. We hold the stare for at least two seconds before Charles, guiltily, wordlessly, turns fast back into the water.

I don't move. I can't move. Something happened. Something was felt. It wasn't just in my mind, else he wouldn't have left me so fast. Oh God, this is the only thing in which I believe, that people do pass wordless messages when they desire the same thing at the same time. But it scares me. He is Luke's father. If he had lifted his hand to me I would have taken it. He is Luke's father. If he had touched me, I would have welcomed it. And he is Luke's father. If he had kissed me right then, I . . . But no: it is absurd, ridiculous, I must be drunk from lunch, from last night. I am not thinking straight. I have to get out.

Before Charles has turned at the other end I swim to the steps, climb out of the pool and wrap myself in a big towel that covers me to my thighs. It was imagined, Pea. But it wasn't. I reach into my bag for a cigarette, but I am stupid and impatient because I soak the tobacco and have to dry my hands and pick out another. I light it and look back. What is he thinking? I curl a finger under the elastic at the back of my swimsuit and yank it down further.

'Is that it?' Charles asks, smiling at me quite casually. 'A few lengths and then a puff?'

'I only wanted a dip.'

'Get one of those lazy boys to make you a cup of tea.'

'I will. Bye.' I skip on to the path, then scream out, 'Ow.'

'Are you all right?'

'Stepped on something.'

I hop back to the chair and lift my right foot onto my left thigh. Rose thorns. I sit down. One comes easily out, leaves a tiny orb of bright blood, but when I pull at the other, it breaks, and I can't get at it. Must have pierced deeply. My sole is white and soft from swimming. I hear a splash. No. He is getting out of the pool. His trunks are quite low on his waist. I can see the white of a tan line, the very top of his pubic hair.

'Let me have a look.' Again, that insouciant smile.

'It's fine. Just a thorn.'

One side of the towel falls off my shoulder as I lean forward. Quickly, I pull it tight around me. There is a crack from Charles's knees – fifty-four, Portia – as he sits on his haunches and takes my foot in his hand. I am conscious of the sound of my breath, then of raised voices from the croquet lawn.

'Pair of tweezers and we'll have him out in no time. Victoria has got some inside.'

Quickly, I suggest, 'Luke can find them, can't he?'

'They're playing their game. I'll finish my swim later.'

I wear Charles's blood-red shoes as he leads me towards the house. I am glad we take the long way around, on paths bordered by lavender, far from the players. Inside, my skin grows goosebumps as we walk up the back stairs. The house is eerily quiet. I wonder what these walls have seen over three hundred years. Is nothing new? No amount of love and deceit? Now, our footsteps are soundless on the carpeted corridor, leaving nothing for the walls to recall.

I follow Charles to his bedroom and wait outside as he goes in. A drip sneaks from my wet costume in between my legs. I pat it dry, jumping when he calls my name.

'I might find it hard to perform surgery with you out there.'

'Does it need surgery?'

'We shall see.'

The carpet is soft and warm under my feet. As Charles rootles through a tiny drawer beneath his wife's dressing-table mirror, I cast my eyes around for anything revealing and personal but, if there is heat, it is hidden.

It is another immaculate room, larger than the other bedrooms, but cosy with its softly plastered, low ceiling. In photos she looks tough, Mrs Bingham. She has a solid, regal hairstyle and wide hips, but the bedroom is feminine – two small, light brown, upholstered chairs, more flowery fabric, pastels framed in round-edged, bleached wood frames and some delicate, antique furniture – without being too cute, too fancy. The bed itself looks luxurious, it's a king at least.

My parents moved to separate bedrooms when I was five or six. I thought nothing of it then. Only more recently have I wondered what prompted her to go, who was least comfortable with the other. Mother was only twenty-six. If they couldn't bear to be together when they were asleep, how did they manage when they were awake? Or is that question too injurious to ask?

'Found them.'

There is farce in the way Charles and I look at one another when he turns around, both of us half-naked in his bedroom, he holding the tweezers high in his right hand, me looking for a place to sit that isn't the bed, his bed.

'Why don't you sit on the bed?'

'All right.'

He brings up one of the chairs and invites me to lift my foot onto his knee. I wish I had asked Luke to do this. I felt gooey for hours after we had made love. Perhaps that is what I am feeling. A Pavlovian response to pool water, a reminder of yesterday's damp-skinned foreplay bringing on another surge of desire. But who am I kidding? It is Charles who is turning my insides out.

He digs with the needle while holding my foot quite firmly. For a short while I close my eyes and am overcome with a dizzying inner glow, a deep satisfaction such as I used to know when Dad helped me with my homework, translating verbs and calculating sums that had been puzzling me for hours. It is a sort of trance, a sensation of utter calm, a meditation to the sound of someone else's breathing. The sense is of being protected. I don't even mind the slight pain.

'There.'

Charles lifts his quarry on the end of the needle. When I hold out my hand, he brushes the point of the needle against my palm, leaving the tiny thorn behind.

'"But, for Man's fault, then was the thorn/Without the fragrant rosebud, born/But ne'er the rose without the thorn."'

I laugh. 'Who wrote that? I should know, probably.'

He stands. 'Do you know something awful? I have quite forgotten.' He tosses the tweezers back in the drawer. 'Someone like Dryden, I should imagine.'

I get off the bed, saying, 'It sounds anti-feminist.'

'Does it? I can't keep up.'

'That's what we're counting on. Not that I'd make a very convincing feminist in a wet swimsuit.'

'Oh, I don't know. There's no sense ignoring man's weaknesses.'

He caresses me with his look once again. I feel myself redden again.

'Mr Bingham, um, I—' Suddenly, we hear a door bang downstairs, and the sound of the dogs running. Enter, wife. I feel guilty. 'I'd better get dressed.'

In the spare room, I sit on the bed, staring blankly outside. It wasn't like this when I met Luke. Then, it was the desperate hope that he might make me happy that led me to him, but oh, Charles, Charles. It is such a ludicrous siege of oneself to be so attracted to someone and yet I can't deny it. Everything about him appeals to my core. If this isn't love at first sight, what is? But I don't want it. No good can come from it. Luke and I may be very different, but I am trying to love him deeply. I would like, please God, to love him deeply. We have good sex, he loves the way I tickle my hand between his legs when he is in my mouth. And I love his strength and energy and shyness, and we have a full and fun lifestyle and a nice flat and he is good, so very good, kind and caring in his bluff, boyish, British manner. And he seems sometimes proud of me, my looks for sure and the way I can make people laugh and also this faintly sexy, distinguishing Canadian accent and the past I have, these things he himself imported, like Drake's tobacco, yes, he is proud of that. And he changed my life and I should love him for that, shouldn't I? But do I? From the centre of my heart? After these few weeks, the answer I think is no. Not like I love his father having met him only one hour ago. So what now?

The door bangs open and Luke barges in with a victor's sprightliness.

'How's the patient?'

'Fine.'

'I thrashed them all again,' he says with a grin. 'Come on, Jo's cooking drop scones and Mrs Rider made us a drizzle cake.'

'In a minute.'

The kitchen has changed in mood now that Luke's mother has returned. The boys have become very well-behaved; their cigarettes put away, the swear words swallowed. Mrs Bingham bustles noisily. I am introduced. She and Charles went to what he called a relaxed lunch party today but she appears dolled-up for a night out in her navy-blue skirt and emerald-green silk shirt and pearls.

There is more of Mrs Bingham in Luke than in either of his siblings. If a police composite was created of either him or his mother, the same facial strips – forehead, eyes, nose, chin – could be used. But she has these feminine, buffed cheeks that sometimes surprise one in older women and remind us of how the journey is not so long. Warily, we shake hands. Victoria's grip is surprisingly loose. She is checking me out, I know she is. But then, I am, her.

'It's lovely being able to put a face to your voice, Portia.'

'Yes, for me too.'

I had seen photographs, but in person Mrs Bingham is more

intimidating than her static images suggest. It has something to do with the fact that her thighs could no doubt crush a veal calf to death.

'I hear that those beastly sons of mine have been making you do all the cooking and cleaning.'

'No, not at all.' I glance towards the others who are all, except Jo who is dripping batter on to the stove, sitting at the table pretending not to be listening.

'But I hope you've been having a nice time.'

'Yes.'

'Wasn't yesterday lovely, absolutely lovely?'

'Yes, it was.'

'You have been extraordinarily lucky with the weather since you arrived,' she says, intimating that my luck has been undeserved.

'I know.'

'Of course, the watering's been a nightmare, it's all so awfully dry, but what can one do?'

'Nothing.'

'It's been such a struggle keeping the border looking pretty. Have you had a chance to enjoy the sunshine out of London?'

'I went to see my aunt in Constable country.'

'Really? How nice. Does she know the Williamson-Smiths, I wonder?'

'Um, I don't know.'

'I'm sure she must. Julia's very busy with the Conservatives and whatnot.'

Luke, sitting neatly at the table with a cup of tea and a slice of cake in front of him, says, 'I think Portia's aunt might be more into the not than the what.'

Shut-up, Luke! Just as yesterday seemed complete and perfect, today has been marred by this odd, dislocated atmosphere. Or is it just what Charles has done to me?

Mrs Bingham won't give up. 'They live in East Bergholt.'

'Oh, well, we went there.'

'Who are the other people who live there, Charles? The other people we know there?'

At the end of the kitchen table there is a larger wooden chair in which Charles is reading the newspaper. He has half-rimmed glasses that add ten years to him. I don't mind the look.

'Four across, five letters,' he replies.' The clue is "loveable finches".'

'Charm,' I say at once, then, after a pause because I don't want to seem smug, add, 'Charm of finches.'

'Bloody hell,' Luke asks. 'How did you know that?'

I half turn towards him. I am keen to end my interrogation, get away from Mrs Bingham, but feel I shouldn't. Shouldn't. The word is usually a red flag to me. Is this good behaviour contagious?

'My dad was an English professor, Luke, you know that.'

'Camilla's dad was a vicar,' Jim pipes in, snorting a laugh, 'but that doesn't make her Joan of Arc.'

I think: pity, I'd have helped carry logs.

'Charm fits,' Charles announces.

'Now is it the Penningtons who live there, Charles? Or are they in Norfolk now?'

'I know Charlie Pennington,' Killjoy tells us, which comes as no surprise to me. Everyone knows everyone else on this island.

'Isn't he gay?' asks Jim.

'No, darling,' Killjoy replies, 'I went out with him.'

'Maybe that did it,' I say lightly, as a joke. I am glared at.

Mrs Bingham has picked up her stinking Jack Russell to give it a kiss when she says, 'I think the Penningtons moved to Norfolk. Charles, did they?'

'All right, Portia cleverclogs, here's something you won't know,' Christian says loudly, smiling (I think, I hope) at my Camilla joke. 'What do you call a group of starlings?'

'Please sit down, Portia,' Mrs Bingham says. 'There's a pot of tea somewhere on the table. Come on, Luke. Be nice.'

'I'll get you a cuppa, Goose,' says Jim. 'Milk?'

'Um, yes, thanks.'

'Why Goose?' asks Charles, looking up.

'Christian, cut Portia some cake,' orders Victoria.

'Not for me, thanks.'

'Really? Do. Mrs Rider made it. It's lemon drizzle.'

'Come on, professor's daughter. It's not a charm of starlings, I can tell you that for nothing.'

'Murmuration,' I mutter.

'Fucking Jesus!'

'Christian,' Mrs Bingham barks. 'Really, I won't allow it.'

'Sorry, Ma. I meant, I thought I was the only person in England who knew that.'

'I was taught all the collectives when I was young. They've sort of stuck.'

Charles looks at me, pats the table next to him, where there is an empty seat, and says, kindly, 'We should have you here more often.'

'Yes.' I feel another sudden flush in my face and my heart is straining as if my blood has thickened. I want to leave now, now. It is a mistake sitting down. I don't like all this attention. I try to take a deep breath but my lungs seem to have halved in size. Can people see that I have begun to sweat? The mug of tea is too hot when Jim hands it to me. And the table seems crowded: mugs, biscuits, milk jugs, papers, plates, people. I have Charles on my left and Jim on my right. Mrs Bingham has taken her place next to Luke, Christian is by his dad. Clearly, this is how the familial alliances have formed over the years.

I notice we are using the same china that Luke has in his London flat, even the tea came out of the same kind of glass jar kept by the stove. It's just one long, smooth ride, isn't it? Luke and Jim and Camilla and Chris and Jo already have more than enough money for smart cars and pretty homes and dinners in good restaurants, so what is left for them to do but upgrade everything? To get a faster car, fill a bigger house with more of the things that their parents have, eat in places more pricey, spread out in five bedrooms instead of two? But does anything evolve, inside or out? That's what I don't know.

'Is it your father's sister, Portia, in . . . is it Essex or Suffolk?'

'Essex. Yes, it was his sister.'

'Was he from there?'

'No. Cornwall.'

'Luke said he went to Cambridge. Charles was there, weren't you?'

'Yes, Trinity. Now, come on Portia, everybody, seven letters, the clue is, "block a passage," beginning in "O".'

'We'll be having none of that passage blocking here, Pops.'

'Christian, does everything have to be filthy with you?' Mrs Bingham wants to know. 'I can't bear it.'

'He's at that age,' says Killjoy, brown-nosing.

'Occlude?' I suggest.

'Absolutely. It is occlude. Are you a keen crossworder?'

'No, not at all. I just used to like words.'

'I like drop scones,' says Jim. 'How are the drop scones, Jo? They smell yummy.'

'You watch that paunch,' Killjoy warns, 'Or I'll leave you.'

Eat, Jim, eat.

I catch Luke's eye, but he looks away, towards his mother. Jo has been ladling batter on to the Aga top and now produces the plate of scones for us. It is the first thing she has done this weekend. Mrs Bingham is beside herself with gratitude. I am pleased for the momentary respite though my body feels sticky.

The mistress of the house won't leave me for long. 'We can't wait to read one of your newspaper articles. What are they about?'

'Oh, lots of things. Prostitution, child sex, Luke, that sort of thing.'

'Are they? I thought that—'

'I think she's pulling your leg, Ma.'

'Well, we'll have to get hold of some, won't we?' she says, in a can-do, rub-two-sticks-to-make-fire-girls' tone. 'How can we?'

I know she wants me to say I'll send some, but they are my world. My writing is the one thing that's me, not Luke and me. I want to keep it to myself.

'I can get Carole to send them,' Charles says.

His sister-in-law. I had forgotten. How dumb. 'Please don't.'

Luke announces, 'Portia calls Carole, the editing ant.'

'Does she, darling? Why?'

'I think because of the way I talk.' I take a sip of tea, my pulse racing with what I know I can't resist saying. 'I don't say "aren't". I say ant. Like in asshole.'

Christian claps. 'I like it.'

A silence falls. Eyes are avoided. It is stupid.

'Joanna,' says Mrs Bingham, 'there's blackcurrant jam up there if you don't like the strawberry.'

It is in front of me, the blackcurrant. Am I being criticized? I feel like I'm being watched, studied, not just as a new girlfriend but as a foreign girl. No one else seems uncomfortable.

I have my tea to my lips when I am asked, 'And, Portia, do you have brothers and sisters?'

'No, just me and my mother.'

'Does she live in Canada?'

'Yes, she's in Toronto. She's a nurse.'

'Is she? I take my hat off to her,' says Charles, looking up at me, kindly. 'They are absolute saints, nurses.'

'Actually, my mother's a sinner who happens to be a nurse. Excuse me, I just have to—' I push my chair back and walk briskly down the cool corridor and lock shut the bathroom door. I sit on the toilet lid. I am being paranoid, aren't I? Tea is what the English take at five, I have seen it a hundred times on TV and in movies, and this is how the English are when they are being polite. But, fuck it, I get so awkward having to be dainty and well-mannered. It is not me. I don't know if I can ever be the person Luke will expect me to be. Whatever I may think of Charles, I should run. Now, before it is too late.

I light a cigarette. Seems like it has become a no smoking house since the parents got back. How old are we? They get like children, Luke and the others. He is such a Mummy's boy, so deferential and honey-tongued. I noticed how Charles gets away without lifting a finger, it's like stepping back forty years. Serena was even buttering his toast. Bet her husband misses that. And there is me stuck in the middle saying all the wrong things.

  I get up to tap my ash into the water, then focus on one of the photographs. Charles has changed little. He was handsome at school, a good sportsman. Tennis, real tennis, rugby, cricket, he made all the teams. I don't know if he has been flirting with me because I'm me, or whether this is how he is with all the girls. Sportsmen always flirt, I don't think forty years is long enough to filter such confidence out. Even Dad was a flirt with some of his students. But I like Charles. He seems younger, somehow, than Luke. More interested in life. He seems to be questioning things that Luke thinks he has answered. Can that be? I know he must have felt something in the pool. I didn't imagine the tension in his bedroom. Charles likes touching me. I like Charles touching me. And yet . . .

  I take another deep drag and throw the cigarette away. After swirling unconvincingly around the bowl's edge, the filter, thank God, is sucked in. When I return to the kitchen, the talk is of leaving. Killjoy has suddenly noticed the time, and has things to do in the city. Luke catches my eye. We nod. Already we have our signals.

  'Before you go, I want to show you something, Portia.'

  'If it's his etchings, say no,' says Christian.

  'Are you packed?' asks Luke, gruffly it seems.

  'No, I'll get my stuff from the spare room,' I say with a glance towards Mrs Bingham, who I catch eyeing me suspiciously, as if she is able to read what is going on in my mind.

Somewhere in suburbia, travelling in silence, Luke and I are snailing along in traffic. All is ugliness, our mood and the surroundings. To fill the silence he turned the radio on but I switched it off. My mind is too full for pop.

  'Sorry,' I said. 'All that coke gave me a headache.'

I knew the answer would appease. It is within his realm, his circus ring. It does not matter that it isn't true.

I feel almost sinful, being trapped in the car with Luke. Suddenly, I feel so little love towards him. Was it really only last night that he made me feel so ecstatic, his face between my legs and the birds singing beyond the open window? But stop. I mustn't get nostalgic over twenty-four hours. It is no wonder that now is a trough. It is Sunday night and it is raining and we are hungover and tired and it is life to be down having been so up, we cannot expect to escape that. Thinking about it, the coke probably is taking revenge.

And yet . . . and yet with a snap of my fingers I would replace you, Luke, with your father. At this moment I would. I can't stop thinking of Charles, of when I am going to see him, of how complete I felt with him. Isn't this how love proves herself? By being parasitical, cruel? Emerging only at the expense of another? But I would untie the knots inside if I could. I have spent too much of my life loving a man I cannot have. If I could only love Luke, imagine what a breeze life might be.

I don't know if it is to relieve the pressure or to test the waters that I say, 'Your father wanted me to go to an exhibition with him,' in a tone that I am frightened must sound guilty.

After Jim and Killjoy had left, Charles took me on a tour of the house, pointing out which parts were eighteenth century, and which later. The thing he wanted to show me was a first edition of *Jude the Obscure*. How could he have guessed how many times I have read and re-read Hardy's books, how Dad turned me on to them, how I haven't turned back since? I held its soft leather in my hands like the thing of beauty it is. Why didn't Luke bring me to see it, too? Charles was dismayed that I hadn't known Hardy was a poet. He has lent me a collection of the poems.

He told me, too, about some places I should visit in London that I knew nothing about – Sir John Soane's house and the Courtauld Gallery and some Christopher Wren churches off the beaten track. Then he suggested he and I should go to the Royal Academy.

'The old man's probably trying to pick you up.'

'No, he just wants to take me to an exhibition. It's not as if you've been deluging me with invitations to the Royal Academy or – or anywhere.'

'Sorry, I didn't know you expected sightseeing as well as accommodation.'

'Fuck off, Luke. I'm not a tourist.'

'Cool it. I was joking. *Joking*. Maybe you should only do one line next time.'

'It's not the coke. I was just saying that. Anyway, I'd be perfectly happy only doing one line. It was dumb bringing any to the country. What's wrong with grass?'

'There's enough grass in the country.'

'You know what I meant.'

'Coke's fun. It makes everybody fun.'

'You guys think you're in the movies, or something. It isn't as wicked and exciting as you all think it is. If only you knew what me and my friends used to get up to.'

'Oh, right, all your friends. So what is it precisely that Aunt Barbara and Uncle Keith do for a laugh? Throw pennies into that fountain you told me about? I'm sure you'd rush to show Lady Joanna that.'

'Don't be a snob. I hate that in you.'

'You were the one sucking up to Jo because she's got a title.' He hits the gas but, for once, doesn't ask, 'Feel the turbo kick in?' We overtake a couple of cars, then slow down again. 'Anyway, what started all this? I thought you had a nice weekend.'

'I did. It's probably the coke.'

'You just said it wasn't.'

'Hormones, then.'

It is usually the explanation men find for our inconsistencies, our character, so can we be blamed for lobbing it back?

Luke is tapping the steering wheel with his hand, calming himself down. He doesn't like to argue, he'll take a detour rather than confront a problem. After about ten minutes, he says, 'It's a family joke about Dad,' as if he has been mentally following a string through the maze of our argument and, by starting again, thinks we will find clear sky if we retrace our steps.

'What is?'

'That he asks my girlfriends out to lunch or an exhibition, or something.'

The words hit me like a punch. And yet, I don't know if I am angry with him or upset that I am not unique, that I read too much into Charles's attention. 'Do they all go?'

'Um, I don't know. Maybe Jemima used to. Not that they get on so well. But Pa liked you.'

'Did he?' Then, calmly as I can, 'Well, I liked him.'

'Good,' says Luke, smiling at me as he reaches across to touch my leg.

I can tell from the way he is patting my thigh that he thinks the matter is wrapped up, all over. I am his pretty girl again, soon we'll be back in London and back in bed and he'll nail me to his body and bed. I turn from him and try to look through the window, but the rain has thickened and fat drops are sliding across the pane blurring my vision and sending my gaze back to myself, where I am not sure I want to look.

SIX

Make a point of devoting some time every day to physical relaxation that takes your mind off your problems. If you go for a walk, concentrate on what you see around you instead of thinking about your problems.

AMA Family Medical Guide

It is a Saturday afternoon, five weekends since this great, dull phalanx of cloud moved in to sweep summer's unthinking bliss away, and Charles Bingham's fingertips touched my own. Luke is shooting in Norfolk. I let him go alone. Life is not as it was.

I make myself a vodka, return to the computer. The week's storms have stripped the plane trees outside the flat's windows, allowing into the room more of October's grey-blue light. It has been an ashen London day, the light barely changing from dawn to dusk. The damp has soaked into my bones and made them ache. The flat never feels warm enough. Here, nowhere does. The English are cheap when it comes to heating. Wherever you are here it's like being grilled in a freezer, pockets of heat wrapped in clouds of damp air; much like the English themselves.

My computer screen teases me with lime-green malice. I am cheating, plagiarizing, editing other articles – failing, I suppose, to do what I should. I think the editing ant might fire me, but for some reason I can't seem to resist taking the easiest route.

I am alone this Saturday night. Kaz, my most reliable, animate saviour (my hidden vibrator I count, ungenerously, as inanimate), is with Charlie being distinctively unvirginal in some British Virgin Island. I miss her. I cannot imagine living in London without my friend. She is as lazy as I am underemployed. When we are not forced to be working, we spend days together doing precisely those things with which daylight is not usually associated. We go to the movies. We get drunk. We rent videos. We get stoned. We eat too much. We siesta, actively, so it has become, for us, a verb. We never seem to do much together, but that is half the point. She and I simply enjoy each other's company. We are soulmates, I suppose.

It was popcorn that sealed our friendship. We had been to a movie, something romantic and forgettable. I was fidgety throughout, distracted by the noise of someone eating a family-sized tub of popcorn. Outside, I asked Kaz her opinion of the film. 'Why popcorn?' she replied. 'Why not marshmallows or rice pudding or something soft and mushy?' Then began one of her famous monologues, this one on the miseries of popcorn in movie theatres, the munching and crunching, the gasps of air as it's thrown in, 'the way it smells all popcorny and buttery and urgh'.

After that, it didn't take long to discover we share a thousand pet hates and loves, have wondered independently about exactly those things that people like Luke find inconsequential. On the Brompton Road we discovered a mutual distrust of cars at pedestrian crossings. Though the mere flash of a 'Don't Walk' sign makes me want to rebel, we won't jaywalk. Neither of us can understand why fat men invariably buy suits that are too small for them or why, if no one has ever heard of anyone who has died from sticking a knife in a toaster, it is considered so hazardous. Both she and I love to eavesdrop, but think it strange that people so often re-live dull days by explaining in great detail just why they were so dull. We have both wondered why there is no pop-up Kama Sutra and think international postage quite something. So, too, are radio waves and separated twins who marry sisters quite by chance. We get a kick out of making waiters repeat the specials and remain convinced that the interesting conversations invariably take place at the other end of the table. It has occurred to Kaz, as it has to me, that ginger-haired men are more likely to sport goatees. We do things to prove we can, whether they are right or wrong, and have lived to see one of our parents take their own life. Such things, and countless others beside, constitute as immediate a friendship as any I have known. Only in one great respect do we differ: Kaz considers herself happy, and I do not. She has taken it upon herself to change my mind, and I am going to try since her refusal either to pity herself or to apportion blame humbles me.

We have spoken only briefly about her mother. She died four years ago, without warning. The note left was horribly simply: 'I was not happy, darlings.' It was addressed to no one in particular, and included no apologies. Kaz thinks her father may have been having an affair, but has never asked. She knows only that her mother did not want to live. Deeper than that, and despite the hours she has sat listening to me wonder about Dad, she will not dig. 'Imagine if I discovered,' she told me, 'there was something I could have done.'

I remain undecided about such British reserve. In some ways, it is a relief not being regaled by people's problems as soon as one meets them, yet it means I never get the sense that I know people. I can proceed only so far, despite my doubts that the seas within Kaz are as calm as she would have me believe.

I light another cigarette. Got to give up, I smoke more than ever now. Still, my Camel Lights make me happy. Perhaps my column should address happiness this week – how we Americans are not happy until we have answers, while the British prefer not to look. It has been on my mind, recently. Since the summer so abruptly ended (since, I suppose, that unforeseen, unbidden moment with Charles Bingham in his pool) life seems to have narrowed. It is probably churlish of me to resent Luke and his friends for their contentment and yet their existence seems so pre-ordained and unimaginative. They hope to repeat their parents' lives, play by their rules, aim for their goals. Not that I have found an alternative. My wooden-legged mind does not know what I need do to soar. I should avoid petty, everyday concerns – what to eat for lunch, when to do the washing, what tripe to write for the paper, with whom to go to which pub or movie or restaurant – and yet my life with Luke has found its predictable routine. I don't understand how some people manage to expand their lives when the details of living contrive to choke exploration and pursuit. Before I met Charles, the orderliness of life with Luke seemed an answer I had not expected to find. Now, being with one man in one city seems uninspired, a weak hum. It seems wrong to unteach ourselves the curiosity we learned as kids; to draw back from the open door, the unturned corner. We unravel from our foetal question marks to exclamation marks when we die. Is that the struggle? Learning to turn from the silken eyes? Ingest the knowledge we have rather than dreaming of what we have not? I am not desperate for the answers, it is not looking that scares me.

Or am I wrong? Am I killing myself trying to find Dad's answer for him? With no divine retribution or heavenly reward to concern us any more, does it make any difference if I reach the end of this life knowing nothing? If I haven't read Proust and can't make a lemon zest soufflé? Whatever happens I can only have scratched the surface of truth, there is so much to know and I don't have so great a mind.

I should not complain. I am comfortable, healthy, have a job more varied than most. In trying to understand this city, I have interviewed greyhound trainers, riding teachers in Hyde Park, a BBC weatherman (a cushy job here requiring only hand gestures while back home they have to walk from one side of the map to the other), presenters from Live TV, a woman who keeps eighty-three cats in Kensal Rise, Indian immigrants who run corner stores, bus conductors, an assistant to Prince Charles, the deputy editor of a daily tabloid. I have spent a day at a stall in Portobello and another behind the bar of a pub in Brixton. I have flown over the city in a Tiger Moth and taken tea in the Orangery in Kensington Park. When I can, I take myself to Islington and Camden and to the glorious parks. Yet, I am required to write only a thousand words a week, and I am lazy in searching for other freelance work. I occupy myself with work for less than two days a week. For the rest of the time, I watch TV and kill time, with or without Kaz. Those things I used to slot in after work (doctors, laundry, bills) now eat up hours of the day. Now, without Kaz, and with no Luke to give my day a frame, I feel my dissatisfaction more acutely.

Come on, to work. I write:

For all the majesty of the towers and spires of Cambridge University the town has a village-like feel to it that

Recently, I squeezed myself into the passenger seat of my friend Kaz's old Citroen deux cheva cheuvo chuvaux

My father went to Cambridge University, and so it was with great anticipation that I

Readers of this column over the last few months might be interested to know that I think I have fallen in love with my boyfriend's father. I sometimes sit here dreaming of his fingers in my pussy. It turns me on, makes me wet, makes

There is a Salvation Army shop near me in London that not only carries the same tarnished silverware, old plastic coffee makers, *Reader's Digest Best Short Stories of 1973* collections and gnarled oddly sized leather shoes that are in my local store in Toronto (and I mean the same ones, there is a conspiracy here) but smells the same, too. I mention this because I recently met a Viscount's daughter who was wearing a cardigan six times too small for her. It sported the musty tang of a second-hand store. 'Salvation Army?' I enquired. She seemed as proud as if I had recognized a top designer's style. 'Yes. Isn't it too divine?'

There is an odd thing going on among the British Upper Classes. I call it down-classing, and I don't think it could happen anywhere else in the world. Of course, capitalism has it that the rich rarely become poor and the poor seldom rich and in this society it's even harder to move between one's

One of the first things any visitor to Cambridge notices is that there is an almost Chinese devotion to bicycles. If one was needed, it gives the town an archaic, old-fashioned air that

Some men become incredibly attractive with age. Charles Bingham is so sexy. Charles Charles Chaaaaaarrrrllessssssssex

I went to Cambridge last month to visit my father's college. It looked much the same as I imagined it did in the fourteenth century, something we Canadians . . .

Oh, fuck it.
    I change the CD, replace an old Smith's album with Elgar. I read recently that his Nimrod variation was considered the most quintessentially English three minutes of music ever written. Dad used to play it all the time. I would sit on his lap against his chest and he'd tell me to close my eyes and imagine England's fields.
    Back at my desk, I rub my hands over my face, and close my eyes. When I was a kid I used to play this game with Dad in which I had to remember all the items I had seen on a tray before he hid it underneath a tea towel. I was never any good since there was always one item that interested me above all others, lime marmalade, say, and an image of that alone would crowd the other pieces out of my brain. I think I would be better these days since, with my eyes closed, I can remember almost everything on the knotted pine table in front of me. There is an empty coffee mug, this a cornfield-clad souvenir bought in Constable country as a joke for Luke, my Camel Lights, a Safeway's freshly squeezed orange juice carton, empty, the

Guardian, an ashtray stolen from Quaglino's containing half a joint stained by Plum Turner's crimson lipstick, copies of *Cosmo*, *Tatler*, *The New Yorker*, a Penguin Classic *Canterbury Tales*, a cereal bowl, Luke's Zippo, the fluorescent orange spiral notepad I bought on my last day in Toronto and on the first page of which is written the world ENGLAND then, uncharacteristically for me, a list of superlatives (harmonious, decorous, gorgeous, splendid) about this neighbourhood scrawled in swaggering handwriting to match the happy self-belief held then that I had the imagination and artistry to gift-wrap a nation and its people. Also, a national lottery scratchcard, a book of matches from a bistro in Notting Hill, a Boden mail-order catalogue for, by and featuring people of Luke's narrow class, a credit card bill I can't face, another from William Hill bookmakers which, thank God, I'll be sharing with Kaz (typically, our luck ran out just as we became greedy), Blisteze, a five pound voucher courtesy of Lancôme for visiting their counter and creating the idea I should be given one, a scented candle with peculiar sprigs of heather and bracken suspended in the wax, two Pilot pens, the laptop, my vodka.

Write about something that matters to you, sounds Luke's voice in my head. So I will . . .

> It should have been a happy life. In many ways, it was blessed. Clive Mills was born in 1928 in the village of Maslyn, close to Land's End in Cornwall. He weighed a little under eight pounds. His mother, Rose Mills, née Dickerson, was the daughter of a prosperous businessman. She was an educated women, more so than the man she loved. It was she who encouraged the young Clive to study th

The door buzzer interrupts me. Probably a mistake, most everyone I know is out of town. 'Hello?'
'Is that Portia?'
'Yes.'
'It's Charles. Charles Bingham.'

Oh, Christ! 'Oh, hi. Um, Luke's out.'

'I've brought him something. May I bring it up?'

'May you? Oh, sure.' I press the buzzer. Help, it's messy in here. I wish I had put make-up on, that I was dressed in something other than Luke's baggy sweats and oatmeal shooting socks. I look at myself quickly in the mirror, then shake out my hair.

After a brisk tap at the open door, Charles takes a step in. He is wearing a surprisingly bright polo shirt. I am by my computer, one hand on the table as if I have just pushed myself up off my chair. That's stupid, of course, since I opened the door.

'Hello.'

'Hi.'

'I'm so glad I caught you in. Luke's grandfather wanted him to have this.' Charles is carrying a framed print under his arm which he rests against the chair by the door. It's of a grand building somewhere, probably Luke's school or university. They don't let go, this crowd.

'Thanks. I'm sure he'll be grateful.'

'You were hard at work, I see. That's very diligent for a Saturday night.'

Is he alone? He's hovering. 'Is Mrs Bingham with you?'

'No, Victoria's still with her father. We've just moved the old boy down to Surrey. I had to pop by the flat to collect some papers. I should have rung you first.'

'No, don't worry, it's nice, um. Come in, if you'd like. Please.' So formal, I'm being. So English.

'Thank you.'

He closes the door behind him. Did he know I was going to be on my own? We stand silent, the music between us.

'Did Luke have a wedding this weekend?'

'No, he's in Norfolk.' I'm nodding, aren't I? I can feel myself nodding and I shouldn't be. 'Ah, would you like some tea, or—?'

Charles raises a palm. 'No, I mustn't keep you.'

'I wasn't busy.' I lean gently on the computer screen. Its convincing click is proof of my intent.

'Very well, thank you.'

'Or would you prefer something not tea?' I lift up my half-empty glass.

'I'm already on the vodka.'

'Are you, now? Well' – he looks at his watch, sees that it's past six – 'I think my arm could be twisted.'

'Oh, good. I think Luke has one of those Glen-somethings.' I bend down to the cupboard where Luke keeps his booze, demurely so, with knees bent, not with my arse sticking in the air. 'You guys drink that, don't you?'

'We do, but I think I might like some vodka for a change. Keep you company.'

'OK, then.' In the kitchen, I nearly drop one of Luke's expensive glasses. I'm fingers and thumbs. 'Ice and a slice?'

'Whatever you have, please. And only a little. I mustn't stay long.'

I hadn't noticed an increase in the volume of Charles's voice so am surprised by his sudden presence at the kitchen's entrance. He leans his shoulder brazenly against the door's frame with the looseness of a younger man. He caught me thinking what a relief it was that I hadn't been anticipating the visit. Now I wonder if it showed.

'You must think I'm some kind of alcoholic,' I say, 'drinking on my own.'

'Not at all. It lubricates the mind, doesn't it?'

'Well . . .' A rectangular shard of ice slides off the surface of the ice tray as I crunch and twist a couple of lumps out. The piece shatters at my feet. 'I think I was hoping to disconnect my mind, if anything; not oil it. Say when.'

'Stop, stop.' One of the ice cubes cracks noisily in the glass. 'Sounds ominous.'

'The ice?'

'No, no,' he says with a chuckle, 'your reply did.'

'We're both cracking up,' I tell him with an apologetic tilt of my head, 'or something. Here you go.'

'Thank you.'

No touching fingertips this time as I pass Charles the glass, though I am shaking a little. 'Actually, it was just a bad day.'

'Was it? Tell me why.'

'Oh, you don't want to know,' I mutter, reddening a little.

'Yes, I do. Very much.'

Why is it that Charles makes me nervous? He is less judgemental than his son and has the natural conversation of a diplomat. His questions are shaped to make one feel comfortable with disclosure. I shake a packet of Kettle chips into a bowl. Charles leads the way next door. I am glad I chose this rich Elgar rather than pop. It lessens the gap in ages.

Charles stands with his drink by the armchair, waiting as I turn off the overhead light and switch on a couple of the lamps. Did that seem flirtatious? No, it's friendlier now. He sits only when I have done so. Was Dad so old-fashioned and polite? I don't remember. He was not strict. Canada may have rounded his sharp British edges.

On the sofa, I lift my feet up under my legs. Relax, Pea, relax.

'He certainly knew how to pull on the heart-strings, didn't he?'

'Excuse me?'

'Elgar.'

'Oh, yes, I know. Somehow he manages to be incredibly English and incredibly passionate at the same time.'

Charles laughs. 'I wasn't aware they were exclusive of one another.'

'Well, you know.' I find myself blushing and sweep a hand through my hair in an attempt to hide it. 'Um, Jane Austen may be great but she's not exactly passionate.'

'Oh, but she is. Absolutely she is. All the more so because it's brewing inside.'

'I guess.' I balance my drink on the sofa's arm, then think better of it and hold it against my knee. A drip darkens the grey of my sweat pants. Charles has leant back in his chair, staring at me. Our eyes lock for a second before he leans forward for a potato chip. 'I hope Luke invited you with him this weekend.'

'Oh, yeah. I just—'

'You didn't feel like it.'

Oh, his smile. I'm on your side. This is charm. 'No, I thought I could use some time on my own.'

'And here I am interrupting.'

'No, I like, ah, you. I meant some time away, some space.'

'Ahha.'

The church clock strikes the half hour. Now I long for the minutes to move slowly. Before, I was expecting the evening to expire sadly, like a sigh.

'So! You were about to tell me about your bad day.'

'I was?' With my heart beating faster after the stare, I say, 'It's not important.'

'I hope Luke hasn't done something.'

'No. Not at all, he's so nice to me, it's ... it's more complicated.'

'I'm very happy to listen,' Charles reassures me, wiping the greasy salt off his fingertips.

'I don't know.' Unconsciously, I reach for a lock of hair in my fingers and then, consciously, continue to play with it, happy for Charles to think I am reluctant to talk about myself. 'Thing is, I don't know whether I'm getting homesick or not trying hard enough with ... with Luke but I feel like life's going the wrong way. Like a wedge of cheese, you know?' I make a V of my hands, my fingertips pressed together, 'that I want to be the other way around.'

'I'm sure everyone feels that way at times.'

'But that's it. They don't.' I swing my legs onto the floor. 'I'm surrounded by people here who are totally satisfied with where they are and where they're going. And I don't know whether I resent them for thinking they've got all they need or dislike them for not having enough imagination, having no real aspirations.'

'I'm sure they do have aspirations. Perhaps they are merely different from your own.'

'But everyone's on the same path. I don't want to know what's going to happen next. That's when life trips you up – when you think you know what's going to happen.'

'Then what is it that you do want?'

'Me?' I say, feeling myself blush.

Charles nods, then leans back, legs crossed. What is he? Shrink? Father-in-law? Flirt? My first period came thirty-four days after Daddy died. I was child, not woman, with him. But we would have talked about such things. 'I used to just want my dad back but now, I don't know.' I gently rattle the ice in my glass and look to its base where large bubbles are trapped in the green glass. 'I suppose I can't say I want to be happy, can I?'

'No, that would be cheating. Happiness depends – doesn't it? – on getting what one wants.'

Then you, I think, with me. Leave this imperfection behind.

'I thought the whole point of chivalrous romance was that bliss came from being denied. Not that I necessarily believe that,' I add, meeting his eye again. 'Self-denial's not really my style.'

'Oh no? You have to exercise some, surely. We all harbour desires that are mutually exclusive.' Charles spins the drink in his glass around. Women of fifty-four would kill for skin like his, wouldn't they? I can't deny that I have thought of pressing my lips to those cheeks, those lips. 'We would self-destruct if we tried to live all of them out.'

He is pensive for a moment. I wonder, is he remembering our swim? Can he feel our fingertips touching in the water? The skin of my leg while I was sitting on his bed? What destruction would follow if he lived out his desire for me? I am sure it exists. Why else is he here, now, when Luke is away?

'I try to deny myself as little as possible.' As if to prove my point, I reach for a Kettle chip the top of which, ironically enough, is folded over like a hotel bed sheet. 'It's healthier that way.'

'Unless that's the root of your dissatisfaction. You risk never being satisfied with what you have.'

'Maybe, but the flip side is that if you're totally satisfied with what you've got, you'll never push yourself to reach for more. It's too depressing to look around and say, "This is it. Here's the sum total of my aspirations." Wanting more is proof you're alive.'

'I think you might be on rocky ground,' Charles says with a wry smile. 'There has to be a point at which one's own gratification is less important than other things.'

'Really? Like when?'

'It's wrong to be happy at the expense of others.'

Is he right? Has that been my mistake? How much happier would I be if Dad had lived for me, instead of killing himself for himself? How much freer and more able to dispense my own happiness on others? I tip my glass back and take in my mouth one of the cubes of ice. Charles has shifted forward in his seat. He looks a little awkward. I wonder what he has denied himself for others? Me? Others, before? He cannot have been satisfied with that wife for all his adult life?

He sets his glass down. 'I don't think I'm being much help, am I?'

'No, it's not ... I mean, there's nothing to help, in a way. You're right. I just have to figure out what I want. I used to think just coming to England would be enough, that it would somehow feel like getting Dad back, but it obviously hasn't happened quite like that, so—'

'It's not what you expected?'

'Not really. But then, nothing ever is.'

In the silence, Charles finishes his drink. I want him to stay, all night I would like him to stay.

'Oh, I just remembered I've got your book.' I skip past him to the bedroom to fetch the collection of Hardy poems.

When I return, he asks, 'Did you enjoy them?'

'So much.'

'I thought you might.'

I fan through the pages. 'There was one, "The Going", that I found incredibly moving.'

'Yes, isn't that one lovely? "You could not know/That such

swift fleeing/No soul foreseeing, not even I, would undo me so."'

'That's it,' I tell him, reading it myself. 'That's it exactly. It made me think of my dad. I want to write it down. I don't have a memory like yours.'

'Then you should keep the book.'

'Oh, no, I didn't mean—'

'I insist.' Charles stands, takes a pen from beside the phone, and returns to sit on the sofa beside me. I am almost paralysed by memories of sitting beside Luke, though I never wanted him like this. Not like this.

Although the two cushions are separate, the sofa has a different tension to it now. It mimics us. For half a second Charles rests his hand on mine, where I'm holding the book. I give it to him. As I watch him write an inscription I think, if this was a movie I would reach over and touch his shoulder, and then I would kiss him and because he is a fifty-four-year-old man and I a women in the prime of her young womanly life, a woman whose looks make fifty-four-year-old men break their stride, he would accept my kiss; understand it. He would understand how I could make both of us happy, and we would proceed from there.

'Here you are.'

He has written: 'For Portia, some honest English passion! with love from Charles Bingham', followed by the date in Roman numerals.

'Thank you. I'll treasure it, I really will.'

And then I do what I had decided not to. I act. I lean across to kiss Charles on the cheek, but as I do so he dips his head slightly, like a little boy away from a grandmother who has bristles on her chin, and in that second I lose my nerve and aim to kiss him instead on his forehead, lifting my torso higher, and so pressing my mouth quite firmly against his skin because my balance is off, the lean too severe.

We both lean back after the kiss and reach for our drinks as if we have been caught *in flagrante*. I can feel the throb of my pulse in my whole body. I wonder if Charles can, too, across the sofa's fabric.

Neither of us speaks for a moment. I fish the crescent of lime from my glass, and wince at its tartness.

'Portia, I should be on my way.'

'Don't leave on my account.'

'No, I must.'

'I was going to cook something. I mean, you're welcome to—' Stay, please, stay.

'I'd love to, but I had better get on.'

At the door, I find the courage to ask, 'Did you get to see that, ah, that Giacometti exhibition yet?'

'No, no, I haven't. I want to do that.'

'Because I remember you saying—'

'Absolutely, let's go soon, shall we?'

'Yeah,' I say with a breathy laugh, 'That'd be good.'

He smiles, leans in to kiss me, and then, boof, he is gone, leaving me feeling giddy, rather like a teenager in love.

'Kaz.'

'Portia.'

'You're back.'

'I'm back.'

'And?' by which I mean, 'and did Charlie propose?' Kaz has been convinced he would. It's in the air. Emma the teacher has just netted herself a rich banker, which Kaz says is all she ever wanted, and next weekend, Dominic Hasbury is getting married. I have been invited.

'No, not a squeak out of the lad.'

'Thank Christ, eh?' I switch channels on the muted TV. There is an item coming on *Richard and Judy* soon about older women screwing younger men. I want to watch.

'He doesn't want me, Pea.'

'Well, you don't want to marry him.'

'That's quite beside the point. He could at least want me to, couldn't he? Or want me to want him to. He couldn't care less.'

I light a cigarette, put my feet up. This hour, between ten and eleven, is most often spent gossiping with Miss Katherine. 'Did something bad happen between you?'

'No, sweets, it was bliss. But I couldn't enjoy the sunsets at all, which quite frankly is half the point of flying across the world with a loved one. There we were every night happy as two peas in our terribly toasty Caribbean pod with our pina coladas and creamy coconut whatsits held lovingly to our rather gorgeous sun-kissed nut-brown bosoms—'

'This is going somewhere, isn't it? You're not just trying to make me jealous, are you?'

'Nothing of the sort. I'm painting the mood for you, it's terribly important. Pathetic phalluses and such.'

'Fallacy.'

'Exactly, Pea.' Hearing me inhale my Camel Light must have put Kaz in mind of a Silk Cut herself. There is a pause filled with the click of her lighter. 'As I say, there we'd be watching the sun go down feeling all nice and juicy after a bit of how's-your-father in the plush beach-side bungalow and all I could think of was Chaz-the-Caveman dropping unceremoniously to one knee in front of all these frightfully smart folk so he could swear undying love to me. It quite spoiled the mood, no matter how many cocktails he poured down my throat. I couldn't relax for the life of me.'

'So how many did he pour down you?'

'Lord knows. Too many, most nights. I remember a somewhat embarrassing incident with a flying lobster.'

'Lobsters don't fly.'

'That's rather the point, Peadle-pea.' She sighs. 'Anyway, the long and the short of it is that even though I don't want the fool to make a decent woman of me it was all something of a let-down. Rather like when we all had to sprint down to Cranborne Chase because we'd been told mummy's mummy was about to finally go belly up and guess what she was doing when we got there.' Pause. 'Pea? Guess what she was doing.'

'What?'

'Cleaning the chicken run. Didn't want the old dear to die at all, but it was still a let-down once we got there.'

'That's nice. Marriage being like death.'

'I knew you'd understand. How's Luke?'

'He's murdering wildfowl.' Huh – I would never have used those words back home. Kaz influences me. 'He's going to Canada soon.'

'Tell him to stay away from the saucy birds this time. One's quite enough. What are you doing today?'

'I don't know. Working.'

'Don't be silly. I'm the one who should be working. You have to see me before this tan has completely faded. It's already a shade lighter.'

'I've got to work.'

'Work? Pea, is something wrong?'

'No. Yes. No. I don't know. I think, maybe. You're no good at secrets, are you?'

'Darling, I'm Queen Mute when I need to be.'

'So you won't tell anyone.'

'Of course not.'

'Charles came here when Luke was away.' Oh, just saying it relieves me.

'Charles who?'

'Luke's dad. He was here on Saturday night.'

'Night?'

'Evening.'

'So?'

'So I like him, Kaz. I mean, I really like him.'

'You mean you've got a crush on your boyfriend's father.' She can sound scary, Kaz, when her voice becomes deep.

'It's not a crush, it's something else. More, than that.'

'Of course it is. Crushes always are. That's what makes them crushes.'

'Kaz, don't. I don't know what to do about it. Luke came back yesterday and I just felt so, I don't know, so nothing towards him. I really like Charles.'

'Pea, please stop sounding so serious. "I really like him,"' she glumly repeats, mimicking my accent. 'You don't think you're the first girl in the world to fancy their boyfriend's father, do you? Lord knows, I've always preferred them myself. Quite frankly, I'd say it's rude not to.'

'This is different.'

'It's not in the slightest different. It's good news, if anything. Shows you'll love Luke when he's sixty-four.'

'Fifty-four. Charles is fifty-four.'

'And doesn't look a day over forty, I know. I wouldn't worry about it at all. Just don't tell Luke. Boys get very competitive. Now, why don't we have lunch at JK's? I'll treat you.'

'You think it's a phase, then? It doesn't feel like a phase.'

'What else could it possibly be? Sweets, I know these things. That's why I stopped going to my shrink.'

'You never told me you had a shrink.'

'I only went until I realized I knew much more about myself than she did.'

'Well, I don't know what to think about this.'

'Pea, if anyone's going to fall in love with a boyfriend's father, it's you. Obviously. It's all terribly predictable and Freudian.'

'This hasn't got anything to do with my dad.' Of all things, this I'm sure of. I am not so naïve.

'Of course it hasn't. Nothing at all. I couldn't be more wrong. Now, I'll be there at one. No arguments. Really, there's no point me flying half-way around the world if no one's going to see my tan.'

I am awake when Luke touches me; of course I am awake. I have woken before six every morning since Charles was here.

'Porsh? Porsh?'

I do not respond to Luke's whispering. Can he tell from the pace of my breathing that my eyes are open? I used to pretend I was asleep when Daddy came in to wake me for school. He would stroke my cheek knowing all along, I think, that I wasn't asleep at all.

Luke's hand is softly stroking my naked thigh. It's sex he wants. I used to adore being woken by a lover excited to have me by my side. Now I wish he would stop, stop.

He cups his right hand over my right hip and pulls me onto my back. I know what will happen now, and how. He will part my legs with his right hand. Perhaps he might kiss me. Once my legs are open a little he will lever them further apart just above the knee so he can slide his hand between my thighs. There he goes now. He is pressing with the nub of his hand against my pubic bone and feeling, adroitly, for my clitoris. I think he is not self-taught, though such efficiency is more likely than passion for Luke. He takes his time. He is well-mannered even when tired and erect. As ever, I admit one finger and he persists with the second. A nail scratches slightly where I am dry. I keep my eyes closed. The daylight carries truths I am reluctant to face.

Suddenly, his fingers are gone. I hear a tick of spit. Oh, he wants to speed this up. We are going to Dominic Hasbury's wedding today, and will probably be late. He is quiet, surreptitious, so as not to criticize my body's ability to lubricate itself, but he cannot stop the cold licking my skin when he lifts the sheet with the back of his cupped hand. His foamy fingers feel better when they enter me for the second time. I smile. Luke must have noticed because his lips are on mine before I have relaxed my own.

'Morning,' he whispers.

I open my eyes in time to see him lower his tongue first to my left breast and now to the right. Within moments, he is on top, inside. We rarely kiss in the mornings, Luke presses his face against my neck or on to the pillow. We are tired, but this is the way he likes to wake up and I do not complain. It is neither hell nor heaven. Sometimes an angle or thrust will rip me from my thoughts and excite me, but mostly I think of other things. Sometimes, I think of other men. Of course, I have thought of his dad. The other day, for my sins, I even thought of my own.

On Monday night, I had a dream in which Dad and I were

swimming in a pool similar to the one at the Old Rectory. Dad was teaching me to swim, I could feel his strong hands underneath me, warm in the water's cool. Then I felt them were I wanted them most – on my neck, my breasts, between my legs. I continued to splash, pretending to ignore him. An innocent swim. Wouldn't you swim better without your suit, my Pea? I agreed I would. He kissed my neck as he undid the straps. I turned on my back and he held me in the water. He put his hands then lips on my breasts. When he entered me, I felt a complete and shameless joy. Then, we descended into sleep. The next morning, I made love to Luke with such back-scratching passion that my feelings for him were almost restored. Almost.

Today he comes, vigorously, then gets up almost immediately to shower.

'It's getting late,' he says when he returns, a towel around his waist. I prefer him unshaven. 'Are you getting up?'

'Give me a minute.'

As Luke busies himself with his wedding uniform (he loves the meticulous detailing of it, the detachable collar, the gold studs and cufflinks) I wonder what kind of woman I am, to be lying in his bed when I dream of his father. But what can I do, when what I feel, feels like love?

It feels like love, but it may be nothing of the sort. Beyond the brief dreamy coddling of one's mind, the emotion has no common diagnosis; beyond its epiphany in erotic lust, I am no expert. I have seen love stretched until it burst when Dad killed himself instead of losing me, but I have known almost none since his death. Lesser men have come and gone and I have thought it would be liberating to love and be loved by them, but none have given me what I once knew. So why does this seem different? Can I trust this feeling now?

I do not know. I understand that I cannot be in love with Charles. He and I have spent almost no time together. Nor am I blind to the obvious, that he is avuncular, stimulating, sexy and, I know, old enough to be my father. Kaz is right. Those crazed shrinks to whom mother insisted on sending me when I was just fifteen and things had turned sour would have a field day with this attraction. Twelve years ago, they took it upon themselves to help me release 'the anger I felt towards Daddy' by trying to get me to cast him as some kind of criminal, a pervy academic, an incestuous Humbertian paedophile. They didn't understand it was Mother I despised, that the perversion was theirs in attempting to implant a history that did not happen. Mother must have primed them, but the twisted way in which she tried to make me hate Dad – how could I conceivably 'let go' of something I had never felt? – merely damaged herself. I loved him, no tricks could change that. And now I think I love this man, this older man, my boyfriend's father.

Oh, it feels like love. I tense and weaken at the mention of Charles's name. I stare at photos of him in the flat. I don't need to close my eyes to picture him stepping from the pool or to see the drips down his body become my tongue. Thinking of it, of kissing him from head to toe and back, makes me ache inside with want. I regret my cowardice for not asking him to kiss me when we were alone. For not kissing his lips myself. I have excited myself with dreams of that kiss and it has left me exhaling, with every breath, the sigh of his name.

And yet it doesn't make me smile. Falling in love should feel like spring, but the dots have been thrown into confusion again. I have no life in London that does not include Luke, and Kaz, and our mutual friends. Should I leave it all behind for something that may, as Kaz insists, just pass? No, I don't have the courage for that. And, besides, I have spent my life running.

'I'll get up soon,' I say, but soon becomes later, of course, because I'm me. Then we are running late and Luke begins giving me the silent treatment, pacing back and forth wearing his jacket and jangling his keys, which of course is completely unnecessary and makes me take even longer with my eye shadow, just to serve him right. We leave with him refusing to speak to me, which in a way is a relief. There is a void in me where there used to be gratitude and love. We take a cab.

The church is full when we arrive, and it seems the whole

congregation turns to stare at Luke and me when we come in. I feel underdressed (Luke couldn't resist a little dig about my unshowy grey skirt and black jacket) amid such finery – hats huge enough for ospreys to nest in, outfits that might as well be sown from fifty pound notes, so precious is their fabric and cut. The women frown at me. I feel as one does when there's a kid who won't quit staring at you on the train: bad for no good reason. To make it worse, we are led to a pew behind Luke's ex, Jemima March-Phillipps, who is wearing the jazziest hat of all under which, literally, I feel shadowed. I was so keen to be invited, now I wish I could run away. It makes me feel homesick for the gang back home. Kally Dieter's was the last wedding I went to, and the most fun I have had for years. This feels like a funeral.

The mood lifts little through the service. Dominic's bride is a believer. She has chosen a young vicar steeped in an untemporal earnestness. In his address, he likens marriage to a temperamental house plant. I am uncomfortable with the message, which would no doubt please him. The truth is that I have done almost nothing to nurture my relationship with Luke, and with the first bloom gone, I feel helpless for the future. There are readings: the soppy 'Desiderata' and something whimsical about trees; then songs: two arias from *The Magic Flute* lacking magic. It is a relief when the service is over.

The reception is being held in a house by the Thames. It is a bright, cool afternoon and with the sky blue for the first time in weeks it feels good to walk beside the fast-flowing river. Luke reaches for my hand, and I let him take it. It is because of my guilt that such gestures make me fond of Luke, and it's because I have something to hide that I am more explicit with my affection. I tighten my grip.

'That's a good crew,' he says, pointing out a passing Eight sending pretty, even waves to lap against the pebbles at low tide. There is a splendid perfection to the slicing of the blades into the river. I think the precision seems particularly Anglican, and enjoy it.

Ahead of us is the bride's Georgian house where the reception is being held. I can see the top half of a marquee behind the tall brick wall separating the garden from the river's towpath. It's directly into this that we are led.

It's an impressive and beautiful sight, easily the grandest tent I have ever been inside. It smells faintly of wet grass, of canvas and flowers and, in fact, there are flowers wherever I look – in displays at the centre of each of the thirty or so tables, in huge vases at each corner of the tent and, most prettily of all, curling with ivy up each of the marquee poles. Luke seems less interested in them than in a board to which are pinned details of the seating plan.

'We're on the same table,' he tells me.

I am relieved. Three months on and still I feel nervous and foreign coming into large groups like this. The truth remains that I am not plugged in to this tight network of British people. I don't know their schools and houses and cousins and histories, their gossip and small talk. When Luke's friends are kind to me it feels like pity. The stray mongrel who wandered in and will wander out. I am patted, fed, housed. And today I am in the grip of a deeper fear, the result of my mental treachery. If discovered, I would be more outcast than outsider. I wave at Kaz as if we have been separated for months.

She is clustered in a group with the usual suspects: Jim, Killjoy, Tom Henessy and his girlfriend, Bibi, Jemima March-Phillipps with wedding hat but minus yacht, Charlie, Rupert Swan and Emma the teacher. They are all decked out in their finery. I wish I had worn something else. Even the boys, with their bright waistcoats and ties, outshine me.

As we approach, Charlie begins to applaud. Luke mumbles something under his breath and drops my hand. 'Garton, are you causing trouble again?'

They have a habit, these men, of using their surnames to address one another. I figure it has something to do with the schools in which, mentally, some of them seem to be still boarding.

'Nothing to do with you, mate. It's Goose we're celebrating.'

'I'm always celebrating Goose,' Kaz says with a grin. I give her a kiss hello. She saves me.

Smothering me in an embrace, Charlie asks, 'Any chance of a Chinese together?'

'Oh shit.' I say, playfully pushing him away. 'Don't tell me you've got one of my articles.'

'Oh yes, I do.' Triumphantly, Charlie waves a crumpled page of fax paper in the air like a political orator with his speech. 'In fact...' from another pocket, he pulls out a bunch of other pages. I recognize my photo and by-line at the head of each. 'I have in my hand articles written by Miss Portia Mills on, what have we got here? The Englishness of Piccadilly ... prostitute ads in telephone boxes ... how the English drink their tea with teabags not from tea pots ... Prince Charles planting a tree in North London ... this one I like: how English boys have "cocktail-party relationships with their parents because they were shipped to school aged seven".'

'Let me see that,' demands Luke.

'All in good time. These two you'll like more, one about how England "has been forced to parody herself since the world has decreed England the home of fancy writing on cookie packets, of a manner of speech for car ads, of butler uniforms and proud manners, and another...'

'That's not very nice,' says Jim, pinching my butt. He is looking red-faced. Been knocking back the champagne, most likely. This crew drinks more than any people I've met.

'Oh, and Luke,' he continues, ''fraid I can't let you take the wife off to Sezchuan Garden again. Can't trust you.'

Luke glares at me. 'Porsh, what's this about?'

'Oh, he doesn't know,' whinnies Killjoy. Then, to Luke, 'Don't you know?'

I can't figure what Luke sees in Camilla. They've a history, I think; before Jim. 'Rusty roof, damp cellar' is what Charlie says about her, and he claims to know. I find it distasteful to think of her naked with that spread of blue-white skin gingers have, the veins visible like handwriting through a cheap envelope.

'How the hell are you, Portia?' asks Rupert Swan. He speaks like a nasally bagpipe, you can tell when he's about to begin because of the warm-up. He gives me a beery kiss that's all grin and no lips.

'I think I'm OK, thanks. Except Luke's giving me that queer look of his.'

'He's a master of queer things,' Charlie informs us wryly. 'Aren't you?'

Luke says, 'I don't like not knowing what you're all talking about.'

Charlie announces that to save Luke the misery of tumbling over any more double negatives ('I tell my classes just to cross them both out,' Emma interrupts with a giggle) he will read to him one of the pieces he had sent from Toronto. 'This article is entitled "Spring Rolls and Silver Linings".'

'We've already heard it once,' Killjoy protests.

'I'm going to find a drink,' I announce. Don't want it assumed I asked for this attention.

'Hang on, hang on, Goosey. This isn't a pub. Besides, there are a couple of things I want to know.'

'Why are you doing this?'

'He's trying to get your attention. He wants to fuck you,' says Tom Henessy in that matter of fact way British people have when they are being obscene. The remark gets a disdainful look from Bibi, Tom's half-mad, half-Swedish girlfriend. The darkness all Scandinavians have seems to have fermented in her, become something less manageable. Tom, an investment banker of some sort with big hair and a rugby player's physique, seems to me to have everything – looks, wit, brains, a highly paid career – and must, I suppose, enjoy the challenge Bibi presents. Me, I like her skewed vision of things.

Charlie continues regardless. 'All I want to know is, one, do you mean, Miss Goose, when you write, and I quote: "My duck pancake reminded me of a rolled-up carpet filled with a dead body, just like the one I had watched Jessica Fletcher discover on *Murder, She Wrote*, but it tasted much more delicious," end quote, that your pancakes tasted more delicious than Jessica Fletcher aka, as we all know, Angela Lansbury, or more delicious than a carpet?'

I say, 'I'll be back soon.'

'One more thing. You write, "I ran to the local grocery store with its quaint stacks of chocolate biscuits, jam, tinned soups and unappealing fruit and Indians." Do you mean the Indians were unappealing? If so, I'm going to have to lodge a complaint with your editor.'

'I meant the fruit was unappealing.'

'Actually, that's unclear.'

'Do you think I should practise my clarity of speech?'

'I think so.'

I smile, 'Go. Fuck. Yourself. How's that? Now, who wants a drink?'

Don't know why, but Charlie has upset me. Must be because I'm questioning being in London and being here with these people who have all been to the same schools where they were either fucked up the arse by the same boys or toyed with the same fluffy bunnies that Princess Diana once fed and groomed. As I push my way through them, all of them melding into one with their morning coats and pointy noses and guffaws, I feel a surge of homesickness for Kally and Moira and Iain. I rang him at *Crow's Nest* a couple of days ago, a mistake because he was full of gossip about Amy finally getting into Jamie Hendrick's pants after four years of wanting him and that made me feel as if I had deserted them and taht they would never have me back – falling out of touch with people is such loss, I feel it deep in my stomach. And these the same few I wanted to run from three months ago. But the grass was not really greener there, was it?

'Hello, Portia. Glad you could make it.'

'Oh, Dominic. Congratulations. How does it feel?'

'Like S and M,' he whispers. 'Bloody good even though I've got an effing great rope around my neck. But don't tell the wife. Where's Luke?'

'Over there with Charlie.'

'You two'll be next, eh?'

He gives me a knowing kiss and leaves. Dominic's nice, he seems to have escaped that English coolness. I pick up a glass of champagne from the table and turn back towards my man. Look at this scene. Admittedly, it is movie-perfect, and yet everyone is so well-behaved and middle-aged, standing upright with their champagne flutes tit-high while wearing those people-pleasing smiles that ensure the true feelings are kept wrapped tight as the canapés themselves. You should have seen me and Moira at Kally's wedding last year, we were dancing on the tables and kissing strangers and whooping it up with the excitement of two people who looked like they'd found each other's match. Despite his assurances otherwise, I'm not sure I give Dominic and his bride a year if their ceremony is any clue to the smoky dampness to come.

Since I know only a sprinkling of people, and they are all with Luke, I make my way back to where I left them. Kaz stops me halfway.

'Don't leave me,' I plead.

'Darling, do you want me to pee on the matting? Oh, I better warn you that Luke's somewhat shirty about that thing you wrote. He thinks you've stepped over the line.'

'I never know where he draws them. That's my problem.'

'I've got to go, I'm bursting.'

I sidle up beside Luke, who barely turns towards me, and then stand feeling like a sixth-grade exchange student in a foreign land while Jemima, dolled-up in pricey pastels, shoots daggers at me (she wants Luke back, I know it) while Luke and the others talk and joke about people and places that remain foreign.

Three months has made no difference at all. It is as if I am stuck in the porch of a house I can't get into. Perhaps this is the way it was always going to be but I arrived assuming that, because of Dad, because of my blood, I would be more in tune with the community of England I had imagined. Isn't that the way countries work? You don't need to know everyone from your land to share habits and jokes and values and beliefs?

Listening to the conversation here – a beater's shoot at Freddy Somebody-somebody's place, speculation about characters on a soap opera (*Brookside*) I have never watched, the Tories' chances, *The X Files*, a football player called Eric Cantona, rumination on who has a crush on Chandler from *Friends* – I realize the only thing that really links me with the others is the American TV shows. But I can get that anywhere. I don't want to belong to some polymorphous, borderless, *X Files* watching, thirty-something clan, as if we are just so many tiny satellites listlessly floating in space. Worse still, I now find myself getting bored by the racist, anti-feminist, chauvinistic witticisms and put-downs that two months ago I thought clever and funny and proof that I had landed on an island of intellectual kings. Now I don't know whether I am supposed to laugh, or to clap at how clever the joke-teller has proved himself to be.

From behind me, a waiter arrives to refresh our glasses. As I hold mine out my jaw literally drops open. It's Derek. I don't believe it. He hasn't changed a day, it seems, he is the same scrawny skinhead he was ten years ago. 'Derek?' I say. 'Derek?' The man looks at me, quizzically. 'Oh, God, I'm sorry, you're someone else. Sorry.'

The others have fallen silent. I am blushing, I know it. How stupid of me. Derek must be thirty-plus now while the man I approached is probably no more than twenty-two. Everyone in our circle is looking at me.

'Who do you know that looks like him?' asks Luke. He is trying to distance himself from me. That's cheap.

'Derek,' I reply, looking him in the eye. 'He looked a lot like Derek.'

'Who's Derek?' Rupert Swan enquires, sounding strict and parental.

'Derek was some English boyfriend Portia had,' Luke explains, dismissively. 'He was a homeless skinhead she met begging on the street.'

'She is standing right in front of you, and he had to Luke,' I say sharply. Is he deliberately trying to annoy me, Luke with his smug laugh and boyish face and job in the city? 'I told you that. Remember?'

'Might we have struck the weeniest of nerves?' stirs Charlie, thinking he is being funny. The boy's a lawyer through and through. Won't let anything by. It is a very English habit to pick people apart, look for the weakness in characters. Charlie is the worst of our friends but he is not alone. God knows, I had to get away from Canada, from its healthy chirpiness and bicycling shorts and goodwill, but there have been times I have found myself craving some pure Canadian enthusiasm. For all the British pride in decency, I find it somehow indecent that they find fault in so much.

'I'm not the one getting wound up, Charlie. It's Luke who has this thing about Derek. He's paranoid I've been mixing with the wrong sort.'

'Or worried that's precisely what he's doing.'

'What do you mean?'

'Nothing. Nothing. Only joking.'

To my right, I catch Emma making a face at Killjoy. My heart plummets. Is that what they all think? That I am to be dispensed with because I am not well-bred enough for Luke? That I am no Jemima March-Phillipps with her mansion in Wiltshire, her yacht, her Armani this and Voyage that? That I don't carry a beloved Yorkshire terrier in a fucking Prada bag or drive a matt silver Alfa-Romeo or have friends called Tara and Jock and Hugo and Minty and Gus and Porks and Jasper and Ness and Giles? It wouldn't surprise me.

'I think a skinhead beggar sounds delightful,' chimes Killjoy.

'Oh fuck right off, Camilla, would you?' I say, surprising even myself with the vehemence of my tone. Although of course I mean it, from day one we two have been chalk and cheese, I know it is a mistake, that I should have kept it swallowed.

Somehow, despite all the noise around us, we seem to have created and contained a silence in our circle. My hands are shaking, I don't know what has made me this upset, perhaps the pressure has been building slowly. I am going to let it go.

I can't let it go. I say, 'I'm sorry, but it bugs me that Luke has dismissed Derek without even meeting him. Just, just because he didn't go to some school Luke's heard of and just because he doesn't know any skinheads himself.'

Luke has straightened his back with annoyance at my attack. 'Portia, you told me he was deported from Canada for throwing bricks through BMW windows. What am I expected to think?'

'We've got a Beemer,' Jim chips in. Chirpy, chippy-in Jim, he's never rude. He is thick, of course. Maybe the rest are too smart for their own good. No, that can't be. Jemima is no brain surgeon. She is a party planner of sorts. Of this sort, I think.

'I'm sorry, Jim. Derek used to think people with BMWs had too much money.'

'And we're expected to like this person?' asks Killjoy.

'No, but if someone hurled a brick at me, at least I would want to know why.'

'I've got some suggestions,' says Tom, grinning.

'It's not funny, Tom. I never guessed you Brits would be so insular. I mean – people not being able to get the right sort of jobs if they're wearing the wrong kind of shoes? That's petty.'

'What?' says Jemima.

Good, Jemima. One syllable's about it for you, isn't it? Christ knows how you manage with vol-au-vent. Then again, double and triple barrels are probably your territory.

I say, 'Ask Luke,' and light myself a cigarette.

Luke is disdainful of my inability to distinguish between people who are common and those who are not. He explains to the others, in an unspeakably patronizing tone, how I am unable to determine a man's class from a glance at his shoes. There is a mumbling, and it is agreed that men's shoes matter. If I am to understand and write about England, they tell me, I need to know that shoes matter.

'The moccasins don't make the man,' Charlie explains, seeming pleased with himself, 'but they say a lot about him.'

'Oh so, so, so all Derek had to do was go to one of those tweedy shops in Saint whatever street—'

'Jermyn.'

'Right, Jermyn, and kit himself up and he'd have got a job, would he?'

'He wouldn't go there,' suggests Emma. 'He wouldn't. That's why it's an easy way to tell those people apart.'

'Exactly, thank you. To discriminate against those people.'

'Not at all,' Tom says. 'It's a way of telling whether someone's going to share your values and background without needing to ask.'

'Shoes first, ideas second, equals discrimination in my book.'

Luke says, 'I had no idea know you were so PC.'

'I'm not PC, Luke. But if I don't dress in the right clothes, does that make me one of those people?'

As if it was rehearsed, three people speak at once. 'It's different,' they say, 'You're Canadian,' or words to that effect.

'Out of the loop,' adds Bibi. It is one of the first things she has said, she's had that drugged expression on her face, but in her smile I can see that she is resigned to her situation, that she thinks I should be too. Do what you like, you're out of the loop.

But it doesn't end there. Now I am lectured, for what seems like hours, about how England is what it is because of the hidden class pyramid, everyone wanting to do good by the person one rung up the ladder, all the way up to the monarch. Hidden pyramid? Some fucking camouflage with this crowd. I don't think the Toms and Jims and Lukes of this land have anything to do with its greatness. They are deluding themselves.

'Porsh, don't make that face. We were only pulling your leg.'

'Have I missed something?' asks Kaz, returning.

I pull Luke aside. 'I'm going. I've got a headache.'

'Don't be silly, Porsh. You can't leave now.'

'I can.'

'You can't, possibly. You've got a place-name, and everything.'

'I don't care. Tell Dom I wasn't feeling well.'

'But, Porsh—' He grasps my arm but I twist away.

'No, Luke.'

Even when I hear Kaz call my name, I don't turn back. I can't face seeing all their gloating faces. I stride out of the marquee, through the garden and onto the towpath where, suddenly, I feel ridiculously overdressed. But it seems fitting that I am walking against the flow of the river now.

I was waiting for something to crack. Everything that has been great was founded on nothing. Luke's friends, Luke's money, Luke's apartment, Luke's body, Luke's love. It has all been so flippant. It makes me feel lonely. Why do I even have to think? Look at Jim, he's happy and he doesn't think. But my heart feels heavy. Is that pathetic? I don't know how much pain others feel when they are burned and scratched and broken. I can't begin to fathom the extent of other people's suffering, know how often they too have thought of leaping into a busy road or jumping off a bridge into a river such as this. We all of us cry more than we admit, at least I am wise to that. Mother accuses me of self-pity, with all the weakness that implies, but I can't help sinking so fast and deeply that I get scared I won't climb up again. Sometimes it begins as a joke – look at me, I'm not smiling – but then I find myself up to my knees then my waist and over my head with sorrow. What is that, if not genuine?

Oh, I do feel shame that there is bravery and decency and love wherever I turn, when I see the dying and the homeless and the sick, yet what can I do when, snap, fast as that, I sink into this space that is already inside, that Dad's hanging shaped. It feels real to me. It was real after he died and, when I am jolted like this, it feels as it did back then when the earth opened up black under my feet. But I can't seem to cling to a melancholic grey.

A couple are walking their dog towards me. I don't want them to see me crying. I turn to face the river, my elbows on the rough, concrete wall. Now that the sun has dipped beneath a building, the river has become more forbidding. It is low tide and in this shady light I see a large sodden branch that looks at first like a body on its side, one shoulder lifted in pain. Around it, lumps of wood are sticking up in the mud like hands from Pompeii's lava. What are they saying? That death is terrible or that life is worth clinging to?

This river has been cleaned up since Charles Dickens loved it, but there is debris enough to prove it runs through a living city: rusting cans, a spokeless bicycle wheel, glass and plastic bottles. The sleek Eight have left the current to create its own patterns and eddies. Now there is menace in it. And yet, as I stare at the water's surface it lifts me to think how much the river has seen. Two thousand years of suffering so much worse than my own. Plagues and fires, not a father but a whole family gone. It has seen traitor's heads skewered to the Gatehouse at Southwark, it has lapped over bodies mauled by Boadicea's swords, heard tragic prayers whispered by Lady Jane Grey and Anne Boleyn. And I am here. I am here. This is what I wanted, to be in London. Luke and his friends can try as hard as they like to shrink my England with pettiness, but it's still here if I want it. I belong to this river. History is reflected in its depths. Henry the Eighth and Shakespeare and Wren and Gladstone and Orwell and Cromwell, Hogarth's drunks and earls and queens, Guy Fawkes and Wat Tyler, Thomas à Becket and Chaucer, I know almost nothing of London's history but this drop that I have thrills me. The Thames is Dad's blood and my own. Britain is not great because it is run by men with the right shoes, Luke Bingham, whatever you say. Nine hundred years and no class revolution, there's the mistake, the apathy. It is great because of what the Thames has seen, because of what it was, because of its passion. That can't be taken away. It just can't.

I wrap my coat around me and walk in the direction I think is home. Thing is, I don't want to get there too fast, sit there with nothing but the TV for company and knowing what a fool I made of myself. I am not good company for myself.

After half-an-hour or so, my route takes me through an ugly working-class area. Grey, quadrilateral towers, bald squares of grass. If I had come to England with Derek, I know it would have been to a place such as this. Would I have felt any more at home? It is not the England I had imagined. Instead of the softly lit pastures this is a land of patchy grass, mud and trash. Instead of villages and churches, these forlorn trees, these shops that wouldn't inspire anyone to consume. A Spar with a broken window-pane; John's video store with Jean-Claude Van Damme and Arnold Schwarzenegger posters in the window and a fluorescent orange sign reading 'We Stock Adult'; a fish and chip shop; a newsagent, its windows shielded with meshing. Huh, there are people there. Of course, it's lottery night, a rollover week. Eight million, I think. I don't play because the disappointment of not winning every week would affect my life more than the prize itself. Eight million pounds would buy none of the things I most want.

But is this the real England? Cheap and shoddy goods? Graffiti-strewn walls? A bleak outlook, whichever way you look out? Suddenly, a group of kids running my way scare me. Probably, I shouldn't be here, dressed like this. I don't know, it's not my city. I can't even trust my fear. I pull my bag closer to me, but they pass. I am lost, unsure even of the right direction, so as soon as I see a mini-cab office I decide to give up this cheerless walk and return back home.

Inside at Luke's, my keys crack against the wooden table. It makes me think of the proverb about a sheet of paper seeming empty only when the first mark is made. The noise underlines my loneliness.

I look outside. The streets are quiet, though there are windows bright around the square. I can't help thinking those lights are shining on lovers being lovers, making lover's love. I can't help hearing the noise of the marquee in my head. Memories sieve discontentment with staggering speed, and tease us with snippets. I hear Kaz calling my name, and Dominic welcoming me sweetly. I imagine my empty space at the table and Luke making his excuses. I feel ashamed, like a little girl, sulking for the sake of it. Oh, but this is not what I dreamed.

Was it only a week since Charles was here? I wish he would come back. He would tell me what to do. He is wise like that.

I turn on the TV, but it is insidious how quickly it drains and deadens me. Anyway, it's terrible here – not enough choices. Music instead? Baroque is meant to calm the soul. Now I roll a joint that I admire for its tidy thinness. It's a professional job. I close my eyes, and lean back on the moss-green sofa and take solace in this edge-softening drag. Maybe Mother's right, perhaps I am scared of happiness. I could find an unquestioning contentment with Luke.

Mother! She has had fourteen years of such loneliness wondering 'what if'? We speak often these days. The ocean between us has helped mend many of the tears in our relationship, but it has also given her license to start offering the sort of advice most mothers give. She has accused me of developing a European attitude by seeing my problems as insoluble. North Americans, she said, assume that every problem has a solution. Is there one? Whichever way I look, the future scares me. Leave Luke? Go home? Start again in England? Oh, if Charles would only do what's right for us. He must know that it would be right.

I finish the joint, willing Charles to call. Suddenly, the phone rings. I rush to it, answer it eagerly, but it's a double-glazing firm. But why should I wait? Perhaps he is waiting for me. I dial the house in the country before I have had a chance to change my mind. It rings three times, and then Victoria picks up. Quickly, I hang up, then wish I hadn't. I can't think straight today. Like this I was even before I got stoned. The phone rings again. I answer it.

'Hello, it's Victoria.'

'Oh, hi.'

'Did you just call the house?'

'When?'

'A moment ago. I pressed 1471 and it gave me your number. Perhaps it was Luke.'

'He's not here.'

'Well, that's very strange.'

'Maybe, I . . . I could have hit the redial button. I was about to use the phone. Sorry.'

'No, no, no trouble at all. There was just nobody at the end of the line.'

'Sorry if it was me.'

'That's all right. How are you, Portia?'

'Same as usual, you know.'

'Good, good. All right, then.'

'All right.' I pause, then quickly ask, 'Now I'm on the line, is Mr Bingham there?'

'Yes, he is. Can I pass him a message?'

'Well, it was about, he said I should call him, sometime, about, um . . . what he said was that I should call him about maybe going to an exhibition one day.'

'Shall I ask him?'

'Thanks.'

It will be a sign if he comes to the phone.

'Hello.'

'Hi, it's Portia.'

'Yes, hello.'

'I was wondering about the exhibition. I saw it was on.'

'Well, I'd love to go. Let me think. Why don't I call you from the office when I have my diary in front of me?'

Oh, he doesn't want his wife to hear . . .

'Great, I'll be here.'

'Jolly good then, we'll speak on Monday.'

When I hang up, a smile breaks on my face, and I feel suddenly not so bad after all.

I am stoned and probably more than a little drunk by the time Luke comes home, sooner than I expected. He glares at me, says nothing, and then disappears into the bedroom to take off his suit. He is wearing rust-red moleskin trousers and a navy Ralph Lauren shirt when he returns. He sits opposite me, and lights a cigarette.

'Luke, I'm sorry about before.'

I can tell that my apology disarms him. I am usually stubborn. I hold out the new joint I'm smoking, only my second, but he shakes his head. The way that he is perched on the edge of the sofa, it's clear he's unhappy.

'I think you like deliberately trying to bugger things up,' he says, carefully tapping ash into one of the shell ashtrays his cleaning lady brings him, and which he is too polite to throw out. 'You like things being upside down.'

'Perhaps my normal's your upside down. Anyway, I'm an upside down girl, like in that Billy Joel song.'

'That was "Uptown Girl". You know that. Don't try to be annoying.'

'I'm not. I'm trying not to make too much of it. I've said I'm sorry.'

He takes off his glasses and wipes at one of the lenses. I think he looks sweet with his eyes all screwy. He needs to do this more often, to see the world out of focus, disordered.

'Well, I think you should call Camilla and apologize.'

'You are kidding, aren't you? For what?'

'For telling her to fuck off. I really don't understand what you don't like about her.'

'Her hair. I hate people with ginger hair.'

'Don't be ridiculous.'

'Her teeth, then. I don't know. Because she makes me feel like an outsider.'

'Rubbish. You've invented that.'

'Please don't be mad,' I say, joining him on the sofa. I owe Luke. I might even love him a little, for all the reasons I hate him. I love him because he is so English and decent and predictable and kind and because he thinks that he knows what's best for me, and wants just that. And yet he doesn't make me struggle for breath as his father does. No, not breathless with you, Lukey. Look at you, wanting to forgive but feeling you shouldn't. You can't look me in the eye, can you? But not because you hate me. I know you don't hate me.

'You don't notice how your friends make me feel like an outsider.'

'It's always somebody else's fault with you, isn't it?'

'No. Yes. I don't know. I said sorry. Besides, today, I was just being me.'

Luke looks suddenly serious when he gazes at me, and his reply sounds rather forlorn. 'Yes.' His eyes move to the TV control. He picks it up, switches the box on. 'Yes, I do know that.'

SEVEN

In order to cope successfully with the tensions of difficult experiences in life, everyone should have a healthy attitude and a healthy body.

AMA Family Medical Guide

When you eat *shabu-shabu*, a wooden skimmer is provided so the scum can be scooped off the surface of the boiling broth. Since the Japanese are conscientious about such things, I've wondered whether they have a similar tool for the grime and skin and semen that gathers in the soap's lather to float on bath water and collect against the dams where skin touches porcelain. I can't understand what the English have against showers. Baths leave me feeling less than clean.

And there is something else. Is Luke's sperm still alive in my bath? At North Toronto we were taught that it can live for up to six days, not Luke's in particular (that would have been odd) but the feisty seeds in general. I thought it cause for celebration and optimism. If the will to create is so strong in such a mindless purse of genes, and against such odds, shouldn't we at least acknowledge our debt by living our lives in an equally upbeat manner? Wouldn't living simply for our bodies, each of which has its own mulish momentum, allow us to bypass such unnecessary complications as purpose and morality and value? It seems odd, almost tyrannical, that our minds should submit to our bodies when we are hungry or thirsty or cold only to conspire to deny us through guilt and logic and perceived goodness other less physiologically vital desires. As I lie in the cooling water I can feel my body craving something that my mind wants to repel. My body wants my lover's father. It craves Charles. It has included him in its meaning. Try as I might, and as I have, there is nothing about that I can do. It has been almost a month since he surprised me in the flat and though through circumstance my longing has been less immediate, although I have continued to exist as his son's lover in and out of bed, I have not purged Charles from my thoughts. Not at all.

I close my eyes and lather soap onto my shoulders and breasts and dream these are his hands. My palms linger against nipples engorged by the thought of him. I bend my knees and brush the sponge down my thighs to where I long to feel him caress and enter me, and I catch my breath even with this inanimate, watery touch. Today, though, something will be decided. Today, at last, I am seeing him. My heart is pattering a thrilled rhythm fast as the excitable footfalls of a child. Though I am nervous, perhaps scared, certainly guilt-ridden, my body is celebrating the fact that the day has arrived.

Out of the bath, I dry my washed hair and it's not bad, there is an ad man's bounce to it when I'm done with the dryer. Don't want to look too primped, not for lunch, but it can only do me good to look my best. I go easy on the make-up, just a little on the lips and eyes, no need to exaggerate. I envy the prettiest girls here, the Lady Joannas and her type, for having a pale, natural beauty that seems old-fashioned. Their skin would be spoiled with colouring. I am too imperfect.

I dress in a Katharine Hamnett pinstripe jacket I found in a thrift store in Camden Town. I would never have worn something like this in Toronto, but Luke's crowd dress themselves expensively, and I feel shoddy enough as it is.

At twelve, I leave. It is drizzling again. The cloud cover has returned and, although the greyness suits the city and its people, blends with the slate roofs and heavy stone buildings and dour dreamlessness, it has made me feel claustrophobic, questioning. I have lost entirely that old sense of abandonment.

I can still relish the luxurious feel of London cabs. In this one, a laminated advertisement for a dating agency is attached to the back of one of the fold-up chairs. A couple exchanging a glance, he on an ascending escalator, she descending. 'Have you ever wondered?' it asks. It reminds me of meeting Luke. If that was choice instead of fate, is this? Should I ignore Charles? Keep walking by? No, I can't do that. I am not so strong.

I am a few minutes late to the museum, but Charles isn't here. I wait where we arranged, upstairs beside the shop, worrying I have got the wrong day or that he doesn't want to see me after all, when I see him coming up the stairs, two at a time. Luke wouldn't do that in a place like this. He wouldn't think it right.

'Portia, hello.'

Oh, the flesh of him is everything I remembered it to be. I blush scarlet red when he cups my upper arm and gives me a kiss.

'I'm terribly sorry. We've had something of a crisis at work and—'

'Oh, if you don't have time for this, then—'

'No, no, absolutely I do. This is a treat for me.'

'Me too.'

'Good. I must say, you're looking lovely.'

'Thanks, it's just, um—'

'I'm sure you'll distract people from the sculptures.'

'I doubt it.'

'We shall see.'

We skip the line for tickets. Charles flashes a membership card and signs the book, plus one. Plus one of me. Exhibit A, your worship, in Bingham versus Bingham. 'I could tell they weren't father and daughter,' the guard would testify. But lovers?

No, we don't look like lovers. You can recognize lovers in art galleries, it says something about art's power how it turns couples touchy feely, allows each their own romantic interpretation. For months after Dad died, I saw morbidity in every work of art. Even youth contained the promise of death.

The first gallery is devoted to Giacometti's early paintings; self-portraits and family members. The stillness in this room makes me feel tense. I walk slightly ahead of Charles, my heart beating with such bullish determination I find it hard to focus when I am next to him. The sensations of last month have not diminished at all. I wish I could touch him. He is leaning in and looking at the canvases in detail. I can't keep my eyes off him. I want to touch him.

'I'll be next door,' I say.

'All right. I'll catch you up.'

It is more crowded here where the sculptures begin. The pieces contain such explicit sexual tension that I am slightly flustered by the creation of such intimacy among we strangers in the gallery. I wonder if anyone else is as breathless as I. Is Charles? I move to the far side of a cabinet from where I can spy on him. I want him to look at me, to prove I'm in his mind. I decide to give him ten seconds. At eight, he glances up. Although he doesn't see me, he skips a few canvases to come my way.

I have turned to an abstract wooden sculpture when he reaches me. We stand opposite one another to view it. The transparent case seems too flimsy a separation, and the piece itself is almost pornographic: man and woman, a cupped vulva, a sharp, violent phallus. I am embarrassed. Is this why Charles insisted we come? The museum seems to have become even quieter. I am shaking. When I lift my eyes, Charles is looking directly at me.

'It's wonderful, isn't it?'

'It is.'

Again, I have to walk away. Now this, a bronze: *Woman with her Throat Cut*. It's obscene and beautiful at the same time, bones and guts and an orgasmic arch to the body. It's me for the last month. Did Charles want to tease me? And more, more of the same, always, it's the man violating the woman or else men striding while the women are upright, in control of the space around them. So unlike me here.

I am usually distracted in museums. I walk through them wondering around which corner the exhibits will finally end, when I will have added the experience and the postcards to my life. Not today. These sculptures are making me feel curiously raw. When I reach a plaster titled 'Hands holding a void' I feel a remarkably sensuous connection with the artist that hits me before any intellectual response. It's as if the piece was created for me alone.

'Charles,' I say, reaching for him and taking his arm. He has let me hold him, I suddenly realize, 'look at this.'

'I recognize this. I believe he sculpted it soon after his father died.'

'You're kidding.' It is as precise a representation of the hopelessness and horror I felt after Dad's suicide as anything I have seen. It was a void nothing could fill, an emptiness I was convinced could never leave. Charles has such an uncanny understanding of what must appeal to me.

We reach soon the most famous sculptures, the willowy bronzes that made Giacometti unique. None affect me as the piece before, but I do feel an empathy with them such as usually alludes my aggressively self-conscious mind. Recently, I have been feeling similarly alone, separated from a richer world.

'I never realized quite how imposing they were,' says Charles, whispering in my ear. Oh, I want to suck that breath into my body. 'Or how tall.'

'They make me feel sad, a little.'

'Do they?'

'I wonder if he was as lonely as this. Do you think so?'

'I see it the other way around. If we have evidence that others have felt as we do, that makes us feel less alone, doesn't it?'

'Perhaps it does.'

Is there a message? Shouldn't I be scared of what I feel for him? I want to ask him. I can't keep it inside any more.

We buy postcards, then it isn't far to the restaurant. Thank God there were no dating ads inside the taxi, instead one about saving money if you buy flowers from Interflora, which I say is ridiculous – if you wanted to save money, you shouldn't buy flowers at all. And there I was taking you for a romantic, Charles said, flirting, so I told him that I was romantic, only flowers weren't inspired enough. He said obviously Luke has to work hard to please me. Not hard enough, I didn't reply.

It is snug coming in from the cold, and the smells – warm bread, fried fish, coffee – are good and inviting. The restaurant must seat about thirty people and is crowded now. Yet despite the low ceiling, it is not noisy. There are a few photographs of famous patrons, actors they look like, in wooden frames on the walls. No chrome or track lighting.

Our coats are taken by an ageing Italian man who is missing two of his front teeth. I worry for his footing and spine, but he is surprisingly nimble as he disappears through a swing door. It's a theme restaurant of sorts since the old, Italian staff are hamming it up, playing their parts. They are the type to crowd around a table to sing birthday greetings. Charles is welcomed warmly by a man whose brown suit matches in colour his thick eyebrows, down to the flecks of grey. I am a little disappointed that Charles and he seem to know one another. I had expected to be taken somewhere more discreet, though it is to Charles's credit that he chooses for us a table tucked in a far corner from which two chains of shiny blue and gold Christmas decorations loop amateurishly across the room. I sit with my back to the wall.

He leans forward. Huh, there is mint on his breath. 'They're terribly friendly here, but they have a tendency to dawdle. I recommend we order something to drink straight away.'

'Sounds like my usual restaurant policy.'

'Good. Now, might you want oysters because there's a delicious entre-deux-mers if you do,' he asks, beckoning the waiter back.

My smile is a shell half open; a hint of pearl. 'Ah, no aphrodisiacs for now, thanks.'

'Then what would you say to a white burgundy?'

'I'd say good. Not that I know a burgundy from a Beaujolais.'

'Well, it's a lovely wine,' then to the waiter, 'That one. Yes, twenty-four. Thank you very much.'

Most of the thirty or so people eating here must be forty-five plus. Not that it is stuffy. There is a vacant table to our left and beyond that a middle-aged couple I take to be American since they are wearing bright checks and suntans. I hope they don't want to share with us their impressions of Big Ben. No, that's terrible. I am judging people fast as Luke. In truth, I'm glad they are there. The English become reticent around one another and I want Charles to speak his mind.

The crisp tablecloth on our square table has a pique weave similar to that of Charles's pink shirt. Oddly enough, there is even an ironed crease that jumps from table to man; a connection between the two of us. Charles is looking quite the dandy, come to think about it. His blue silk tie is patterned with neat yellow flowers. I would look twice at him across a crowded room.

'Do you mind if I smoke?'

'Absolutely not.'

I pinch a cigarette from its packet and am about to light it when Charles surprises me and strikes a match from the slim box left in the glass ashtray. I glance down at the cigarette's tip.

'No, no, at me, Portia. Look at me.'

I smile back as much as I can without letting the cigarette drop from my lips. So we are both playing, are we? It may be corny – eyes meeting as a cigarette is lit – and it may have been stolen from the movies of Charles's youth, but I feel an absolute sexual jolt as I stare into his dark brown eyes. I think it a large step taken.

The coordination is not as easy as I would have imagined, and I laugh when I finally feel the smoke come. Charles has to shake the match quickly out of his hand. It must have hurt.

'Did you burn yourself?'

'That would be telling.'

I laugh again. I'm feeling lightheaded, as if I have been cast in an Audrey Hepburn film where everything will smell of roses and look like diamonds and work out right. It is on the tip of my tongue to ask, 'Now that we've found love/What are we going to do with it?' (the song lyric a joke between Kally Dieter and me) but I hold back. This is the best and worst feeling in the world; a painfully sweet anticipation. I lean back.

'Six months ago I would never have dreamed this is where I'd be now. Never.'

'I've always thought it particularly lucky for you and Luke to have run into one another as you did.'

My heart thumps. I have to ask, 'Why?'

'You don't think you were?'

'I don't know. We're different.'

'That's a positive thing, surely it is. Victoria and I disagree all the time.'

'And that worked? Works?'

Say no, give me a hint, it can't be an Eden, can it?

Charles smiles and, I think, evades the answer by lowering his voice to say, 'It does when I make her change her mind.'

I turn my side plate half a revolution. Yes, I am spinning plates. It is a matter of trust, confidence. Don't let go, Pea. I am bold enough to meet Charles's eyes when I say, 'If I hadn't met Luke, we wouldn't be here now. That's what was lucky.'

Charles's eyes widen, just enough for me to notice. He, too, flattens a hand on his side plate. 'There's that as well, of course. Yes.'

It is going to be hard, this lunch, not pushing aside the table, kissing those lips. I get impatient.

The waiter returns with wine. Charles knows what he is doing when he tastes it, I can see that. His approval is given and even I can taste why when I take a sip. I suppose it is what they call complex and I, expensive. Our glasses are tall and thin-stemmed.

The restaurant must be able to absorb the cost of their breaking. In Verdura, our glasses were a half-inch thick.

'Thank you, Charles.' The feel of his name in my mouth is oddly intimate. We chink our glasses together. I try not to think of my first meal with Luke in Toronto. 'It's nice being in the corner, isn't it?'

Charles lowers his eyes, and picks up the menu. He is being more stand-offish than the last time I saw him. I suspect it is the restaurant, they know him here. I take a bread stick from a tall glass and peel off the prophylactic wrapping. Though I crunch the paper tightly in my fist, it unfurls on my side plate. Ha! There's an excess of energy at the table. I smile inwardly as I scoop on to the crisp bread more butter than is good for me. A happy memory has come. I once bet Tom Montino that I could break a grissino to the exact length of his erection; twenty dollars I couldn't afford. We both snapped. Tom went long, I short, and a lesson was learned.

Charles closes the menu. 'How is Luke? I don't think I have seen him since I last saw you.'

'He's going to Canada for a couple of weeks.'

'Yes, Victoria mentioned that. Have you thought of going with him? I'm sure your mother would like to see you.'

'I'd rather be here.'

'That sounds more encouraging. I was a little concerned about you after our chat.'

'Things changed.' I take a drag on my cigarette, grateful for it. 'Didn't they?'

'Well, that is good.'

Didn't Charles hear, understand? He must know what things and how they changed. How we changed them.

'I didn't tell Luke I was seeing you today,' I say. I need Charles to realize where my loyalties lie. I crunch on my bread stick. 'Then again, he tells me you take all of his girlfriends out to lunch, so I don't think he'll be too shocked.'

'He said that?'

'Yes.' Then, casually, 'Don't you?'

'One or two, perhaps. But a long time ago.'

'And did you go swimming with them all?'

'Now that I can't remember,' he chortles.

'I would have thought you would. Remember.'

Why is he suddenly making me do all the sweating, all the work? Why isn't he picking up the scent? Thankfully, the moment of awkwardness, of my fearing I have gone too far, is saved by the waiter's return.

'Portia, do you know what you'd like?' Charles asks.

I catch his eye. Yes, I know: him. Me in his bed every night instead of that wife he has. But he is asking about the food, isn't he? I saw two people being served whitebait. The dish seems out of fashion these days, like crêpes Suzette. I don't know whose strings the fish were pulling to get such a break, but I love eating them, as Dad did. They will remind me of him, but I don't think my mood will be jolted. I am going to follow it with Sole. Something light. I might not be able to stomach too much food later. The waiter pushes a house salad on us too, one for both of us. I like that, the sharing. My glass is filled again, from the dripping bottle. I must have gulped that first one down.

'My father used to eat whitebait at this great place just outside of Toronto. I'd get fish and chips and he'd have the whitebait. I think I must have inherited the same taste.'

'You were obviously very fond of him.'

'Yeah. He was, is, a hard act to follow.'

'In what way?'

'Well, um,' I rub my palm across the table's grainy cloth. 'It's not easy meeting men who can match him.'

'He was a teacher, was he?'

'Yup.'

'Tell me about him. What did he teach?'

'Medieval literature, English mainly – Chaucer, Langland, you know. And he was an expert on French troubadours' lyrics. I remember him showing me lots of lines like, um, like, "A man is really dead when he does not feel some sweet taste of love in his heart." That kind of thing. It was perfect for him because he was a real romantic.'

'Did he move to Toronto for your mother?'

'No. Well, I don't know. I think he stayed for her. She was going to enroll at U of T in his course and they fell for each other when they met. I think it was love at first sight. She wasn't even twenty and he was, I guess, forty already.' Is Charles calculating the equation too? Dad twice Mother's age as I am half Charles's.

'Did your mother ever take the course?'

'No,' I laugh. 'She had me instead.'

'Was your father published?'

'Yeah, he wrote a book on the similarities between Boccaccio and Chaucer, and he published articles here and there, but he was working on his big project for years. I never knew much about it. It was kind of taboo at home. I think it may have had something to do with sex in early literature, but I don't know. Mother gave most of his papers to the university.'

I never read any of Dad's book, but guessed at its illicit nature since he put locks on three of his desk drawers as the work continued. Nor was I allowed near his office when he wasn't at home. It was his only strict rule. Yet I remember the pages piling up. He must have been close to finishing. I have wondered whether it was disappointment in his work which drove him to despair. It is a manageable notion, and one to which I have sometimes clung, but in truth I doubt it.

'I have often regretted not becoming a teacher myself,' says Charles. 'It's what I wanted to do.'

'You would have been good.'

'Oh, I don't know.'

'Yes, you would. You're like Dad was. You're still interested in things. You've got . . . you've still got the wedge of cheese facing the right way. Of course, you'd have had to deal with all those student-professor crushes.'

Charles sniggers. 'Oh, I can't imagine there'd have been too many of those.'

'I disagree.'

He doesn't laugh a second time but seems, rather, to have retreated for a moment into himself. He says, 'It comes as a rather galling shock when you realize that you've run out of time to read the books and learn the languages and instruments you used to think you had the rest of your life for.'

I lean forward on my forearms. 'You're beginning to talk like me. I'm always accused of moaning about what was instead of thinking about what could be.'

'Are you? Well, it's only human to look back now and again. We are all exiles from some state or another.'

Sounding like me, thinking like me. I wish I could stroke that brow of his, run my fingers through his hair, sleep against his chest. 'Luke doesn't think the way you do.'

'He will when he's my age, I'm sure.'

'No. Luke likes knowing what he likes. Makes him feel secure. All of them, actually. They all like being on the same Ferris wheel.'

'I think you're being a little harsh. Every culture has to keep its integrity. It's what we have habits and customs for.'

'But you need some new ideas too.'

Charles leans back and lifts his eyebrows. I adore the creases of his forehead. 'It could be that you're looking in the wrong place for ideas. A friend of mine who owns an art gallery admitted to me that he tries to persuade his artists into debt so they are forced into producing their best work. That's why capitalism is good for art. It makes people hungry. I may have made my son too comfortable.'

'Still, it pisses me off that people do what they do because it's the easiest option. I mean, you could be lying back on your sofa by now, couldn't you? But you're not.'

'You didn't know me at thirty. I was very like Luke.'

'I doubt that.'

'You shouldn't. I am sure that Luke will have a very sure sense of himself for twenty years or so and then he'll probably begin to question aspects of his life. You're Serena's age, aren't you?'

'Yes.'

'Oh, please,' he lifts the dripping bottle from its bucket. Oops, that's me on my third glass, and when he fills his second, the bottle is dead. Bottle in hand, he nods at the waiter for another. I am beginning to feel deliciously hazy. The dank world beyond the restaurant's panes is fading from my conscious mind like the lights in a movie auditorium. The alcohol is beginning to lift, one by one, my fingers off the grip I have on myself.

'I think it's a terribly difficult age. You're an adult but perhaps you don't feel as if you have earned that position. And then when you reach my age, you are suddenly faced with the prospect of becoming an old man and still you feel that you are only scratching at the surface. You are years from being young, but you feel anything but old. It's why you'll see us fifty-somethings chasing young women around.'

My wine glass is held close to my lips when I say, 'It's lucky some of us like to be chased, then.' I lock my eyes on to his. It is now. The moment may have snuck up on us, but it has come.

'I wasn't referring to myself.'

'I was.'

Oh, to see inside his mind. Why hasn't he replied yet? The way he is touching his chin reminds me of Luke. I should feel guilt, but the power of my emotion negates everything but this present moment.

With his eyes lowered, Charles picks a crumb off the sleeve of his jacket. Then he looks at me, 'Portia, please forgive me if I'm misinterpreting you, but—'

'I don't think you are. I think you know you're not.'

Charles is giving nothing away with his expression. Or is he? He doesn't look overjoyed. When the wine is brought, he doesn't even taste it, just asks for some to be poured in my glass, and none in his own. The first courses arrive as well. He is eating seared tuna. Now, I am frightened by the silence. I squeeze the lemon over my fish, not wanting to look up. Suddenly, there is a crash of plates, a tray dropped behind us, a lull in noise, then a rush of voices. Charles turns back my way.

'They look good.'

'Yes.' My throat is dry. I take another sip. I am shaking, now I am. The whitebait have a nauseatingly strong smell. 'Charles.'

He lifts his eyebrows.

I take another gulp of wine. 'I have to say something that might, that will change things. It will.'

'Change them in what way?'

'Between you and me, and me and Luke, and maybe Luke and you,' I jabber. With a thumbnail I scratch at the tablecloth. See how much I'm shaking. I feel nauseous. 'Sorry, I think I may have drunk too much. Excuse me.'

I am dizzy when I get to my feet. Charles stands too. I walk clumsily to the bathroom. Am I going to throw up? The bathroom is quite large, with two stalls, but I lock the main door and lean my back against the wall sucking in great heaves of breath. I won't be able to cope if he doesn't feel it for me. He must. Please, he must. Calm down, Pea, calm down. I'm hyperventilating, got to stop, got to stop, stop. Come on, now, calm, calm. Breathe in. I used to have these attacks at the most unexpected moments after Dad died. Times when I should have been calm, when everyone around me was.

Now I am hot. A sob bursts to the surface. But he hasn't said anything, has he? He hasn't said no. I couldn't cope if he said no. I haven't imagined this all, have I? I could not have done.

There is a hand at the door. I make myself lower my shoulders. I can do this. Charles is being careful, that's all. He is a married man, and I am his son's girlfriend, of course he is being careful. I pat some water on my face. My eyes are bloodshot. I don't want him to think I've been crying. I take a few more deep breaths, stretch the muscles of my face and return to the restaurant.

The prim, English woman waiting for the bathroom is not much older than myself. She smiles pleasantly at me. She is wearing a wedding band. What would she think of what I dream about? Home breaker? Adulteress? Hussy? Yes. But for love, for *love*. Wouldn't she understand that?

'Don't, please,' I say to Charles, when it seems as if he is going to stand. I touch him on the shoulder. I take my seat and drink a glass of water.

Charles has not yet started his food. He asks, 'Are you all right?'

'Yes. I think. Sometimes I get these . . . no, nothing.'

'You mustn't let your whitebait get soggy.'

'I don't think I can, I'm not hungry. I'm sorry, I'm suddenly not hungry.'

'We should go, then.'

I take the plate of fish and put it on the table next to me.

'Can we not, Charles?'

'Of course, if you don't mind watching me eat.'

'I meant, can we not keep talking around it.'

'I'm afraid I don't follow.'

'Us,' I say, too loudly, so that the Americans look our way. I feel suddenly angry with them, I want to swear at them, but they have politely turned back to one another. I lift my glass and rub my hands on it. My sweaty skin skips in tiny jerks. Wish a genie would appear, make it all turn out right. I would have Charles, not Dad back. Have I ever thought such a thing before? 'Don't say that it's all me. Please.'

'You are looking so worried, Portia. You'll have me worried soon. What do you mean, "all you"?'

'This, that's happening. Now, and before. When we met and in the pool and, God knows, all the time. Please don't look like at me like that. In your bedroom with the splinter and at Luke's the other night, and all the time. Everything.'

He does look surprised now. He takes a sip of water. No wine. Keep a clear head, your son's girlfriend might not be sane. 'No, Portia, I'm sorry, you've taken me a little by surprise. What exactly are you saying?'

'I don't believe this.' I drink some more water. I am not feeling well. I say, 'I'm going to have to go.'

'Are you feeling sick?'

'Do you really not know?' For a strange second everything around us seems to freeze. 'What I feel for you?'

He has that particular, English stutter when he says, 'Feel? Portia, you don't know me.'

'I know you enough to be attracted to you.'

'But I'm fifty-four. I'm old enough to—'

'Don't say that. Please, not that. It isn't why.'

The more agitated I am, the more composed Charles seems. How can he look so calm. How can he possibly sound this calm?

'Portia, I don't for a moment presume to know your mind, yet from what you told me earlier about your father I really must wonder if—'

I bring my hand down hard on to the table. Yet again, people look. 'Don't you start too. I never wanted to sleep with him. Never,' I say in a stage whisper, 'but I can't help—'

He whips his head to the right to see if anyone heard. 'I don't think I want you to finish that sentence.'

'I've said it now.'

'I simply can't believe you mean it.'

'I do. I do.'

'Does Luke know?'

'Of course not. No.'

'Well, I think he should.'

'What?'

He is angry now, isn't he? He's speaking in a harsh whisper. 'My son. I thought you two were settled. You seemed very happy. He thinks you're happy.'

'We're not at all. Don't worry about that.'

'Can you imagine what on earth he'd do if he could hear you now?'

He is siding with Luke, isn't he? How stupid I am. There I was worrying about Victoria and it is his goddamn son he's loyal to. And would any father do less?

'This is not about Luke. It has nothing to do with Luke. It's you.'

Charles makes a fist of his right hand then relaxes it. 'I wish you hadn't said anything.'

'How could I not tell you? I thought you'd be glad.'

His hand is shaking too when he picks up his water. He glances at his watch. Now he won't look at me. 'I never expected this.'

'But what about when we were in the pool? When we were standing at the end. I saw how you were looking at me. Don't say you weren't looking at me.'

'Simply because I'm fifty-four doesn't mean that I don't sometimes think—'

'And it doesn't mean that I can't love you. I thought you felt something. I'm not a complete idiot, am I? I thought that's why you asked me to lunch, why . . . why . . . why you were lighting my cigarette that way. Why everything.'

'I'm terribly sorry if you misunderstood me. I may—'

'And don't say you weren't flirting with me. You encouraged me, paying me all this attention and by, God, by so many things. Giving me that book. I can't believe I've been imagining it all. I won't believe that.'

He is shaking his head. He thinks I am insane. He wishes we had never met. Yet he knows how he behaved. He knows. 'Believe me, Portia, I never dreamed that you would take me in the wrong—' he shakes his head. 'Perhaps, I am partly to blame, but . . .' He reaches out and I feel his palm cover my hand in a paternal, caring way, as if I'm mentally ill. We've come to see you, dear.

My heart is beating so violently I have to take small, tight breaths. Charles lifts his hand to draw it away, but quickly I turn my palm upwards and take hold of one of his fingers. I stroke it with my forefinger and thumb. Soft hands. No turning back, now. Not ever. Nothing will be the same. I look into his eyes, but something has scared him and he pulls his hand back.

'Portia, if I had known that my—'

'I don't want to hear.' The legs of my chair scream against the tiled floor when I rise to my feet. 'I'm going. I can't stay here.'

Charles stands and takes hold of my arm as I try to pass him. His keeps his voice low, but stern. 'Please, Portia. Sit down and we'll talk. Let's try not to make a scene.'

'Fuck what people think. Let me go.'

'I can't let you—'

'Why? Why can't you?'

Everyone in the restaurant is trying to look without looking. Just like the fucking Canadians, now I know from whom they got their do-nothing apathy. Nobody wanting to confront anything that might hurt them. Not that I can bear to look at Charles. I can't trust what I would do if I looked at him.

Without replying, Charles releases my arm. I push my way past the waiters and run from the restaurant. On the street, I don't know which way to turn, where I should go, what to do. I can't go back to Luke's, can I? I can't let myself be touched by him again. Not now. Twenty-seven years and I've never so much as asked for a drink from a man I haven't been sure about. Now this.

It is freezing out here. I need my coat but I can't go back inside. I am going to take that cab. I'll go to Aunt Barbara's, that's what. Nothing left to hide from her. Then somewhere far away. The countryside. Cornwall. I've saved some money now. I'll, I'll . . .

'Portia.' Now Charles is by my side on the street. 'Be sensible, please do.'

I turn to him. Oh no, I want to kiss him. I want to lick every last inch of his body, I would stick my tongue up his arsehole if that's what he craved. How could he say that he didn't feel anything? You can't grow feelings like mine out of nothing. There has to be energy from elsewhere. Or was he lying? Is that why he followed me out? Because he was too scared to tell me the truth inside? Look, he hasn't let me run.

'Portia, please, I feel awful about this.'

His words make me cry, suddenly. I hadn't expected to, but the tears have started to flow. He hands me a handkerchief. It smells of him.

'Please try not to cry. I don't know what to do to make it better.'

'Yes, you do.'

'It's all so absolutely out of the blue.'

'Not to me, it isn't.'

'Can we go somewhere quiet to talk about it? We can't stand here on the street.'

'No, I'm leaving. I'm getting that cab. I can't be with you.'

'Please, it's awful seeing you so upset.'

He lays a hand on my shoulder. I swing my body away from him. 'Don't touch me.'

But I want to touch him. I want him holding me. I lower my eyes.

'I feel I must be partly to blame.'

'Why do you keep saying that?'

He shakes his head. Now I can't help myself from reaching out to touch his cheek. He takes a step away and looks from side to side. He is not being paranoid; it's true, we are drawing attention. 'Portia, we need to talk about this.'

I'm crying when I say, 'I can't, I've told you, I can't. Not unless you've got something else to say.'

'Honestly, I don't know if I have. But I hate to think of you going home to Luke like this.'

'You think I could go home to Luke? I can't. I don't love him. I love you,' then, more quietly, 'I love you.'

He steps forward and opens his arms and I hug him so tightly I can't bear to let go. I start to sob into his shoulder.

'You miss your father, don't you?'

'It's not that, it's not. It's you.'

'Tell me you'll go home now. Mm? Go home and settle down.'

I lift my head back. 'Maybe.' I don't care what he sees. 'Will you call me? If I go will you call me?'

'Look at your face. Where's that handkerchief?' I hand it to him and he wipes at the tears on my cheeks. See how he cares for me. Loves me. He doesn't want me to run. He wants me where he can find me. 'Let's get you a cab.' He raises his hand.

A driver sees and steers to the curb. I'm suddenly frightened now, with the cab waiting to take me away from him.

'Promise you'll call.'

'Yes, of course.'

I nod. Charles will call me. I need to give him time, now he knows how I feel. 'Thanks. I'm sorry, Charles. I am.'

'Don't worry. It's all right.'

He gives the cab driver my address, and opens the door for me. I let go of his hand – how can we be sweating when it's so cold? – and he slams the door.

'My coat,' I say.

He nods, and raises his hand in a little half-wave. He has a peculiar lost expression that I wouldn't have expected to see on his face. I don't think he knows what to do with me.

As the cab pulls away, I turn and look back at him through the oval window. Now I see it again, it strikes me that the expression looks uncannily like the man's face in the dating agency ad. I'm not imagining it. *Have you ever wondered?*

Oh, Jesus, what have I done now? What have I done? I slink into the corner of the cab feeling as if I am shrinking into nothing.

I am cradling the phone in my lap when it startles me.

'Hey, it's me.'

Luke. I expected Charles though he has already telephoned once.

'Hello? Portia, are you all right?'

'Not really.' I had been lying on the sofa half-watching TV. I sit up. 'Not feeling well.'

'So I heard. I just spoke to Dad.'

The words shock me like a punch. Charles promised that he wouldn't talk to Luke. He said that we would meet next week, once Luke had left for Canada, that we would 'sort everything out then'. Whatever everything is, whatever 'sort out' implies. But I am heartened that he wants to be with me soon. He is not repulsed by me. He must have been lying in the restaurant, I could hear him weaken on the phone. It is why I wasn't in tears when I answered Luke's call.

'Did your dad say anything?'

'That you were feeling sick.'

'He rang you?'

'No, I had to call him about something. Why?'

Oh, thank God. Charles couldn't help that. It wasn't he who dialled.

'Was he angry?'

He sounds confused by my question. 'No, he was worried. Why do you ask?'

'Because I had to leave lunch quickly. I told you we were having lunch.'

'You didn't actually, but that doesn't matter. Anyway, he says he's got your coat. I'm going to pick it up on the way home.'

'Don't.'

'It's easy.'

'No.' It is as if there are a million creatures under my skin pulling my nerves in different directions and I am helpless to do anything about them. It makes me want to scream. 'I've got another coat. There's no need.'

'I can, easily. I'd be happy to.'

'It's fine, Luke, really. Go to the party.'

Emma, the mini-skirted teacher I met on my first night, is having an engagement party tonight. The clan is celebrating.

'I'm not going without you.'

I can't cope with such kindness from Luke. His goodness has always fettered me, left me with no room for my faults and tempers and selfishness. I feel obliged to mirror his benevolence. 'Go. You want to go. I'm not feeling sick any more.'

It is true, the Valium I took has made me feel better. Earlier, after lunch, I threw up; breakfast and bile. It was horrible, clinging to the bowl with my face wet with tears and mucus and shame. I felt squalid, sick with myself, wished I too could be swallowed into the sewer's bowels. The bathroom light I had switched on this morning to beautify myself, to make myself into anything but the resistible person I was, still shone down on me. The mascara and lipstick were open under the bathroom mirror, ridiculing me. Every object in the apartment knew what I did not.

It was the same when Dad died. Then it seemed wrong that those everyday objects he had worn and used and touched, his black glasses, identical ballpoint pens, wrinkled briefcase, scuffed jacketless books, clothes, the possessions that possessed themselves of a hundred thousand fingerprints, the inanimate objects that had become almost animate from the smell and shaping of him, should have survived unchanged and unmoved by his death. That they should have been so dumb as to wait for his hands again. A day or two after Aunt Barbara left us to go back to England, Mother and I, in unity then, swept through the house gathering six boxes full of Dad's things and delivering them to Cynthia Maynard, my soon to be ex-piano teacher, for her to sell beside her perennials in aid of some third world country or other. In later days, I stole back some of those things, but we needed them gone at first. They were too full of his life, just as the make-up in the bathroom laughed at me for having expected too much.

'Whatever I do, I'm going to come home early to see you,' Luke says. 'I don't like thinking of you all alone.'

'OK.'

'Promise me you'll look after yourself, Pea. Drink lots and lots. I'll be home in about an hour.'

I stare at the telephone after we hang up. How dare I elicit sympathy from a man I am hoping to betray? I have never had sympathy for criminals who plead insanity at their trials to lessen the actual and moral burdens of their crimes. And yet right and wrong and good and bad mean nothing to me since Charles has become my one horizon. Charles coming here, summoning me, lifting me from this. I have read that laboratory animals will attempt obviously impossible leaps towards food when, with patience, they could survive and be fed later. And here am I, wanting nothing in the world but Charles, readying myself for the leap. Oh, you stupid, stupid girl! You baby girl, you! How did it come to this? How, Daddy? How?

I have to tidy up, don't want Luke to see how much effort I went to for his father. In the bathroom mirror I catch a glimpse of myself. There is no doubt I have a sickness of some sort. The mind pours its misery like water into one's body and face. I weigh twice as much as before I left, though I feel completely empty. My face has aged five years in three hours. My skin is colourless, my eyes swollen and sad.

I gather together the make-up and move into the bedroom where clothes are scattered over the bed and floor. I don't know what Charles meant on the phone. He was using contradictory words: surprised, flattered, shocked, culpable. I now hope that the notion that I, a twenty-seven-year-old woman, am happy to give my body to him must be too great a temptation for him to resist. Won't it be? In the last few hours, hasn't he been able to imagine me doing what I have imagined I would? When he lies down to sleep, won't I be undressing at the foot of his bed? When he looks at his wife, won't it be my body he envisions? I have that power.

I have poured myself wine and am wrapped in our spunk-smeared duvet watching TV when Luke returns carrying a huge bunch of flowers. Ranunculus, yellow roses, irises. He always does the right thing. It's a little of what's not right he can never seem to do.

'You poor thing.' He lays the flowers flat on the table and sits beside me to kiss me. He strokes a hair from my face. His tenderness makes me want to cry.

In some ways, his return from work at the normal time and my preparing for it have made the horrible events of the day seem implausible, an unlikely dream. Aside from my state and his attentiveness, this is how we are every day. Do I have to complicate it so? Perhaps Luke is a better man than his father. He would never lead me to bloom, as Charles has undeniably done, then cut the stem. Nor would he lie to me as I have lied to him. So why, then, why am I screaming for one man to love me when I have another gazing at me with an expression that looks like love, like love? Which one of us is more blind?

'Poor you. You look drained.'

'Mm.'

'What do you think it was? We ate the same things yesterday, didn't we?'

'I think so. It sometimes happens, that's all.'

'I brought you some flowers.'

'How sweet are you? Thank you, they're beautiful.'

'I'll put them in water.'

In the kitchen, I hear the sink filling. Finding a vase would be too much like woman's work in Luke's mind, nor would he want to intrude on a task he presumes that I, as 'woman in his life', would enjoy.

'I brought you some Coke,' he calls from the kitchen.

'Coke? Jesus, Luke.'

'A cola. Coca-Cola. It's good for upset stomachs. You want some?'

'Oh, sure, thanks.'

Why doesn't he see that I am bad news? A waste of his time? He thinks of our future together, I know that. Doesn't speak about it, that wouldn't be his style, but he thinks of marriage more than any man I have known. Most men are like Iain. He once told me he likened marriage to being given a composite of all the menus he had seen, then being forced to choose just one dish from that moment on. I should be happy to have a man I can hold and have. Luke wants to marry soon. More than half of his friends are hitched now, starting families, moving up that inevitable rung. Has he seriously considered me as a mate? I don't know how important he thinks love is.

I take the drink. There it floats, my one iced heart. It is dissolving fast, not cracking. A slow fading of love. Is that it? Always how it is? But, for my sins, I have never loved Luke solidly.

'You will go to the party, won't you?'

'All right, for a little while. Everyone will be sad not to see you.'

'Heartbroken, I'm sure.'

'They will, Porsh.' Luke takes my hand in his. 'I don't know what to do to convince you.'

I shake my head and close my eyes. 'Don't. It doesn't matter.'

'It does to me.'

I open my eyes. 'Why?'

'It just does. Of course it does.'

'Why? Why to you, Luke?'

'Because I want you to be happy here, of course. I want you to feel as if you fit in. And because,' he lowers his eyes, concentrates on his thumb moving against my fingers, 'well, because, because I love you.'

Oh no, not this, not now, Luke. I don't have the courage for love from you now.

'Oh, Porsh, please don't cry. What is it?'

With his thumb, he wipes off my cheeks the tears I can't seem to keep inside. 'I'm sorry. Guess I'm feeling low.'

'Right, that's it. I'm going to stay. I'll call Emma.'

'No, go, go. I want you to have a good time.' I sniff, wipe at my nose with my hand. Don't want Luke seeing the handkerchief Charles gave me and which I'm still clutching. 'You never know, you might meet some nice English girl. Another Jemima, or, I don't know, someone who wants a baby and a house in Clapham and—'

'I don't want some nice English girl. I want you.'

'No, Luke, I can't, I can't.'

'You can't what?'

'Don't, please.'

Why is he being like this today, of all days? Luke, the cool son of a passionate man. Luke who is too English to talk to me about what he feels; too English to feel what he feels. Luke who won't say he loves me unless the lights are off and he is inside my body. Why today, of all days?

'I can't do it, Luke. I can't be who you want me to be.'

'What are you talking about?' Joking, he asks, 'Are you delirious?'

It is on the tip of my tongue to tell him the truth but I don't have the courage. He looks so young sometimes, like a little boy. How dare I hurt him? 'I think I should move out for a while. Just until I get my head straight. I think I can stay with Kaz or . . . I don't know. But I can't change, I'm sorry. I don't think I'm going to change.'

'Have I ever asked you to? I've felt the same about you from the moment I first saw you in Toronto. You know that.'

I am shaking my head as I say, 'I thought you were just looking for someone to have dinner with.'

'I was, but—' He takes a swig of his beer and then smiles. 'You know, I saw you before.'

'What do you mean?'

'In a chemist's down the street from where we ate. I'd had to go in to get a razor or something, and you were coming in as I was going out and I remember getting that jolt you feel when . . . well, you know. You looked so beautiful and I wished I knew you, but I didn't so I left and went to look for somewhere to eat and suddenly out of the blue there you were. I didn't think I'd have the guts to say anything but then—'

'You said um.'

'Did I? Um was probably all I could manage. Talking to strangers is not the sort of thing I'm normally very good at. But you—'

'Why are you telling me this? Why now?'

'I don't know. It came up. I thought it might cheer you up.'

I sigh from the heart of me. It is unbearable for him to tell me this now. Why has he told me none of this before? After so many weeks of bludgeoning the mystery and romance out of our affair with his rational, almost bureaucratic logic? The tears well again in my eyes.

'You're really not very well, are you, sweet?'

I shake my head.

'Come on. Let's get you to bed.'

'Luke, no, you can't lift me,' I say, when he bends down to push his hand under my back. 'You'll break your back.'

'You're a feather,' he replies, as he gently lifts me out from the duvet and towards his bed. 'A sick little bird.'

'You're being so sweet.'

After he has laid me flat on the mattress with such precision anyone would have though he had feng shui on his mind, he kisses my forehead and leaves to get the duvet. I think he likes seeing me helpless like this. And I don't mind playing the victim. It helps absolve me of my guilt. Sick, I cannot be blamed for my actions.

'I see you've been stealing my handkerchiefs,' he says, returning to lay the duvet over me.

'Have I?'

'I'll get you another.'

Top left in the chest of drawers, Luke. You like them neatly ironed, don't you, my sweet thing? I am glad he thinks the handkerchief one of his. Charles suddenly seems an Iago in my mind. I didn't ask for his attention in the pool, in the house, in the restaurant today. I didn't want to fall in love with him. I have a man here who loves me, who would be good to me, who could turn into another Charles for all I know.

'That's funny. Here's my blue handkerchief.'

'Oh, I remember now, your dad gave me that one.

'See how my family looks after you—' He flicks a clean handkerchief on to the bed. 'There you go.'

He wouldn't suspect anything, would he? Why should he? Now that I am in bed, I feel suddenly tired. The day seems to have lasted for ever. I lay my head on the pillow and then feel Luke's hand, stroking at my hair.

'I'm going to do something,' he says, 'to make you feel better.'

'What?'

'That would be telling.' He bends over to kiss me. 'I love you.'

'I love you, too,' I whisper. I know I shouldn't, but in this moment, it is true. Curiously, it is. 'Remember that, won't you. I mean, whatever.'

'Ssshh.'

He kisses me again before leaving the room. I curl into a ball, listening to the thud of water in the bathtub. The sound is so soothing I am soon floating on the water's surface, so quickly and deeply asleep it must seem as if I am dead.

Though it is only the first week of December, Christmas is on everybody's lips, bauble bright, a speck of gold in the alluvial sludge that is London in midwinter.

I have dreaded and hated every Christmas since 1983, though it was the first year without Dad that cast the longest shadow. Back then, Mother and I were relying on one another for comfort. It made us friends of a sort, though neither was able to give the other what she truly wanted. At thirty-four, she needed a new man, a new body to enjoy, a chance without a child in her life. I, of course, wanted nothing but the old body back.

The first Christmas without my father, Mother offered to take us to the Caribbean. For a few weeks I kept our holiday brochures by my bed and gazed at the images of long, golden beaches wondering whether in such an unexplored paradise my loneliness might recede. Those dreams were scuppered by my grandfather. Despite his manifest iciness towards Dad, Mumpsimus had spent the previous few Christmas holidays with us in Toronto and I suppose he thought he was returning the favour by inviting Mother and me to L'Estrie. I didn't want to go. Mother, thinking it too cruel to leave her dad alone, accepted. So it was that we packed the car and drove not to the airport but towards Montreal, me sitting glumly in the car, full of self-pity and sadness.

That Christmas set the tone for years to come, made me dread the onset of each holiday. At the last moment, Mumpsimus had invited a woman as dour and earnest as he who, within six weeks, he would make his second wife. Over Orange Spice tea on Christmas Eve, Mother and I learned that he and Clara had met on a cycling tour for seniors around North Hatley, each soothing the other's sore muscles and lonely hearts. I couldn't have cared less. I just wanted Clara gone.

I had loved Grandmamma Bec. She was the most life-loving person I have ever known. It makes me smile to remember the fury she'd fly into if ever I said I was bored. 'Bored is for boring people, Portia,' she would insist. When she was still strong and well, she would pick me up like a child's doll and carry me outside so we could find something to do. It didn't matter if the snow was thick on the ground or if an icy wind was slicing into our skin, within moments my crossness would ebb and I would find myself laughing with her, glad to be picking up twigs off the lawn or feeding the hens or sanding a door for Grandmamma to paint, or plunging my hands between the cold, waxy apples in search of rotten fruit. She and Dad have been the only two people in my life whom I have loved unequivocally. Remarkably, since they shared the same *joie de vivre* and were born only three years apart, the two of them were cool towards one another. Grandmamma even called Dad 'rotten to the core' once, unaware that I could hear through the floorboards of their eighteenth-century house.

I was ten when she died. At the time, I remember feeling angry with her for deserting me. She was the best thing about her family. My grandfather Mumpsimus was as good and dull and predictable as Toronto itself, so much so that Dad used to say that persuading a beautiful, young Francophone from Montreal to marry him was grandfather's one act of creativity. It must have been a slight against Mother, too, though I was too young to pick up on such things. Looking back, I suppose Grandmamma's death marked the point at which I began to feel distant from Mother. She was too like Mumpsimus, too full of reason and Canadian common sense. It was I, not she, who inherited Grandmamma's Gallic, chocolatey eyes and hair. I think Dad was scared of her when she was alive, but when she was gone (when, I guess, she wasn't there to act as a rival for my affections) he encouraged me to see her as the source of much that was sparky about me. Mother was the carrier of such genes but they never bloomed within her.

Was it any wonder, then, that I should have considered Clara an impostor, the holiday a punishment? In those months after Dad's death, Mother and I were as close as we had ever been, but I was intolerant of the others. Clara tried to cheer me up, but failed. In truth, I don't think anyone could have made me happy. There was too much to miss about Christmas with Dad. He and I were responsible for decorating the house while Mother put food on the table, and every year he would nail fairy lights with tacks to the garden shed, not in the haphazard fashion of most men, but in a decorative pattern that set our garden apart from everyone else's. We usually had a party at which I switched on the lights. My parents would play the happy couple with such conviction that sometimes the deceit even fooled me.

Clara understood none of this. She tried to stuff us with jollity. Once, with inexplicable cruelty, she said, 'Smile, this isn't a wake, you know.' I don't think there was a single minute when I didn't wish I was somewhere else, that someone else could have my life, and me, theirs. It is strange to remember that, up until then, I had considered life a wonderful thing. Is it really out of my reach to think it again?

This Christmas I am, of course, expected at the Old Rectory to take part in the whole fairy lights and mistletoe charade with the Bingham family. I wonder, as what? Luke's girlfriend? Charles's mistress? I can't imagine. My mind spins variations like a fruit machine rarely hitting the jackpot. The faces come up: Luke Luke Me; Luke Charles Luke; Me Me Me; Charles Luke Me; Charles Charles Me; Charles Charles Charles. Luke's confusing declaration of love made me fond of him again, but since he went to Toronto, a passion I can't prevent has built again. I have been thinking of nothing else but seeing Charles tomorrow. It hurts to wait.

I am writing when the door buzzer surprises me. Charles again? Oh, please. Please.

'Messenger.'
'Who for?'
'Ah, Por . . . Porteea Mills.'

I sign my name downstairs and rip open the cardboard envelope on my way back up. Inside, there is a single white envelope. My name is written by a fountain pen on its surface. I recognize the writing from the countless times I have stared at Charles's inscription in my book of Hardy poems. What can't wait?

I sit in the chair next to the door to read.

Dear Portia,

Since our meeting last week I have been able to think of little else and, after much sleepless consideration, I have concluded that it will be better for all concerned if we did not meet this Thursday. I do hope this letter will adequately explain why.

'No.' Tears burn at the back of my eyes. 'Please, no.'

When we had lunch, and again later when we spoke on the telephone, you led me to believe that I was responsible, in your own words, for sparking a fire that turned into a flame. If that is indeed the case, I must apologize from the bottom of my heart.

I would be doing you a great disservice were I to deny that, because I have always considered you a very attractive woman. I have behaved towards you in a manner that I thought was complimentary and flattering and that I now understand you interpreted as otherwise. You have opened my eyes to the folly of my behaviour, and it has left me remorseful and rather ashamed.

I am horrified at the thought that, however inadvertently, I could be responsible for damaging your relationship with Luke. I am sure he would permit me to tell you that he is very fond of you and believes that you and he could enjoy a long and happy future. I would give much to be able to turn back the clock, yet since that is clearly impossible I can only offer my sincere apologies for having misled you. I must stress again that an involvement with you was never my intention.

    I am sure that you must understand, dear Portia, that we could never extend our relationship beyond the friendship and advice that I hope I shall be able to provide. I cannot deny that I am flattered by your willingness to see beyond these crow's feet and shadowy eyes, nor that it is with a certain degree of ruefulness that I accept our fate. However, to acknowledge your charms is not to succumb to them, and it would be an abhorrent mistake were we to confuse the two.

    I am absolutely confident that in time you will agree that this is the best course of action. Despite my age, or possibly as a result of it, I am not entirely without feelings in this matter. I fear we might be tempting fate were we to meet. Although I do not presume to know your mind, I suspect it would be foolish to deny some connection between the unresolved sadness you feel as the result of your father's untimely death and the attraction you have said you feel for me. I am not qualified to offer useful advice in such matters except to suggest that any kind of intimacy with me, given my relationship to Luke, would surely deepen the wounds.

    I realize that I am taking something of a risk in putting these thoughts on paper and sending them to you at Luke's, but I do hope and trust that you will either destroy this (as I would prefer) or keep it very well hidden from Luke. Although neither of us has acted improperly (I do not, of course, berate you for your emotions in the restaurant) he would suffer from any knowledge of this.

    Portia, I understand that my son is not faultless, none of us is, but he is trusting and generous and, I think, very decent. I wish you had been witness to his kindness towards Serena. We English are not always comfortable wearing our hearts on our sleeves, but we are not, as you must know from your father, a heartless race. It would give me the greatest pleasure were you able to give Luke the time to prove that to you. He is really very much like me. If you are honest in your feelings for me, I have no doubt you could find much to admire and enjoy in him.

I understand from Victoria that you are expected here for Christmas, and I look forward to seeing you then. I do hope that we can put this behind us, as we must, so that we might enjoy a more realistic and fruitful relationship in the future,

With my very best wishes for your continued health and happiness,
Charles

No tears, just anger, anger. He cannot do this. I will not let him. We cannot put this behind us. I will not allow him to brush me off. I love him. He made sure I loved him. I cannot bear wanting you and not having you, Charles. I know that it seems impossible and abhorrent but I cannot extinguish my love with one letter. It is strong like fire under water.

I sit to read the letter again, five times. Thank God, it is not as bad as at first I thought. It is only fear that's holding him back – fear of tempting fate when that's all fate's good for. He is 'rueful' about not having me. He is 'flattered by my attention' and disappointed by the obstacle of his son. And he is scared. I need to tell him that I am scared too. I am frightened of everything. The world will not end for us if we follow our hearts. It is only once in a lifetime and then only if you are lucky that a love like ours comes along. And it is because we do not ask or look for it that we cannot ignore it. Of course it is because of Daddy. Everything is because of him.

I fold the letter and return it to its envelope. What now? I have to speak with him, but I know from before that he won't answer my calls at the office.

I have to get outside. Everything inside these walls contains the oppressive weight of Luke. I am part of the furniture, an object for display. I think he assumes that I am willingly transforming myself into the woman he has wanted me to be. I am not required to think or speak for myself. It is the way he has always wanted it. He has loved the idea and look of me more than anything else. It is a curse as well as a blessing to have a face that makes heads turn. It makes it harder still to convince others that you are not necessarily the person they take you to be. Too much is assumed, not least that you love yourself above all others.

Yet, perhaps Daddy taught me to do just that. Be oneself first. Love oneself first. Love before rules. Truth before manners. Honesty before everything. What was that T-shirt I had? 'Love life, live love.' Cute, but true. I will love this life if I can live the love for Charles, if he'll only let us live our love. But my mind trips over the longing as my tongue trips over the 'l's. The hell of it. Oh, what should I do?

Last night Luke called from Toronto to say he was missing me in his king-size hotel bed and had he left his diary in the bedroom, could I check? I found it for him and when he had hung up, I flicked back to August. 'Portia arrives,' he wrote, 'H'throw, 6:18 a.m.' Somehow that private contract with me, that considered act of kindness, meant more than most of the things he ever said to my face. It is black and white proof that I have altered his life, even when I wasn't here I had imposed myself on him, made him slide out of bed before dawn, diverted the course of his thoughts. I can't walk out without leaving my stench. There are consequences, there will be consequences. But I love Charles. What can I do when I love him?

The pressure doesn't subside on these streets. It is almost the shortest day of the year and the darkness like death has its hand on my shoulder. The streetlights punch orange holes in the blackness. I can't bear to think of spending the night alone. I was longing for the space that Luke's trip abroad was going to give me, but now I am desperate for someone to talk to, to stop me feeling insane. Kaz is the only person, and she is in Kent, at a jewellery fair.

When I return to Luke's apartment I feel like screaming, but what's the point if no one can hear? We learn that much soon as we know how to think. I dial Charles's number, then hang up. Damn him! I fear we may be tempting fate ... But we have already eaten its apple. Charles can't run away from that. I have to see him. What is stopping me? I can go, can't I? Yes.

Yes! The knowledge that I will be seeing Charles fills my empty soul much as the water I am running fills this bath. I lie against the enamel surface that has seen and felt Luke's naked body countless times. Despite this sense of him around me – the curiously quaint badger-bristle shaving brush, the Penhaligon's cream, the natural sponge that, just here, has one of his hairs threaded into its dry honeycomb – I feel numb, guiltless. I can't lie. I feel possessed of an awful honesty that justifies everything I do.

I wet the sponge and wash between my legs, not with Luke's musky sandalwood soap, but with the scentless bar from the sink. I want the odour of me and nothing else for Charles. He won't be able to resist me now. He can't – not when this is meant to be.

Simple make-up, no bra under my sweater, my smallest white cotton panties then it is up to Earl's Court where I take the tube standing next to boys in suits coming home after work. They are wearing the same shiny shoes and chalk-striped suits as each other, their faces puffed up from client lunches and boozy dinner parties the night before, enjoyed, most probably, in cosy, cramped Fulham houses with the baby toys pushed into an overflowing pine chest in the corner where the sickly sweet smell of babies and breastfeeding lingers in the air despite the smog of Silk Cut smoke that rises again when the nippers are put down to sleep. I don't envy all these new mothers. Giving birth makes you futile, used up. The tunnel those tiny hands spring from is the same we sink into. I am not ready for that. I have not loved life and lived love long enough for that.

At Sloane Square, I look around for Charles as the wooden-slatted escalator carries me into the ticket hall. Up here, a

Samaritan's Santa Claus is rattling a tin. It is a rich neighbourhood, and he is being ignored. I give him a pound coin; am thanked. For all my sins, the good citizen.

With nothing to lose, I am bold in approaching the dark-red building that houses Charles and Victoria's London 'pad'. The buzzer plate is of polished brass. I press 3a.

'Yes?'

Strange, I'm caught off guard when Charles answers. I was not sure he'd be home.

When I announce myself, he is momentarily silent. Then, 'I'll come down.'

'Can't I come up? I'll be quick, I promise.'

Another pause, then, 'All right.'

He buzzes me in. It is expensive here, much like Luke's only the carpet's pale green, not blue, and the renovation is less recent. A pile of property magazines is squared against the far wall. There is a slight smell of cats. I climb the stairs, slowly. There are two apartments to each floor. I listen for the eager click of a lock above me, but hear nothing. Yet when I turn on the third floor, Charles is waiting at the open door.

'Hi,' I say, lightly as I can muster.

'Hello, Portia.'

He is not going to kiss me, is he? In my dreams and conscious fantasies, he has been unable to resist me. He has ripped at my clothes and been gentle with my body. He has kissed me until that alone has made me come. Now, he has the look about him of his letter. Circumspect, obdurate, a little superior.

'Did you receive my letter?'

'Yes.'

'It seems you didn't agree with it.'

'Not really.'

He nods. 'I have to be honest. I am a little reluctant to invite you in.'

'Please, I can't go back to the flat, yet. Please. Please, Charles.'

My use of his name unlocks something in him and he steps

back, though his expression remains rigid. Through a small corridor there is a small living room that is pleasantly if unexceptionally furnished with two comfortable-looking sofas that have between them a glass and metal coffee table that seems seventies in design. There are books on its surface. *London in 360 degrees*; *English Country Gardens*; a few issues of *Interiors* magazine; a magazine from a classical music club, at an angle. It has been read since the cleaner last came.

'It's cosy in here.'

'The heating's on a thermostat.'

'It was getting cold out.'

'Were you waiting for me?'

'No.'

'I only just arrived back myself.'

'Must be fate.'

The word bothers him as might the mention of an ex-lover. I notice a tightening around his eyes. Is it too many years of wincing at what is painful to our ears that makes us look old? I need him to soften, please, I do.

'Did you try to call me?'

'No. I didn't think you'd rush to invite me over.'

He doesn't reply. We are still standing. I am wearing my coat and Charles his suit. The only lights shining are those in this room, patterned lamps with large, salmon-coloured shades. Very Victoria; Camilla; Peter Jones.

'Can I sit down?'

'I'm not sure you should be here, Portia.'

'You think I'm going to bite?'

He refuses to smile. But how strange, Charles is more nervous than I. He says, 'I'm afraid I can't imagine any good coming of this.'

'Do you think it'd be better if I arrived at your house for Christmas without us even talking?'

'No.' His hands sound dry when he twists one against the other. He takes off his jacket. I am half-expecting him to roll up his sleeves, too. If there is a fight, it'll be of wills. 'I was about to have a drink. Would you like something?' he asks without enthusiasm or encouragement.

'Yup, a vodka tonic, if you have any.'

'We do.'

The we was on purpose, I'm sure, though I know Victoria is seldom in London. She has the horses, and now Serena. Has she never suspected Charles might get lonely?

I sit and watch him. It is a sweet torture to be in the same room as he. He places two thick crystal glasses on an antique side table beneath a framed oil of what looks like brown heathland in Yorkshire or Scotland. Or is it Cumbria, where Victoria comes from? She has a hand in everything, it seems. I see a variety of different bottles of liquor on a tray beside which are tins of mixers, as if we are on an aeroplane. Charles pours me a Smirnoff. There is a brisk 'tssht' when he opens the can.

'You like ice, don't you?'

'I like ice.'

He leaves. An ice tray is cracked. He returns. I can feel the redness in my cheeks and at the top of my neck. For himself, he has J&B whisky, no ice. Two fingers, or more, and a splash of water. Just as Luke likes it.

'Do you mind if I smoke in here?'

'No.'

Charles brings in a china ashtray decorated with a peacock. I have no clue what non-smokers do in moments such as this. Bite their nails? Sweat? Cancer's a risk I'll take.

Charles drags a wooden dining chair across the carpet. When he sits, his suit trousers look too tight at his thighs. He says, 'I rather hoped what I said in my letter might have lessened your feelings.'

'Is that how it usually works?'

'I am not an expert.'

'I meant do you think people usually change their minds because others tell them to?' I hear the cynicism in my voice. I suppose it's nervousness making me pushy. 'Stop wanting what they wanted.'

'This is not a question of desire.'

'So you do admit it.'

He lowers his eyes, unable to look at me. He has lost much of his physical confidence. He is hunched.

'I thought I was going to go mad today,' I concede, 'after I read your letter. I can't talk about you with anyone else.'

His shoulders fall slightly now. There is some logic to my being here. He flattens his hands as if in prayer. 'I understand, but I simply do not believe that any good can come from us being together. I don't.'

'It might stop me jumping off Hammersmith Bridge.'

'Please don't say that.'

'It runs in my family,' I hear myself reply, though it is inexcusable. Like everyone else, I have thought of suicide a hundred thousand times, but it has always seemed like disappointment heaped on disappointment. More of a question than an answer.

Charles looks tired. 'Sleepless consideration', he wrote. If he had been sure about me, he would have slept soundly, wouldn't he? He must have been imagining me too. His glass clacks against the table when he puts it down.

I ask, 'So, what do you think we should do?'

'Do? In what way?'

'About us.'

He smoothes a hand across his forehead again, and is slow in replying. 'Nothing. Nothing.'

'What if I can't do nothing? What if I don't believe nothing's the right thing to do?'

'I'm sure in a couple of weeks—'

I am so quick in moving, it's almost a surprise to myself. It is not the soft, sweet kiss that I have longed for, yet nor has he pushed me away; not yet. He has let me unseal his lips with my tongue. I am kissing him, kissing him, kissing him.

I can feel how he has craved this. Though his hands remain still by his side he has not turned me away. Without breaking the kiss, I cup his face in my hands, and then move so I am sitting on his legs, facing him, my knees against the stiles of the chair like a cabaret whore. I hold his head between my taut fingers as his tongue responds to mine and yes, now he lifts his hands to my back, squeezes me tightly to him. His breathing has become more excited, and he is hardening against my buttocks. I knew he would, like a young man. I pull back from his mouth, run my tongue over his lips, then lower my hand behind me to feel him.

Suddenly, he breaks the kiss.

'Portia, no. Stop it, please. We have to stop it.'

'Shssh.' I kiss him again. 'Sshh.'

'No.' His legs tense as he tries to stand.

'I love you, Charles,' I whisper in his ear. 'I love you.'

'You can't.'

'I do. Please look at me.' Now he does. 'I love you, I—' I press my lips to his again, but he turns his head sharply and I feel ugly, animal, my lips rudely grazed by the stubble on his cheek. He is trying to lift me off, to stand.

'You have to go.'

'You can't make me, not now.'

And yet I cannot stop him rising to his feet, so lifting me to mine. Off balance, I fall back on to the sofa. He is quite frightening, standing above me, his eyes sharp, his lips still wet with my kiss. 'I won't let you do this to me,' he urges, breathlessly.

I stand. I feel stronger than him. I am freed by knowing myself, by having given myself. 'It's not our fault.' I step close and take hold of the shaking hand that Charles is holding out to keep me away. He draws it sharply back.

Something snaps: 'For God's sake listen to me, Portia,' he shouts. 'This cannot go on.'

'Why? When it's what we both want.'

'This does not stop with us. You are too intelligent not to see that. There are always consequences.'

'But you wrote that you had feelings for me. Don't you?' He closes his eyes when I touch his cheek, but doesn't flinch or move away. 'That was the truth, wasn't it?' I ask. 'That you have feelings.'

'Yes,' he answers, placing his hand over mine, 'of course I do.' He closes his fingers around mine and lifts my hand off his cheek. 'That's why you have to go.'

'Don't make me,' I whisper. I turn my hand around within his and squeeze it tightly. 'No one will know.'

Charles looks at me, apprehensively. Quickly, I step away and lift off the pale-blue cashmere sweater Luke bought me last month. My breasts rise with the fabric then fall from its ribbed bottom. Charles lowers his eyes to them, speechless. I step closer, reach for his right hand and turn the palm towards my chest. I press it to my left breast. The warmth of his skin makes me catch my breath. He is touching my breast as if it is a thing of mystery; measuring the weight of it, its indistinct malleability, its softness. The sight of his slender fingers, dark against my pale flesh, doubles the beat of my heart, halves the weight of me. The pattern of his skin touching mine contains and spreads over me the complex web of his life. Gently, he increases the pressure. Tears come to my eyes.

He brings his other hand to my right breast. I lift myself onto my toes and kiss him again. Now he welcomes me. His hands are firm on my naked back. I tug at the back of his shirt, I need to feel his skin too. With our mouths pressed together I pull the shirt from the waistband of his trousers and slither my hands under the fabric. The solidity of him entrances me. I shiver. I can feel his erection through his trousers at the base of my stomach, and press myself against it.

I want to be naked for him, stretched out on his bed for him. It turns me on to think of how filthy I will be for him, whatever he wants from me. I let my hands fall down his back and to his buttocks and then, more slowly than last time, to the front. His prick feels huge in his trousers. I tickle my fingers around it. There is only forward from here.

'Let's lie down,' I say.

This much has reddened him, brought into relief a vein on his neck. But am I losing him? His expression contains shock like a paper made translucent with a spot of grease. He steps back and runs his hands hard through his hair, erasing the wrinkles on his forehead and so becoming, for these seconds, a younger man such as I don't crave.

'We mustn't.'

'Let's lie down,' I repeat. Returning to him, I lick his ear and whorishly whisper, 'I want my tongue over every inch of you. I want to swallow you.' As I speak, I touch him again. His hardness is undiminished. He needs me to be the seductress, is all. Absolve him of some of the guilt.

I take his hand and he follows. I don't turn on a light in the bedroom, there might be photographs in here, something of Victoria's that will wrench him from me. He reaches to unknot his tie, then sits on the bed to undo the laces of his shoes. Quickly, without poetry, I strip naked for him. The charcoal light allows only indistinct edges. Charles is still unbuttoning his shirt when I step out of my knickers. The air kisses my warmth. I climb on the bed. The mattress is soft, giving. From behind, I help with the last buttons and ease the shirt off his shoulders.

He twists his upper body towards me and says, 'Lie down.'

I want to. I want him to fuck me for being the naughty girl I am. Punish me for seducing him.

'Close your eyes.'

Knots twist and loosen in my stomach as I wait. Then I feel his fingertips touch and glide over my eyelids, my cheeks, the line of my jaw, my neck, now they circle my breasts, tease my nipples so that I can't help but open my eyes and arch up to kiss him, the need coming like a surge of blood. Charles pushes me back. I close my eyes again. His touch floods every cell as his hand passes by. Now he is tracing the line of my torso, over the crest of my shoulder, down my arms to my fingers then to my hips and, please yes, gently, so gently, they press against my mound, his fingers soft in my pubic hair. I want them inside me, his fingers, his prick, his body inside me. I arch my body up, sluttishly I guess, and one of his fingers slips inside. He is staring at me as if he has never had sex before, but I am the one who feels this is a new virginity broken. Something denied me when Dad died I have found in this man. I am becoming a woman for the first time. Have I ever been so in love?

'Touch me.'

He continues to run his fingers down my leg to my feet. He is drawing me to life, creating me for himself. Within the outline, I am his. I wish I could see inside his mind, know whether his happiness is as absolute as mine.

When his hand completes its cartography, I am open, unzipped, whole. He is looking down at me, still half-dressed himself. I push myself up and kneel on the bed behind him, stroking his shoulders. His skin is dry and he is tense, not just from now but from too many years of keeping his spine straight. Oh, it is so British the way he is wearing his trousers and socks; most men would be at me by now. My hands drape over his chest, no wonder he hasn't Luke's firmness up here, but the slackness gives me the sense of reaching more deeply into him. Luke's muscle doesn't yield so. My hands drop lower. The touch of my nipples against his neck is almost unbearably thrilling, I can sense how wet I am below. I push myself against his back and now my arms are around his waist and at the buckle of his trousers. Dad wore trousers with buttons, too. Charles doesn't help me as I undo them, and then I can't wait until he is naked, I flatten my palm and slide it against his stomach, under the elastic of his boxers and lower to touch his penis with my fingertips.

But he is soft, he has lost his excitement. The disappointment shocks me. I climb off the bed and kneel in front of him. I kiss him through the fabric. I slick my tongue against him through the slit in his shorts. I would eat him all, I want to be filled with him. It would not be possible to get enough of him.

'Portia.'

Kneeling, I look up.

'I can't,' he says.

'Yes, you can,' I kiss his right leg by his knee. 'I want to make you happy.' Softly, I scratch my hands up the inside of his legs. They like this, some men.

'He's my son.'

'I don't love him, Charles. I don't.'

'But I do.' Haltingly, he strokes some hair off my forehead. 'You know how much I wish . . .' he begins, then turns to look away towards the door so lighting his mournful eyes.

'What?' I whisper.

He shakes his head, slowly.

'You wish what?'

'Look at you. You're very beaut—'

'Let me,' I say, staring at him while I run my right hand back up his thigh and inside the leg of his shorts. 'Let me.' He covers his eyes with a hand as I begin to touch him. Slightly damp, men are, between their balls and their legs, as if there is always energy here, a will to produce. I am gentle but persistent. Slowly, I feel him harden again. He looks full of sorrow when he says, 'No.' His gloom is an insult that stifles my own sense of breathtaking abandonment. Suddenly, he stands. 'We can't.'

Like a priest offering benediction, he presses a hand on my head and then his fingers trail through my hair as he steps over me and walks swiftly into the living room. I pull the sheet off the bed and run to find him sitting on the sofa creasing his brow with his hands. I sit beside him, saying nothing. Bubbles blip stupidly to the surface of my vodka and tonic. A bus rumbles and accelerates outside. I touch his shoulder. Lightly he lays his hand on mine, then lifts my fingers off. 'I'm sorry, Portia.'

'I feel stupid,' I say, and it is not all for effect. 'I thought you wanted that.'

'I did.' He shakes his head again. 'Of course I do.'

'Then, why?'

Interrupting, he says, 'What do you think you will do for Christmas?'

Sometimes you can feel the position of your heart in your chest. Charles's tone is so unspeakably cruel that mine shifts, jolts crooked; a paper mobile with one of its strings snapped. I know the sensation from before. Every one of the strings snapped when my father died. I tied them together with knots that loosen too easily.

A long pause, then, 'I thought I was coming to your house.'

'With Luke there?' he asks, with a disbelieving shrug of his eyebrows. It is a teenage expression.

'I don't know what else to do.'

'What about your mother? Have you thought about going back to Canada?'

'No.'

'If it's a matter of money, I'll happily—'

'What?' I jump up. 'You haven't even fucked me and you're trying to pay me off.'

'Portia! Please, grow up.'

' Oh, I'm sorry, I forgot you English hate emotions.' I pick up my drink and take a swig. Hasn't he belittled me enough?

'I'm not thinking about myself, I'm thinking about Luke.'

'I don't get why's it such a sin to think about oneself?'

Charles answers by leaving me. When he returns from the bedroom, he is buttoning up his shirt. 'I'm not sure I completely understand you, Portia. How you operate.'

'In what way?'

'You seem so completely oblivious of other people's feelings.'

'That's a horrible thing to say.'

'Have you even thought about Luke? Or Victoria?'

'Of course. Of course I have. But you can't just insulate yourself from all feelings. Life doesn't work that way.'

'Life works the way we work it, Portia.'

'Well, I don't believe that. I didn't ask for my dad to kill himself. I didn't work it so I fell in love with you. Sometimes, things just happen.'

'And then it's up to us to make mature and sensible decisions. Ethical decisions.'

I look away from him, lower my eyes, take a drink. Truth is, there is no point in arguing. I thought he wanted this, wanted me. Quietly, I ask, 'Don't you want me with you for Christmas?'

'Honestly?'

'No, lie to me,' I answer, angrily. 'Be a real man – make me fall in love with you and then lie to me.'

'Then, no. I don't think I do want our mistake staring me in my face every day. Excuse me.'

'Mistake?' I repeat, shouting after him as he walks towards the bathroom. 'Fuck you for saying that. Fuck you!' I run to him, the sheet dropping to the floor, to stop him at the door. 'You started this.'

'Portia, please,' he says, smugly. 'Can you let me inside.'

' You started this,' I say, beginning to cry in frustration. 'You—'

'No. No, I didn't,' he says, and then begins to close the door.

'Fuck you,' I scream again. I slap my palm, hard so it hurts, though I don't want to show it, against the door. With a bang, it slams shut. I feel helpless, naked in every way. I take a step back towards the bedroom and then turn and fling my hands, slap, against the wooden bathroom door, crying at the horror of what has been said. 'Don't you know that I love you?' I scream. 'How much I love you?' but there is no reply from within, nothing but the sound of the lock turning once.

EIGHT

Do not hold grudges or blame other people for your problems. Even if you have been treated badly, a constant sense of frustrated hostility will accomplish nothing and can only make you feel worse.

AMA Family Medical Guide

Luke's lips are moving. I try to read them in the murky light. William? Will? Willa? What is he saying?

I used to talk in my sleep. Daddy would listen beyond the bedroom door which I insisted on keeping ajar so that in the soothing sliver of light I could follow the wallpaper's complicated vines and daisy-chains out of consciousness. I never reached a satisfactory end to the complicated weaves and turns, but in failing I would find sleep, just as in life. In the morning, Dad would say that if it wasn't one of the cats I was calling in my sleep, or a friend's name I muttered, I would bark aloud one of the words he had challenged me to learn. Glockenspiel; caggy; polliwog; a polliwog's a tadpole, I remember. Not that it matters now.

Again, Luke mumbles. I used to get scared, years after Daddy killed himself, that the secrets I kept suppressed during my conscious day would bubble to the surface and release themselves like pus through my lips to whomever was sharing my bed. But

I have never slept as soundly as my men (is it the loss of sperm that drains them? Is it thinking? Or carrying that hair and brawn?) and, anyway, it seems my habit died not long after Dad did, as if it was only he who could fill this bucket of a brain to its brim. The bucket's empty now. The more I begin to resemble Mother, the more I become her intellectual equal. There's nothing inside to overflow.

Still, Luke knows something is wrong. How could he not? He came home two days ago to find me drained and weak, the apartment unclean, my work behind schedule, the phone messages from his friends unanswered. I lied to him, said that since it was Christmas I was depressed about Dad. After all, I couldn't have told the truth.

I hate Charles. I loathe him so deeply there are times I think I may even have stopped loving him. He has been cruel. He has denied me access to his body and heart when they are all I have been craving. He has abandoned me and will not tell me why.

We argued more before I left his flat. Hot, still, from the thrill of what had almost been, I flashed my Kantian trump card, said that our human capacity to choose is the greatest proof of our creative brilliance. Couldn't he agree that this should be celebrated, respected above notions of ethical good or moral rightness? Charles was frustratingly immutable. A respectable, adult relationship, he talked about; or nothing. I left feeling disconsolate and alone. He refused to kiss me goodbye. That night, I cried until dawn, the music of sadness thrumming in my heart.

Every deep sadness reminds me of Dad's going. That pain's a fever which remains in my bloodstream. I sink so low so fast that the future becomes too terrifying to contemplate, a house of cards that has already blown down. The apartment has been a living hell. I have been soundlessly screaming, my thoughts trapped in an exitless maze, my mind spinning, setting my body on edge, making me clench my hands in frustration and shame at my impotence. I have been hurling things across the room just for the sense of something solid in my hands, something controlled. Charles hasn't even had the decency to talk with me.

'So, what have you been up to?' Luke asked.

Do I know? With the clocks gone back, the dark sweeps in as fast as a tide before I have made progress with the day's sandcastles. The hours pass as listlessly as children impatient for their parents outside the school gate. Clouds hang sluggish over the damp city. I have stared at the miserable rain dripping off bare trees in the square. I have written twenty letters to Charles, half of which I have sent. I have clumped with beating heart to the door each morning hoping for a reply, despairing when there was none. I have walked after dark drenched by rain and frozen by winds and whistled at by lecherous men. Most nights, I have pummelled my head into the pillow, crying with hatred and love and despair that he and I met at all. Only with the comfort of dawn have I fallen asleep knowing I will wake later feeling dead, wishing I had the energy and will to follow my dad back to the blackness of being unborn.

I am old. My bones ache. What have you been up to? I have looked inward at myself and seen maggots. I have spoken with no one except Kaz although, since I have not been able to confess to my nakedness with Charles, our conversations have seemed shallow. She is the one person I might have turned to, but our friendship has become like a CD one listened to too often at first. We have tired of each other's tunes. I am sure my feelings for Charles have come between my new friend and me. She has refused to take my love for him seriously, whether out of loyalty to Luke or because I have been unable to tell her the complete truth, I don't know. And yet, she has shown concern for me. It was she who pointed out, without malice, that I am looking thin, that I have lost colour, that my hair has become lank. And it is true – my body is weak, handicapped with the weight of my mind. Amid the gloom, a nightly panic has set in that I will never succeed in finding peace, never open the right door to the right rose garden.

Oh, but I thought I had. Why won't Charles let me close to him? We could be happy. I have spent hours on his street, waiting for his return, but he has shut the door in my face, uncaring that I have been left crying openly on the street. He has ignored my phone calls, my pleas, my presence, our past. He has refused to listen to his own heart. Does he hate me or is it that he hates himself? Can't he even let me know?

Luke stirs. Gently, gently so he won't wake, I lay a hand on his shoulder. Look at him, back in his bed; our bed.

I have become a constant surprise to myself. I was terrified of him coming home and contemptuous of myself for lacking the courage to move out before he did so, and yet, when he woke me two days ago (his flight from Canada having arrived early in the morning) I held him so tightly he might naturally have assumed it was from missing him that I had been at such a loss, unable even to clean the dishes in the sink.

I think having an unstructured girlfriend gives his life just the right amount of deviance. There is something perverse about his desire to hear of my troubles. A rather dense calmness takes over his face when he listens. But, he loves me. I think he really does.

Soft as a breeze, I touch the skin behind his ear where it is so white and clean and taut over the bone of his skull. Do all men have such neatness, only look here how tidily the dark line of his stubble runs below his ear. I hear a slight sigh ease itself from his lungs. It is beginning to get light outside. I hope when he wakes he won't expect sex. I denied him last night with a temper that shocked both of us – evidence of a spirit stirring in me, at least. For days, that spirit has been dead. Shock turns you moribund, but like snowdrops after winter Luke has returned, forcing me back to life. He had with him a bag of presents from Mother, and something from him: it's a secret, he says. He seems, in ignorance, to believe this – whatever it is – will cure my ills.

'Por . . . ssssh.'

Aaaah. That's as good as reading my name in someone's diary. Porsh what? I think I love this man a little when he sleeps. He becomes a harmless boy to whom I am doing harm. Looking at him, I can't escape nostalgia for the thrill of the week after we became lovers when he and London were shiny and new.

We have been to four parties in two days, one to celebrate Killjoy's pregnancy, she prissy and proud and already on the Aqua Libra. In getting me out of the house and into restaurants and even, for a while, to think of something other than his father, I can't deny that Luke has made me happier. He couldn't keep his hands off me at Killjoy's. And yet, filtered through a mind so saturated with Charles, my life as Luke's girlfriend has lost its authenticity. I am an actress. At our Christmas parties, I have joked and gossiped and drunk too much sickly mulled wine and beer and vodka and then I have flirted with all of Luke's flirtatious friends and kept hidden everything in my mind, though it has often been on the tip of my tongue to speak of the torment of last week, of twice beginning to pack my bags; of the alternating waves of self-hatred and conviction in the purity of my love; of the belief that my future cannot possibly contain Luke. Perversely, amid the generosity of the season, I seem to have been accepted with nothing but grace and friendship. Tom, all wobbly as he splashed a drunken glance at my cleavage, admitted last night that most of Luke's friends thought I 'wouldn't last the summer'. Now that I have, I am being accepted with much the same defeatist shrug urban citizens give recently built eyesores. I no longer arouse passion. I just am. It comes as little surprise, life being how she is, that I find myself included when it's no longer what I want.

Luke makes a noise, turns my way, croaks, 'What time is it?'

'Seven, just after.' I wonder if there is one minute I have not seen pass on the red digital display of our bedside clock.

'Why are you awake?'

'Thinking.'

'My head hurts.'

'Mine too.' From thinking, I don't add.

'You didn't drink half a bottle of Talisker.'

'No, you win, I didn't.'

'Did you take Nuros?'

'Unhunh. But they're here.'

'Give us some, would you?'

I pop three shiny Nurofen out of their packing and pass them and the half-empty glass to Luke. He drinks, his Adam's apple bobbing up and down. Then he dribbles, as an old man might.

'When are we leaving?' I ask. I am scared of today, of going to the Old Rectory for the holiday.

'After lunch.' He turns his pillow over and moves it out of the way of his shoulder. He can't rest, I know, if there is any pillow under his shoulder itself. He gets fussy like that. 'Go back to sleep.'

Probably doesn't want me fidgeting beside him. I slink under the covers and, though I turn my back on Luke, I move my bum to touch his. He feels for me with his foot. He has an area of rough skin on the side of his big toe the scratch of which has become curiously reassuring. I rub my soft sole against it.

In a moment of unforgivable selfishness, I turn to Luke and spoon his body in mine. He hums his appreciation, and sloppily touches my thigh. The future is wrapped as the presents at the foot of the bed, and there is nothing I can do now, but wait.

As soon as our car comes to a halt outside the Old Rectory, Christian runs out. He is wearing a pair of colourful Afghan socks the leather soles of which have been chewed by one of their dogs. His skin looks bleached, like mine. Too much partying, I'd have thought, too many drugs. I wouldn't be surprised if his sweat was toxic enough to damage the plants and trees he landscapes.

'Quick,' he whispers urgently, 'back in the car.'

'What's happening?' I stretch my legs and shiver in the clear, country air.

'Hi, Goose. Happy Yuletide and all that bollocks.' He kisses me on both cheeks, flicks his cigarette on to the gravel and then climbs into the driver's seat. 'Come on, bro, get in. Where are the keys?'

'What is it this time?' Luke asks wearily, lifting one of the bags from the trunk.

'They want us all to decorate the tree and you know what

Mad Fish gets like if it's not the way she wants. Let's hit the Carrier's Arms for an hour.'

'I decorated the tree last year. Anyway, Portia's here.'

'So what? Ma'll rope her into it too. She thinks it's fun for the family.'

'I'm not going to abandon them. Why don't you try entering into the spirit of things?'

'Rather have some spirits entering me. What d'you think, Goosey?'

'About your joke?'

'Nah, the pub.'

'I could be thirsty.' Truth is, I'm terrified of facing Charles. I sat helpless in the car hoping something would delay us. Road works, a breakdown, Christmas cancelled due to endemic faithlessness.

'You two can walk if you want,' says Luke.

'It's two miles, Luke. Don't be such a cunt,' Christian complains, though I think he knew he never stood a chance. He hadn't bothered with shoes. 'Oh Ludo, I haven't got you a present. We had a pact, didn't we?'

'No, we didn't, and you say that every year.' Luke hands Christian the huge Harrods Stilton for which we had to do a U-turn on the Brompton Road, he huffing and puffing and trying to blame me because I hadn't remembered that he always forgot. It is the only sign of temper he has shown all week.

'Bring the rest of the stuff will you? Come on, Porsh, he'll do it.' Christian dumps the cheese on the roof of the car and slinks his arm around my shoulders. 'You say you love this man?'

'Actually,' I whisper, 'I'm in love with someone else.'

'It's me, isn't it?' He pulls me closer. He would be the most forgiving of his father, wouldn't he? If the truth were to emerge.

'That's right, I can't keep my hands off you Binghams,' I say, my mouth becoming dry with terror as we walk inside.

I see Charles immediately. He is dressed in baggy, faded green corduroy trousers and a cardigan with leather patches on its sleeves. He has a string of white fairy lights in his hands. So far, the tree is undecorated. It is planted just off-centre in a bucket wrapped in red tissue paper and, in its natural state, looks incongruous inside the refined hallway – much as I feel I must. 'Hello, Mr Bingham.'

'Charles, please.'

Serena and Christian watch as I take the four long, loud paces across the stone floor. I hold out my shaking hand but he leans forward for a kiss. I want to linger against his cheek.

'You're just in time for the tree.'

'Don't Dad!' says Serena. I kiss her hello, too. 'Don't let him rope you in.'

'Oh, I don't mind being roped.' Serena would despise me if I stole her father away. I would be blamed. Men above fifty are thought, almost endearingly, to be too incapable of restraint to be morally responsible.

'Just tell me what I can do.'

'Didn't you bring anything in, Porsh?' asks Luke, returning from the kitchen. 'I don't really mind being your butler, but—'

'Sorry. You said Christian was going to do it.'

'Oh, cool. Can I be your butler?' Chris pleads.

Mrs Bingham follows Luke as her lumpish ass follows her. 'Ah, here we all are. Splendid. We can all decorate the tree now.'

'Ding bloody dong,' chimes Christian. Oh, I like him.

'Merrily on high,' sings Serena. Something's pleasing her. I'm glad of that.

'Happy Christmas, Portia,' Victoria barks before offering me one cheek to be kissed. 'Christian, didn't I ask you to fill the log basket in the telly room? Grandpa's getting cold.'

Luke's maternal grandfather is the other guest. There will be seven of us in all.

'Somebody should tell him he's not in India any more. Oh, Luke, ten quid on "Darjeeling" later, yeah?'

'Make it twenty.'

'I'm a gardener.'

'Please, boys, can we not have that ridiculousness this year?' Victoria urges.

Such private language is the only thing I envied in families larger than my own.

'Does the door really have to be wide open, Luke, darling? Grandpa does get so cold. And where's Betty?'

'Out digging her grave,' Christian says with a smirk.

Betty is the golden labrador on her last legs. I try not to laugh. Victoria is suspicious of me as it is.

'Please, Christian, can you at least try to be a little more charitable. I don't know what Portia must think. It's so unbecoming over Christmas.'

'Porsh,' Luke complains, being a tad whiny, 'it's your stuff in the car, too.'

I look at Charles, wanting to confirm that he and I have discovered something to keep us above this, and for a moment he meets my eye, yet his look is so glazed with reproach that I trudge away, already fearing the hell I am sure this Christmas is going to be.

With dinner finished, there is talk of church. I am skipping the service. The others are not believers. They are going because not going would make them feel dislocated. I will not be alone. The old boy is already in bed, too close to checking in full-time with his maker, I would guess, to want to drop by tonight. His epithet's disconcertingly accurate since both his body and brain have begun to regress to childishness. He has, too, a distinctly boyish glint to his eye. I overheard him telling Victoria that I was a 'damn fine looking filly'. Charles, who was also there, said nothing. He could have ridden me, and knows as much.

'Come on, Porsh,' Luke urges, 'everybody goes to Midnight Mass.'

'I'm not everybody.'

'I know.' We are alone in the pretty dining room in the candlelight. He pulls his chair close to me and gives me a sexy kiss. Tongues, too. He is being so adorable, so tactile and passionate, I am almost falling for him. I have even begun to taunt Charles with Luke's attention and, in doing so, have fallen a little into my own trap. See how good it feels? And in its way, it does; it does.

'I'd better go and put on a jacket and tie. Ma hates it if we're not on time. If you're in bed later, I'll creep in.'

'I'm tired, Luke.'

'OK. But I can hardly wait.' He is excited. He has that flutter in his voice.

'For what?'

'For you'll see, naughty.'

He leaves. We have cleared the magnificent oval dining table but for a few glasses and half a bottle of claret. I fill my glass. This is my favourite room in the house. On the panelled walls hang handsome portraits of Charles's and Victoria's ancestors. They watch me. I doubt they would approve of my presence, though tonight I am being good.

We were set to task by Mrs Bingham. The holiday's a 'terrible worry' to her, she keeps telling me. Tonight, the tree had to be decorated, the silver cleaned, the dogs fed, wine brought from the cellar, holly cut from the garden (satisfying, this, because the berries are plump and abundant and shone brightly, festively, in the torch light) and, three times, I had to scrub the pots and pans filling the kitchen sink. I have always resented such effort. Victoria was cooking mince pies and mixing stuffing for the turkey and there was tonight's dinner on the go as well: a pheasant stew from the freezer, the potatoes peeled by me.

She is greedy to know about Dad. I have told her almost nothing. In between my silences, she talked a ceaseless chatter about the horses and the weather and the dogs – they like me, so I was told, which is just my luck – and about London in the fifties when she was a deb. It is called being polite, I guess, but it is tough going between us: she reminds me often, as Camilla does, of the different textures of our foundations. And it is precisely the quality I am sure Victoria most admires about herself, her jolly heartiness, that I find tiring and dull. When she wasn't watching, I made a face out of one of the potatoes and stabbed the knife between the eyes. If she were gone, I keep thinking, Charles would be free.

I look again at the smoky paint of a portrait of Charles's grandfather. Did he sit in this very room? The two share the same sexy eyes. When the others are at church, I am going to trespass into Charles's bedroom to touch and smell his pillow, his clothes, his things. It is this I am thinking when Charles himself steps into the room.

'You're not coming with us?' he asks.

'No.'

As he turns to leave, I call out his name. He wraps his hand around the door and looks back towards me. Dressed in his tweed suit, he looks so handsome in the soft light from the fire and candles. Why won't he kiss me again? Everyone else is upstairs, I can hear the floorboards creak.

'Is it going to be like this all Christmas?'

He shoots a glance into the corridor, then looks back my way. There is no kindness in his face. 'What do you mean?'

'You know. You know you know. Being so cold towards me. It's Christmas.'

'Portia, I don't think this is something to joke about.'

'I wasn't. How was that joking, for fuck's sake?' God, he can make me angry.

'Will you please keep your voice down. What would people think if they heard you talking like that?'

'The people are upstairs.'

'Walls have ears.'

I nod towards the portrait I was admiring. 'Yeah, and his eyes are moving too.'

Charles pours a taste of red wine; the martyr's blood. Can't he wait the half hour until communion? 'I don't think it's so very much to ask. You are a guest in my house.'

'So much to ask what?' I hate him being pompous. It was the fingertip-touching, ankle-holding, cock-hardened Charles who engaged my heart.

'That you respect Luke and Victoria. And myself, for that matter.'

'And I don't deserve any respect? It wasn't just me who got us here, don't forget.'

As he steps towards me, a log spits and crackles. His voice, an angry stage whisper, seems to contain the same ferocity. 'And I have apologized to you for that, Portia, time and time again. I am very sorry that you misunderstood me, but I will not be held responsible any longer for what you imagined I felt. Really, I can't be. You know precisely how I feel now so please, please, for all our sakes, grow up and accept it.'

Suddenly, the crackling log, shifted by its own internal energy, rolls from the fire behind me. Though the grate keeps it from rolling on to the wooden floor, it is billowing smoke into the room. I jump up and try to lift it in with the brass tongs, but the hinge is loose and I drop it again. I hate my feminine feebleness sometimes. Charles has to come to my aid. He takes the tongs from my hand. When he drops the wood back, a plume of sparks leaps and crackles from the embers.

'Please, Charles. Why are you acting as if you hate me?'

'I am spending Christmas with my family,' Charles says, his teeth actually gritted. 'It is beyond me what you expect me to do.'

'You could try not hating me.' I lift my hand to his cheek, but he tightly grabs my wrist and pulls it down. The orange flames splash satanically against his church-going face.

'Don't you dare touch me when Victoria's in the house. Never. Not now, not tomorrow, not ever.'

'Why? Because you want me to?'

He lets go, and lowers his eyes. 'You're going to force me to say something to Luke.'

'Say what? You wouldn't.'

He speaks quickly. 'I thought you two were going to . . . to break things off. I can't have you making eyes at me while he has his hands on you. I don't know how you have the heart to treat him like that.'

'You think he'd prefer the way you treated him? Or me?'

'I treated you with all the respect I could. How dare you suggest otherwise?'

I want to cry. I can't bear it that he hates me. 'Charles, please, what have I done?'

'Haven't you understood what I have been telling you? Whatever your mind imagines could happen between us is quite impossible. It's something I would never conceive of doing—'

'That's a lie. You know it is.'

'No. I am appalled by you, if you must know. Aren't you aware how serious Luke's intentions are?'

'Yeah, he'll leave me the second some nice marryable type comes along. I'm a curiosity to him.'

'And have you told him you think this?'

'I need to tell him what he's thinking?'

A door bangs upstairs, then Victoria's voice, 'Come along, boys, or we'll be late.'

Charles and I back away from each other. I sit again.

'Portia, I am asking you to please tell Luke what's in your mind. You owe him that.'

'You mean tell him about us?' I ask, incredulous.

'Charles,' comes Victoria's voice.

'No, of course not, but at least be honest and make it clear that—'

'Charles?'

'In here,' he answers, crossing the room.

Victoria bustles in looking regal in a black velvet jacket that just about stretches over her hips. Her diamond brooch picks up the candlelight. I feel I should stand up or something. Curtsy. God's getting all the finery tonight. Even Christian, appearing behind her, is wearing a tie. It makes him look more like Luke.

'Not coming to church, Goose?'

Act normal. He will probably assume my cheeks are red from the fire and the wine. 'Don't worry, I promise I'll say my prayers before I go to bed.'

'Oh, there'll be none of that praying. I only go for the wine and Mum goes to see who else is there.'

'Sometimes I don't know whose son you are, Christian. Really, I don't.'

'God's,' he says with a smirk. 'Later, Goose. Don't steal the silver.'

There is a bustle over lost dogs and car keys then suddenly the house is quiet, eerily so. The clocks tick on, the logs cackle. 'Don't steal the silver!' Am I really nothing but an impostor to the Binghams, a common thief? Charles is surely treating me as if I had tried to steal him from his family. To do unto others what was done to myself. Is it true? I don't know. My weakening love for him feels neither destructive nor evil. I thought I had learned from Dad's death to live a life that was enthused, alive, that fear itself was futile, that nothing brings death faster than cynicism and detachment. But whenever I engage my emotions, do what I believe honest and true, I am greeted by a world that won't allow me to be me. Only sometimes do the words fit the tune. I thought they had with Charles. I believed without malice that he and I were meant. So why this discord? How can I be so wrong? What if I have been mistaken in trusting as my teacher a man whose life ended in such abject misery; in no life at all? Or have I had no choice? Perhaps within his genetic casket is a will that is tarnished. Or is Dad out of the equation? Should the blame for my unglistening existence rest with me alone?

Glass in hand, I saunter through the mellow house to where the tree's lights sparkle with the curve and span of an elegant ball gown. This should be contentment. For half of my life, I have longed to belong to such a family in such a house. It is my dream of England come true. Yet, when I sit on the bottom step of the stairs and lower my face into the open prayer-book of my hands, I cry not with joy but mad impotent frustration at my ignorance, my aloneness. Shouldn't I be the one at church praying for guidance out of this mess? Not Charles, the man who would not commit adultery, who would not lie and cheat.

Not Victoria or Serena, who has already been unfairly punished. And not Luke.

No, not Luke. An image of him kneeling in prayer confirms to this sinning unbeliever his goodness. It makes me feel suddenly guilty, not for the accident of my love for Charles, but for doing to Luke just what I hated his father doing to me. I have given hope to his love. I have allowed him to believe in us after I have lost faith. That much was in the hands of no one but myself.

The white fairy lights kaleidoscope into prisms through the tears in my eyes when I lift up my head. It isn't fair to blame too much on Dad. It wasn't he who made me wrap ten empty boxes to put under the tree for Mother one year. Or to ignore her presents to me until, eventually, she took them back to the shops. And was it because of him that I dropped out of going to college, he who had forged an academic career out of an inauspicious, rural life? Was it because of the man he was and the manner in which he reared his only child that I acted towards Luke as I have? I don't know. I don't know why I never considered his desertion a challenge, as a chance for him to redeem himself through my successes. Me as Canadian nation after his loyalist defeat.

Or have I been trying? I write for him. I have been searching for a man who will love me as well as he did. I am living his desire to return to our land. I could never have guessed it would lead to this.

I choose the back stairs to bed, away from Charles's door. I have lost the desire to step inside. There is no better proof of greatness in a person than goodness, and Luke is good. He is good. He would never have hurt me as Charles has done tonight. However I act from now, I must never forget how I owe him for that.

I wash, get to bed and close my eyes on the soft, clean pillow. Someone has flattened my sheets with care. It feels luxurious, privileged. I have been greedy wanting more than I have already been given. Maybe through Luke I could stop this running. Luke, who is anchored in this house, this country I love. Luke who loves me, loves me, loves me.

It is with such thoughts in my mind that I curl my body into the shape of a smile and relax. Downstairs, the clock chimes the midnight hour. It is Christmas Day, and all is surprise.

There is a hand stroking my cheek. I open my eyes. Luke.

'Hey, sweets. Happy Christmas.'

'Thanks. To you, too.'

Last night's cold and clear weather rinsed out Christmas Eve, but the particles are busy again with noises of people active downstairs, with cosy heat from the radiator and faint smells of bacon and coffee and bread burned. A rich winter sunshine has argued its way through the pale curtains to make more creamy the worn eggshell paint of the frames. The room is gracious. Something in me feels settled, answered.

'Why'd'you wake me?'

He brushes his lips against mine then whispers, 'You've been sleeping for hours.'

'You were just in my dream. There was an elephant. And a man with a big head.' My body leans to where his own depresses the mattress. Strange dream, it was. The man with the large head offered me a job as an advertising copywriter in Toronto. My first assignment was on the roof of a skyscraper. A photographer was taking shots of an elephant sitting cross-legged on a chair. I could make out the faces of old friends in the clouds. My desk was precariously perched at the edge of the building. The wind was strong and I was scared I would fall. I couldn't think of anything witty to write, of anything at all. Then, suddenly, Luke was there. He secured the table, wrote my copy for me and left me with the praise.

Awake, my gratitude lingers. I think this man would fly across the world if a friend needed him. He is selfless and generous in that way.

'What time is it?'

'After twelve.'

'You're kidding.' I push myself up. 'Have I missed all the presents?'

'No, we always wait until after the Queen's speech.'

'How polite!' I twist some sleepy gunk from my eye. 'Did I miss anything else?'

'Not really. We took the old boy for a walk in the orchard. Serena got a surprise stocking from Hugh and—'

'Hugh was her husband, yeah?'

'Is, yup. What else? Um, Dad's in a filthy mood for some reason but apart from that we're all just waiting for you, really.'

'Sure you were.'

'I was.'

'Were you? Why?'

'Because I love you.'

Oh, but we are simple. There are tears in my eyes when he kisses me again. I take his face in my hands. For all our flights to the moon and bombs dropped and babies saved and computer chips built, despite everything and anything any philosopher has surmised from Heraclitus to Heidegger, we are simple. Everything collapses in on itself under the weight of our need to be loved. And Luke loves me. Contained within his promise is the extraordinary fact that he, to whom I have promised nothing, is willing to forgive everything.

'Porsh.'

'Mm?'

'I want to . . . I mean, do you think you would ever think of?'

'What?'

'Actually, doesn't matter.' He stands, suddenly. 'Come on, I'll let you get dressed.'

I laugh. 'You don't have to leave. You've seen me naked before, I think. In fact,' I flip the duvet onto the floor, 'voilà! Here's a Christmas present that's already unwrapped.'

'Better not. Mum's around. I'll, um, I'll see you in a minute.'

He smiles, but not conclusively. Something – I have no idea what – is up. Not that I mind such a pleasant sense of anticipation returning on Christmas Day. It beats the sense of gloom I most often feel. And I do feel curiously optimistic and renewed, not merely by my restorative sleep, but the sense that I have found the strength to shield myself from Charles. I have not felt such indifference towards him since the day we met.

It is Luke I have to thank. His loving declaration cocoons me through our smoked salmon lunch and beyond, rendering Charles's Scrooge-like malignity stingless. And it calms me deep within, lifting the weight from my shoulders. After lunch, I feel genuinely happy and calm as we take the dogs for a walk across the softly undulating fields. Charles can ignore me all he likes. I have Luke, and he loves me. He loves me. There is the promise of snow in the air, but the early afternoon clouds withhold their gift, much as the Bingham family hoards its presents until after the Queen has demurely addressed her subjects at three. Then we gather in the drawing room where, amid oohs and aahs and kisses, a very English Christmas is acted out, reflected in the opulent shine of the drawing-room's furniture.

I sit beside Luke and am thrilled by almost every present I receive. Christian gives me a printed T-shirt with the familiar McDonald's 'M' spelling marijuana instead; from Serena I receive some silver earrings not entirely dissimilar from the earrings I have given her. For Luke I bought a leather overnight bag, which I now realize contains within it the suggestion that he and I will be travelling together. He gives me a slim leather address book with Toronto/London embossed in gold on the outside. It makes me suspect he is keeping something else for later. From Charles I get a sterile science book about the discovery of longitude. He wrote Merry Christmas on the card, underlining the truth that he doesn't want me happy. I am hawk-like while he unwraps the sky-blue pyjamas I bought for him, so see how quickly he hides them by the side of the sofa, though not so fast that Victoria (avian herself) fails to notice. His behaviour gives my gift an adulterous hue made more so by the quizzical look Victoria sends me, and to which I remain expressionless.

It is only after we have cleared away the tea cups and Christmas cake and Serena and Victoria are tending to the horses that I walk in on Charles adding logs to the drawing-room fire, and we are alone for the first time today. I turn at once to leave.

'Portia, could we have a word?'

'What about?' I won't have him puncturing my mood.

'Do you think you could push the door shut first?'

'Luke and Chris are watching *Indiana Jones*.'

'All the same, please.'

Around the room, on the carpet and chairs, clusters of presents make manifest each of our characters. Christian has CDs, sunglasses, a hip flask, funky shirts with big collars, while Luke's pile includes some golf clubs along with single malt whisky and socks. He might expect little different over the next thirty years. I don't think it troubles him. Charles moves the grate in front of the fire. 'I was wondering whether you had spoken to Luke yet.'

'No, I haven't.' Already, I feel self-conscious, the way I get when I become aware of my hands and don't know what to do with them.

'I thought we agreed that you would talk to him.'

'No, you agreed I would. I don't want to today, OK?'

Odd, I guess I didn't mind feeling the little girl with Charles before (maybe there was something in Kaz's assertion of Freudian transference) but today he has no right to talk to me as if he's my father. Nor will I let him take his moodiness out on me. All day he has seemed malcontent, as if he has wanted to hit me. Now he stares at me, coldly. 'I rarely consider it my business to become involved in my sons' relationships, but the way that you are behaving with Luke is so completely at odds with what you yourself told me you felt that I really must ask what it is you think you are playing at. You two couldn't keep your hands off one another this afternoon and—'

'Oh, my God—' I take a small step back. Charles is jealous,

jealous. That's what this is, what yesterday was. Jealous of his son's hands; of mine on Luke. It makes me in an instant think less of him. 'You don't like it that we're happy, do you?'

'Don't be so absurd. I am not thinking about myself.'

'No, of course.' I smile, ungraciously. 'You never do.'

Angrily, Charles retorts, 'Portia, we are not all governed by such self-interest. It was you yourself who told me that you no longer had feelings for Luke, so, clearly, clearly, I am no longer an impartial observer. He believes you.'

'Good. I want him to. I feel differently about it, now.'

'Since ten days ago?'

'I felt differently about you after ten seconds. Remember?'

Charles has been addressing me as if he had our conversation prepared, but I think my answer has him surprised.

I speak again, less aggressively. 'It feels like a choice, this time. Not just chance.'

'As long as you can promise me that you're not doing this to make me—'

At the sound of footsteps in the corridor, he breaks off, and luckily, because it's Luke who comes in. 'Hey, Pops. Um, Porsh, I'm going upstairs for a bath. Do you want one first?'

'The immersion is on,' says Charles, 'so there'll be plenty of hot water.'

All this here, I think, and hot water still a luxury. Calvin lives.

'Shall I leave the water in for you?' Luke asks me.

I make a face. 'I think I'll pass on that, thanks.'

'All righty. But you are coming up, soon, are you? You're—'

'In a minute.'

When Luke is gone, leaving the door open, Charles lowers his voice to say, 'You won't make any promises before you are sure of things, will you?'

'What do you mean?'

'To Luke.'

I laugh. 'Well, I'm not about to marry him, if that's what you think.'

Charles shakes his head, but I wonder if his shoulders didn't just drop a little or if the knot that had been tightening his brow didn't loosen, as if my marrying Luke was precisely what had been on his mind.

The bath I lie in after Luke has had his is a huge tub with an archaic plunger that leaks where the washer has perished with age. I fill it so deep that I can almost float without touching the sides. By the time I get out, the air is dense with steam and my fingertips are soggy and white. I wrap a towel around me and scamper briskly on my tiptoes on the worn-out, dog-hairy carpet that, inexplicably, covers the corridor between bedrooms. I close the door of my room then almost leap with shock when I see Luke sitting on my bed. He is dressed in black tie for dinner and has a huge glass of whisky in his hand.

'Hey, you. You look like James Bond.'
'Where have you been? I thought you must have drowned.'
'I was swimming. I love that bath.'
Beside him, I run a hand through his hair. He kisses me on my stomach then, parting the towel, runs a cheeky finger up the slit of my vagina. But instead of going further, he takes another gulp of his drink then rises to walk to the window to peek through the curtains, as if he is expecting someone. I lift a foot onto the bed then dry my legs. Here if he wants me.

He asks, 'Had a nice day?'
'Yeah, it was real nice, thanks. You made it nice.'
Now he is playing with something in his jacket pocket. While I dress he keeps looking at me, then back outside. Something is making him jumpy.

'Porsh?'
'Yeah.'
'Um, next year, shall we maybe go on holiday? Africa, or somewhere.'
'Maybe.' Planning, I don't like; mice and men and all.
'So you weren't thinking of going back to Toronto?'
'No. I mean, I don't think so.'

'Oh, OK. Because you, you didn't seem very happy before Christmas.'

'I know.'

He drinks some more, lets the curtain fall from his fingers. 'I thought maybe you weren't enjoying London.' His frown makes him look older. It is rare. One thing about Luke, he doesn't possess a troubled soul.

'I get like that sometimes. When I think about things that happened.'

'You shouldn't look back so much. Maybe if—'

As I rub cream under my eyes, I see in the mirror's reflection Luke coming closer. 'If what, sweet thing? You keep starting your sentences and not finishing them.'

'Oh, doesn't matter. Here, I got you something, I—'

I turn and stand. From his pocket, he has taken a present.

'Happy Christmas.'

The gift is a small box immaculately wrapped in thick, silver paper – the type a jewellery shop might stock and . . . Oh no, Luke. Oh, no. My heart doubles in size, shrinks, triples. You wouldn't have. 'Luke, what is this?'

'Just something for you.' He has that nervous flutter in his voice.

Oh, my God. Suddenly, the pieces slot into place: Luke wanting to meet Mother. Charles urging me to take Luke seriously; Luke himself all jittery with excitement over his surprise; his talk of making me a decent woman and of the future; his affection today and his drinking now and, oh God, what will I say if it is a ring? I rip at the paper, see the blue-black jewellery box beneath. I don't think I can bear to open it. 'Luke, what have you—?'

'Go on.'

With my shaking hand, I flip open the lid then clasp a hand to my mouth. Relief floods through me. Inside are two diamond stud earrings. 'Oh, Luke, they're beautiful, they're—' They're not me, not really, not the kind of earrings I would have dreamed of wearing or wanting just a couple of years ago when I had my right ear pierced a further five times, and yet I adore the look of them the moment I press them into my ears. They are Cinderella's slipper, I should be dancing at this ball, shouldn't I? I belong on this boat.

'I love them. Thank you.' The sparkliness of the gems make me light on my feet as I slop my naked arms over Luke's black-suited shoulders. I have to lift myself on to the tips of my toes to kiss his lips. 'What did I do to deserve these?'

'You were you.'

'And that's enough?'

He smiles the same warm smile I first saw outside my apartment in Canada. 'More than enough.' Another kiss, then, 'Porsh.'

'Yes, Luke.' I answer slowly. Don't know why, but it seems he needs humouring.

'Do you think you'd, you'd—'

'I'd?'

He nods like a simpleton. 'Do you think you'd like a drink? A glass of champagne?'

'To go with my diamonds? Yeah, I'd love one. But I'll come down.'

'All right. Dinner will be served at eight-thirty.'

Usually, infidelity (even when unconsummated) makes you hate your lover for his stupid, senseless trust. A part of you wants to shake him out of his ignorance, his refusal to fight. Now my renewed sense of guilt is causing me to accept Luke's emotional and actual generosity as a priceless, undeserved bequest. I am flattered and surprised by it. And 'Dinner will be served at eight-thirty.' How cute! How English!

I dress in a simple black dress with my diamonds. I feel like Jackie O before the tragedies. Feelings of fortune are flooding back. The dining room is lit only by fire and candlelight and the table is congested with silver cutlery and candlesticks and Christmas decorations and crystal glass and decanters filled with heavily breathing wine. Delectable smells of roasting turkey, which my mind translates into images of glistening, crisp skin, are making the evening seem even more palatable and appetizing. I think of Mother alone in her kitchen and of the years I left her alone when I promised to come home. I should work to repair such damage, not just let it heal with time. I would be happy if Mother could be here now. She would love such finery as this.

Now when I catch a glimpse of my candlelit self in the mirror above the fireplace I think my face is well-suited to this mood. My sharp features look softer. The diamonds twinkle. The colour has been found for that black-and-white image seen in Heathrow. I would love Moira and Iain to see me now, living the high life. And Dad. He would be proud.

Vintage champagne awaits me in the drawing room. The men stand for me. Charles's expression is more benevolent than before, less threatened. The drink fizzes merrily on my tongue. I walked in on Luke and Christian playing 'Darjeeling' with their grandfather. The old boy spent years in India and the continent is never long out of his conversation. The object of 'Darjeeling' is to see who can tempt him to name an Indian city of their choice. Five pounds are riding on a hill station in the south.

Though he has large ears, the old boy is going deaf. He has a long face and thick, straight white hair cut short at the back and sides in a style I imagine has changed little in the past fifty years. He looks distinguished in his black tie.

'The church last night, Gramps,' says Christian, 'was the smelliest place in the world.'

'You've never been to Bombay. Stank to high heaven. It was bloody hot and bloody smelly but you couldn't help loving it,' he recalls, laughing to himself.

'That's why you had to go up to the hills, isn't it?' asks Luke. 'To that place. What's it called?'

'Absolutely. Get the ladies up to the hills.'

'Where did you go again?' asks Christian.

'What's that?'

'They were asking where you would go when you went to the hills in India,' I explain. 'Near Bombay.'

'Ooty, do you mean? Have you been to Ooty?'

Christian whispers. 'That doesn't count.'

'Bollocks, you owe me.' Luke grins. 'She's half-mine.'

'I've never been,' I say, though I heard what Luke said.

'Double or quits on Trivandrum.'

'Oh, you must go,' the old boy urges me. For a military man, he has soft and kind eyes. 'It's a lovely place, absolutely lovely. Beautiful light on the lake. We went up there to escape the heat. It's actually called Ootacamund, but everyone calls it Ooty.'

'Come along boys,' says Victoria, 'can't we talk about something else?'

'We could toast the baby Jesus,' suggests Christian.

'I say we toast Portia for looking so lovely,' Luke says.

'I'd better go and check on the turkey,' Victoria responds. 'Charles, can you come and carve in a moment?'

I am tipsy on champagne and compliments (my dress, my diamonds) by the time we sit down to eat. Again, I am beside Charles though, for now, he and Luke are serving the feast. It makes me smile inside, dinner being served by servile father and son. I would say the two of them enjoy the roles because they know how far they are and have always been from being waiters themselves. It's their upbringing they're atoning for.

Over the civilized clink of dinner I listen to the Binghams discuss what matters to them. They talk of the dogs and horses and pheasants and little people in the village; of the women on whom Christian has had his eye since the Lady Joanna left him for New York; of whether she'll make it as a model; of nothing memorable. Because I am on the wrong side of sober, it doesn't much bother me as it can do in London – all those interminable conversations I have had with Luke's friends about everything that couldn't matter less.

Victoria says, 'Charles, I forgot to tell you: Betsy asked would we go to a Conservative curry lunch the week after New Year.'

'I suppose that we can, if we must.'

'I don't know which'd make me more sick,' says Christian. 'The Conservatives or the curry.'

'Christian, your Labour lot are taking the country to the dogs.

Really, they are,' Victoria says. 'You can't remember the last time.'

'I don't think they're changing shit,' I say, then, quickly, 'Help, sorry.'

'Nicely put,' says Christian.

'Portia's got a point,' says Luke. He's with me tonight; every tiny step. Makes me want to cry.

'Tony Blair's just like Clinton,' I suggest. 'Too keen to please all the people all the time to get anything done. I think you have to upset people if you're going to make a stand.' Like Dad used to, I don't add. I remain proud of his fights with the university.

'Nothing can be gained if you upset the wrong people,' Charles points out.

'Yeah, but you can never lose if you say what you believe. Can you?'

'Luke,' asks Victoria, out of the blue, 'is your friend Kaz still one of those Vegan people?'

Luke lies, says she is, then Serena compliments me by taking the conversation back to the British Labour Party, though now the discussion is of their dress sense, the wrong ties to go with the wrong shoes, until we are offered more dry turkey and over-boiled Brussels sprouts and good, fatty, roast potatoes that I squidge in gravy with my fork, indelicately, before Serena and her mother clear the plates. I am drinking too much. My chirpiness makes Charles seem stuffy. He hasn't relaxed as he used to when we were alone.

Suddenly, the lights are turned off and Mrs Bingham, trilling as she goes, rushes in brandishing a plate on which our plum pudding, stabbed in the top with a sprig of holly, is burning. I think it is meant to be. I can't say I like the look of it, but am persuaded by the promise of brandy in the sauce. I wish I hadn't been (the pudding tastes like wet socks) although it isn't me but Luke who has trouble eating his share. He is edgy, each of his sentences is prefaced with an um. He is drunk, too. Then again, so am I. Must have had six or more glasses of wine on top of the champagne.

'Go on, give us some more, Mum.' Christian holds out his pudding plate.

'No one's got the sixpence yet.'

'Have you asked Portia, or Grandpa?'

'No more for me,' the old boy says. 'Watching my weight.'

'Portia?'

'I'm good.'

'Um, you could . . . I mean if you get the sixpence, it's lucky,' mumbles Luke.

'I'm lucky anyway,' I say, catching Charles's eye as I reach for my crystal water glass.

Christian fails to find the elusive sixpence and I clear the plates. Victoria tells me I shouldn't have, but the look she gave me after the turkey made me think I should, so I have. Back in the dining room, Luke has swapped places with his brother to sit beside me. He is looking sheepish.

'Have you got a cracker, Grandpa?' asks Serena.

'Yes, it's lovely, isn't it? I've got some. I never cared for French cheese.'

'A Christmas cracker. From the table.' Serena won't join in the teasing and now hands her grandfather one of the chunky crackers that had been criss-crossed around the decoration in the centre of the table.

'This one looks different,' I say to Luke as we fold our arms across our chests.

'They're all from Harrods,' Victoria assures me.

'It looks cut at the end,' I say. 'Look, Luke.'

'It's fine,' he answers, not looking.

'Did you do something to it?'

He reddens. 'Sssh. It's just for you.'

'Luke, what are you playing at?' Victoria asks. 'I think you've drunk too much. Charles, I think he's drunk too much.'

'You've got to hold it more over the table,' Luke insists. His concentrated urgency reminds me of a little boy out of whose reach something is being held.

'Why?'

'Well, I'm pulling,' says Christian, starting the chain.

When I tug against Luke, the cracker snaps much too easily leaving me with the prize. I am sure he cut it. The tube is stuffed with tissue scarlet as turkey guts. I whip it out as if I am a magician. Something bounces off the table onto the Persian rug. My shoulder bumps against Luke's as we both look down.

'Portia,' says Charles, 'I've got your insides.'

I lift my head. 'I think Luke's got something else for me.'

Luke has fallen desperately to his knees but quickly finds what was lost. He is clasping the object in his right hand when he sits back in the chair. 'You've got to read the message first,' he insists. He has folded into a tiny square the rectangle of paper that usually reveals a fortune or joke. It is fiddly in my shaky, nail-bitten fingers. 'Just not out loud.' His hand remains tight on whatever he dropped.

I read the message: When I read it again, and again, my heart seems to stop. A tiny death. I suppose it is my expression that has turned the table quiet.

'What's the big mystery, Goose?' Christian wants to know.

I turn to Charles, then back to Luke whose expression is less excitable now.

'What's it say?'

Will you please marry me? Luke has written. Simple as that.

Now he extends his hand to me. The ring has dented its shape in his palm. I take it, turn it slowly in my fingers.

'Glory! I don't believe it,' declares Victoria. 'Luke, you can't have. You can't have.' It's an admonishment, though whether for his intent or its timing I can't know.

'What has she got?' asks the old boy.

'It's an engagement ring, Gramps,' says Christian. 'Luke's popped the question.'

'Popped what?'

I turn to Charles. He looks winded, pale, almost as if he is about to cry. His eyes leave mine for Victoria's. I focus again on the beautiful ring. The clock chimes from the hall.

Luke says, 'I did ask your mother.'

I shake my head, as if it could matter.

'You asked her mother too?' Christian jokes. 'That's rich.'

'Portia, your mouth's bleeding,' says Serena.

Oh, I taste it now. I've bitten my bottom lip.

To my right, Charles has stood. 'Luke, was this really the wisest time?'

'Portia?'

Poor Luke looks quite dumbstruck. I guess I do as well. I am silent as the others rise to their feet. A rabbit in headlights. We are being left alone. My heart is thumping. I feel completely lost, unable to connect thoughts to my brain or cogent words to my tongue. I have been here before, not a proposal but as overwhelmed, as addled, as this. I loved acting at school, was good at it, used to get the lead roles often as not, but then when Dad killed himself I said I couldn't do it, not any more. And only because Mrs Killian had seen her eldest son die on Highway 401 and swore she understood such things did I let her talk me into it ('a talent's a terrible thing to waste, Portia') so 'the girl whose Dad hanged himself' got the lead role in *Romeo and Juliet* opposite Craig Chamberlain, no less, the handsomest boy in the school. It should have been my moment on opening night, he professing his love, but I knew it was a mistake, of course it was, just two minutes after I got on stage everything froze black and the only voice coming into my head was Mother's repeating, 'It's Daddy, darling. Something has happened to Daddy,' so that I forgot not just one line, not even one speech or one scene but my role in its entirety, as if my memory had been erased.

'If you want time—' I hear Luke begin now that we are alone.

'No, Luke, I—'

'Don't say no without thinking,' he whispers, touching my hand. 'Please, just—'

'I'm me, Luke. I'm me. You're good, you're so good and—'

'And I want to marry you. I love you, Portia.'

When he touches my cheek, the tears come. I take hold of his hand and squeeze it tight and close my eyes. Oh, he loves me. He forgives me. He is offering me more than I will ever be offered again. Isn't the ring nothing less than a map of life's maze? The blood from my engorged heart seems to be flowing into those fingertips against my cheek calming me, calming me. As the pressure subsides so the unfocused whir of thoughts slows to a roulette ball's determined clack. Clack, clack, clack and now to a stop. How can I say no?

When I open my eyes, Luke seems so very unhappy, as if he has done something very wrong, as if he could ever do something wrong, and it makes me wonder why I was so blind and self-obsessed as to betray the man willing to offer this much trust and belief in me. Why can't I put it right now, do something for someone else, this lovely and loving man? See if my happiness, ours, can't spring from his.

'Yes, Luke,' I whisper. 'I will.' I kiss him on the lips and let my tears drop from my eyes and run on to his cheek just as my blood must be flowing into his mouth to mix with his own.

When, with shaking hands, Luke slides the ring on to my finger (it fits, I am Cinderella) a bubble of excited laughter bursts through my mouth. Mrs Bingham of the Old Rectory? That's near Oxford, yes.

We kiss, the best of first kisses multiplied a hundred thousand times. I am dizzy on my feet as Luke leads me to the kitchen. Only look where your baby girl is now, Daddy! See where I have finally arrived.

'Hey, everyone,' Luke calls out as we turn into the kitchen, but only Charles is inside, clutching to the sink, his back to us, his head bowed, here where I first set eyes on him. When he turns and sees Luke with his arm around mine, he can't hide the dismay. My heart dips; a little, it does.

'Hey, Dad. Where's everyone?'

'In the drawing room, I think.'

'Guess what?'

'What's that, Luke?' There is nothing glad about his eyes.

'Da-daaa.' Luke lifts my hand to show the ring. 'Meet Mrs B-to-be. Look at the ring.' Hugging me from behind, Luke walks me towards his father until I am sandwiched between father and son. I lift my hand for Charles to take. His is shaking, as is mine.

'Got the DT's have you, Dad?'

'I am getting old, Luke. But this is lovely. Did you get it from Johnny Stamford?'

'Yep.'

I don't recognize my jewelled hand. It is someone else's, I have given mine away. The ring is exquisite, a rectangular emerald with a small diamond on each side of it. The mounting tapers in an elegant curve. I am suddenly feeling more drunk than I did in the drawing room.

'Let's tell the others. Dad, is there any champagne in the cellar?'

'Of course, Luke. I'll bring it through.'

I ask, 'Do you want help?'

'No, Porsh, you've got to come with me,' Luke insists, kissing my neck. He and I are almost out of the door when he turns back. 'Hey, Dad, you didn't congratulate us.'

'Didn't I?' His voice is unmistakably shaky. 'Well, congratulations, Luke. And Portia.'

'Thanks. See you in the drawing room.'

Luke's beaming face broadcasts my acceptance the moment he and I enter the drawing room. Victoria can't seem to muster a smile, but Serena's lips curve into a genuine and lovely grin. Christian lifts me in the air and swings me around so vigorously that my feet knock a small table to the ground, spilling to the carpet silver-framed photos of the family. The sharpness of Victoria's rebuke exposes, I think, her displeasure at Luke's match. She won't make it explicit, but I have never won her over. She is hesitant in her congratulation. Even when the champagne has been opened and Luke and I are toasted, she is behind the others.

When the initial excitement is over, the old boy excuses himself to go to bed and the talk turns to the wedding itself. At first, everyone has an opinion – the ceremony should be held in London rather than Canada or at the Old Rectory; perhaps a small service since not so many of my friends will be flying over; probably not a sit-down, considering; maybe even the Turf Club for a reception. Luke seems to have all the questions answered as in other countries a woman might. He has assumed I will want a white wedding with all the British trappings. I am less sure. I don't see what our promise has to do with anyone else. Why can't we be married quietly, just us two, alone?

'Who's going to be your best man?' asks Christian. 'Charlie?'

'I thought Jake.' Jake is Luke's cousin. 'Hey!' He leaps up. 'I'm going to call him now.'

'Luke, it's half-past-ten,' Victoria says. 'You know Betsy goes to bed early.'

'Mum, come on. You don't think she'd want to hear this?'

With a tilt of her coiffured head and a glance at her husband, Victoria answers no to Luke's rhetorical question without saying a word. With Luke gone, an uncomfortable silence settles fast during which I realize that, since we began talking, first Charles, then Victoria and then Serena withdrew from the discussion and into themselves. If this was a party, we would all be heading home. The atmosphere is depressingly flat.

'What a long day,' says Victoria. 'Serena, darling, you look dead on your feet.'

It is not an inaccurate description. Ever since I met Serena, I have thought there was something ghostly about her, not merely in her appearance, though her demeanour is always pale and drawn and her prominent cheekbones remind me too forcefully of the skull underneath, but emotionally, as if she edited the superfluous from her life and was surprised by how little was left. Clear out life's junk and you are left with an empty room. It is difficult to justify a life that is not reproductive, and this is how Serena most often behaves, as if she is wombless, hollow, a purposeless shell. She has seemed happier this holiday (the generously filled stocking from her estranged husband brought her real joy) and yet I recognize in her moodiness the private remembrance of painful things. Her face changes fast as the surface of a lake when the wind gathers and the sun is hidden by cloud.

'I'm fine,' she says now. 'Just tired.'

'Then have some more champagne.' Hedonism for Christian is an all-consuming answer. He lifts the bottle from the bucket but has misjudged the mood and receives no takers. I flatten my palm across my glass. Even before the champagne I had drunk too much but now its bubbliness in my stomach has begun to make me feel sick. The tiny burps I have been sneaking from my stomach are failing to ease the nausea.

The new mood dampening the room has deepened my unease. I feel as if I have done something wrong. Charles has barely spoken a word, only now does he say something about the shoot at Toby Yarbridge's tomorrow, it's an eight-thirty start, apparently, and I'm expected to go to serve drinks or perform some such wifely, servile duty. I am not looking forward to it.

'Mum,' Luke announces as he bursts back into the room, 'Betsy wants a word.' He fills his glass with what's left in the bottle. 'Jake's said he'll be my best man. I bet he ties me naked to a train after the stag.'

'He's a bad boy,' says Serena. 'Always cheats on his girlfriends.'

'He's going to be in London next week. We should have a party, Porsh. Shouldn't we? Maybe on New Year's Eve.'

'Maybe.'

'Are you OK?'

'Yes. I just feel. I need some water, that's all.'

'I'll get you a glass,' offers Serena, sweetly.

'No, I will.' I need to be out of this room. I don't want a party and I don't want a big wedding and I don't know if I want to tag along as the latest addition to Luke's settled life. Why can't he just promise to love me when being loved is all that counts? Help, didn't think I was this drunk at all, no wonder I can't think straight. Can't walk straight. When I collide with the corridor wall, I almost knock a print of Trinity College to the ground. As I am setting it straight, I hear Victoria mentioning my name on the phone. I tiptoe closer, hear with shock her saying, 'Yes, well, it sounds as if he was terribly common, her father . . . That's right, English, mmm. One simply can't tell with the accent she has . . . Well, he killed himself, Betsy. Awful, I know . . . Hanged, I believe. Well, quite. The problem is she's lovely looking . . . Yes.' She sighs, as if I am a terminal disease contracted by her favourite son. My heart thumps like a fist into a punching bag. 'It's just such a terrible shame he's at that marrying age . . . Did he? Well, I can't say I'm at all surprised . . . Of course, Charles is dead set against it, too. He thinks Portia's not terribly stable, Betsy, and quite honestly, I must say . . . Yes . . . Yes, well, quite . . . She has to work. A nurse, I believe . . . Well, that I don't know. From what I understand she won't have the money for the kind of wedding that . . . No, nor do I. I don't see why Charles should have to pay for it all. One doesn't expect to, does one? But we can't let poor Luke get married like some, I don't know, some, some . . . Well, exactly . . . Isn't it? Such a shame the silly boy wouldn't take Jemima back. Upper Park would have been lovely. Diana has been so clever with that garden . . . Oh, do you? Well, let's hope so, at least. One never knows . . . All right, Betsy. Yes, I'd better. Bye.'

I turn quickly after I hear her hang up, though I am not the one who should be ashamed. No, I should turn back and slap Victoria. How dare she call Dad common? He was an uncommon man who couldn't find his way to fit into the world. And fuck Charles for talking about me like that, for his jealous disapproval.

I don't want to go back into that drawing room now, me the silver-thief stealing the favourite son. I feel like crying and I don't know if Luke would understand. I am scared he thinks he can change me into the kind of woman his mother wants me to be. He has been talking as if it is marriage he craves, not necessarily me.

'Portia, you look quite lost,' Victoria says, emerging from the corridor and finding me trapped with my gurgling thoughts and stomach.

'I was going to go to bed. I was going to say goodnight.'
'Oh.'

With the fire blazing, the room feels claustrophobic and hot when I enter it again. I waste no time in bidding people a good night. Charles shakes my hand. Luke looks a little bemused. He has a drunken look in his eye and embarrasses me with his explicit kiss.

'I'll see you in the morning,' he whispers with a wink and a squeeze of my hand that makes it quite clear that I won't have to wait until the morning at all.

I grip the bannister tightly as I climb the stairs. I am dizzy, scared I might fall. Unstable, Charles called me. Fuck him! Fuck him and his fucking wife. I should turn around and tell them all: this man's word cannot be trusted. This man made me love him. I have been naked with this man. I would have given everything for this man. He is jealous. He did not have the courage to give everything up for what might have been, yet he cannot tolerate seeing his son have me instead. Oh, God, now my legs buckle and I twist and end up sitting on the stairs looking down on the top of the tree. Why couldn't Charles have approved? I can't be hated, not hated. I don't know who is right and who wrong any more. I don't know what I would do if Charles picked me up from these stairs and carried me into his room. I don't know if I would let him. No, I hate him. But yes. Oh, I would go with him. I would.

People are coming. I pull myself up. My legs have lost their solidity, just as they did when Mother told me about Dad. The mind buffers such shock with disbelief, but the body loses its strength at once. I lost the strength to do anything, even when I didn't believe it was true, my body resigned itself to the horror.

I hurry to my room and push the door shut. Please, Luke, don't come, please. I fall onto my bed. Ugh, head spin, horrible head spin. The mattress is tilting at such an angle I have to grip to its sides. The framed silhouettes of Luke's great and good ancestors lift off the wall and circle my face like angry insects. I want to lose consciousness. I want the new day to come and bring with its sunshine the conviction that it is not a sin to marry this man. That I am doing it for us, not for me, not because I long to fill this hateful void.

How can I be getting drunker still? I'm dribbling like a baby on to the bedspread. Got to get under the sheets.

Time passes. I keep falling half-asleep then finding the light bright in my eyes. There are noises. People in the corridors. Victoria is whispering: common man, common man, he hanged himself, not a wedding like Luke my son deserves, she's picturing Dad's rope being tied around her own lovely son's neck. Would I ruin Luke? I don't know. I imagine the church but cannot picture myself in white at the altar, only Luke's sad face as he turns to look down the aisle.

Somehow I pull my dress over my shoulders and turn off the light and am sinking into a fretful sleep, until I wake with a start, my heart pounding, sweat dampening my body. Ugh, my head is spinning still and my tongue is stuck to the roof of my mouth. What woke me? I don't want to be awake. It must be three or four, I don't know. I reach for my water, then hear a sound, like a giggle.

'Hello?'

'Hey, Pea.'

'Christ, it's you. You scared me.'

'Sorry, um—' There's a thud as Luke knocks a chair onto the carpet. 'Ow,' he says, then giggles some more.

He is drunk. He must be. When I said goodnight, Christian had just poured him a glass of Glenlivet so large I am surprised he can walk.

'I can't find the light, Luke.'

'Don't. I've got a surprise.'

I close my eyes again. I was dreaming. Random images float by like Polaroids washed from my hand. The dream was unsettling. Dad appeared at the wedding. Luke told him he couldn't come wearing that kind of suit, those shoes. There was no one at my side of the church, not even Mother.

I hear what sounds like a plate being put on my bedside table. I try not to flinch when Luke touches, like a blind man, my face.

'Hey, baby.'

'What time is it?'

'Time for some fun.'

'Oh, I—' I turn on my side. I can just make out that he is taking off his clothes. I can't refuse him, I know. Through sickness and health. Till death do us part.

'Let me in.'

'I'm very sleepy.' I turn my back on him. Sleep, please, Luke. But he is nudging his erection against my buttocks and now boorishly thrusting a hand between my legs. He lifts his torso up and leans across me to whisper in my ear. My body under his sinks into the mattress.

'Roll on your back.' The alcohol is thick on his breath.

'Luke, I'm sleepy. I don't feel well.'

'Go on, Mrs B. It's our engagement night.'

He kisses my tired mouth and then lowers himself to lap between my legs. I feel numb. I let him ease my legs wider apart, part me with his fingers. Now his tongue pushes into me with a drunkard's slobbery determination. 'I want to do something. Can I?'

'What is it?'

'I couldn't eat, earlier.' He sits on the edge of the bed, reaches for my hand and places it at the base of his willy. 'Mm, that's nice, that's nice.'

I play with it harder, a slick tick. At least it'll be painless if I can make him come like this.

'Can I do something?' he asks again.

I can't refuse him anything, can I? I who whored out my body to his father. I deserve whatever he wishes to do to me. I flop back on the bed, close my eyes and then feel something cold, food it must be, being pushed between my legs. Then his tongue.

'Luke. What are you doing?' I ask, without much urgency.

'It's Christmas pudding.'

Oh, that's vile, revolting. I should stop him, but then it is not him, it is me who disgusts. He should recoil from me. The tears gather and drip from the sides of my eyes. I feel nothing, my sensations have hardened. I clutch my hands on Luke's head and call out his name, wanting him to stop, but from the way he presses his lips harder against me he must think I am excited.

Suddenly, he utters a muffled cry of joy. 'Pea.' He clambers up on hands and knees. 'I've got the sixpence. I've got the bloody sixpence. Here.' He kisses me. His mouth tastes horrible. 'It'll be our lucky coin.' Now he slides the coin from his mouth into mine. I almost choke on it before spitting it out.

I feel dirty when he enters me now. It hurts. He is fucking the pudding hard inside me, treating me as if he knew the worst. He doesn't seem to care that I am motionless. Before long, he is through, hurting my arms as he clutches me and grunts in orgasm. He lies breathing heavily into my neck and slowly relaxes his shoulders. I think he is falling asleep.

'Luke, you're getting heavy.'

'Mm.'

'You're heavy. Can you move?'

He shifts to the side and then thumps onto the floor. The walls shake.

'Shit,' he says, but he is laughing.

'Are you OK?'

'Better go to my room,' he whispers, 'before the folks find us.' It is a game to him. He bundles his clothes in front of him like a refugee then, after colliding with the upended chair, says, 'It'll be fun, won't it?' before leaving me alone feeling sordid and used, and as if it is precisely the fun itself which, at last, has come to an end.

I sit up, drink, grimace at the taste. I have a headache though the spinning has ceased. It is two forty. The lights are on in my head. I am scared and cold. Soon as I hear Luke's door close, I rise shakily to my feet, wrap a towel around my nakedness and tiptoe to the bathroom. The silence in the house is so deep I am convinced he and I were heard. It shames me. It shames me to think of Charles awake and listening. It shames me, God knows why, to think of Victoria saddened by what Luke has done. Most of all, I am ashamed that I didn't want to be touched by the man I have promised to have and hold.

Keen not to wake the others, I dribble water from the hot tap into the bath. I wait some minutes but, since it remains tepid, I fill it only a few inches, and squat to wash myself. This bathroom is so very pretty with its soft yellow wallpaper and antique fittings. On the wall hang Victorian prints of flowers, roses mainly, in polished walnut frames. Its Anglican quaintness makes me feel sordid, here with my soapy hand washing the filth from between my legs. I shiver. Freezing rain spatters the tiny window. The drain gurgles when I lift the plunger. If only I could wash away my shame so easily.

I am cold, cold. My sheets are stained and disgusting. I can't face lying awake with the doubt eating at me so I dress in pyjamas, socks and a sweater and creep downstairs to the kitchen where, for once, I am not bothered by the dogs. Two of them lift their eyes to me, but they are not interested. I fill the kettle.

I feel like a trespasser in this kitchen. I wonder, would I feel this way if I kept coming here for twenty years? The tick of the kitchen clock sounds like someone tutting at me. While I wait for the water to boil, I gaze at the photos adorning the fridge door. See? All my life I have celebrated such a British past only to be undone by Luke's authentic history. I think it odd that it should have been this fairy-tale ending, this princely proposal, that exposed the myth of my romantic England. I have no place in such reality. The weight of the Bingham history cannot rest on my incapable shoulders. I am not a trustworthy progenitor. I am from different stock. There is no point lying to myself any more. I will not do.

Footsteps. The dogs and I lift our heads to see Serena, dressed in a pale cream dressing-gown, coming in.

She smiles, 'Ah, a fellow insomniac.'

'Did I wake you?'

'No, I think that drunken brother of mine was taking a bath.'

'Was he? Oh. Well, I'm, I'm making tea. Do you want a cup?'

'Thanks.' She fetches for us some camomile from the larder. 'Usually, I'm down here alone. I think the dogs are getting used to it.'

My mind is functioning less well than usual so it is in silence that I make the tea and bring it to the table. The situation does not seem so unusual. The tranquil are never aware how many of us sit out the small hours of the night.

Serena says, 'I'm sorry if I seemed quiet after dinner. I started thinking about me and Hugh. Except Hugh wasn't into it like Luke seems to be.'

'Luke's "into it" because he doesn't trust me when it comes to things like that.'

'I'm sure he does.'

'No. Anyway—'

Serena smiles, reflectively. 'I'm not surprised you're awake. I was so excited after Hugh proposed I couldn't sleep for days.' She pauses, looks into her cup, says, 'It's strange, isn't it, how the very thing you most wanted can suddenly feel like nothing at all?' Now she looks at me sharply, as if about to accuse me of something. For a frightening second I think she knows about me and Charles, but it's herself she's angered by. 'Oh, Portia, I'm sorry, that's a terrible thing for me to say.'

I shake my head. 'Don't worry.' What does Serena assume? That Luke is everything I most wanted? No. No. I should confess that I don't love him as deeply as I should. That it is not excitement keeping me up.

'Hughie first proposed to me when we were ten. At a pony club meeting.'

'Did you accept?'

'I can't remember if I liked boys yet. Probably not. Still—' She spoons the sugar into a heap in its bowl and we watch as the mountain collapses. 'I think I always knew it'd be him. It was almost inevitable.'

'Do you think that ... I mean, you know when something

doesn't feel like a choice, it makes you forget it's what we wanted all along. Do you think that could have had—'

'Something to do with why I left Hugh?'

'Mm.'

'Probably. And I think I was a little scared at how perfect it was. Something had to go wrong.' Serena collects her hair with both hands and twists the back into a knot. She looks into my eyes. 'About a year after we got married I started thinking Hugh was having an affair with one of his stable girls. I was convinced by it.'

'Was he?'

'No. No, I don't think he was.'

'So why did you suspect him?'

'I don't know. Because I couldn't believe it would stay as good as it was and because I was pregnant so my hormones were playing up and because I was stupid, mainly. And then . . . and then I suppose there was the whole thing that happened with Mum and Dad. I thought, if it can happen to them, then why not to Hugh and me.'

'What do you mean, happened to them?'

'Oh.' She pauses. 'Has Luke never mentioned anything?'

I shake my head.

'No, I suppose he wouldn't have. Help, I don't know if I should tell you now.'

'So don't.'

'Then again, I suppose you are almost family.'

I look away. 'I suppose I am.'

She lowers her voice. 'Dad had an affair about three years ago. With some friend of Luke's.'

'Oh, my God.' My heart plummets. 'Some girlfriend?'

'No, some French friend of a friend. Looked a lot like you, actually. She came here once and then . . . I never really wanted to know what happened after that.'

'Did your father admit to it?'

'No. God, no. Mum found some lipstick on his collar or a letter or, I don't know, something like that.'

'And she didn't leave him?'

'Mum? No, she just told him to stop being such a baby.' It makes her laugh. 'Just like that. Told him never to see the woman again.'

'And do you think he did?'

'No, I think it worked.'

'God, I can't believe—' I can taste the anger, the bile, at the back of my tongue. I want Charles here now, this second. I want to hear him apologize for those lies he spewed. '*It is not something I would conceive of doing . . .*' How dare he? How dare he? What was wrong with me that was so right with her? I ask, 'Did it just happen once, do you think?'

'Oh, yeah. I don't think Dad's a serial adulterer. We all decided it was some mid-life crisis. It's that little French floozy I'd liked to have strangled. I mean, when she came here she went swimming with him in this skimpy little bikini and I know, I just know she was trying to—'

'Wait, you don't know that, do you?'

'She knew he was married. She knew he was married and what she was doing.'

'Maybe it was more complicated.'

'I don't think so. When you're married, there's only black and white. You'll see that.'

'Perhaps.'

I don't know why, but Serena has made me scared of tomorrow, of telling Luke that I can't marry him after all, of what this family will think. She trusts me. Haven't I sinned against her, too? And yet I am still indignant with anger at Charles. I want to confront him. He had no right to talk to me or to treat me as he did. Not if he had already broken his precious vows once.

'I'm going to take my tea back to bed,' I say, 'if you don't mind.'

'No, of course not.'

I am almost out of the door when Serena calls out, 'Portia, um, I probably shouldn't have told you that. About Dad.'

'Don't worry, I promise I won't say a word.'

'Thanks. You know, you mustn't worry. Luke would never do what Dad did. Not in a million years.'

I nod, because she is right, and then turn to climb the back stairs.

Of course, I can't sleep, not at all. The dirtiness of the sheets seems too obvious a symbol of my degraded self. Instead, I wrap the blankets around me and sit in the window. The rain has stopped and the strong wind has ripped the earth's own blanket of cloud just enough to allow the full moon to paint silvery-grey the large croquet lawn where once I was happy, to brighten the neat paths into slug trails of light and, over there, to highlight the top few bricks of the lovely old wall which encloses that swimming pool where twice, at least twice, Charles Bingham has seduced women half his age, and threatened to tear his family apart.

I had not noticed before how the garden, like the house, is divided into squares and rectangles of border, lawn, tennis court, pool. It is neat, structured. Yet doesn't decay and disease tear through it as fast as in one left wild? Serena's ordered, tidy life, which could, save for the cars and drugs and movies of the twentieth century, have been lifted from a Jane Austen novel, was disrupted as easily as mine, leaving her just as sad, just as lonely. For a few hours, I thought Luke could save me by giving my life an adult shape. I thought wrong.

Though we are less than a week from the shortest day of the year, it doesn't seem so very long before the first traces of light make watery the inky black of the eastern horizon. The garden in time regains its sullen, wintry aspect; much as I do. My festive mood was an aberrance like a ball thwacked temporarily out of shape. It is said by some neurologists that we mature with a foundation of happiness that is little altered by the dramas and tragedies and joys in our lives. An optimistic, vivacious man losing the use of his legs is no more likely to deviate for long from his character than a curmudgeon will skip gleefully through the streets many weeks after winning a lottery jackpot. Yesterday, I should have recognized my alien self would not reward Luke with the love he deserves. I would not be content as country wife and mother. I preferred the English castle I constructed within my head.

I close my eyes, willing sleep to rescue me, but voices play in my head as if I am turning a radio dial. Mostly, I hear Charles and his pontificating, self-righteous voice. With each throb of my headache, my anger at him seems to rise. To think he knew how history might repeat itself when we swam together. To think he visited me at Luke's having hurt his son once. To think he led me to this slaughter.

A diffused light brings the garden to life. The path's stones have acquired a mossy sheen since the summer but, of course, all the lushness has sunk back into the earth. We croquet-playing swimmers are ghosts on the lawn. The trees along the wall have dropped their fruit and bring to mind prisoners facing a firing squad. The vegetable garden is barren. A frost clings to the greenhouse windows.

Rabbits have been chasing each other on the lawn, but now they scamper to safety as one of the dogs races onto the lawn. Someone – Victoria, I guess – has let them out. I peek from behind the curtain. When I see that it is Charles, I don't hesitate. I dress hastily and, though my headache is like a nail being hammered behind my eyes, run, following his footprints on the frosty grass. I reach him as he is climbing the stile into the horses' field.

'Portia! Good morning. You're up bright and early.'

'I saw you from my bedroom,' I explain, catching my breath.

Charles zips up his waxy coat. It's a defensive gesture. 'Did you not sleep well?'

'No.'

'No. Well, if it's any consolation, nor did I.'

I brush hair from my forehead and face him. 'Was it your guilty conscience keeping you awake?'

His lifts his eyes towards the house, I think in surprise, then lowers them to me. 'It may very well have been, yes. I should imagine that is something we share.' Now, he continues over the fence, whistling for the dogs. I follow until I am parallel, my breath smoking the cold air.

'I need to ask you something.'

'Yes?'

'Why didn't you tell me about your French woman? Why didn't you tell me it had happened before?' Charles has increased his stride so that I have to take two paces to keep up with his one. The tall grass wets my jeans. 'Charles?'

'I didn't think it your business, if you must know.'

'None of my business how you'd, you'd never conceive of doing something "like that" to your family? Or how you were so shocked by what happened between us? I don't think you were surprised at all, I—'

'Portia,' Charles interrupts, speaking over me. 'This is quite unnecessary.'

'No it *isn't*!' I scream. A cloud of crows, disturbed from one of the huge oaks bordering the paddock, spatters the pale sky, cawing ominously. Oh, I didn't realize how much I still loved this man. 'It is not. You can't keep acting as if nothing happened between us. How can you be so cruel?'

It must be the tears in my voice that make Charles stop and turn back. He puts his hands in his pockets and sighs. 'Portia, I am not willing to discuss it with you. It was a private matter between Victoria and myself.'

'But you took her swimming, just like you took me. Why can't you admit you were trying to seduce me, too?'

'Because it isn't true. Nor do I want to have to go over this again and again. Especially after last night.'

'I think you're lying to me. I think you've been fucking Luke's girlfriends for years.'

Charles's right hand visibly tenses. 'Somebody really ought to smack you.'

'Go on, then.'

He looks at me with what seems like hatred, and then strokes his hand across his newly shaven cheeks. He dips his head, and then his shoulders. It's as if the fight has suddenly left him. His tone, too, sounds defeated. 'Don't do this, Portia. Please. Aren't you aware what you have already done to us?'

'If you tell me about her, I promise I'll never ask again. Why her and not me, Charles? Why? What did she have that I didn't?'

Charles wraps one of the dog leads around his hand. 'Honestly?'

I shrug, nod.

Charles looks me in the eyes and says, 'She didn't have to beg,' before turning his back on me once more, and striding towards the copse.

I stand motionless, hollowed out with shame and anger. Charles slapped me harder than if he had used his hand. Tears burn at my eyes. Beg? I never begged. I press a hand to my mouth to stifle my sob, but with the tears comes anger and I can't keep it in, I shout out once in this early silence, a hopeless yelp which echoes back to me. Charles doesn't flinch.

When I run back to the house I'm a little lost girl again, clueless as to which way to turn, the panic and fear freezing my mind. Is this what happened to Daddy? That he knew of no place to run? In the grey light, stone upon stone, the house looks like a fortress. I should never have been let in, me the Trojan horse, twenty-seven years of poison hidden inside.

The cold gravel crunches harshly under my feet as I run to the back door then into the kitchen where I almost collide with Victoria. She looks shocked by my presence, as she has done from the day we met. I do nothing to hide the tears coursing down my cheeks.

She sets down her cup of tea. 'Lord, Portia, what on earth has happened?'

'Ask him!' I shout as I run on, ignoring her calls, on through the hallway and up the stairs towards their bedroom. Fuck you, Charles. *Fuck you. I begged for nothing, I asked for nothing.* Everything suddenly feels like his fault, everything that went wrong between Luke and myself, every chance I had to find a new peace here. I run into his dressing room and press my face into one of his shirts and howl with my hatred. My hands clench and pull at the fabric and then, suddenly, the shirt tears and almost before I know what I am doing I rip it in two. Try flattering and flirting and seducing in this now, Charles Bingham, or in this, or this, or this. Red, blue, white, like the colours of the Union flag the ripped shirts fall at my feet. I am tearing them with ease now, and the sound is beautiful, like clearing the phlegm from one's throat. The buttons pop off fluently as honeyed compliments. I am relishing this. I sweep my arms across the shelves pushing sweaters and cardigans and socks and belts to the floor, spilling his gold cufflinks and studs. My hand is bleeding from something sharp so I am smearing blood like a warrior across his white, painted shelves. Now the suits, off their hangers, one by one by...

'Bloody Hell!' Luke, at the door. He is wearing an old school dressing-gown which makes him look like a child. 'What are you—?'

'Don't look at me!' I scream, and, although Luke tries to hold me as I run past him, he is too sleepy or shocked – from the look on his face he can't believe what he's seeing.

It is over. I have no time to waste. Before Luke has caught up with me I have run to my room to collect my purse and now I am taking the front stairs two at a time. The car keys, thank God, are in the silver bowl in the hall and although the old door sticks when I first pull it, I'm soon outside and in the car. The doors lock with a reassuring sound.

I am not excited as I might be, just purposeful, even though the engine seems dead when I turn the key and it is like every clichéd scene from every movie thriller when I see Luke running desperately on his bare feet, screaming for me to stop. I turn the key again and again, and only now, just as Luke reaches me and flattens his hands, slap, against the window does the motor rev alive. I glance at him, framed against the gorgeous façade, for no longer than I did when something about his face and manner made me stop on that Toronto street six months ago. Yet, I am as sure now of this ending as I was of our beginning then. I press my foot hard on the accelerator and lurch forward, the car's back wheels digging a groove in the driveway. The skid-marks of an accident. Briefly, I stop at the road before swerving out, and then I am away, away, running again.

I am sure I will be followed so I keep the speed up. I think Christian will drive Luke, leaving Charles with his wife and my recrimination like a knife in her hands, but at this speed they won't chase for long, not without knowing which route to take.

Which route? London, I suppose. Collect my things and then head ... where? Cornwall, perhaps. Or Nottingham or Cambridge. Somewhere I might get a sense of Dad, of why I wanted to come here at all. The rich are a different country, this exile no great surprise. It calms me to be in control of this car, of my destination. Luke has let me behind the wheel only when he has been drinking, and then he has been a testy passenger, concerned for his paintwork, for my choices of lane and speed and direction. But I am free now.

That the inside of the car feels huge without Luke adds to my sense of liberation. Cars are an escape I have always loved. I passed my driving exam a few days after my sixteenth birthday then took a bus to Buffalo with Ronnie Carp whose cousin had a stolen Oldsmobile cruiser he needed off his hands. It was a beautiful boat of a car, which glided along at sixteen miles to the gallon while I steered it with the palm of my left hand, smoking cigarettes that I kept between my lips so that, too often, I had to cruise in it like a one-eyed pirate girl as the rising smoke stung my eye and the Scabs wailed angrily out of the speakers. Luke's Saab is heavier, but now I feel what he meant when he spoke of the turbo's kick. I think it's the power I feel in making progress towards something new which is negating much of the horror of what I have just done. I drive on, surprised at my level-headedness and resolve, concentrating on the car and the road.

It was right, what I did. Charles deserved nothing less, while Luke, poor, good, lovely Luke, deserves so much more. I know he will be loved. And the relief I feel at leaving him is the only proof I need that it was stupid and wrong to accept his hand. The ring, cocky and boastful on my wheel-steering hand, looks misplaced. When I hit a stretch of clear road on the motorway towards London, I ease the diamonds off my finger and with a little metallic click, drop the ring in the car's ashtray.

NINE

Once you have decided what you want to do about a problem you can do something about, act quickly and firmly. Positive action is usually helpful.

AMA Family Medical Guide

My optimistic sense of purpose is kept afloat by the ease with which I find my way into London and to Luke's flat, yet is deflated almost as soon as I am inside and listening, with nervous shame, to the seven messages on the answering machine. Six are from Luke. His tone in each conveys a growing understanding of what occurred. The last message is from Kaz. Seems calling her will be the best way to get word to Luke. I dial her number in Somerset. She lifts the receiver after two rings, clumsily, as if she has been waiting for my call.

'Kaz? It's Portia.'

'Pea, where are you?'

'London.'

'I've had Ludo mad as a mad thing on the line. What's been going on?'

'What did he say?'

'Nothing, really. He wouldn't say anything.'

Of course, he wouldn't. It is his reputation I am threatening. Such things still mean something over here.

'Pea? He says you drove off in his car like a mad thing. What's going on?'

'He asked me to marry him.'

Audibly, like a bad actor, Kaz sucks in her breath. 'And then what, Pea? Pea, then what?'

'I said yes and then this morning I had a fight with Charles about how he's been treating me and—'

'Oh, Lord, what are you thinking? You can't possibly still be going on about him. I thought you were over that little—'

'You always make it sound like nothing, Kaz,' I interrupt, angrily. 'It wasn't nothing.'

'Please don't shout at me.'

'But you've never understood.'

'I understand, sweets, that you and Mr Bingham can hardly have—'

'*We did*. That's the whole fucking point. We did.'

'Did what?'

'Love each other,' I say, the words sticking briefly in my throat. 'That's why this has happened. How could I have told Luke that?'

There is a silence at the other end of the line before Kaz says, 'Why do you say Charles loved you? Did something happen between you?'

'Yes, sort of, it did. OK, it did. That's why I've been so upset. While Luke was in Canada, Charles and I—'

'Actually, Portia,' Kaz says, sounding upset, 'to be honest I'd rather not even hear this.'

'I haven't told you what—'

'I don't want to hear. Luke's one of my oldest friends. Poor lamb must be—'

Now it's me getting mad. 'You don't understand.'

'I suppose that's what Ludo was arguing about with his father.'

'How do you know he was?'

'He told me. They didn't go to Toby's shoot. Luke said he was going to leave the Old Rectory, the poor love, and come back to London.'

'Luke was?' Oh God, no. I cannot be here when he arrives. Not if he knows. 'Kaz, I'm going to have to get out of here. I promise I'll call you.'

'You're not going to stay to see Ludo? Portia, you have to.'

'No! Jesus, I thought you were my friend. Not my mother.'

She doesn't reply. Angry impatience rushes through my veins. It is exactly how I used to feel when I argued with Mother.

'Listen, I haven't got time to hang around. I want to talk to you about this, but—'

'When Luke proposed, you said yes to him, did you? You told him yes.'

'I don't want to talk about it.'

'Why? After you had—'

'I've got to go, OK? Please, Kaz,' I say, my voice breaking. 'I'm going. Goodbye.' I burst into tears the moment I slam down the phone. Why? Why? Why does it always end up as me against them?

I gather the clothes I am going to need, my tears dripping on to the suitcase just as they did when Mother and I had found the courage to clear Dad's possessions from his study and bedroom. We worked in silence then, as I do now, each item warmed with memory like stones still tepid with sunshine after dusk. Dad's most loved books caused me the greatest heartache, especially those he had annotated with enthusiasm and excitement. Some still carried dirty fingerprints like fossils in amber. Now, it is trivial items that keep my tears flowing: the bright velvet bikini Luke bought me in Harvey Nichols one sunny afternoon after a boozy lunch with Kaz and Charlie; the spiral notebook filled with superlatives; ticket stubs kept ostensibly as receipts but in truth as souvenirs; the shirt I was wearing when Luke and I first made love; the leaflet I picked up at the exhibition with Charles. I have made fires with such things in the past when I have wanted to forget. Now, simply, I am leaving them behind.

My eyes, red from crying and lack of sleep, are sore in the bright sun as I lug my cases into the car. I throw everything in the trunk and then drive quickly away without looking back or even knowing where I am going. At one intersection close to the flat I look to my left to see through a huge window bordered by holly and pretty white lights a family enjoying a drinks party in their spacious living room. The explicit airiness of the room and the openness of such smiling faces exaggerates my claustrophobic condition in a car that only this morning thrilled me as a means of escape. Fast as I can, I accelerate away. I just keep driving through London towards the Thames. The traffic is so light I reach the city's landmarks in quick succession, barely noticing the ugly shops and offices. Harrods, Buckingham Palace, Westminster, Big Ben connected by the green, green parks which I so love. I never found such majesty among the people. No, not as I expected, Mother. I want to start again, in the countryside this time, without judgements and enemies, without anything to live up to at all.

When I pass St Paul's and the extraordinary Tower of London, the roads becoming unfamiliar and a slight panic joins hands with my sadness. I stole a litre bottle of Luke's vodka to keep me going in the cheap hotel I expect to stay in tonight, but now I am not sure I can bear such loneliness. I bring the car to a stop and almost at once see a sign to Liverpool Street station from where I took the train to see my aunt. Of course, of course.

I find a pay phone and dial her number and even though she's not there, I don't feel discouraged. I wait for a while and dial again. Though there is still no answer, I decide to go anyway. I can pick locks. Barbara won't mind finding me inside.

I get lost and lost and lost again, but in time find the road I need, and, although I take the M25 in the wrong direction, before too long I am safely travelling towards Colchester and my aunt's home. In the town, I follow the signs to the train station, then remember the simple journey from there to Devonshire Close. It is dark when I pull up beside number 48 but, to my relief, the lights are on inside.

I feel an immense tiredness when I step from the road. My back aches. My face feels too heavy to smile. The car's engine is making ticking noises that sound in my ear like tuttings. I walk a little reticently to the front door and ring the chiming bell. A light is turned on in the hallway.

I was expecting Keith, but it is my aunt who opens the door. 'Portia, hello. What a lovely surprise. Keith. Ke-ith.' The manner in which Barbara cleaves into two her husband's name sounds nagging, but I am sure she is only wanting me to feel welcomed by both of them. 'It's Portia. Portia's here. Come in, dear.'

My aunt's house feels tiny after the Old Rectory. I could touch the walls either side of me. It has been decorated with looping strings of plastic holly and berries along which tiny green clips at four-inch intervals clasp a variety of Christmas cards.

Keith emerges from the living room wearing leather slippers and carrying a small knife. 'Don't be alarmed. Armed but not dangerous,' he declares, chuckling to himself. 'You caught me peeling an apple.' I can feel the slight stickiness when he shakes my hand.

'Would you care for something to eat, Portia? You look like you need feeding up,' Barbara asks, touching my arm.

Such motherly concern, combined with Barbara's dumb, kind ignorance, makes me want to cry. 'No, thank you.'

'A drink, then? A nice cup of tea?'

'I'd love some water, please.'

'Keith will bring it for you. Won't you Keith? Oh, Portia—' She rubs my arm. 'It's lovely to see you. Really, it is. We were just talking about you. Weren't we Keith?'

'Yes, as a matter of fact. Not long ago.'

'It's such a pity, you've just missed Paul and Tony,' Barbara tells me as she leads us to the living room. 'They all went to their in-laws today. They were asking after you.'

'Were they?'

'Oh, yes. I showed them the photographs we took in Flatford. They couldn't believe how you'd grown up.'

'Yup, I'm all grown up.'

'Well, come on in.'

The living room is L-shaped. At the near end, a large TV the picture of which seems three shades too orange is on but muted. From on top of it, Barbara hastily tidies away a card and envelope. She tucks them into the lacquered box from which last time she took the photograph of her grandfather, then plumps the cushions of a wide, beige recliner that has beneath it a footstool attached by hinges and on which, I suppose, she wants me to sit.

'Sit yourself down. Come along, now.'

Barbara herself sits in the couch opposite me. I want to turn the gas fire down, there's no air in here.

'I thought you said you were spending Christmas in – where was it?'

'Near Oxford.'

'That's right, so . . . ?'

'Barman arriving,' says Keith, bringing my water. 'I'll just put it here.' He sits next to his wife then, holding a crescent of apple in front of his mouth, asks, 'What brought about this unexpected visit, then, Portia?'

'I thought it'd be nice.'

'Will you be staying the night?'

'If I can.'

'Of course she can. Of course you can, Portia. Biscuit?' Barbara offers me a shortbread round. 'We were just thinking the house seemed empty, weren't we Keith?'

He nods. Though I have not eaten since last night, I decline the biscuit. My stomach feels awful, I'm not yet over my hangover. I take a sip of water. Perhaps this wasn't such a good idea. I don't want to have to explain, not now. Barbara isn't Dad, can't be him. On the drive down, I was thinking of the 8mm films of our holidays in England, whether seeing him living, breathing, might suggest to me a way to act. But I can't muster the energy to be polite.

'How's your young man? Remind me of his name again.'

'Luke.'

'You should have brought him with you.'

'He's with his family.'

'Couldn't you stay?'

'Well, in fact we, we sort of had a, a fight, I guess, so—' Thinking of Luke arriving in London and finding me gone makes me suddenly sad for him. I can't help wondering what was going through his mind this time yesterday, and what he will be thinking now. And I didn't even leave a note.

'You'll probably patch things up soon enough.'

'Maybe.' I look away, trying not to cry.

'You can call him from here, if you'd like,' begins Keith, but Barbara lays a hand on his arm.

She says, 'We were about to watch *Barrymore*. Do you like him?'

'I don't know.'

'He's ever so good. Keith, where's the flicky doo-dah?'

The sound returns and although the show is inane, I am grateful to Barbara for recognizing my desire not to talk. It's so warm, I keep half-dozing off to sleep, my head sinking and then jerking up. I long to sleep, sleep, wake to find this mess resolved, for Luke and me to be happy, but I don't need to be reminded how futile such hopes are. Was it only last night that he proposed? With my tiredness comes a despondency, an utter lack of hope in the future. I cannot see a way beyond this. I close my eyes.

'Portia?' Barbara is gently shaking my shoulder. 'Hello, dear. You went out like a light.'

I yawn. Oh, I feel awful, like a little girl sick in someone else's house. Truth is, I do want my mummy. I want her back, stroking a hand across my brow and tucking me in. Even though Dad would read to me, always Mother came in to see me to sleep. She was good that way.

'You must have been tired.'

'I'm sorry.'

'Oh, never mind us. Usually, it's Keith who falls asleep in front of the telly.'

'You say I do,' says Keith from behind me. He sounds playful, as if he's been at the sherry. 'You say I do.'

'Portia, dear, we've got tea on the table if you'd like.'
'I think I'm fine.'
'Come on, you look like you need food. What would I tell your mother?'

There is no arguing. At the table, I drink tea. Keith insisted on heating his turkey in the microwave, and it looks disgusting now, like abandoned leather soles. Barbara thinks it funny that he heated the coleslaw, too. It has been steaming unattractively, like fresh shit. I've no hunger, anyway.

I ask, 'Did you ever get your projector fixed?'
'Oh, yes,' answers Keith. 'It wasn't much.'
'You think I could see that film? The holiday in Cornwall?'

Keith looks over the rim of his glasses at Barbara as if accusing her of telling me something she shouldn't have; that or else he needs her approval.

'I'm not sure where it is.'
'I'll find it,' Barbara assures me. 'But I can't work that contraption on my own.'
'Very well,' he replies, 'but I'll finish my tea first, if I may.'
'There's no rush,' I say, though the truth is that I become impatient as the meal drags. More turkey, more tea, then crème caramels that I hear were going cheap 'on account of their sell-by date' in Sainsbury's, then mints (brought by the boys, my cousins, about whose families I have to hear) and only then does Keith rise from his chair to clear the plates with his wife.

'I'll just get the screen,' Barbara says on her return. 'Portia, you sit yourself in Keith's chair again.'

Keith sets up the screen on its spindly tripod legs. Inexplicably, he smirks at me as he unpeels the casing, as if he is some kind of magician or a dirty old man on the subway.

'Here we are then,' Keith says, after he has tut-tutted over the fiddliness of the film. 'St Ives, Cornwall. The year is 1973 when we were all younger and not so wise.'

'Oh, come along now, you.'
'Lights down, then, Barbara, if you please.'
The spool clicks on. The film is as jumpy as I. First, sky: blue

but for a few clouds, followed by a jerky move to the hotel where we stayed. It is less handsome than my mind has constructed. The beach I faintly remember. I smile as I watch myself on film running flat-footed while the adults set up on the beach a windbreak patterned with wide, horizontal strips. After a short blank, Dad comes centre-frame.

'There he is.' Barbara points, needlessly, towards the screen. 'There's your dad.'

I tighten my grip on the chair. I am in the picture too, then when I was all the picture. I am wearing a floppy yellow hat tied in a bow under my chin. I remember the hat and the navy swimsuit, although this I envision folded in Mother's basket or bundled at my feet while I shivered and rubbed at the sand still clinging to my clammy, hairless skin. On the beach, I am digging in the sand with a tiny red spade. Dad is leaning over me, shadowing his five-year-old daughter. Has nothing changed? Still I dig under his shadow; still the waves sweep on.

Aunt Barbara, less plump then than now, chuckles carelessly when she sees herself gesturing towards the castle I was building. The subtle celluloid colours make us seem rich and happy. It is something of a miracle that my father should be so alive in front of my eyes when he has been dead for half my life. I stare with such longing for his presence as he plays the fool for me that my eyes sting and I have to look away.

'Didn't he have a lovely smile to him?' Barbara says, the question floating unanswered between us.

Now I am on Dad's shoulders, giggling. I see Mother, looking so young, younger than I am now, lift her arms to take me down, but I grip Dad's neck. He reaches up and tickles my ribs until I'm laughing so hard I almost fall. So excited am I that I slap his cheeks, hard. He winces and must have said something because the next thing I know I'm rubbing them better, the child nurse, excited by my capacity to help, and in awe, I suppose, of his wondrous, exotic stubble. Sometimes at night he would fall on my bed, pretending to be dead, and I would run my fingers against the growth of his bristles to wake him. Remembering makes my fingertips tickle.

Now Daddy is spinning me around like a helicopter before lowering me to his face for a kiss while I kick my feet behind.

Keith stands. 'I have my book to finish.'

'Don't go, Keith. It's not long, is it?'

Without an apology, he darkens the screen as he walks in front of it. 'I've seen enough, thank you.'

Something about the manner of his leaving creates a tension that spoils our mood. The camera turns to us all having lunch. Mother is being maternal and diligent. My cousins run in, grab sandwiches, and leave. There is a shot of me running from a short-haired thug of a boy who clearly has my bucket in his hand. A break, then a frame of Dad making a toast with a plastic glass towards the camera. The film skips and then, in an instant, all is white. The suddenness of Dad's disappearance is unintentionally poignant. I don't move as the projector cackles on.

Barbara slowly gets to her feet, muttering about not knowing what's what as she turns off the machine, but with a click it is done. She switches the lights back on. I blink back the tears. I was wrong. Watching it hasn't helped me at all.

'Did Keith never like Dad?'

'What funny things you say sometimes, Portia.'

'Didn't he?'

'They were different,' she says as she tidies. 'Very different. Clive was ... well, he was different to Keith. They had their disagreements. Now, I wish you'd have something to eat.'

I repeat that I am not hungry, the film having made me even less so. I think of calling Luke but don't know what to say. Poor baby, not even knowing where I am. And his precious car gone.

'We could play cards,' says Barbara.

I used to play gin rummy with her on my bed after Dad died, game after game to keep the demons at bay. I say, 'Fine.' Keith joins us. Our conversation is on the game (I keep winning, lucky at cards and all ...) and not about any issue that might upset me. One thing about having had a troubled existence, others handle you with care. A damaged boat mustn't be rocked too hard.

It is still early, before eleven, that Barbara and Keith say they're going to bed. I think I tire them. I am shown my room. It smells of air freshener and is small and clearly not often used. Its inertness defines it. The books are dusted around. There's a suit-press that has dented its shape into the lime-green carpet and, when I hang my jacket in the cupboard, I am repelled by the smell of moth balls. Dad hated them, too. Complained that Mother was obsessed with them. 'She's even got them between her legs,' I recall him saying over dinner one day soon before he died. I think I laughed, but I remember the comment not because it was funny or mean, we said such things every day, but because, for once, she screamed back. It wasn't often she let the cracks show.

I am quick in the shared bathroom and then slip uncomfortably between the sheets. What am I doing here? Beneath my closed lids, my eyes stare at nothing. Can't stop thinking disconnected thoughts. A straight-spined man my imagination has conjured stands behind a glass cabinet asking Luke my finger size. An undertaker planes a coffin of unfinished wood. Noise at the Old Rectory, dogs barking, Victoria shouting. Christian meets me on a street and won't say hello. Luke is alone in his flat and sadder than he has ever been. Some kind of hateful satisfaction flares in me: now he understands how less-than-charmed lives feel. The crackers snap. The ring. Oh shit, the ring is still in the car. I was just getting warm under these blankets, but what if someone stole the unlocked car?

I dress, tiptoe downstairs and out into the drizzly air. The car's interior smells of my cigarettes. Luke won't like that. Maybe with my money saved I can buy a car of my own, later. I open the ashtray. Stupid! The ring is covered with ash – I forgot it was there.

Back inside, I wash it in the sink and leave it to dry. Now, I need tea. As I wait for the kettle to boil, I can't help wondering where I would be had I not wanted tea during the night last night. At the Old Rectory still? Warming to this idea, this marriage? Too late now. We die with 'what if' on our lips, all of us. It's Dad's 'what if' I've been searching for since he died.

Something about cheap heating, it goes as fast as it comes. The living room is cool now. I light the fire again. Shouldn't have watched the film. It is impossible not to stare into the captured eyes of people who have killed themselves, looking not only for a reason for their actions but an excuse for why we shouldn't follow as well. What is mine? There is not much to keep me here. I wonder if Dad's eyes ever gave anything away? There are photos of him as a younger man with Barbara, I remember, in the lacquered box. I fetch it. On the top of the pile is the Christmas card I saw Barbara tidy away. It is of an icy Richmond Park. Inside that is a folded sheet of pale blue writing paper. I glance over my shoulder before reading the names – Richard, Peter, Diane – signed in one person's looping hand. The address is written, not printed, at the top.

Diane is the one who wrote it. She begins by thanking Barbara for her card and letter. Yes, she writes, she'd love to visit one day, she knows someone in Aldeburgh and enjoys that part of the world. Possibly in the spring? Peter (husband? son?) is very busy these days. The hospital's hectic as ever. She's in maternity now. Prefers that. I yawn one of those yawns that lasts and lasts and stretches one's jaw and brings tears to one's eyes. I wipe them, read on. Richard's working in Oxford still. Writing a book on the social consequences of the Black Death of 1342. 'Isn't it strange,' she continues, 'how he should have inherited an interest of Clive's?'

In the second I stop reading I know who this is, and why it was hidden. Diane. Diane the nurse. Remarried. We keep in touch, Barbara said, Christmas cards sometimes. It is Dad's first wife. My hand is shaking as I read on. Diane is sure that Richard would like to visit, too. He rarely gets to see his aunts and uncles in Ireland. He enjoyed meeting Paul and Tony at his birthday party. Thirty-two. 'Hard to believe!' It was so nice of them to come.

I stop again. It is late and my brain is so overloaded I am finding it hard to think clearly, logically, but this equation a child could manage. One plus one equals one other. I read the sentences again and again and again. Something is absolutely wrong, as wrong as it could ever be. This child, this writer, this academic at Oxford, is thirty-two years old. He 'rarely gets to see his aunts and uncles in Ireland'. She means his other aunts doesn't she? Other than Dad's sister? Thirty-two. Easy sums again. Thirty-two years ago Dad was in England and he was married to this woman, Diane, and she has a son who misses his aunt.

Snap. The memory comes. I throw the letter down and start flicking on to the carpet those shots that don't matter. How stupid I am. Something in me recognized his face when I saw the photograph last time. He enjoyed meeting Paul and Tony at his birthday party. Oh God, no. I am really shaking now, praying to a God I don't trust that I am being human and getting it wrong as I get everything wrong, wrong. But, help me, here it is. I flip it over, and retch when I read what's written. Paul and Tony meeting Richard. February 21, 1996.

Does he look like me, too? Perhaps something in the lips and forehead. But he is Dad. It's all there. I can't look. I light a cigarette and pace, my nerves too on edge to let me sit down. I stare at the picture and read the letter again. It has to be a mistake. They wouldn't have all known and not told me. Not Dad. Not if I had a brother and he a son. It is not possible.

But I am wrong. Dad would not have deserted a child. He adored me. And if I had a brother, I would have been told. Mother, Barbara, Keith, someone. Brains understand their own alleyways so well that self-deceit becomes a game. I know it. I saw Dad's coffin and knew he was inside, but still I waited for him to wake me, still I looked out for his car, for his briefcase at the bottom of the stairs. About some things the brain chooses to be dumb.

I sit, smoke another cigarette, spill tea because my hand is so unsteady. The house is unnaturally quiet. I can't keep my eyes from the photo, from this man with his pint of beer. I look again at a photo of Dad at roughly Richard's age and now I can't deny what I see. They are father and son and everything I have ever known means absolutely nothing at all.

Doesn't matter that it's twelve thirty, I'd ring this Diane if I knew her number. There is no hope of sleep. I will have to wake Barbara or Mother . . . that's who.

I toss my cigarette in the kitchen sink and dial the number of the Ashbridge Bay Home where Mother often works evenings. They take twenty rings to answer, as always, but then tell me she is not there. I ring her home number. The connection is quick. She answers after three rings. She sounds bunged-up, like she has a cold.

'It's me.'

'Hello, Portia. I was wondering if you'd ring. Happy Christmas, darling.'

'Did you know about Richard?'

'Who?'

This is how we were. Bland, accusatory statements took the place of pleasantries.

'Do you know about him or not?'

'Richard who, darling?'

'Richard, Diane's son.' There is a silence at the other end. 'Do you?'

'Where are you?'

'What does that matter? Just tell me.' Then, more softly, 'Please.'

'I didn't know.'

'What do you mean, you didn't? What do you mean?'

'I didn't know and then I did. Barbara told me.'

'When?'

Silence.

'When?'

'After Clive died.'

'How soon after?'

'Soon after.'

'And you didn't tell me? You didn't *fucking*—' With a scream, I crunch down the phone. I can't talk to her. I feel sick. I am going to be sick. I turn the cold water on and lean over the kitchen sink.

'Portia?'

I swing around. It's Barbara in her dressing-gown.

'Portia, what's going on? You're all dressed. Who were you talking to?'

She steps forward as if to hug me, but I lift my arms to shoo her away. My action shocks her. Oh, the last person I could trust, truly trust, is enemy. Dad's own sister. There is nothing left. Such awareness is too much.

'What on earth's the matter?'

'Why wasn't I told about Richard?'

She looks at me blankly. The phone rings. It'll be Mother. Keeps one of those dumb telephone books that pop up on a chosen letter of the alphabet – she'll have found B for Barbara quickly. With my arms crossed, I stare at my aunt as she speaks into the receiver. I would run if I knew where to go.

'Yes . . . well, I heard from upstairs. Diane wrote to me, Angela, so perhaps . . . yes, she's standing right here . . . do you want a word? I'll—'

I am shaking my head. 'No, she can fuck off, *fuck off*! This is it. This is it. She can, she can—' Violently, I grab the phone from Barbara's hand. '*Goodbye for fucking good bitch!*' I scream. Then I hang up.

Now it is Keith's turn to pitch in, arriving at the door in a dressing-gown himself.

'What's happening?'

I push my way past him and run into the tiny toilet downstairs. I lock the door and fall to my knees and cling to the seat. I want to cry but there are no tears and nothing to vomit up. There are three soggy coloured strands from a party popper floating on the scented blue water of the bowl. I flush. The bowl gradually fills before the spiral hastily sucks the water and strands away. Then it settles. My own vortex won't dissipate. I don't know if I can ever get out. About what else am I so ignorant?

After a few minutes, there is a knock at the bathroom door.

'Portia? There's no point you getting yourself in a state, is there?'

'What else?' I demand through the closed door, 'don't I know?'

'Come and sit down. I made you another tea.'

Like something burned through, I am suddenly at a loss. Maybe it's my utter impotence making me so.

'Your mum just called again, Portia. I promised her I'd explain. Come along.'

'Where's Keith.' I hate him. Don't know how, but he's somehow complicitous in this, in Dad's death. 'I don't want him there.'

'All right, Portia,' he answers. 'I'll go upstairs.'

I wait a few moments more before stepping out. I feel sick. Acid is stinging my stomach. My eyes are sore. Barbara is keeping her distance, as if I can't be trusted. Me not being trusted, that's rich. When I have been lied to so.

The photos have been cleared up and the box hidden somewhere else, everything hidden from me like bottles from an alcoholic. The clock ticks with an empty, tinny sound. I sit. I can't drink the tea I am given, how strange to think I could. Keith has snuck back upstairs. Barbara, I remember, was composed like this after the suicide. She fusses with the knot of her dressing-gown cord. We sit in silence. She hands me tissues. I blow my nose, ask for water. 'I'm not missing anything, am I? Getting it wrong. He is Dad's, isn't he?'

'Yes.'

I nod. Barbara at least understands that straight answers will appease. Weird how I can't stay angered at her. Not as I do with Mother. But Mother is dumb, and she is nothing. Dad understood that she was nothing. I was stupid to forget that.

'He never knew, did he?' I ask. 'About Richard. She didn't tell him.'

'Clive?' A pause, then, 'Clive knew.'

'Oh.' I had not expected that.

'Diane took Richard with her when she and Clive divorced. She thought it was for the best, seeing as Clive wasn't going to be in the country even.'

'Was she having an affair with someone, then? With this Peter guy? Is that what?'

'No, nothing like that.'

'Then—?'

'He was a mistake, I think, Portia. The baby.'

'But Dad wouldn't have left. I can't believe he'd have left.'

'Yes, he did. He went to Toronto.'

'But why? I can't believe—'

'Come on, Portia.' Now Barbara joins me on the sofa. 'Try not to get yourself in a state. Would you like a pill to help you?' She has tranquillizers, I think, in a tube on the table by the letter. I don't want them. I want to be aware. I need to know everything.

As Barbara is picking up the pieces of torn tissue I have inadvertently dropped to the ground, I ask, 'Why have I been lied to? Why wasn't I told about him?'

'Diane thought it best if you never knew. It wasn't really our place to say anything, mine or your mother's. You mustn't blame her.'

'What fucking right did Diane have to stop me knowing?'

'Don't get angry at her, too, Portia. Come along. Everyone thought she was doing the right thing.'

'And I didn't count? Even though he was my brother, I didn't count?'

'Perhaps if you'd been in England, then—'

'What fucking difference does an ocean make?' I scream.

'Now, it's no use getting upset, is it?'

I do try to breathe more slowly. I want to be clear-headed, not miss anything obvious. 'Had Dad done something to her? Something bad? Is that why she didn't want to know him?'

'I wouldn't worry yourself about all that.'

'You're saying yes, aren't you? He did something.'
'They weren't very fond of each other at the end, no, Portia.'
'Why?'
'You'd have to ask . . . her that.'
Him, she nearly said him.
I stand. 'What's her number?'
'I don't know it, I'm afraid.'
'Please.'
'I don't know, Portia. Not since they moved.'

'Then I'm going to have to go there. I'm going to go.' I say, making for the stairs.

Barbara runs to me, grabs my sweater. Her grip is strong. 'No, Portia, you can't. It's the middle of the night. You're tired out, you know you are. Go to bed and we'll have a talk tomorrow.'

Should I listen? I am so tired after last night's lack of sleep I am not even sure I could make it to London. Not in this rain. I could have a pill, I guess, chase it down with some whisky. Or take all the pills, end the questioning for ever. Why not?

'I don't know.'

'Come on, I'm going to give you one of those sleeping pills and tuck you into bed. It's never good to think about these things in the middle of the night.'

'Really?'

'Really, come on, come along upstairs.'

I let her lead me. She has to put on her glasses to read the label on the bottle of pills. She tips one into her hand, and then, after a pause, another. I drink them down. The idea of Richard becomes less plausible and focused. I lie down. Barbara strokes my hair. I try to connect the why's with their answers, but the chains disintegrate. Can't fight the pills. I'm glad, I think, I'm glad. The light is turned off and . . .

I wake, sharply, not from a dream but the sense is with me at once that something is wrong. Could be any time. In fact, it's early. I'm surprised. The pills must have been strong since they knocked me out so fast. I sit up, peer beyond the net curtains. It is evidently damp. Luke's silver car gleams from the rain but there is nothing precious about the day. No hint of jewels. And somewhere, out under these clouds, Richard, my brother, sleeps.

I hear a noise. I don't want to face my uncle and aunt after last night. It's Diane I need to speak to. What if . . .?

I dress and pack fast (taking the pills) and manage to sneak downstairs before the others are up. It is seven a.m. Diane's letter takes some looking for, but I find it in the kitchen and moments later, having scrawled a note telling my aunt not to worry, I am out the door. I follow signs to London with the radio turned loud. Radio One spills the Spice Girls, Mariah Carey, Oasis; soft rock I don't need. I change channels. It is easier driving this way. I stop once at a Little Chef for a watery coffee, but I am eager to push on. The traffic becomes more dense as I near the city, but it does keep moving, and soon I am past the Tower and back on roads I recognize. I pull over to find Diane's road on the map.

The route takes me west past Luke's and then up the Goldhawk Road towards Acton. It is an unappealing, soulless part of the city. The streets all look the same with two-storey, pale brick workers' terraces. Ridgedale Road is no exception. I park by a builder's skip and check my face in the driver's mirror. Urgh. There's no blaming the typically brutal perspective of the Swedes who make this glass, my eyes truly are sunken and bruised. I put on bright lipstick, to shift the focus.

Now the new day has come, I feel more sad than nervous. What if losing this son was the great sadness of Dad's life? Richard lessens me.

I locate number 29, walk by to see the curtains open. When I have found the courage I return and wait nervously once I have rung the doorbell. Inside, a phone rings. No one answers. I ring again then return to the car, and wait.

Once an hour, at least, I ring the bell. My luck never changes. When the local pub opens, I have a Coke, use the squalid bathroom, eat a bag of chips, but still there's no answer when I return. What if she's away? Hours pass. I sit in the car, studying every person walking down the street. In between, images of Richard make my heart plummet as in a dreamer's cliff-edge fall. What went wrong? Did Diane's leaving break Dad's heart; his neck? Has it all led to this, my failure as an adult? Camilla and her cronies will feel justified by my actions. Never should have trusted me, they'll say, we didn't, not from the start. Religion and politics at the dining table on her very first night. Couldn't get a grip on her. 'One simply can't tell with the accent she has,' said Mrs Bingham. Fucking bitch. I despise her. Luke deserves a better mother than she. And yet, did any of them deserve what I did? I am sick of myself. It did not purge me, that brief madness.

Where is Diane? I walk the block again. When I return there is still no reply. A soupy December darkness seems to have risen like fog from the grey sidewalks up to clouds stained yellow by the city's unfaltering bulbs. And what if Richard is home? The soft-boiled fact of his existence is still meeting opposition within my mind. For fourteen years, my consciousness has considered itself my father's only legacy. I am halved by Richard. Why would I want another, Dad used to say when I wondered about being an only child, when I have my little sweet Pea?

I rub at my eyes, then look again at the letter. She works at the Westminster and Chelsea Hospital now. Couldn't I go there? Can't be many Diane's hiding in maternity. The idea gives me hope.

I find the hospital easily and park in a road so close to Luke's I have to run like a thief into the sparkling glass and metal building. The Christmas decorations do a little to brighten the mood, but it is not a happy place. I am smiled at when I ask for maternity. A sister, they might assume. Me the aunt. But that is possible, now. Richard could have a child.

I take the elevator up. A black woman is mopping the floor. I hate the smell, the lights. Reminds me of Grandmamma Bec dying with tubes in her that seemed to me the child to be sucking her essence out, as if the embalmers had already started their work. It is less depressing up here among the expectant, but the women in their beds look far from happy.

I stop a nurse, a large woman with a stony expression. 'Excuse me, I'm looking for Diane.'

'Diane who?'

Diane who stole my father's child, maybe ruined his life. That Diane.

'She's a nurse, um, she's—'

'Diane Powolski?'

'Oh, I, I, don't know.'

'She's the only one here today. Diane?'

The nurse – a midwife, it seems – had her back to me, attending to some pallid young thing, but as soon as she turns, I know it is she. She is petite, quite slender. She wears no make-up and yet has vanity enough to die her hair a pale brown. The roots, I can't help noticing, need some retouching. But she seems too young to have a thirty-two-year-old son. She can't be much older than Mother. In fact, with her uniform and her short hair, the parallel is shocking. Dad's taste. It turns my stomach. She looks at me and briefly narrows her eyes, as if trying to place me. Then she holds up a hand. I wait, nervously, wondering how I will introduce myself. Now that I am here, I can't feel angry with her. It is just not inside. She tends, kindly it seems, to the new mother, before approaching me, her hand extended.

'Hello, there.' Huh, a soft voice, still something of an Irish brogue in it. 'You must be Portia.'

'How did you know?'

'Barbara called me.' Diane touches my shoulder. 'She was worried for you.'

I shake my head. 'I'm OK.'

I had been anticipating shock from Diane, a rebuke, a confrontation in which I, representing the innocent, would emerge vindicated. Instead, she kindly explains that, even though her shift only recently began (just my luck: today she has been shopping at the sales) she can spare ten minutes if I am impatient to talk. I am. I follow her to the soda machine where she buys me a Diet Pepsi. She has good legs, like Mother. Slim ankles, quick around the wards. Together, we sit in an empty consulting room, a table between us. I focus on the delicate gold cross about her neck. A good Catholic girl? I know nothing. It is peculiar that we, who have shared so much, should be strangers.

'My mother's a nurse, too. Except she looks after the dying. It has always been more up her alley than . . . this.' It is disarming, the little smug smile with which Diane responds. I clean with a nail some dirt from the groove at the top of my can. 'Barbara probably told you that I found out about Richard.'

'Yes, she did.'

'Apparently, you didn't want me to know.'

Barbara sits composed, her hands folded in her lap. 'No, that's right, I didn't.'

I suspect Diane, like Mother, is skilled at answering difficult questions with composure. Is my blood level dangerous? Will I walk again? Any hope of a hand-job under the blanket? 'Can you tell me why? I mean, he is my brother.' I meet her eye. 'Isn't he?'

'Your half-brother, yes he is.'

'Hasn't he ever wanted to meet me?'

She smiles again. 'I'm sure he will.'

'But before,' I say, almost relieved that the anger has returned, 'I mean, if I hadn't found that letter, you think I'd have gone through my whole life not knowing I had a brother? Was that up to you to decide?'

'If Richard had wanted to contact you, of course I wouldn't have dreamed of standing in his way. He was the one who asked to meet Barbara. But he has his own sisters. Three of them.'

'And I don't count? I'm somehow not real?'

'Of course you are. I hope you will meet him, I do.' She glances at the watch hanging from her uniform. An arriving elevator dings from the corridor.

'I recognized him from a photo even before I knew. He looks like my father. Our father.' Who art in heaven, I think in the silence. I would guess Diane does, too. 'I can't imagine having a dad like that and not being allowed to know him.'

'Richard considered my husband his father. I married again before he was two. It was better for him.'

'How could it have been? Jesus! I'm sorry, but Dad was the best father I could have possibly had. Don't you remember how fantastic he was?'

Diane straightens her back and runs a hand along the top of one thigh, pushing flat the creases of her pale blue dress. 'My memories aren't perhaps as tender as yours.'

'Why?'

'It was complicated.'

'Why? I need to know.' I am tired. I don't have the taste for argument, nor can I be calm with such perplexing questions left open. 'What was complicated?'

Diane shakes her head. 'We haven't the time, now,' she says.

'Barbara said she thought you were too young.'

'Or not young enough,' she says, quietly.

'What does that mean?'

'Nothing,' With a hand, she waves the comment away. 'Forget I said that.'

'I can't. Please tell me. Please, please,' I beg. 'It's important to me.'

And I am owed, I don't say. Who knows for how much?

Diane now holds up her hands as if in surrender. 'I'll tell you this much, and then I am going to have to get back to my work. After Richard was born,' she pauses, casts her eye towards the window, says, 'Clive lost all interest in me.'

'How? In what way?'

'As man and wife. And since I was only nineteen, that—'

'Isn't that common? Don't people take time to re-adjust after they've had a kid? I can't see that's such a big crime.'

'That depends what you call a crime, I suppose. He left me without anything, and he left his son, and I had to hear people talk, in the university. Say unpleasant things. About how he liked us young. About how I was already too old.'

'Too old? At nineteen?'

'That's what was said. I don't know how old your mother was when she met Clive, but—'

'Seventeen.'

She makes a face that says, 'there you are, then'. I try to swallow the phlegm in my throat. 'But they said things in Toronto,' I tell her, 'and they weren't—'

Weren't true, I was about to say; only rumours. That he made passes at students. Had relationships. That one girl had been considering charges against him. That he was cornered. Mother would have relished the stories had they been true. Anything to discredit him.

I ask, 'You didn't believe them, did you? The things people said.'

Diane stares at me, and it seems she is about to speak when there is a commotion behind us, a nurse running. Diane glances over her shoulder, stands. I stand too.

'I mean,' I ask, unable to hide the panic setting in, 'that's not why you divorced, is it? You never knew anything, did you?'

'I knew he wouldn't even look at me after Richard was born. He could be cruel. He used to use words I didn't understand.'

'Words?'

'He enjoyed making me feel stupid.'

'Words.'

'That I couldn't be expected to know.'

The blood seems to rush from my head. I stumble, half-fall, half-sit.

Diane is by me in a second.

'I'm sorry, I—'

'Sshh-shh-shh. Why don't you come and lie down for a moment. Barbara said you hadn't eaten and—'

'It fits,' I whisper. 'It can't.' The fights with the university. The separate bedrooms. The way Mother changed after she had me. Her face in the photos. Her sadness. Of course she resented me, why wouldn't she hate me? Twenty-one, a life over. And the words made to make her feel wordless herself; worthless, silent. It terrifies me to think. But since then, the years since. Why hasn't she said? If he wasn't 'interested' in her, why wouldn't she have said?

'There's a place you can lie down through here.'

'I don't want to. You have to tell me if it was true.'

'He wasn't a bad man, Portia.'

I want her to assure me that it doesn't fit. All the questions from Mother and her shrinks. Had he touched me? When he put me to bed, were sometimes his hands where they should not have been? When I was in the bath, would he come in? Did he help me to dress? Did I let him draw me naked? 'Don't feel ashamed, Portia, but did he ever ask you into his room?' No, I would answer, no and no and no and *no*. They had no right to discredit him.

'Was it true?' I ask again.

'No, I'm sure it wasn't.'

'So why did he leave you?' Not one but two families deserted, I am thinking. 'Why did he come to Canada?'

There is a nurse at the door, looking towards Diane. 'They're taking Tracy Norton through now,' she begins, 'so—'

'Thank you. Portia, I'll bring you a glass of water but I am going to have to attend to this—'

'I need air.'

'I think this window opens.'

'Outside, I need some air.'

'I think you should lie down.'

She is right, I am dizzy as I walk, but I need to be somewhere alone. To think. What she said can't be true, he was not that kind of man. He never touched me. 'No.'

'There's a café on the ground floor, Portia. Why don't you have a sit-down there, get yourself something nice to eat and I'll join you in a few minutes. How's that?'

'OK.'

'Diane?' comes a voice.

'I'm sorry, I have to go—'

'Yes.'

'But I will come down. Unless I can make you lie down here?'

'No, I'll go.'

She walks me to the elevator. She has a kind, empathetic nature, this woman. Not dishonest. Not the lying type. She squeezes my hands and tells me not to worry and makes me promise again that I will wait. Before the elevator doors have closed, she has turned to run where she was needed. I am looked at with sympathy in the elevator, as if it is obvious I have been visiting the sick.

Downstairs, I keep walking past the café and out the front door. I continue until I reach the car. Worse, it is, than I would have ever imagined. I sit in the passenger seat and turn the mirror towards my face. There is nothing there. Deadness. His flesh and blood. Am I in my crimes no better than he?

A man passes the window who looks just like Luke. I am only two minutes from the flat. I have to go, to go. I start the engine, almost hit another car as I accelerate away. Don't know where I should go. I don't have family left to run to, not now. Have to get away, that's all for now. I turn off the Fulham Road and soon find I am in Hammersmith. I make a left then a right and park close to the Thames. I run to its edge.

Too many thoughts to think about. Too many nightmares forming. Don't want those long nights to return. In front of me, lights from a house boat illuminate slivers of the river close by. It is high tide, and the current is moving fast. I would jump in if I had the guts. Just let myself go. The only anchor I could trust has snapped. Was he just waiting for me to grow? No, no, no. *No!* It is all obscene.

I must speak to Mother. What if Diane, in her guilt for leaving, was lying, creating an excuse for stealing his son, making evil a man who was anything but? Near me is one of those old-fashioned red boxes the tourism offices have us believe abound but which, in truth, are far between. I run to it and pull on the heavy door. Someone has pissed in here, and it reeks of that, and of old smokes, and there are a few ads for prostitutes, boys mainly. Always, there seems to be a link between rivers and male hookers, can't say why. I dial the operator, hear in time Mother hurriedly accepting my call. Never once has she let me down.

'Portia, where are you?'

'I'm sorry I spoke to you that way this morning. I'm sorry, I'm sorry.'

'Where are you?'

'I'm in London. I met Diane.'

'Are you all right?'

'She said things and I don't know whether they're true. Mum, I don't know if they're true.'

'Where are you, darling? Luke's been calling me all day.'

'Luke?'

'He wants you to go to his apartment.'

'Luke does?'

'Yes. Will you go back and I can call you there? I hate it not knowing where you are. I've been so worried.'

'She said that Dad wasn't interested in her after she had their baby. Is that true? Is that what he did? Is that why you moved to separate rooms?'

'Clive and I weren't particularly close, were we? You knew that, darling.'

'But never told me why, Mum,' I begin to cry again. 'Not why. I didn't know that about him, I didn't know that about him, none of it—'

'Calm down, darling, please.'

'And that he hit on his students. Is that what he did with you?'

'Darling, will you go to Luke's? We can't have this talk on the phone. We just can't.'

'I don't know what I'm going to do. I haven't been sleeping, Mum, and at Christmas Luke asked me to marry him and there are things I haven't even told you. I did something terrible to him—'

'You've got to calm down. He loves you, Portia. Go to the apartment, will you? I hate it that I don't know where you are. Portia?'

The mind is so strange. In an instant, mine feels pure, and knowing, and calm. My tears stop as fast as they began. I wipe at my cheeks, push open the door and inhale London's air. I think I may understand. I may. 'Why did Dad leave England so fast? Was he in trouble?' Mother says nothing. 'Did something happen at the university? Something with a student?'

'Well, I think something may—'

'So it is true.'

It is true, it is. The very thing I adored about Dad, his love for me, was the thing most evil about him. Was every gesture, every kiss, every caress tainted? The world is no longer round.

'Darling, I was thinking of coming over. To London. Luke said he'd be happy to meet me at the airport and—'

I am not listening. I am calm. In the very moment in which she announces that she is coming here, I know where I am going, and why. The dialling code for Penzance in Cornwall is displayed on the first page of the ripped telephone directory. I have vodka, and I have tranquillizers, and I know a place where, twenty-something years ago, I ran from Dad's arms and almost fell to my death. And now I am going back to Maslyn, to where Dad was born.

I am not sure I have the words for this sensation. It is as good as any high I have known. I am over flying over this waste of flesh and blood. In my weightlessness, I am ecstatic. I have all the answers I need. It is pure freedom.

'Portia, will you?'

'What?'

'Go to Luke's.'

'I know it wasn't your fault, Mum.'

'What, darling?'

'Dad. I know that, now. I love you, whatever I said.'

'Are you all right?'

'I love you,' I say again, 'I promise,' and then, before the lump in my throat betrays me, I hang up.

At a Shell gas station nearby, I fill the car with gas. I buy a further eight cans which I store in the trunk. The attendant looks at me as if I am insane. I buy a Patsy Cline tape. *Crazy for Loving You*. It is not meant to mean anything. I pay in cash, leave a tip. A dysfunctional camera records what I do in a hazy monochrome that keeps flickering on and off. I buy a map. In a neighbouring McDonald's I mark out my route. Fittingly, perhaps, I need to drive almost to the end of the country, to Land's End. I like it that there is only one direction in which I can drive. I am calm. Don't know if Daddy felt the same, but I cannot underestimate that. Sweetly, the blackness of being unborn beckons me. It beckons, and I am glad.

I drive in the dark listening to the radio, happy to feel free from the world and its turmoil. If a thousand Algerians die or China connects to the Net or the Footsie dips by one hundred and ninety points, I will remain Portia Mills, the island I am; absolutely inviolable. There are not many people on the roads. I drive slowly with the windows open to help me stay awake. The miles clock up as I pass cities that I once yearned to visit, the names of which were poetry to my foreign ear. Even the yellow brick road was less magical than Salisbury or Winchester, Shaftesbury or Exeter. Except now I can picture the urban centres as I know them to be, their hearts ripped out for uninspired malls, their souls paved over, all mystery gone. I think they have lost as much as I. It makes me feel hopelessly distant: much the same, in fact, as I did with Luke after I had cheated him, as if my spirit had kicked back, given up, folded its arms, made me pay for my sins by denying me feelings at all. If I was able to cry now, I think I would stop this car in the fast lane, fling open the door and howl into the night. But there are no tears. I am empty as the malls, eerily so, since in them, as in me, clamour and commotion can still be heard; a faint, haunting echo.

I break again at a late-night service station near Salisbury, and fill the tank once more. That should do it. I buy tonic, too, to help the vodka go down. My party for one. The man in the kiosk tells me I've 'a ways' to go yet; a few hours, four or five, so I drive into the parking lot, recline the seat and even manage to sleep for a while. I do not dream.

When I begin again, it is past two and the country road seems almost deserted. Nothing seems alive. Fallow fields curve into the bleak sky and down out of sight. Gas stations look as if closed for months. The dim interior light of a white car in a lay-by exposes nobody inside. A sign reading 'Dwarf Rabbits for Sale' is nailed to an open hutch door. To keep myself awake, I steer the car to clump along the cat's eyes and try to guess how many minutes will pass before a car approaches or overtakes. I would play that game lying late at night in the back of my parent's car. I used to love being right because it made me believe what Dad insisted: that I was unique, that the world was shaped for me and not the other way around.

Now I wish my mind would stay clear but as I drive my memory is insistent. The car's headlights turn into film projector beams, casting back against the windscreen distinct images from my near and distant past. Here, Dad singing behind the wheel while I tickled his neck where the hairs curled tightly on themselves. Mother and I would urge him to sing an English song about Henry the Eighth that would make us laugh. ''Enery the Eighth I am, I am/'Enery the Eighth I am I am/I got married to the girl next door/I've been married seven times before.' Is that how it went? Mother and I used to sing it through tears and smiles after he died. I used to reel off the names of Henry the Eighth's wives with breathless speed. Katherine of Aragon Anne Boleyn Jane Seymour Anne of Cleves Catherine Howard and Catherine Parr. Dad would cheer with each one I got right.

I hear him now, see his profile as I lean forward through the gap in the seats. Then, suddenly, Charles's face replaces my father's. He is looking over his shoulder at my naked body on his bed. Now, snap, I am high on Dad's shoulders and tracing the circle of his baldness with my fingers. Luke in his dressing-gown, running to the door. Dad, driving again, then, Mother, old beyond her years, holding the phone as I hung up, then Luke, giving me the ring. The ring! The ring is at Barbara's. But she will get it back to Luke. She will.

This is how I spend the hours, trying to keep my thoughts and memories down. The white lines in the middle of the road seem to flash through the windscreen. Once I take the wrong route, and panic for a moment that I might lose with my route my resolve. But I find without much trouble the right road again, and my choices diminish as I near Cornwall.

I reach Penzance. Dad's town. I drive through the town with the sea to my left, glad it is so quiet. The weather, too, is milder than of late. The clouds are low and dense. By the time I arrive at Maslyn, dawn is just stirring. I park by a forge where the road tapers to a lane and a dairy cow on the ice-cream flag slaps its rump lazily in the wind against the granite wall of a tea shop selling scones and clotted cream and postcards so faded they seem antique already. The air carries the Atlantic's brine in its fog. I am alone when I step from the car.

It is an extraordinary shock that I should remember this place. I don't think anything has changed. In the chest at Mother's there is a photo taken on the day we visited Maslyn, either before or after my near-escape. Daddy and I are outside the store, smiling showily. We are holding our cones in the summer sun. Mine has a stick of flaky chocolate planted like a flag in its snow-capped peak. I am smiling a conqueror's smile. I have the expression of someone who is where she wants to be. Daddy is holding his ice-cream high, like an Olympic torch, and saying something towards the camera, chiding my mother, no doubt, for being too close or too far away or for having her finger dipping over the lens or for any number of faults he perceived in her and complained about to me. 'What is she?' he would have whispered, his breath tickling my ear. 'A technophobe?' I might have answered, delighted with the sound of one of our newest words. 'An electrophobe?' he'd ask. 'A neophobe?'

From the back seat, I take two bottles of tonic and pour half of each onto the ground. The liquid fizzes on the soil, a white spawn, and then is absorbed. In one of the bottles, I empty all of the pills I stole from Barbara. There are six. I swirl the liquid until I am sure the pills have dissolved, then fill the bottle to the top with vodka. I take a gulp, and another, and another. I was thirsty.

I leave the keys in the car's ignition and do not turn back as I set off from the forge towards the sea. Dad and I must have walked this same path before. Mother was probably lagging behind, carrying the picnic while Dad may have carried me. I can't remember now, nor do I try to as I step through the heavy mud towards the ocean, watching my step, wary of the gorse roots stretched like wires across the path. I walk carefully around the puddles. There is no voice inside my head pleading for mercy. There is nothing soft; I am charred.

About a half-mile walk from the teashop the tall hedges die out and the coastal path opens onto the cliff, offering a first rewarding view of the shore. I was here before on a bright, sunny day. The vista, captured on my photos, was ravishing. The shallow waters of the inlet were seductive pools of Caribbean blue, jewelled earrings on the Atlantic's elephant-grey skin. I remember now we saw seals lounging on the tremendous angled planes of granite, undaunted by the people two hundred feet above. But today I am alone, glad to have no witnesses.

The headland's lifelessness is fitting. In every way, it is an unenchanting morning. A dense mist, not quite bold enough to be fog, has fused sky and sea to shroud me. I take another swig of the drink. It is fiery and unpleasant in my throat and makes me cough – a weak, sorry sound lost in this vastness. Beneath me the sea is almost silent, the swell rising and falling as the belly of a sleeping man. I have been walking briskly, with an outdoorsy, Canadian determination. Now I am on the cliff top. There is little wind. Ahead of me, I can see a crude wooden sign signalling DANGER in stencilled red letters shiny from the damp. I am here.

Slowly, I approach the edge. The sound of the waves is magnified in the hollow, making the fall seem further. I peer down into the great geological divorce. Shiny black pinnacles point skywards like the fingers of a drowned sailor, their peaks visible only when the ocean sucks the tide back out. I take a slight step closer, just as a surprising gust of wind slaps my back. I scream, jump backwards, my heart pounding. God, I can't do it. I don't have the strength. I am scared of heights, for God's sakes. And yet, I can't turn back. I am him. How can I live with that?

I sit, drink as much as I can from the narcotized bottle. I step again to the edge. My pulse thuds in my throat. I have become breathless with fear. I only need one jump, one little jump and I will be free, free. And yet . . .

For the next half-hour I must look a pathetic figure, stepping forward and back, talking to myself and closing my eyes and looking to the heavens and never being able to push myself far enough on. I am drinking as much as I can from both bottles, hoping that the pills will take effect just before I jump so that I may fall sweetly and without pain, silent as a crash test dummy.

Yes. Now, now I have the courage. I start to move, one step then the second, three, four, nearly there, Pea, nearly there . . . but my body, my stubborn, demanding body that has never had enough is fighting my will. Above me a gull shrieks, perhaps in encouragement. I watch it swoop towards the sea and check its glide before rising, angled, to borrow a current of wind. I hate it for being so dumb, so unknowing. I envy it for being able to escape while I have bankrupted my life with betrayal and misplaced love.

I finish one bottle, drink some of the other and quite suddenly feel a lightness in my fingers and head. I sit on the edge of the cleft, my legs pointing towards the rocks. I can feel the pull of gravity on the back of my thighs, a gentle, stroking invitation. By now my head is spinning, so I close my eyes and begin to rock with the rhythm of the waves, my arms hugging my body. Soon, sings the sea, soon, soon, soon, soon. It's easy never to open your eyes again. I relish my new calmness. This is how I had imagined it would be, mind and body as one. Even the rock's painful details are blurring before my closed eyes. I should go, just go. Now that I can.

Shocking me, a fog horn sounds from a lighthouse I can't see. It jolts me. I clasp my hand on to the rock. I remember it now, a comforting sound through the night. 'Who do the keeper men talk to?' I wanted Dad to tell me. 'They talk to themselves.' 'Aren't they lonely?' 'Some people like being on their own.' 'Not you.' 'No, not me.' He would have smiled then, perhaps given my nose a pinch. 'How could I be lonely when I've got my Portia Pea?'

'Damn you, Daddy,' I say aloud now, and then in a moment the sweet tears swell beneath my eyelids and at last I am crying, softly at first then in sobs that rock my whole body. 'Damn you. It was not my fault.' Dizzy from the drink I tip my head back to suck in a wide yawn and as I do so I suddenly feel myself slipping. I scream, terrified, and push my body up and back with the heels of my hands but I am losing, slipping, screaming with effort and terror. Help me. '*Help!*' My mind is dizzy and the pain in my arms too much and I can't keep myself up. I am going to fall. I kick with my legs and suddenly my heel finds purchase and I manage to push my body up and back. I fall hard on to the stone behind. Sharp stabs of pain shoot from where I hit my skull on the stone but I am hugging the cliff like a lover.

But now I am panting, violently. Everything is spinning. I want to get safe, but when I try to get to my feet I start to spew hot rushes of bilious, stinging vomit. I fall again to my hands and knees, retching so fiercely I have to struggle for breath. I am not going to survive, now I want to I won't. On my side I tuck my knees under my chin. I am shivering and moaning to keep myself conscious, jabbering words that make no sense, thinking that I will never stand again, that I will roll down the rock and be lost in the tide, that my death will change nothing, that it won't make me understand why Dad was the way he was, that it won't make Luke and Mother and Charles love me for being me, that it won't make them believe that it wasn't my fault, that I did nothing wrong when everything was for love, because I loved and wanted to be loved, because for half my life I haven't been able to trust anyone because of him, because he swore, he swore, he swore that I was his stars and sky and sea before he left me, before he tied that rope around his neck without saying goodbye.

The sky spins. A hotness soaks my jeans between my legs. The clouds open. 'Mother!' I scream, 'Mother! Mother! Muuummy,' and then the blackness comes like a shroud.

TEN

Be more sociable and more physically active than usual and stick closely to your daily routine. At times of stress a familiar pattern of regular meals and activities at the usual hours can encourage a sense of security by providing an orderly environment.

AMA Family Medical Dictionary

My friend Ulla is at the door with groceries in a box: potatoes, fruit, milk, eggs. I am dressed in a towel. 'I was thin once,' she says, coating me with a gaze. 'Like you.'

Ulla Jeubratt is still thin but, at fifty-one, seems to be troubled more by the furrowing of her handsome, long face and the greying of her shoulder-length hair than the loss of either of her husbands or the distance she has put between herself and her native land. Today she is wearing a faded navy fisherman's top finger-painted haphazardly with grey slip from her potter's wheel, tight black jeans and brown leather boots that look as if they were bought for Stockholm in the sixties but now carry dried Cornish mud up to the calves.

Six days have passed since Ulla found me on the cliff at Maslyn. I was unconscious and soaked by rain that had washed the vomit and urine from around my body. She lifted me to safety and asked, on waking me, only simple, commonsense questions. Had I been attacked? Had I come with a man? Did I want the police? A doctor? Had I been sick before? Was that my car by the forge? Would I go with her to her house? Not once did she ask what had happened or why.

She drove Luke's Saab. Neither of us spoke. Ulla's black mongrel, Silas, sat with his muzzle on my jeans and his eyes fixed on mine, but she herself was not so questioning, neither during the brief ride nor at home where she prepared a bath for me, then bed. I accepted each offer with genuine but wordless gratitude. Later, when I woke, it struck me that Ulla had acted with such fluent grace because she had known worse either in herself, or in others.

'Always a long sleeper, mm?' she asks now as she slides the box of groceries on to the kitchen counter of the apartment that has become, suddenly, my home. 'Like a sloth.' I relish the elongated 'o' from Ulla's sing-song Swedish tongue. It weights the word with a fitting onomatopoeia.

'I don't sleep upside down,' I say over my shoulder as I move to the bedroom to fetch a sweater. 'Besides, I was up late, writing.'

'Good.'

The economy of Ulla's speech mirrors her modest temperament. Now I join her by the sink where a vase containing dried flowers casts a pretty shadow on the stained enamel surface. Magnified through the window panes the winter sunshine feels surprisingly hot.

Ulla's cottage is about five hundred yards down a lane towards the sea. I am in a flat that was converted, along with her studio below, from a cattle shed. She rents it out during the holiday season and it has the feel of summer about it – pale yellow and blue daisy-patterned curtains, bookshelves painted white and carrying fat paperback novels that are wrinkled with age and tanned from exposure to the sun, a line of mottled shells and beige stones along the window sill and, everywhere, fine traces of sand from the beaches closer to St Ives. The books are mainly pulp-fiction paperbacks, quite a few from the seventies mired in great disasters on trains and planes and flights to the moon. In the freezer I found a promotional Jurassic Park ice tray, empty, and two choc ices, one of which I ate though it tasted of animal fat and its own wrapping, as if it had melted and frozen again.

Ulla starts for the door. 'You know where I am, if you need.'

I make coffee then sit by the window, looking out across the fields towards the sea. The tightness has eased. A couple of days were crowded with horror and, occasionally, I cannot stop myself from shaking with the memory of my escape, or at the shame of how I treated others, but I am finding something very close to peace here.

Ulla persuaded me to leave a message on Luke's answer machine saying I was alive and well. I owe that, at least.

Lovely Ulla says she is happy to rent me this apartment for a nominal fee. I feel safe here. All day yesterday, the silence was punctuated by the same fog horn that saved me from my own darkness. The haunting sound didn't haunt me. It has made me feel as if both my feet are on the ground, that my state is solid, enviable. All will begin again, from here. I live the days as they come.

I spend the day reading and writing in a journal. I am giving myself a sense of wholeness through the words on the page such as I never felt with the column I have deserted. These pages seem to be separating me, much as a plasma membrane will separate one organism from another, from my now shameful past.

It is almost four when Ulla knocks at the door again with word that an Atlantic storm is racing in and she is heading to Blazey Point to meet it. She has come brandishing a bright yellow waterproof jacket and a pair of red Wellington boots, neither of which I could afford when I went shopping in Exeter three days ago. Ulla had to take some of her pottery to a gallery in London that sells it during the winter months when Cornwall's tourist river has dried to a drip. I wanted more clothes than I had brought, some cash, a typewriter. She decided to drop me in Exeter, far enough from here to keep others in the dark if they try to trace my credit-card withdrawals. Such subterfuge is unavoidable if I am to remain isolated. In London, Ulla left the Saab at Luke's flat and posted the keys through his letter box. We met later on the evening train, me with all the money I could withdraw, and the few items I needed. Strange how running away should feel like finding myself.

Ulla's dog, Silas, has come with her now, barking with excitement. He is a wiry black mongrel found abandoned on the coastal path. Ulla adopted him much as she has adopted me. 'You coming?' she wants to know.

She is wearing a purple bobble hat and oversized white plastic sunglasses although it is midwinter and the sun is hidden behind clouds that seem to me a hundred miles thick.

'It looks dingy.'

'Agh.' Ulla swipes away my complaint with the hefty, rubber torch she is holding. 'Come on, it's good for you.'

I give in and stab my fists into the sleeves of the green sweater I bought in Exeter. It is shapeless and unflattering, but I love it for that. For once in my life I bought clothes with thought only to how they would keep me warm, how they would last. Such indifference to the opinions of others has given me a winning sense of resurrection.

Outside it is drizzly and cold, but the green of the surrounding fields has borrowed strength from the towering trunks of white and charcoal cloud. I am glad at once that Ulla has persuaded me out. I feel a hundred thousand miles from everything I left behind, a light year from last week.

England feels ancient and unblemished down here. Less than a mile from the cottage we pass two semi-circles of megalithic granite slabs standing vertically like mysterious gravestones, motley patches of lichen gripping their faces. They thrill me, make me feel a part of something unbroken. Dad must have seen these stones, as would his paternal ancestors. It is not nothing.

I have yet to search out his living relatives. My feelings towards him are complicated and unsettling at the moment. My whole self has had him as its foundation and I would collapse without any of that. He was a good father. He showed me patience, and love, and he taught me, and I have tried to live up to his high standards, and none of his behaviour was sexual, at least not until the day before he died, and it is impossible to erase and replace these memories with an image of him as a perverse and cruel man.

The storm is picking up. The wind keeps flipping Silas's left ear on to the dome of his head, outing the inner pink. Below the hem of my jacket my jeans are wet and cold. About us, the green of the land has become grey, and through the muffled colour the roar of the somersaulting waves has burgeoned into something quite frightening. The view through Ulla's dark lenses must be apocalyptic but, unlike me, she is keeping her head high, walking fast and upright towards the headland's point a hundred feet ahead.

Suddenly, she breaks into a run. 'Come on, you.'

I jog behind her on the slippery roof of the cliff. The prevailing wind is so powerful it is sucking the breath from my lungs so I let Ulla, twenty-four years my senior, surge ahead. When I approach, I am nervous of standing as close as she to the edge. I lift the hood of my jacket over my head, but with a whump the wind pushes it back off. Ulla turns to me. She has removed her sunglasses. The excitement in her eyes takes years off her, and pleases me. 'Isn't it unbelievable?' she shouts back to me in the wind. She takes hold of my left hand. The slate-grey sea is tumultuous below, a shuddering maelstrom. The waves are pounding against the rock face, like canons firing. I can feel the cliff being battered under my feet. The wind is fearsome, it takes effort just to stand still. I shiver as a trickle of rain tickles my neck behind my ear.

'Open your arms,' says Ulla, making a crucifix of her frame, 'and lean in.'

I do so. She is right, it's exhilarating feeling the power of the wind, as if hundreds of tiny hands are keeping me from falling on my face. Even the rain in my face, I don't mind.

'I love it!' Ulla screams. 'See those lights?' she adds, pointing. 'You should speak to them.'

There is a huge vessel, maybe an oil tanker, far out, the lights of which we can see as it is thrown about on the swell. The body of the ship is lost in the murk.

'What?'

'To the ship men. On the boat there.'

'They can't hear.'

'The wind will carry your words.'

'It's freezing, Ulla. Let's go.'

'Hello to you, my ship men!' Ulla screams. She is mad, my Swedish friend. It makes me laugh. 'This is Portia.' Then, to me, 'Say hello.'

'You're crazy.'

'Say hello to the nice ship men.'

'Hello,' I say, without conviction.

Ulla laughs, 'Come on, shout. Shout!'

'Hello, ship men.'

'No, like this. From here.' She bangs her palm against her stomach. Still holding my hand, she makes us step right to the edge of the cliff. I let go her hand and grab her body. 'Hello, hello, hello,' she hollers.

'They can't hear you.'

'So? It doesn't matter. You have to try.'

'Next time.'

'You want to go?'

I nod.

'OK, come on then.'

Silas seems glad when we turn to home. Away from the cliff's edge, the wind drops and, though strong still, it feels calms here. The tenebrous light is an atonement with the earth as our battle was with the sea. We have become blissfully indistinct. We walk in silence, hand in hand, until we reach a path where the gale is less loud.

'When I was a girl in Sweden,' says Ulla, 'I believed you could hear things from the past blowing in the wind.'

'And could you?'

'Oh, when I wanted to. But the past has to be invited if it's going to mean anything. Otherwise, passhoo, it's gone.'

'I don't agree. I think it has meaning all the time.'

'No,' she says with a laugh. 'You make that up yourself, Portia. You like it like that.'

'No, I don't,' I say, annoyed with her suddenly. 'I'm just saying, you can't undo the stitching.'

'Yes, you can. You start from here, where you are. Oh, Portia, don't look so serious. Come on, I'm going to cook for you tonight.'

'I need a bath.'

'So, I have a bathroom. Then you can stay for food. We'll eat early.'

Ulla's cottage is small and simple, painted white and built of hefty granite blocks. The buildings here have to pay homage to the force of the weather. It feels absolutely right for me to begin again amid this austere Cornish architecture. Man has left little impression, and where he has, it has been as servant to the elements. Ruined tinmine chimneys seem scarcely more modern than the megalithic stones that preceded them by four thousand years. Cottages have been left deserted. Dad bequeathed to me a sense of the magic in Cornwall, not merely the many ancient fables of screams heard from shipwrecked boats or sightings of mermaids and giants and witches, but its unique refusal to be subjugated. He told me we were of the same stock. I am less proud of that now.

The cottage is wonderful. From the worm-ravaged beams of the kitchen hang bunches of dried flowers and a few old pots and pans. The room is cluttered with Ulla's stoneware pottery and the spoils of her beachcombing walks. Arranged on an old, oak church pew are fingery spindles of bleached and salted wood; a few green and brown bottles, message-less but barnacled; a lacquered abacus which looks antique to me and is missing, as maybe Ulla is herself, a few of its beads; a length of thick, frayed rope beautifully knotted at one end; the pear-shaped sounding board from an acoustic guitar and, strangest of all, a brilliantly coloured stuffed pheasant that she found on the beach on New Year's Day. She is convinced it has meaning.

Ulla's most prized possession is an unmarked old barrel she heaved and rolled all the way from Gallow's Bay and which now stands proudly on the tiled floor at the end of the pine table. Though the staves on one side are warped and the hoops buckled and dusty red with rust, it is sturdy enough to be used as a seat and is one of the few items, along with her collection of smooth sand-coloured oval stones, that she has kept in the cottage for years. She replaces everything else, she told me on my second day, as often as she can. She seems to have made it her mission not to become too attached to anything she might lose.

'Why don't you go and have your bath? I'll bring you some Glögg when it's hot.'

'Don't you want—?'

'No, you go.'

Sinking into my rose-scented water I listen with delight to the clatter of raindrops against the tiny window pane. It makes the cold sound colder. With the tub hard against the nape of my neck, I lean back, close my eyes and form a cinematic vision of myself standing, arms wide, on Blazey Point – a gull's eye view that captures acres of land and sea with myself the tiny cross of an unmarked grave on the cliff's edge. I don't mind at all that I should seem so small.

I slide under the hot water and begin to count. Two, three, four. Dad would sit on the seat of the toilet with his watch in his hands to time me. After a while I learned how to ease the water from my lungs as I lay still with the unfamiliar brush of my hair sweeping my cheeks to carpet the water's surface. Fifteen, sixteen, seventeen. How long did I last? A minute? Two? Mother used to complain that one day I would pass out, that no one would know until it was too late. Twenty-six, twenty-eight, thirty. Dad would give me prizes with each record broken, make a big hoo-haa about it, as always. 'Tonight, Ladies and Gentleman and fat old hags and roly-poly monsters with bad breath,' he would announce while I tried to keep my laughter inside, 'tonight you shall witness the most wonderful Portia-Pea Mills make a bold and incredi-bubbly daring attempt to break her own breathholding-in-the-bath record. Yes, indeedy, you will.' Forty. Thinking about it used to make me cry underwater when he'd gone. And forty-seven and eight. If I'd had the guts I would have stayed under after he left, breathed in the water while picturing him, my great, good upside-down god, peeking at me in my sunken world. Fifty-six, splash! I lift my head fast out of the water. My heart is thumping as if it is going to burst. I squeak forward to turn on the cold. Tell me Dad didn't crave what in innocence I displayed. Tell me, someone, please.

A knock, then Ulla comes in. I lean forward, a little coyly, and grab my ankles. She sets the glass down with a little chink against the enamel.

'Come on, I'll wash your skinny back,' she says.

I would say no, but she is quick to sink her hand in the water, and in truth it feels good, my senses rush towards her lathered touch. I have needed another.

'Your mother, does she look like you?'

'Why do you ask that?'

She scoops up a handful of my hair and gently soaps my neck. 'You don't say much about her.'

'There's not much to say. But I guess I look like her, sometimes. I look like my grandmother too, the one from Quebec. You'd have liked her.'

'Is your mother beautiful?'

'She's my mother, you know. So I've seen her . . . crumble.'

Ulla splashes the soap off my back and sits on the square cork top of the laundry basket. 'That's all you can say about her?'

'Well, she's ectothermic, too.'

'What?'

'Cold blooded,' I explain, but the definition sounds mean and hollow.

Dad and I would laugh so hard at the words – ectothermic, coprophagous, rugose, tribadistic – with which we regularly taunted Mother. It makes me angry, now. 'It doesn't matter.' The skin of my big toe whitens where it curls around the tiny loops of the plug's chain. I pull. 'Which towel should I use?'

Ulla wraps me in one and dabs my shoulders dry, as Dad used to. Can't she even dry herself without you? Mother would demand to know. Your mother's lurking again, isn't she? he'd reply to me, even as Mother stood by. She's a lurky-lurky-lurker.

Now I have to wonder whether she was just watching out for me.

'I put your jeans in the dryer,' says Ulla, 'so you can have these.'

I dress in her leggings and a thick sweater. It is always freezing in the cottage. The temperature seems to be knee-deep in its own history, but I put so many logs on the fire before helping to cook the pasta that, after our kitchen supper, the living room has changed in character. With the tapestries Ulla has hung on the wall, it's the cosiest room in the house anyway. The light from the flames makes it more intimate still.

Ulla rolls a joint which we share. I lie on my back in front of the fire. The grass crackles as we inhale. I am aware of the fierce storm buffeting the walls. It makes me feel cosy here.

'Are you my pheasant?' Ulla suddenly asks. From the carpet, her inverted grin looked grotesque. Her teeth are large as it is and for a second I think she is a witch, that she has kidnapped me and is planning to hang me by my ankles in the barn. 'Are you my pheasant?' she repeats, laughing some more. 'The pheasant I found.'

'Am I missing something?' I narrow my eyes. 'Isn't the pheasant, the pheasant?'

'No, it was a sign. I knew something exotic and beautiful would join me. You're my pheasant.'

'Quack,' I say.

'That's a duck.'

'I speak good duck.' I say, giggling at how stoned we are. 'I'm one talented pheasant.'

'I know why Luke kidnapped you.'

'You've got kidnapping on the brain,' I reply, stupidly, because of course I was the one who had kidnapping on the brain. Weird.

'You want more of this,' she asks, pinching the soggy roach in her fingertips.

'Unh-unh, I'm done.'

Ulla throws it in the fire and then flops onto the floor and lies facing me, supporting her head on her hand. She lifts some hair off my forehead, and strokes it back into place. 'I'm happy you're here,' she says.

'Me too.'

'You don't miss him?' she asks, surprising me with the question. 'Luke.'

'No.'

'Do you think he misses you? Was he in love with you?'

'I don't know,' I say, softly, wishing I hadn't been asked. I close my eyes. 'Maybe he thought he was.' I have been writing about such things. In trying to be objective, I am turning detective. I am trying to treat my former beliefs (especially that Luke regarded me as nothing more than an exotic acquisition, a pheasant) with the same polite disrespect that TV private investigators offer cloddish police chiefs. Why, when he barely knew Miss Portia Mills, did the suspect turn her life around? Was it not through honest love and kindness? Would it not be fair to conclude that he fell in love at first sight, that it was Portia Mills who lied and sinned and callously betrayed a man willing to make her his wife? Don't the facts speak loudly for themselves?

The poor, sweet baby. Did he find out about Charles and me, I wonder? Does he hate us both? My crime was selfishness, indecent as Dad's. What if all . . . ? Suddenly, my thoughts are severed by the shock of Ulla's lips touching mine. I open my eyes, see her smiling face. I am motionless, hoping she won't move again.

But she does, only now when she kisses me, I press my fingers to her cheek and push her away. 'Please, Ulla, no.' Though I am dizzy, I rise to my feet. Ulla flops on her back. She is still smiling. I don't know what to say. I collect the coffee cups. 'I'm tired, Ulla, I think I'm going to head back to the cottage.'

Her smile remains in place, but now I think it rueful and forced.

'Do you need help clearing up, or—'

She shakes her head. 'No.'

'OK, then, um, good night. Thanks for the pasta. I'll . . . I can let myself out.'

I hug myself in the cold as I jog towards the cottage. I don't want to think about what Ulla has just done. I don't want to be loved for what she can get from me. Lust leaves too much destruction in its wake. Through her peace and selflessness, Ulla has been making me feel secure this last week. I can't bear to think her motives have been sordid. That we are all sordid and sullied. Did none of us escape the fall?

I reach the cottage as thunder splits overhead. The door is thrown open by the wind, and I have to fight to close it again. I am scared, a little. The barn creaks. Dad used to come into my room during such storms. He would hold my hand and whisper stories to me. Any time of night, he was there. I used to look forward to storms then, but all is tinted differently now. My memories have become rancid. Dad with me in the bath. Dad coming to me in bed. Dad wanting me on his lap as he read. All the time, Dad playing with me and not Mother, his wife. Was it my touch he wanted? It is horrible.

When I get into bed, I have to keep the light on. There is dust under the chest of drawers, it needs a sweep. I'm getting like Mother, wanting the place tidy and clean. I have been wanting to write to her, and to Luke, but I can't risk them seeing the postmark. Like a bone cracked, I need this time in plaster. Yet I need to say sorry, too. I want to admit to my culpability, admit that I have been wrong and they are not to blame and that . . .

I stop myself. My mind the sponge is becoming heavy again. The enormity of my misjudgement is scaring me. What if I have spent my life chasing the wrong star? Forming myself in the wrong image? Wouldn't that mean I am unable to understand what is right or wrong? It is all confused. Perhaps Ulla is right: we have only ourselves each minute of each day. I will not invite the past. It will not have meaning. I exist now. I am breathing, and my heart pumps with blood, my own blood, and all else flows from that.

Two weeks have passed and the kiss has not been mentioned. Could be Ulla was just stoned. I have since become her partner in another way, in her ceramics studio. She thinks I am a natural on the wheel. I have a feel for it, it seems.

I am finding a peace here I think I have never known. Everyone is a little kooky and out of place. Penzance is a town that probably comes into its own during the summer, but the fact that I am here out of season makes me feel as if I belong. The candy stores and restaurants display brightly coloured ads for chocolate nut sundaes and banana splits (kids' menus half-price) and the ads for recreational activities carry photos of sun-drenched beaches where kids on donkeys wear T-shirts and colourful hats. In the brochures, the sea is azure and the gardens in bloom. Yet I am enjoying it now when the wind is harsh and the seagulls' ceaseless cries sound mournful rather than joyous and the sea, carrying its thick blankets of seaweed, lashes vigorously against the rocks. It is almost enough to make me believe in a God.

The road from the cottage into Penzance, past Newlyn with its chorus of halyards ting-tinging against the swaying masts of the fishing vessels, becomes soaked when the tide is high and the wind strong. Waves crash onto the screen of our car. It makes me and Ulla howl with laughter. We drive back and forth trying to guess when the next swoosh of water will fall to blind us.

There is no escaping nature. At night, as the wind rattles the windows and doors, I think of the fisherman and of the animals on the moors hiding in the hedgerows and under rocks, of the men and women who lived here thousands of years ago in simple stone houses not so dissimilar from the granite homes that face the Atlantic today. I think of Dad, and it helps me forgive, because to leave this place must have been torture. I never want to go. Often, I open the atlas in the cottage and pinpoint my place on the map. Land's End. The narrowness of the promontory makes those of us living here seem somehow larger in the universe. It is not possession but belonging.

I walk the cliffs as often as I can. Late this morning the sleet died and the wind tore a great hole in the clouds exposing a shocked, pale-blue sky that has since been covered again. I dressed in my thickest gloves and excused myself from the studio to walk along Maslyn's three-hundred-foot high cliff and then to the village to buy basics for Ulla and myself. Halfway there, I stopped at the point where I almost jumped. I sat gazing in wonderment at the expanse of ocean. An immense calmness, persistent as the ocean itself pushing towards shore, filled me. The cloud cover was dense yet, despite the oppressive gloom, for as far as I could see single wave crests were curving into the light for a brilliant moment before returning to the water's mass. I sat with my palms flat on granite rock as solid as the headstones of my English antecedents and thought that the mere fact that I had clung to it, that I struggled so to grip to this life, is proof enough that we don't need meaning beyond each living moment. We ride our white horses or we do not. Dad chose to jump. I am not yet steady on these new legs but I was excited by the feeling that, in choosing to stay, I have begun at last to walk alone.

Silas and I walk for more than two hours along the castellated cliff before reaching the village. All I need is here. It is a world in miniature. Little shops, little buses, small concerns. I have no deadlines, no lover, no plans to be made for the night.

I approach Maslyn village from the west through the churchyard where the unshielded gravestones have been battered faceless by gales. There is not much sense of religion around here, there is no room for its ritual, but it is a spiritual place and I get the feeling among Maslyn's graves that these souls are no less dead than those of the drowned sailors whose songs, as Ulla likes to tell, can be heard from their wrecks across the waves. I discovered a Mills buried here, a child of eight, fondly remembered in 1864. I hope we are related. The past is the present. I don't need to unearth Dad.

Beyond the church, with its unbuttressed, fifteenth-century tower, is the village square. It is perfect. There is a First World War memorial in the village centre (a Mills here, too), around which are all the basic shops one could ever need – two bakeries, both of which seem permanently deserted save for an assortment of dry white breads and sickly pastries: gingerbread men with misshapen eyes, meringue creams, Swiss buns at twenty-five pence. Here, too, there is a butcher, a fish 'n' chip shop beside a Stop 'n' Shop supermarket where, for one week only, Kellogg's cornflakes, Mr Fry's pork pies, Dettol and Mullen's 'all-cod' fishcakes are on sale. Crossing the road you get to the estate agents and Shirley's barber shop (Ladies' Day, Wednesdays) beside the Tulip Inn – Maslyn's social heart – a bold, early Victorian pub and hotel in what is probably the only attractive building in the square. Beyond that is a carpet shop neighbouring the local grocery and newsagent. I have developed an odd little relationship with Karen, the girl who works there. I kick the mud off my boots and enter the store. The bell sounds. Karen looks up from her *Daily Mirror*. As usual, she has time to read. It is an empty shop she's minding.

'Hey there, what's cooking?'

'Nothing much.'

I am as cheery as can be with the locals I have met. The village is small enough that I have already become known, if not accepted. My whole life I have wanted to belong to one of those communities where people greet and wave to each other on the street. Where they all know each other's names. I want to walk into the Tulip and be able to join any of the tables. I want to run a tab at the village store and have the memory of a crush on some local boy, ideally the older and inaccessible brother of a childhood friend. Befriending Karen, all glum and jittery in her pink and white checkered nylon apron, is not going to change my life all that much, but it is a start.

'Nothing good's happened?'

'Tony won a tenner on the lottery.'

'There's something.'

'Then he lost fifteen quid on scratch cards.'

I shrug. 'Oh, well. Hey, got any new cereal suggestions?'

'Special K?' she suggests, pointing.

'You don't think that's too healthy?'

'Not with enough sugar.'

'OK, it's a deal.'

The shop sells cereal out of scratched plastic containers, like hamster food. It is beyond me why Karen doesn't carry those colourful boxes, like everyone else. The store could use cheering up. I buy a little bag and a carton of milk. I don't care for canned foods or sweeties and there is not much else to buy here. The shelves, made from plywood and lined with squirly blue plastic, are half-empty. Really, that's what they are. Though half the space is filled, the impression is that something's wrong. It is a disabled shop.

'I wanted to be a shopkeeper once,' I tell Karen.

I had, of course, wanted to be plenty of things, but for a long time I had this vision of a perfectly square room with huge glass windows and wooden floorboards and shelves that reached to the ceiling. It was Grandmamma Bec who got me started. Every summer, she and I would set up a stall outside my house. Our stock, much like Karen's, was not as impressive as my imagination: apples in the fall, plastic cups of home-squeezed cider, jam and cookies if Mother made them, and whatever bric-à-brac I could persuade Mother to part with. Grandmamma Bec and I would sit together and I would cross my fingers tightly every time someone came near, cursing them under my breath if they passed. Getting a customer was the most thrilling thing in the world, a rung climbed to an adult world.

'Have you read any of these?' I ask, squeaking the metal

bookstand a revolution. The novels – thick romances by Catherine Cookson and Daphne du Maurier and Barbara Taylor Bradford – fight for space with tourist maps and guides to shipwreck sights and tinmines and gardens open all year round.

'I don't like books.' She hands me the cereal. 'Did that woman find you?'

I stop spinning the rack. 'What woman?'

'The one that was looking for you.'

'For me?' I ask, nervously. 'You sure?'

'I don't know any other Portia's here.' Karen thinks this funny.

'What did she look like?'

'I don't know. About fifty, I suppose. She had an accent like yours and . . .'

'What was her hair like?'

'Short, sort of grey. I told her how to get to Kale's Farm.'

'When?'

'I dunno. An hour ago. I'm surprised she didn't—'

'I've got to run.'

I grab Silas's lead, and I do run; fast as my legs will take me, I run. I reach the lane to the cottage heaving for breath and, despite the light snow that has begun to fall, with sweat soaking my back. Questions came with each stride. If it is Mother (and who else can it be?) how did she find me? Is she alone? Did Ulla betray me? What will I say? How can I say what I need to? I am not ready for her. I have not been able to dispel this quickly half a life's worth of bitterness. My remorse is not unconditional. She remains to blame for hiding the truth from me.

I stop fifty yards from the cottage and bend over with my hands on my thighs to try to catch my breath. Her car is here, parked in front of the house. It is too clean to be local. I stay where I am but Silas has run to the door and will, with his scratching, announce our return. He scratches some more. When the door opens, it is not Ulla but Mother who comes out. At once, I think she is looking too dressy. She loves that beige suit of hers.

She waves. With less conviction, I wave back. She keeps her

eyes on the puddles as she begins to close the gap between us. Still, I can't move. I fold tighter the top of the brown paper bag from Karen's, as if my purchases are all I have left to conceal. Mother nears me and then stops a couple of paces away. We stare at one another like enemies in a duel until something extraordinary happens: my mother smiles at me, a smile that releases from who knows where such a flood of emotion that I step to her with my arms open and, with my head buried against her neck, begin to cry in deep, satisfying sobs.

'Darling, my darling,' Mother whispers and then she, who has always been so very strong in the face of everything I have thrown at her, begins to cry too, her hand stroking the back of my neck. We hold each other for minutes before she speaks again. 'I was so worried, Pea, so worried, so scared. I didn't know what you'd done with yourself.'

'I'm sorry.'

She squeezes me hard then loosens the embrace and, still holding my upper arms, steps back. 'You're looking thin.'

'I'm fine.' I wipe at my eyes with the back of my glove. Mother hands me a tissue. She has one on her, of course. I ask, 'How did you know I was here?'

'Luke somehow found the number of the phone you'd called from. When he said it was from Penzance, Barbara and I thought you may have come here. I asked around a little and the girl in the store knew, so—'

'When did you get to England?'

'Ten days ago, or so.'

'My God.'

'You left everyone so fast, we didn't—'

'I know. I know.'

She shivers, twists her face towards the sea and into the wind. The caramel-coloured cows have turned their rumps to the slanting snow. It is falling thickly, all of a sudden. With luck, we'll get a covering. Flakes are melting on our clothes.

Playing mother, I say, 'You need a coat.'

'Yes.'

'Did you see the flat?'

'No, show me.'

Having Mother in my apartment, which I have been considering a world wholly separated from the one I left, is not unlike meeting a celebrity who has always been in one's consciousness but not one's presence. She belongs elsewhere than at the table where she is sitting, her hands wrapped around her cup of tea like an actress in a soup commercial.

A few moments ago, when I heard Ulla returning to the studio, I ran down to ask her how much she had revealed to Mother about my arrival. Ulla assured me that Mother knows nothing. It is a relief. If Mother knew, I am sure she would assume that my suicide attempt was a cry for help rather than what it was, a logical response to my honest, intense desire to return to blackness and peace. My outlook is different, now. Since discovering this mysterious, innate will to live – a will that I have come to believe exists within all of us, part of a genetic programme that insists life need no reason for her celebration – my effort has seemed embarrassing and absurd. Whether it is a delusion or not, I feel wiser now.

I fill Mother's cup with more tea, and sit opposite her at the table. We have been talking of the coastline, of exquisite Zennor, of Mousehole, St Ives and Penzance. Ulla has already invited Mother to stay for a few days.

Now, she says, 'I saw Luke in London. He's been very kind. He wrote you a letter.'

'He wrote me?'

'Yes, it's in the car. He wanted to come with me, at first.'

'Down here? Luke did?'

'Of course. He's been almost as worried as I have. He's very fond of you.'

'I thought he wouldn't be . . . any more.'

'Well, he obviously is, Portia. And some nice girl called Kaz used to come round.'

'You've been with Kaz, too?'

'Yes,' she answers, somewhat impatiently. 'We've been worried sick. You walked away from Diane without saying goodbye, you put the phone down on me and then—'

'I know what I did. I don't need you to rub my nose in it.'

The silence is uncomfortable. The legs of my chair scrape noisily on the floor as I rise. I take my cup to the sink. Beyond the windowpane, the snow is swirling in huge planes, making clean sheets of the fields.

'I'm sorry,' I say. 'I was incredibly upset.'

'Yes,' she says, and it sounds like a sigh. 'I know you were.'

I turn and lean back against the sink with my arms folded. Now is as good a time as any, I suppose. 'Why didn't you tell me?'

'About what?'

'About Richard. About Dad. I mean, Jesus, I have spent half of my life believing in this guy who I suddenly find out was an A-1 asshole. Why wasn't I told?'

My mother shakes her head, gazes at me, and then looks away. Softly, she admits, 'I made a mistake.'

I wait for more, but she remains sitting still, her hands on the table as if at a tribunal. Is that all she can say?

'And you've only just figured that out?' I ask. 'I don't get it. I've been trying to get it everyday since I've been here and I can't begin to understand – I really mean that – I can't begin to figure out why you wouldn't have told me. It makes no sense. Can't you understand how much easier it would have been for me if I'd known? I might not have wasted all these years looking for some guy who could live up to Dad, for a start, and I'm convinced I wouldn't have stayed awake for night after night after night trying to figure out why he did it. And what about you and me? It's insane to me, it's completely fucking insane of you not to have said anything. If I'd known what he was like, and how he was treating you, and maybe – God knows – what he might have been thinking about me, I wouldn't have hated you like I did for all that time. Ma? In fact, you made the same mistake a thousand times over since it happened, and that pretty much ensured I didn't have a mother, either. You could have got me on your side. Couldn't you? Richard's a whole 'nother matter. I don't know how I'd have reacted to that, but not telling me about Dad was crazy. Insane. It was so wrong of you.'

'I know, Portia. I said that. It was a mistake.'

'And that's all you can say? You don't have a reason?'

'I had plenty of reasons.'

'Such as?'

'Such as not wanting to see you hurt any more.'

'You hurt me more by not telling me.'

'That's cruel.'

'You don't think it's true?'

'No, I don't. When do you think I should have told you about Clive?'

'As soon as he killed himself. Right then, bam!' I clap. 'Get it over and done with.'

'How could I have? You were fourteen, darling. It was awful enough that he did what he did, especially from your bedroom. Can you then imagine telling a fourteen-year-old girl that on top of what her father had done he had nude Polaroids of her locked in his study and, and drawings and underwear and God knows what else?'

'What do you mean, Polaroids? I never once . . . I would have remembered.'

'He used to take them when you were lying in the bath. He used to make you hold your breath underwater – you've probably forgotten – but he'd take Polaroids of you when you had your eyes closed.'

'Oh, God.'

'Should I have told you this when you were fourteen?'

'I never knew.'

'You were supposed to grow up, to leave it behind you.'

'My underwear?'

'Can you imagine what you'd have thought? It was an awkward time, anyway, if you remember. You were going through all your changes. So we agreed—'

'"We" who?'

'Every expert I spoke to, Portia, every book I read. And Aunt Barbara, and Sally, and everybody. I didn't have the first idea what to do but all the advice was the same – that I had to let you come to terms with the shock and to grieve before I could talk to you.'

'So why didn't you?'

'Because you changed. Didn't you? Just like that. You collapsed in on yourself. All of a sudden you decided you were going to hate me and blame me and believe exactly the opposite of everything I told you. Trying to get through to you was like trying to catch a falling leaf. You wouldn't even talk to me, if you remember. You were wasting your time with that crowd you knew I didn't approve of. You were doing everything in your power to taunt me and upset me. If I'd told you then, you wouldn't have believed a single word I said.'

'If you'd told me,' I say, softly, 'I might not have hated you . . .'

'Do you honestly believe that? You were angry at everybody. Weren't you? Who else would you have shouted out? You couldn't bring Clive back. So I thought it would be better just to let things heal themselves. And it was getting better, wasn't it? Slowly.'

'Yes,' I whisper.

I have to sit now. I am not breathless as I used to get (my mind seems to have become accustomed to shock) and yet Mother is confirming the worst of my fears. I bite at a tiny strip of dry skin on my upper lip and wince in pain when it comes loose. Mother comes to sit by me. She takes my hand. Her eyes look bloodshot. Worried sick? I spread sickness. Carry Dad's sins, his disease, this conviction that satisfying oneself is what counts.

I ask, 'If you knew, why did you stay with him?'

'Why do you think?'

'Tell me.'

'Honestly, I didn't know, not at first. He told me nothing about Diane or about Richard or about why he'd had to leave England so fast – as far as I knew he'd been offered the post at

U of T and then, well . . . then you were born and I wanted you to have a normal life, a happy life.'

'But if you knew about him—'

'But I didn't! Not really. Not until you were about six when I found out he was being investigated for harassing one of his students or . . .' She sighs, lets go of my hand, pinches and pulls gently at the skin under her chin. 'There was often talk of that but they seemed less bothered back then. And then he used to go off on these conferences.'

'I remember. He used to send a postcard a day, didn't he?'

'But there weren't any conferences. When he went to Europe, I think he was . . . I mean, I found out later that there was some kind of club or . . . I don't like thinking about it.'

Talking about Dad like this, he has never seemed less real, more dead. These are not the details that keep him alive in my mind.

'And you still stayed with him?'

'I didn't know what to do. He could be so charming, couldn't he? And funny, and good company. And can you imagine how you would have reacted if I had taken you away? I never knew a child who adored their father so much.'

'But if you'd told me the truth—'

'You can't tell a six- or eight-year-old those things, Portia,' she interrupts. 'And I suppose I hoped that we'd all . . . Oh, I don't know.' She stands, feels her hair with both hands. She looks so tired. I want to make her nights more peaceful. She who carried and fed me, who wiped the shit from my bum and the sick from her shoulder. Mother, whose sorrow was a gift to me after Dad died, the only one who understood my sadness as I lay in her bed dreaming of his lifeless body and longing, with my nails creasing sad moons in the palms of my hands, for nothing more than what we had known. Mother, who martyred her happiness for mine. Who do I owe, if not this woman who gave me life?

She pulls out a chair from under the kitchen table, sits again. 'Do you know the one thing I can't forgive him for? I can't forgive him for turning you against me. He was jealous of you.

Remember that hateful language you had between you? It made me feel so horribly separate. It wasn't your fault, but it was hateful, hateful.'

'He didn't mean it that way. He thought he was teaching me. He wanted me to learn.' Mother is quiet. 'Didn't he?' I press.

'No, I don't think he did. I think he wanted you to believe I was stupid and worthless. Remember doddypoll? How you used to call me that? I was being called uneducated by the man who kept me from going to university? Doddypoll and dufflehead and all those words. I used to have to shut myself in my bedroom so you wouldn't see me crying.'

'Don't, please. Please.' I close my eyes. 'Please.'

'Oh, darling, I'm not blaming you,' she says, touching my hand. 'I'm not saying it was you.'

'You don't have to,' I reply. I can feel tears coming again. I don't want them to now. Enough, now; enough. They do nothing to lessen the shame.

'Listen, Ma, I want us to talk but I'm meant to be helping Ulla. I'm sort of paying my rent by working in the studio and—'

'Go then, go. We don't need to do this, Portia. We just don't need to.'

'It's just, I've got to help.'

'That's fine. I'm happy to potter. Oh, potter,' she repeats, snorting a laugh. 'That wasn't intended.'

We never did find the same things funny, but I laugh with her. 'You could probably have a go. If you changed. It's fun, I'm getting OK at it. I made that mug.'

'This one?'

'Yeah, the one that drips when you drink from it.'

She holds it up. Truth is, I needed Ulla to stroke the clay into a handle, but it is the first piece that has been fired and glazed, and I am proud of it.

'It's wonderful. Can I watch you.'

'Sure. It's downstairs.'

There is something generous and calming about the way Ulla treats Mother when we join her. It is a talent. Forgetting, perhaps, that the winters in Toronto are harsher than the gulf-warmed nights of Cornwall, she turns on the heating in the studio, which she rarely does, finds an apron for Mother and insists that I throw on the wheel instead of helping her reconstitute and wedge the old barrel of stoneware clay, a tiresome task we had agreed to share today. She is mixing glazes, now.

'I'll make you a bowl,' I promise, rashly. 'They're the easiest.'

Mother draws up a stool. On parents' days as we met with teachers and showed off our paintings from class, it was always Dad's hand I held, always his approval I craved. Mother was just there. She was always just there; efficient; invisible.

Now I thud a red ball of earthenware on the electric wheel and set it spinning fast. When the clay is wet, I cover it with my hands. I like my pots to be imperfect, misshapen, but first they must be centred or the motion of the wheel will make it impossible to lift and shape the clay. If you are steady and centred yourself the wheel does the work. I apply pressure, hold firm. In time, the clay spins evenly. Ridges of shiny slip remain from the grooves between my fingers. I slow the wheel and make a hole in the clay's centre with my thumbs. Sexily, it yields. I stop with the base sufficiently thick, widen the hole then slow the wheel further. Now comes the magic. With one hand inside the pot and the other on the outside, I squeeze and lift the clay. It rises, just so; as I will it to. I repeat the process. Wet, squeeze, lift, until the edges are evenly thick. With a sponge, I ease the clay into the shape I was after, and it is done. It is thick, and almost ugly, but I am proud, and Mother is impressed, and glad for me.

'It's lovely, Portia.'

'She's good,' Ulla adds, flattering me.

I am hoping to rent the flat through the summer. Ulla doesn't much care for the tourists, and enjoys my company and assistance.

'It's too Woolworth's,' I take it between my hands, and squeeze it out of shape. 'That's better. Mum, why don't you have a go.'

'Oh, I couldn't.'

'Sure, you can. I'll show you how.'

It is fun teaching her when I know so little. We have so rarely done this: acted like friends. We spend all afternoon in the studio, so by the time we are finished it is dark out. The snow is still falling and is thick on the ground. Beyond its brilliant white, the cottage looks stranded and magical. Mother and Ulla leave trails as they walk to the cottage. They are going to cook a chicken. The two of them are a similar age and get on like sisters. I think I like that. Probably, Ulla wants Mum to put out. It makes me laugh. They are almost at the house when I remember the letter from Luke, which Mother collects for me.

Alone, I take it back to the flat and pour myself a glass of wine. Luke's writing on the envelope is small, tight. He has underlined my name then finished it off with a full stop. It is sealed tightly. I rip it open, and begin to read, memories of Charles's letter large in my mind.

My dearest Portia,
It feels so strange writing this not knowing where you are or whether you're happy or even whether you want to hear from me, but I've been so keen to speak to you that I thought I'd take this opportunity to sort out a few of my thoughts on paper. There are so many, I don't really know where to begin. Ever since you drove away after Christmas, a part of me has wished that I could just carry on without you, as if we had never met, but our hearts and minds don't always act in unison, I suppose, and I am finding that when I think of you it's with love, and regret that we did not talk things through before you left to wherever you are now.

I still don't know what precipitated your sudden departure after Christmas. Dad said that he'd spoken to you in the meadow and admitted that he'd been less than enthusiastic about us getting married. I know you've always felt that my friends, and I suppose my family, have been against you because your background is so different from mine, but I promise that hasn't been the case. Dad was probably just worried that you wouldn't want to stay in England with me. Apparently you had mentioned something about it not being everything you'd hoped it would be. I know that Dad feels guilty that he didn't do anything to help Serena in her marriage and I suppose he felt he should say his piece while it was on his mind. We ended up having an argument after you'd gone, which we've almost never done before. I assumed from your reaction (his tailoring bill is going to be huge) that he'd been bloody awful to you, but he swears he wasn't, and that something else sparked off your mood. I wish I knew what it was. Did I do something wrong?

Portia, I've gone back and forth a hundred, hundred times whether I should have proposed to you when and how I did, and still I can't make up my mind. You seemed so low before Christmas that I thought that if I put my cards on the table, and proved to you how much you meant to me, then you'd realize how serious my feelings were. And I think that did happen, didn't it? Even if we never see one another again, which I hope and pray we shall, I will not forget that look on your face when you decided you would marry me. You looked so beautiful, you really did, and so happy and I felt as if everything we'd been through had suddenly come right, and that we were doing the best thing for both of us. I know I got stupidly drunk later, and probably stumbled into your room, but I just can't believe that's what would have set the whole thing off. I just can't think. And yet I can't imagine what else would have made you so angry and unhappy.

It's so frustrating knowing none of the answers. I want to talk to you about your feelings, and whether you have any towards me. I find it too hard to believe we are completely through with each other. Not that much has changed, has it? People don't meet on street corners like we did, and fall for each other in the first second like we did, and then just walk away without talking things through. I know you're very harsh about the English not communicating and not being emotional, but I don't know how much more emotional you can be than saying you love someone enough to marry them. I don't know what more I could have done.

At the same time, I don't want to be blind to the fact that you have hurt me recently – I would never have just run away like that, or dropped the car back at your home without coming in to talk. And I also understand that if we were to try to be together again, we would have to find a new way that wasn't so full of questions and judgements. I know from what you've said to me and to Kaz that you think it's arrogant and typically English of me to go on believing that the way I was brought up was the best way, but why shouldn't I believe that when no one has ever questioned it or complained about it before? And I think the English are quite good at raising solid, happy families, aren't they? Perhaps it is wrong of me to be completely inflexible, but I can't suddenly change into a new person. But I am trying, and I will go on trying if you want me too. It isn't always easy for me to be close to you, because you challenge me on so many levels, but since I have met you I do believe I have become a better person. I am more aware, I suppose, of who I am, and what I believe. And it's not all wrong. You yourself said you liked the English way of doing things, that you liked the history of our culture, so I can't be expected to throw it all away because you feel threatened or judged, or something.

The truth is, P, I don't know what to think any more. I don't know whether to believe we can have a future together. I miss you at night and in the mornings and I miss going out and having you by my side. I was proud to have you as my girlfriend, and I was proud to be getting married to you, not just because you are beautiful and funny and we have fun together – don't we? – but also because you made me feel a little more alive, a little different. I wish you could just settle down and accept all those things I can offer you.

That's it, really. I do not believe I'm the kind of person you wanted loving you, and I'm not sure you were the sort of girl I had in mind. You're certainly not the sort of person my mother had in mind for me, but I refuse to believe that any of the above really, truly matters if we want to be together enough. I think I would rather have you in my bed for one night a week than to have someone else there every night. I was so very happy with life when you came to England, and I think you were too. I wanted a life full of that sort of happiness, and I just don't know anymore if it's possible or not.

Please write or call me after you have read this. I want to talk to you about all the things that have been going on in your life. Your mother – who I like a lot – and I have been talking quite a bit about your brother, and how you must feel about it, and both of us want nothing more than to help you. You must believe that. I know that my life must seem simple and uncomplicated beside yours, but I think our hearts beat in the same way, and I know something now about losing someone I loved. I want to believe there is a way to get her back, but whether that's true or not I simply do not know.

I look forward to hearing from you soon. Please.

With all my love,

Luke.

I read the letter once again. So Luke doesn't know about me and Charles. That makes me happy, for his sake. Oh, Luke! He's not inflexible, is he? His malleability and forgiveness, his love, astound me. I was convinced my actions would have led him to his senses, but it was those senses I misjudged. God, is there anything left for me to get wrong? What about that belief that I could never deeply love him? Was that wrong, too? Might I, again? If he loves me as he says he does?

I light a joint. Ulla has supplies, from who knows where, and is able to furnish me. I smoke a little, thinking how strange it is that Mother is cooking at Ulla's. Her compassion, because of the forgiveness it contains, is doing much to lighten the weight of my culpability. Do I deserve it at all?

Since I am not expected for an hour or so, I take to my bed

with a book, but it is so cosy under the thick blankets, and my brain has been muffled by the smoke, that soon I have turned off the light and feel myself falling into a doze.

I am by woken by the sound of someone coming into the apartment. I sit up, turn on the light.

'Portia?'

It's Mother. I call her. She smiles as she pushes open the door. 'We wondered where you had got to.'

'I dozed off.'

'I'm glad. You looked as if you needed some sleep.' She sits on the end of my bed and rubs one of my feet. 'Are you all right?'

'Sort of, yeah. I'm trying not to let things get to me so much.'

'Take a step back and life looks like one big joke,' Ulla said to me last week. Me, I don't think it's that funny and I don't think I ever will, though on one thing she is right: screw up and there are no second chances. I was thinking of Mother in my semi-conscious sleep, of how courageous and bright she has been despite a life that must have been weighed down with regret.

'I don't want you to think I am angry at you, at all,' she tells me now.

'I'm not. God.' I sit up. 'How could I be? I've been screwing up for fourteen years. More. I don't even know how to begin . . . how—' I stop. Where do I begin? How do I drop into our conversation that I am sorry that I blamed Mother for driving Dad to his death? Or that I threw forks and shoes and insults at her whenever I had the chance? Or that I sabotaged every attempt she made at bringing us closer and, perhaps worse, every stab she made at rebuilding a life for herself? Do I just shrug my shoulders and say, 'sorry'?

'Let's not do this, huh?' Mother says, rubbing my foot again. 'Apologize for all those things we can't change.' Her eyes soften when she smiles. 'I can forgive you, you know. Just like that, I can forgive you for everything you said and did.' Now she leans forward in the bed, and kisses my forehead. 'And I do,' she whispers. 'I do. Now, come on, Ulla's waiting for us.'

She rises off the bed and makes some comment about how I was always a groggy sleeper, even as a baby I was bad-tempered for a long time after I woke, then she hands me my sweater, picking off some hairs before she does so. I feel loose, like a rag doll. I lift my arms into the sweater and then I wrap them around Mother's back. I hug her to me, squeezing her tight.

Outside, the landscape has changed. A strong wind has blown the clouds away allowing a moon not far from full to brighten the fresh snow and turn the night almost to day. I turn off the torch. We can see the details of Ulla's cottage as if it has been floodlit. The yellow light through the windows looks soft and beautiful and inviting.

'Isn't it amazing?' I say. 'Come on, we've got to go to the sea.'

'Now? But Ulla's waiting—'

'She'll want to come. I'll run ask her.' I run in great strides, laughing to myself as the snow crunches noisily up to my ankles. Ulla is in the kitchen chopping carrots. I can see she has laid the table with her favourite pottery, the painted Dutch plates she doesn't use because they chip too easily. She has lit candles. It looks like a celebration. When I ask if we have time to walk to the sea, she lays down the knife and says 'yes', but then insists that Mother and I go alone.

I run back to her and together we head towards the swoosh of the waves. After a minute or two, Mother breaks the silence. 'You know, I spoke to Richard on the phone. Apparently, he's been wanting to contact you for some time, but . . . well, none of us wanted you to know too much about Clive. We didn't think that . . .' She paused. 'I suppose we didn't think it through enough.'

'I don't know what I think about Richard being at Oxford. He sounds so much more like Dad than I am.' I take her hand. 'The good parts, I mean.'

'Oh, you've plenty of those. I promise.'

'But plenty of the bad, too. Right?'

'I thought we weren't going to do this,' she says, releasing my hand to rest her arm across my shoulders. She pulls me closer.

'Besides, I don't think your dad was bad. Not really. He never asked to feel the things he felt.'

'Did he talk to you about it?'

'No! No, of course not. But I think he was very scared that he wouldn't be able to stop himself from hurting you. You were growing up so fast and you looked so beautiful that—'

'What are you saying?' I break loose, stop walking.

'What do you mean, darling? What . . .?'

'You're saying he killed himself because of me, aren't you?' Mother doesn't even know that Dad came into my room. That he touched me the day before he died. That my denial must have broken him. And yet still she blames me.

'No, Portia. No! Listen to me.' She takes hold of my arms. The shadows created by the moon lend her face a frightening, cadaverous aspect. 'It was not you, not you, not you. And it wasn't me. It was him, him. It was him. He hated himself for what he felt. That's why he did it. No other reason than that.'

'How do you know that?'

'Because of tying himself to your bed, darling, the way he did. And because of that note he left you, and that book he wrote and—'

'What book? I thought you gave that away.'

'I did. Darling, I'm getting cold. Shall we go back in?'

'No, I need to hear this. What book? Please tell me.'

'All right.'

We begin to walk again. Since we are nearing the cliff's edge, I turn on the torch so that we can safely follow the path. 'About a year after I gave all Clive's papers to his department, a man came to the house with the manuscript saying that he'd read it, and he thought it should be published, but it wasn't something his department wanted to act upon. Anyway, he left it with me – you must have been at school – and I started reading it and, well, it wasn't academic at all. It was a novel.'

'Jesus. What kind?'

'It was set in England in the Middle Ages and it was told by a poet, like Chaucer, I suppose, who wrote about courtly love.

So, of course, it was very much set in Clive's world. Anyway, at the same time as this poet was writing about noble ideals and pure love he was having an affair with his employer's daughter and that's really what the book's about. It's partly a love story, but it's mostly about his guilt and shame at living up to the ideals he was preaching. So it goes on like this – it was about four hundred pages long – until one day' – she pauses, briefly – 'one day the poet collects all of his manuscripts together and rips them into little pieces and lays them under his mattress. Then he lies on top and sets fire to the paper and he dies and that's the end of the book. I think Clive must have just finished writing it when he did what he did.'

'My God. You think he'd been planning it, then?'

'I don't know. I don't know, Portia. But it must have been in his mind.'

'Where's the book? I want to read it.'

'I've still have it. Perhaps you should take a look. It's quite wonderful in places. You've inherited that, haven't you? Being able to write.'

'Have I? I can't—' I stop myself. 'Mum. Oh, Mum, look!'

We have arrived at the coastal path. The ocean is spread in front of us, breathtaking in its vast beauty. I am not sure I have ever seen it so sublime, so calm. A column of light from the moon has made the surface of the water directly in front of us seem almost incandescent. The wind has died. Nothing but our breathing disturbs the sound of the waves as they tumble against the rocks. Even the grumbling earth is muffled in its coat of snow.

'Tell me that isn't worth the walk,' I say. 'You can see why I want to stay.'

'Do you?'

'Yes. Yes, I definitely do, for a while.' The pebbles far below clack softly as a wave subsides. 'Try and get my head straight.'

'Yes.'

'If I stand here,' I say as I stare out across the ocean, 'I'll be able to wave at you. Canada's right over there.'

'Then I'll watch out for you.'

As she always has, she could have added, as she always will. I should have known.

'They must be glad that storm's over.'

'Who?'

'Those fisherman there.' She points at a fishing ship I hadn't noticed and which, just now, seems to be passing out of the moon's glow into a more shadowy stretch of sea.

'You should say hello to them.'

'They wouldn't be able to hear.'

'That doesn't matter. Go on.'

'Oh, Portia!'

'Ahoy!' I scream. 'How are you doing out there?' I turn to Mother. 'That's what Ulla does. You should try it.'

'Hello,' she says, quietly.

'Louder. Like this . . .' I slip my arm around my mother's waist, take a deep breath and scream as loudly as I can, 'Hello, my fishermen. Hello!' I can feel with my fingers Mother's torso shake with laughter. 'This is my lovely mum!'

'Hello!' Mother shouts, and then again, more loudly this time, 'Hello, hello, hello!'

For a moment, the boat seems to turn our way and I think I see it flash a light, but in truth I know they are too far out to sea. I do not mind that they can't hear. I can hear me. We can hear.

Together, Mother and I shout out again. 'Hello!'

We shout and shout, and are shouting, our voices carrying far across the waves.